T0265725

Perfectly
Wicked

Perfectly Wicked

A Novel

LINDSAY LOVISE

alcove
press

Copyright © 2024 by Lindsay Lovise

All rights reserved.

Published in the United States by Alcove Press, an imprint of The Quick Brown Fox & Company LLC.

Alcove Press and its logo are trademarks of The Quick Brown Fox & Company LLC.

Library of Congress Catalog-in-Publication data available upon request.

ISBN (hardcover): 978–1–63910–953–1
ISBN (ebook): 978–1–63910–954–8

Cover design by Dawn Cooper

Printed in the United States.

www.alcovepress.com

Alcove Press
34 West 27th St., 10th Floor
New York, NY 10001

First Edition: September 2024

10 9 8 7 6 5 4 3 2 1

To my husband. Of all the university summer Spanish classes, I'm so grateful you walked into mine.

CHAPTER ONE

Holly surveyed the acres of blossoming apple trees, the early morning sun gilding the soft new bark and tender buds, and knew without a doubt that her family's apple farm was doomed.

"Isn't it beautiful?" Stacy sighed beside her. Even though the grass was damp with early morning dew, Stacy wore four-inch black stilettos with an A-line skirt and a cream blouse. She was the picture of a professional boss lady, and if Holly didn't want to slap the smug right out of her rival's voice, she *might* have been impressed with Stacy's extraordinary level of put-togetherness.

Holly glanced down at her chunky hiking boots, ripped jeans, and the navy plaid shirt that was unbuttoned over a tank top stained with coffee. Their respective attire perfectly reflected the success levels of each of their apple farms. The Apple Dream was raking in the dough, and Wicked Good Apples was . . . not.

"Yes, charming," Holly said through gritted teeth. "Is this what you wanted to show me?" She didn't know why she'd taken the requested meeting except that she'd had a masochistic desire to see the orchard that was putting them out of business.

"Only part of it. Follow me." Stacy beckoned Holly toward The Apple Dream's rustic barn, its frame the only thing rustic about it. The red paint was fresh, the trim crisp, the doors sanded smooth. Holly's family barn was, well, a barn. Weathered, falling apart, mice-ridden.

Stacy navigated the uneven ground with unfaltering perfection, and Holly was impressed while also hoping a *teeny tiny* bit that her nemesis would face-plant. She didn't.

Once inside the barn, Holly did her very best to suppress her awe-struck expression. She'd never seen the inside of The Apple Dream, apart from the photos on their website which she may or may not have stalked a few times, and it was even cleaner and more efficient than it appeared online. A massive stainless steel cider mill took up the entire far wall, and squatting beside it was a gleaming tank that held the finished cider that would be shipped to grocery stores across the state of Maine. There were old-fashioned apple barrels with cute chalkboard signs denoting the apple type; sleek aerial photos of the orchards framed on the walls; and a cozy couch setup where, in the fall, guests could mingle and sip cider from paper cups.

Holly tried hard not to compare The Apple Dream's customer experience to that of Wicked Good Apples, where last fall a customer had stepped on Prickles, Holly's hedgehog, and had threatened to sue after a dramatic meltdown.

"We produce over a thousand gallons of cider a day," Stacy chirped. She brushed a springy black curl over her shoulder, her cheeks glowing with pride even as she briefly pressed her fingers to her temple as if she had the start of a headache. "We have one of the biggest operations in the state. Oh, did I tell you that I—I mean *we*—just secured a contract to stock over a hundred New Hampshire grocery stores this fall?"

Holly bared her teeth. "That's *great*!"

Stacy beckoned Holly toward a closed door at the back of the barn that had a tiny "Private" sign affixed to it. Holly stepped into a modern-day office that had all the right touches of hipster style, and vowed that when she got home she was buying a new set of pens to do the budget books with. Maybe even gel pens.

Stacy perched on the edge of the desk and crossed her arms over her chest. Her nails were manicured with tiny apples. "Listen, Holly, I know our orchards have had a friendly rivalry in the past, and in the spirit of putting that behind us, I'll admit that your family's secret cider recipe is unmatched. The truth is we'd love to have that recipe—and the old Gala orchard at the back of your property. That's why I asked you here today. I wanted to show you what your orchards could be a part of."

She sounded like a college recruiter. *"Just look at what your orchards could ASPIRE to be!"*

Holly had half thought Stacy had invited her to The Apple Dream just to rub her successes in Holly's face. Holly's apple orchard was going under—had been going under for a while—and everyone knew it. Holly's family strived for an unremarkable break-even model, but in the past four years they'd slowly sunk into the red. Some of that might have been Holly's fault. As the eldest sister in the family and the general manager of Wicked Good Apples, she was adamant they keep their operations on a small scale. Not only was it necessary for their business model, but there were other, far scarier reasons they needed to blend in. Maybe she'd been a little *too* adamant, though, because if Wicked Good Apples didn't pull a profit this fall, they'd have to close. But being bought out by her lifelong rival? That was worse. Way worse.

Holly's eyes dropped to a cider glass on the desk printed with The Apple Dream's name and logo. Stacy had spent all morning humble-bragging about her cider contracts, but Holly *knew* that Wicked Good Apples' family recipe was better. Her great-great-grandmother had planted the orchards by hand to spite a town councilman, and the orchards had been passed down through the generations along with the secret cider recipe. There was no way Holly was giving it up.

Actually, Holly *couldn't* give up the recipe. There was a special ingredient no one else had.

"We're prepared to make a generous offer," Stacy continued, and she gave Holly a sad smile. "We know your business prospects are bleak, but we aren't going to take advantage of that." Stacy pressed one slender hand over her heart. "Our family wants to do right by yours."

Holly swallowed down her nausea and shoved her fists into her back pockets. She always felt vaguely sick around Stacy. She told herself it was because she was allergic to perfectionism, but the truth was she and Stacy had a far more complicated history.

Stacy reached behind her for a folded square of cream stationary and held it out. Holly reluctantly took it. Frig, even their stationary was a class act. When she opened the note, her jaw dropped. "Are you kidding me?"

"That's for the orchards *and* the recipe. We don't want the house, but we aren't going to kick you off the land either. You and your aunts and sisters can continue living there. For now."

Holly counted the zeros six times and then folded the paper and handed it back. "I'll have to consult with my family."

It was the polite thing to say, but she already knew their answers. Her sister, Winter, would curse Stacy out until one of their aunts exclaimed that ladies didn't speak in such a way in *her* day, and Winter would remind her that she was by no means a lady. Holly's youngest sister, Missy, would relay all the latest gossip about Stacy but wouldn't actually commit to weighing in one way or another. As for Holly? She would rather live off potatoes and salt for a year than ever sell the orchards to Stacy, no matter how badly Wicked Good Apples was failing. Their mothers had been rivals long before Stacy and Holly had inherited the farms, and Holly had great respect for tradition.

Stacy gave her a cold smile. "You do that. But don't take too long."

The threat was implicit: the longer they took to decide, the lower the offer would go.

A curl of wind slithered over them, rifling Stacy's perfect hair. Stacy narrowed her eyes, and Holly quickly buried the ember of anger that had flared to life at her rival's words.

Not here. Anywhere but here.

Holly straightened her shoulders, and the errant breeze vanished. "I'll see myself out."

She exited the barn, her boot heels clomping across the waxed floorboards, and she didn't let her posture slump until she reached her 2009 Kia. Once safely inside, she pressed her forehead to the steering wheel and took several deep breaths, calmly reciting all the reasons she was *not* going back inside and telling Stacy where she could shove her offer. The main reason was that Holly was already on thin legal ice after the hedgehog incident.

On the short drive home, Holly rehearsed what she would say to her family. They weren't going to accept Stacy's offer, but it might be a good time to remind them how important this season was to their future. She wasn't convinced the others understood how dire their situation had become. Along with her family's desire to appear unremarkable, there had been a strange and steady decline in customers over the past several years that had chipped away at their margins. Holly wasn't sure what had changed, but what used to work didn't anymore, and Wicked Good Apples was barreling toward foreclosure at an alarming rate.

The view along the winding country road helped lift Holly's spirits. The winter had been long and bitter, and spring had been reluctant to emerge. It was May and it had finally, *finally* stopped raining. Everything was green and flowering and smelled like rain-washed lilacs and daffodils. The air was still a bit cool, but Holly didn't care. It was better than the forty-degree April they'd had, and infinitely better than the single digits they'd suffered through all winter.

She turned left at the rusted metal mailbox with the word "Wicked" painted across the side and smothered a smile. The rest of the name had ostensibly worn off.

The driveway was rutted with potholes—just one more thing they had to rectify before they opened for the fall season. Massive maples with tender green buds arched over the dirt drive, forming a woven canopy of delicate branches patched with blue sky. When the maples were leafed out in bright reds and dark maroons in the fall, the driveway would find its way onto dozens of Instagram accounts.

Holly was in a much better mood when she rounded the bend of the long driveway. It was a breathtaking day, and even Stacy and her stupidly amazing stilettos couldn't keep her down.

Then she saw the truck.

A shiny, forest-green pickup truck with all the latest bells and whistles was parked by the front door of the house. In discreet lettering on the side was the name "Grimm Productions."

Oh *hell* no. Not today.

Holly had already sent two Grimm Productions goons packing a couple months ago. Didn't Grimm understand the word *no*? *No*, she and her sisters did not want him filming his ghost-hunting TV show at their apple orchard. *No*, she and her sisters did not care that several internet fan sites had popped up claiming Wicked Good Apples was haunted. *No*, she and her sisters did not want to know how much money Grimm Productions was willing to throw at their dying apple orchard, because the answer was still *no!*

Holly jammed the Kia in park directly behind the pickup truck and marched toward the house, all of her anger at Stacy now directed toward Grimm Productions. She whipped her hand behind her, and a violent gust of wind slammed her car door shut with enough force that the visor fell open. Holly tried to remember the names of the two men who'd visited a couple months ago. *Kevin and Mark,* she thought. They'd both been so sure she'd fall over herself at the chance to be on TV that they'd been visibly shocked when she'd told them to get lost.

She almost felt bad for Kevin and Mark because they were about to have their asses handed to them. Today was not the day to be messing with Holly Celeste.

Holly threw open the door like a conquering invader and was horrified to hear *laughter* coming from the direction of the kitchen. Good God, was that Aunt Rose's girlish giggle? What on earth was happening? They'd all agreed that exposure in the form of a national TV show would be far more detrimental than the money would be helpful.

Holly wended through the mismatched furniture, pausing only long enough to reach inside the hedgehog enclosure and run her hand along the grain of Prickles's spines. The Celeste home was two hundred years old and as worn and drafty as one might expect from a farmhouse that had been built before modern insulation. Most of the furniture in the house was antique, which was unusual enough on its own, but when combined with the abnormal number of books the Celestes possessed, it made the house seem downright weird to most visitors. Every room had at least one full wall packed tightly with books, the spines ranging from hardcovers to cracked ninety-nine-cent paperbacks. It was a well-known fact that a Celeste *never* gave away a book. Holly's great-great-grandmother had started the collection, and every Celeste had added to it since.

Holly pushed through the swinging door that separated the living room from the kitchen and froze in surprise, the door literally hitting her in the butt and bumping her forward a few inches.

Sitting around the kitchen table were her two sisters, who had the nerve to be *glowing* with happiness, and Aunt Rose and Aunt Daisy, who were blushing and tittering, respectively. Laid out on the antique walnut table was the good china, the kind Aunt Rose reserved for visitors on par with the Queen of England, steam curling from the tops of the teacups. The kitchen smelled of apple scones and apple jelly, and a block of cheddar cheese was lying on a small charcuterie board in the center of the table, a silver-handled knife sticking out of it.

It wasn't the cozy domestic scene of entertainment that stopped Holly in her tracks, but the man lounging at the table beside Aunt Rose. He lifted his head as she entered, and Holly's heart leaped into her throat. It seemed Kevin and Mark had taken her hint after all, because sitting in her kitchen was none other than the *Grimm Reality* TV show star himself, Connor Grimm.

CHAPTER TWO

"There she is!" Aunt Rose exclaimed, beckoning Holly into the room. Morning sunlight glinted off the dozens of rings on her wrinkled fingers, and her green eyes were twinkling just enough to put Holly on alert. "This is Wicked Good Apples' manager and my *sweet-tempered* niece, Holly Celeste."

Connor Grimm stood to greet her, forcing her to look upward to maintain eye contact. She'd seen him on TV before, but in real life he was even larger than he appeared on screen. There were dozens of fan pages devoted to Connor: he was the most famous supernatural hunter to exist in modern times. He and his brother, Erikson, produced the hit primetime TV show, *Grimm Reality*, where they traveled across the United States seeking out tales and experiences of the supernatural. Holly had researched them after the goons had visited; she'd even watched the show, finding it unremarkable and at times downright ludicrous.

It didn't seem to matter the gender or the age of the viewer; Connor was popular with them all. His dark hair was cut short and often rumpled in a sleepy, sexy way, as if he'd just rolled out of bed. He had cool gray eyes that could be cajoling one moment and cold and harsh the next. When he was after a story, he was ruthless; he knew exactly what to say and what to do to crack the tale wide open, and he wielded his power of persuasion like a weapon.

Holly's gaze ran over his jaw, which was solid and shaded with a day's growth of beard. When he flashed her his legendary grin, she reflexively scowled. She'd seen the ghost-hunter memes created by his lovestruck viewers and how they practically fainted over the same disarming smile he was giving her now. On the show he wore a white polo for every episode, but today he was dressed in a simple gray T-shirt and jeans, his skin tanned from the sun. Holly wondered if he'd just flown in from filming in the south. She remembered seeing an ad online for an upcoming episode about the rougarou in Louisiana.

"It seems you're just the woman I need," Connor said. His voice was smooth and deep, but his eyes didn't match the warm tone or the casual smile, and Holly was instantly on guard.

"What do you want?"

The corner of Connor's eyebrow lifted. "Straight to business. That's the kind of person I like to work with."

"I—we—have no interest in working with you. I told your two other employees that when they visited a few months ago. You've wasted your time coming out here. Wicked Good Apples isn't haunted, and it never has been. I'll see you out."

"Holly!" Aunt Daisy admonished. Like her twin, Aunt Rose, she wore enough jewelry to stock a pawnshop, but unlike Aunt Rose, her green eyes were unfocused and slightly clouded from vision loss. "Mr. Grimm came all this way to speak to us personally. The least we can do is hear him out."

Missy flipped her curly red hair behind her shoulder and gave Connor a blazing white smile. "Yes, it's the *least* we can do."

Holly glared at her youngest sister. Missy was a serial dater, and she wouldn't care what Connor wanted so long as it meant the chance to flirt with the supernatural hunter.

Holly crossed her arms over her chest and said, "Fine. Speak."

Lindsay Lovise

Connor gestured to an antique chair. "Would you like to sit?"

It galled her that he was playing host in *her* house. "No, I wouldn't like to sit, if you know what the word *no* means."

"Oh my God," Winter hissed, "sit down, you pain in the ass." She grimaced at Connor. "Usually I'm the jerk, not her. I promise."

Connor's slate-gray eyes were unreadable as he sank into his seat, and Holly reluctantly pulled out the chair at the head of the table, not because it was a power move, but because it was the most accessible spot. The smell of the sharp cheddar cheese made her stomach sour, so she shoved the board away from her.

"As I was telling your family," Connor said smoothly, as if she hadn't just insulted him in front of the entire table, "I understand your reservations about having a filming company in your personal space, but we do our best to minimize our presence, and we always leave the grounds and buildings exactly as we found them."

Holly let her boredom show.

Amusement surfaced in Connor's eyes before he directed his attention to her sisters. "Filming typically takes a few weeks unless the location is worth a deeper dive, and then it might span several episodes, but we wouldn't know that until we began. At the very worst, we'd still be out of your hair before apple season begins."

"You sound dreamy," Missy sighed. Then she sat up straight, alarmed. "I mean *it* sounds dreamy."

"It sounds inconvenient," Holly said. She tapped her fingernails against the top of the table. Unlike Stacy, they did not have tiny perfect apples painted on them. Instead, they were short and unvarnished—the nails of a woman who was routinely up to her elbows in apples. "We'd be tripping over you and your cameramen for weeks."

Winter nodded in agreement. She was Missy's twin, and although they had identical curly red hair, hazel eyes, and spritely builds, they were completely opposite people. Where Missy was easygoing and bubbly, Winter was so stubborn and fierce that Holly was convinced she'd been an Amazon warrior in another life. "Holly's right, it does sound inconvenient. What would be the benefit to us?"

"We pay generously for all of our filming locations, but maybe the greatest benefit is the massive media exposure. When the episode airs, your farm will be flooded with business. People will come from all over the country to visit, and if you're inclined to, you can leverage that publicity. We've had locations open B&Bs, haunted tours, and more."

Missy perked up. She was in charge of publicity for the farm, even though their unique situation mostly kept her hands tied. Holly knew her sister would love the chance to break their apple farm out to a wider customer base.

Holly shook her head slightly. National media exposure was the *last* thing they wanted. Besides, Holly wasn't entirely convinced of Connor's motives. Why was he so focused on their little apple farm in the middle of rural Maine? Hell, there was a haunted movie theater just two towns over that had made it onto a Top Ten Haunted Spots in the US list. Why not go there?

"We want to be known for our apples, not for ghosts," she said.

Aunt Rose took a scone from the plate with a trembling hand and buttered it. "What exactly are you looking for here, Mr. Grimm?"

Connor tore his cold gaze from Holly, his eyes warming when they landed on Aunt Rose. "There are entire websites devoted to this apple farm. Did you know that? My brother and I have scoured them, and we've interviewed at least a dozen visitors who all claim to have seen odd things happen here."

"Odd things? Like what?" Holly pressed.

"Completely dry ground when it has been pouring for days straight."

She rolled her eyes. "We have a good drainage system."

"The opposite too. There was a drought a few years back, and your farm was the only one to produce apples."

"Luck."

"The apple tree disease never touched this place."

"We're remote."

Connor leaned back and rested his arm over the top of the empty chair beside him. A tattoo peeked out from beneath his sleeve, but not enough that Holly could see what it was. "The most popular story, however, is about a man who haunts the orchards at night, moaning of witchcraft and devilry."

Holly's heart blipped, and she was very careful not to look at anyone else in the room but Connor. "I'm sorry you've come all this way, Mr. Grimm, because that is the most ridiculous list of nonsense I've ever heard."

"Call me Connor."

"Connor," Missy purred.

Holly stood. Her job wasn't only to keep the orchard business on its feet, but as the oldest sibling, it was also her duty to protect the family, and Connor Grimm was bad news. "We're not interested."

Connor finally took the hint and stood. He thanked her aunts and sisters for their time, complimented them on their apple jam, and followed Holly through the house. She felt his eyes on her back as she led him to the front door. The moment it closed behind them, he spun so that he was standing between her and the driveway. Without the table between them he was even taller than she'd realized, and she could smell pine and warm spice on him—probably from his cologne.

"You're making a mistake," he said, his voice low enough that he couldn't be heard inside. "I know how much trouble your orchards are in."

Holly leaned one hip against the peeling white paint of the porch railing and tried to forget she had a huge coffee stain down the front of her tank top. "You've been misinformed. We're doing very well."

Connor's insightful gray gaze searched her face. "You're nine months from foreclosure. You *need* this deal just as much as I *want* it."

His arrogance chafed her. "Actually, we just received a very generous offer for the orchards today. We don't need a damned thing from you."

"Why do you dislike me so much?" He took a half step closer and pressed his hand to the door. "The minute you walked in and saw me, you closed off. Most people would be thrilled to have Grimm Productions knocking on their front door."

He was right about her attitude. The moment she'd seen him, she'd known he meant trouble for the Celeste family. Winter was the real seer in the family, but sometimes Holly got feelings about people too, and everything inside of her was screaming that if they let him in, Connor Grimm wouldn't stop until he'd laid bare every one of her family's secrets. Until he'd made them vulnerable to the scrutiny of the world.

"Then most people are idiots," she snapped. "The supernatural isn't real, and these orchards aren't haunted. This place has been in my family for two hundred years, and you want to know something? We make damned good apple cider, and we sell damned fine apples." Holly pushed away from the railing and stepped forward; he wasn't the only one who could command space. Unfortunately, now she was so close she could feel the heat from his body, and she had to look even farther upward to meet his steady gaze. "My great-great-grandmother started this place with pride, and I'm not going to let you turn it into some phony circus for cheap entertainment. This farm means everything to me, and I'll do whatever it takes to protect it."

At the last sentence a glint entered his eye, as if she'd just given away a vital piece of information. He lowered his head and said quietly, "Then I'll leave you my card, because I'm the only offer that's going to keep this place afloat in exchange for nothing but a few measly weeks of filming. When you change your mind, give me a call. I'll be in town until the end of the weekend."

She glanced at the white card he held between two tanned fingers, but didn't move to take it.

He reached forward and tucked the card into the blue plaid pocket of her shirt. "Don't make me wait too long, Holly. There are mysteries here to solve, and you have an apple orchard to save."

"Don't hold your breath, you overconfident spook chaser!" she shouted at his departing back.

Her anger flared further when he only laughed.

CHAPTER THREE

Connor Grimm had met his share of prickly people in his line of work, but he'd rarely met a woman so adept at telling him to go fuck himself with nothing but a look. The moment Holly Celeste had entered the kitchen, he'd known she was the lynchpin of the family and the one he'd have to convince if he wanted a shot at Wicked Good Apples, and God he *really* wanted a shot at it. For four years he'd read of the strange goings-on at the farm with mild interest, but it was the photograph a viewer had sent him that had fanned that spark of interest into a raging inferno. The email address had been a throwaway, but the three separate experts Connor had paid to analyze the photograph had all agreed that the picture was genuine.

He tapped his jeans pocket where he carried a folded copy of the photograph: Aunt Daisy, the thin leather gloves she'd been wearing this morning absent, hovering her hands over a barrel of apples while inky smoke leaked from her palms. Behind her was the weathered Wicked Good Apples barn, its outdoor floodlight casting a cone of light over the older women while an eyelash moon dangled in the background. Rationally, he knew the photo was probably a trick of the light, or a setup. Hell, it was possible the aunt had staged the scene herself. And yet Connor's instincts were whispering that there was something a little off about the Celeste family—something beyond a ghost haunting their property—and his instincts were almost never wrong. The Celeste women were keeping secrets. Every cell in his storyteller blood was buzzing with suspicion, and the investigator inside him was practically itching to be let loose.

Now that Connor and Erikson's show was a success and they had the money and freedom to choose their own sites, Wicked Good Apples had gone straight to the top of their filming wish list. Connor had led the Celeste women to believe the ghost was his main focus, and he fully intended to investigate the haunting, but there were a dozen other locations he could have chosen if that were his *only* interest. Along with the photograph, there were the oddities he'd listed in the Celeste kitchen, and a dozen other strange happenings rumored to have taken place at Wicked Good Apples that he *hadn't* mentioned. In his experience, that much chatter meant something paranormal—and he had plans to take *Grimm Reality* to the next level by exposing whatever it was. His show was a huge hit, but Connor wasn't the kind of person to be content with good when *better* was still out there. They'd investigated paranormal happenings on their show in the past, but they'd never been able to prove anything. He intended to change that, and it all hinged on the cooperation of Wicked Good Apples.

Connor turned onto Main Street and tapped the brakes so a woman with three pugs on leashes could cross the road. Usually, people who were hesitant to let him film at their house or business were simply worried about appearing foolish on national TV, but he didn't think that was the reason behind Holly's reservations. She'd been hostile from the moment she'd met him, so either she disliked him personally, or there was something about Grimm Productions filming on her property that put her on guard. Her desire to send him packing only added fuel to his theories.

He rolled into the cracked driveway of the motel and stopped outside the tiny gray shack with green shutters that he'd rented for the weekend. The porch light didn't work, and the white plastic chairs that sat out front were spotted with black mold. The interior wasn't any better: papered with trippy green wallpaper, carpeted with matted orange shag, and sporting a 1970s polyester bedspread, its only virtue was that the sheets were clean.

Connor sat in his truck for a moment, the door open as he thumbed through his phone, scrolling for any mention of Holly Celeste on the internet. He'd done his research into the finances of the farm, but he hadn't been able to zero in on who was truly in charge, not until the kitchen door had burst open and a woman with dark hair pulled into a sloppy bun had appeared, a coffee stain down the front of her tank top. Holly's flashing hazel eyes had told him exactly who it was he needed to sweet-talk.

Then she'd opened her mouth, and he'd known there'd be no sweet-talking someone with that kind of spine.

He'd found her antagonism perversely refreshing. He was recognizable enough now that most people were fake with him, but Holly had made it clear she didn't give a damn about how famous he was. In the past, women had gone to enormous lengths to meet him, but he knew Holly Celeste would never be one of them. She may have had a soft, curvy body that made his mouth go a little dry the moment he'd seen her, but he was pretty sure her will—and her dislike of him— were made of steel.

Connor glanced at the time on his phone. He was counting down the hours until she called. The moment Holly had told him she'd do anything for the apple farm, he'd known she wasn't going to take the offer she'd bragged about. Whatever her reservations about Grimm Productions, she couldn't afford to pass up the chance to keep the orchards open in exchange for a few weeks of filming. If she loved Wicked Good Apples as much as he thought she did, all of her skepticism about ghosts, her apparent grudge against him, and any worry about secrets were going to have to take the back burner.

His phone rang in his hand, and he grinned as he hit the answer button. It was an unknown number. "That was fast, Celeste. I thought you'd hold out longer."

Silence.

"Holly?"

"This isn't Holly."

No, it wasn't. The voice was raspy, like the caller was on oxygen or trying to conceal his true voice.

"Who is this?" Connor demanded. He didn't bother asking how they'd reached his personal number. He had a system set up where his secretary forwarded him calls that he might find interesting.

"A concerned citizen." The voice paused dramatically, and in the background Connor heard a cat mewl. "Leave the Celeste family alone. Some secrets are better left buried."

Connor's skin prickled as his temper heated. He hadn't pegged Holly for someone who'd hire out her dirty work. If she thought a threatening phone call would scare him off, then she'd sorely misjudged his character. Connor had been voted Most Stubborn Ass one year in high school. He lived for stuff like this.

"What do you know about the Celeste secrets?" he asked. A sleek car tooted hello as it pulled into the parking space beside him. He gave an absent wave to his assistant, Charlotte, who was behind the wheel. He'd already booked her the motel cabin beside his.

"More than most."

"Did Holly put you up to this? What's she hiding?"

The man cackled, but the grating laughter turned into a long fit of coughing before he finally said, "She's wicked, that one. They all are. If you don't leave, bad luck will get you."

"Is that a threat?"

A pause, then: "It's a promise."

Well, he'd set the guy up for that one. Before Connor could ask anything else, the line went dead. He texted the number to Charlotte so she could send it along to their private detective, but he suspected it would turn up as a burner number unless the caller was completely ignorant about how technology worked.

Connor tucked the phone into his back pocket and slammed the truck door behind him as he exited. Charlotte's rear end was sticking out of her car as she fished in the back for her carry-on. As soon as she pulled it out, Connor took it from her and carried it to her motel door. Today Charlotte was wearing orange tights, a purple skirt, a hot-pink halter top underneath a neon sweater, and black lipstick. She'd twisted her dark hair into pigtails that brushed against her collar. At this point in their careers, Charlotte Hernandez was almost as recognizable as he was.

"Good flight?" he asked as he unlocked the door and handed her the key.

"Long flight." Her voice was high and squeaky, and she looked half the age she really was. "I don't know why you had me come out here if they haven't even agreed yet."

"They will." Connor followed her inside and flipped on the light switch.

Charlotte gasped. "Oh my God, it's hideous! This is the best you could do?"

"We're in the middle of Nowhere, Maine, so yeah, it's the best I could do. I've rented the whole place. We'll be filming by next week."

Charlotte arched a perfectly waxed brow and gestured to the luggage rack. Connor lifted the heavy suitcase and set it on top. "You seem awfully sure for someone who was called an *'overconfident spook chaser'* today."

Connor grinned. "I take it you spoke to Erikson."

"He's worried. He thinks you're obsessed with this place." Charlotte's eyes scanned the peeling wallpaper and the two-cup coffeemaker by the sink. Connor hadn't even known coffeemakers could be so small. "God knows why. This town is small, all the people dress the same, and there aren't any vegan restaurants."

"I'm not obsessed." Connor stuck his hands in his pockets and gave her his most innocent look.

"Nuh-uh—I know that look. You're *mega* obsessed."

"I'm slightly interested, and getting more interested by the minute. I just got a phone call warning me off the Celeste family."

Charlotte chomped on a piece of gum, and Connor could smell the juicy grape flavor from where he stood. "Well, that's something. Usually the threats come later."

"I'm on to a story, Charlotte. Strange things have been happening in that apple orchard for years, and I'm going to get to the bottom of it."

"On national TV."

"Naturally."

She sighed and began to unzip her suitcase. "Your instincts haven't failed you yet. If you say there's something here, there is, even though I still believe that photo is a hoax. You really think that chick will come around? What was her name?"

"Holly."

"Yeah, Holly. Erikson said she sounded like a real hard-ass." She laughed again when she caught his expression. "I know that wolfish smile too. The challenge just makes it more fun for you, doesn't it?"

Connor backed to the door and said, "It would be boring if it was too easy, now wouldn't it? Settle in and I'll check on you for dinner. There's a diner about fifteen minutes away that serves salad."

"Why does everyone think vegans only eat salads?" she shouted after him.

CHAPTER FOUR

Three days later

Holly stood outside the motel room door with her hands in her pockets. It was raining, and not the soft romantic kind, but the torrential downpour kind. Her navy raincoat was pulled over her head, and water dripped from the hood to splash on the tops of her yellow duck rain boots. And still she couldn't force her legs to move another inch.

I am going to grow roots and die here, she thought, because there was no possible way she could make herself knock on Connor Grimm's door.

After two straight days of arguments, Holly had been outvoted by the two sets of twins. They'd been as dismissive of Stacy's offer to buy the orchard as she'd expected, but they'd been surprisingly open to Connor's.

"Did you see the money he's offering us?" Missy had squealed, thrusting the paper with the Grimm logo on it at Holly for the fifth time. "It's enough to keep us afloat for three years. And think of all the things we could do with our new status! I'm picturing haunted midnight apple pickings and spooky Halloween barn weddings. This is *it*, Holly. We have to grow with the times, and this is our shot."

"How can you even consider it?" Holly had argued. "You know how important it is that we remain out of the spotlight, how important our break-even model is."

"Yeah, except we're not breaking even now, are we? We're about to lose our house, Holly."

That was true, but still she'd said, "Now, more than ever, we need to keep a low profile." How were they unable to see what Connor was underneath? He wasn't just some handsome ghost hunter with a big ego; he was the real deal. This was a man who dug in and went after what he wanted with pigheaded stubbornness—she'd seen him do it on past shows. She didn't trust that he was there for a simple ghost haunting. He would sniff and poke around, and he wouldn't be satisfied until he'd exposed their family secrets for the entire world to see. He would paint a target on their backs after the aunts had sacrificed everything to keep Holly and her sisters hidden. "We have to find another way."

"There *is* no other way, Holly. If there were, I know you would have thought of it already. I'm tired of playing it safe." Missy had hugged the offer to her chest. "It's one thing to be broke, it's another to be broke *and* boring. It's been four years, and nothing has happened."

Yet, Holly had thought. Four years ago, the aunts had no longer been able to conceal how powerful Holly and her sisters had become. Since then, she and her sisters had done all they could to fade into a rural existence, but a TV show would, at best, put them squarely in the public's eye and alert the *others* to their presence.

At worst, it would destroy their lives.

Aunt Rose and Aunt Daisy had been on Holly's side until Winter had quietly said, "I think we should do it."

That was when Holly knew she'd lost, because when it came to the future, Winter's word was law. The aunts had agreed with Missy that there was no way around it. The Celestes needed the money or they were going to lose the orchards and the house, and after two hundred years, they simply couldn't allow that to happen.

Once it was decided, Holly had tried to bribe Missy into delivering the news to Connor. Holly couldn't bear to witness the smug arrogance on his face, and she knew Missy would jump at the chance. "Maybe he'll be so grateful he'll take you out to dinner!" she'd said, trying to sweeten the pot.

If Missy hadn't had concert tickets, Holly knew her sister would have gladly taken her up on the suggestion. Even with her much coveted concert tickets she'd still almost gone.

With Missy out of the running, Holly had found Aunt Rose in the little glass-paned sunroom at the rear of the house. It had been converted into a cozy indoor greenhouse, complete with burgeoning shelves of thriving herbs and a long wooden table at the center, scattered with glass vials. Aunt Rose was working a stone mortar and pestle that had been in the Celeste family at least five hundred years, grinding what smelled like dried rosemary. Holly had made the case for Aunt Rose to deliver the news, but Aunt Rose had only chuckled and offered her a brave-of-heart potion.

"No," Holly had said on a sigh, although she'd appreciated the gesture. A potion that would help her would only cost Aunt Rose in the long run.

In the end, despite all of her wheedling to nominate someone else, it had been decided that Holly was the person who should negotiate the deal.

Holly hadn't been able to make herself drive to the motel on Main Street until the afternoon, and by then the clouds had darkened overhead, perfectly reflecting her mood. The moment she'd stepped out of her vehicle it had begun to pour, but she'd been expecting that.

The wind ripped through the pine trees behind the motel and Holly shivered, but still she couldn't move. Her phone buzzed in her pocket, and after a few minutes of listening to the rain patter on her hood, she pulled it out and squinted at the text.

Winter: *How long are you going to stand outside his door?*

Holly scowled and shoved the phone back in her pocket. Sometimes Winter knew too much.

Five minutes passed. Then ten. Then twenty.

Finally the door opened, and Connor stood in the doorframe, the yellow glow of lamps backlighting his form. He was wearing jeans and a simple black T-shirt. His feet were bare, and his hair was mussed and damp from a recent shower. His flint-colored eyes met hers, and without any emotion on his face he said, "Come inside."

Holly swallowed and followed him in. The motel room was sinfully ugly, and she couldn't even think about how many people had slept in that bed over the decades without getting the heebie-jeebies.

She unbuttoned her raincoat but didn't take it off. She'd changed out of her high school track T-shirt into a soft pink V-neck before realizing what she was doing, and had defiantly changed back. Strands of hair slipped from her usual bun, and she pushed them behind her ears. Every ounce of her rebelled at being here; even her tongue felt stuck to the roof of her mouth.

Connor gestured for her to take a seat at the small table, but she shook her head. "You've been out there a while," he commented.

Holly opened her mouth and then closed it again. She couldn't do it. She just couldn't. She knew this was wrong; she knew it would end up badly. How could she jump into shark-infested waters with both feet? She loved their quiet little farm and their loyal base of customers who came to pick apples and buy cider every year. It was quaint and idyllic, and yes, it was run-down and their sales had been inexplicably dwindling, but it was comforting and steeped in history, and now she was expected to risk everything and turn it into some cheap spectacle.

It's that or losing the farm completely, she reminded herself.

She took a moment to compose herself by glancing around the room. A black carry-on was propped against the wall, and a few T-shirts were draped over the back of the desk chair where a high-tech laptop was set up. There was not one, not two, but three cell phones scattered across the desktop. A half-empty bottle of water was on the night stand, and the air smelled of pine and warm spice. Other than those few signs of occupation, the room seemed fairly organized and sterile for having been lived in for three days.

"You could have called," he said softly. He'd been watching her with those insightful eyes while she scanned the room. "It might have been easier."

"Yes, well." She cleared her throat. "I don't do anything the easy way."

He rubbed his jaw but didn't say anything; he just waited patiently for her to speak.

Holly cleared her throat several more times. Finally she forced the words through her lips. "I suppose you know why I'm here. My family accepts your offer—with conditions."

He arched a brow and crossed his arms over a chest that spoke to some decent time in the gym. The combination of those intelligent gray eyes with the five o'clock shadow was enough to give her an unexpected flash of desire.

Holly was both caught off guard and appalled. *Get your shit together, hormones!* She wouldn't be interested in Connor Grimm if he were the last man in Maine.

"Your family accepts my offer, but not you?"

"I'm part of my family," Holly said through clenched teeth. Technically the apple farm had passed to her when her mother had died, but in her mind it belonged equally to all of them. She finally hung the dripping raincoat on the hook by the door but didn't walk in any farther. She didn't plan on staying long.

"Did you change your mind after the man you hired failed to scare me off?" His eyes were sharp and hard, his easy stance not giving away any of the anger that she glimpsed in the press of his lips.

Holly frowned. "I didn't hire anyone to scare you."

"So the person who warned me away from the Celeste family had nothing to do with you?"

Holly blinked. Who could have done that and why? "Who was it?"

"He didn't give me a name."

She shrugged. "It wasn't me." Honestly, she didn't care if Connor believed her or not; she wasn't wasting her breath trying to worm her way into his good graces when she had no desire to be there.

Connor kept that hard stare on her for a moment longer before he reached for one of the cell phones, his biceps shifting beneath the tight sleeves of his T-shirt. Again, she glimpsed the bottom of a tattoo. Was it a ghost?

"What are your conditions?" He swiped his thumb over the screen, and she assumed he was opening a notes app.

Holly took a deep breath. "None of us appear on the show."

Connor dropped his hand. "Come on, Holly. My show is a visual record of America's stories, and they always sound better coming from the people who know them best. Is that something your whole family wants, or just you?"

Actually, Missy was dying to be on the show. "All of us," she said firmly.

Connor scowled, but he typed the request in his phone. "Next?"

"One episode only."

"No." He shook his head. "I'm not rushing it. If the story deserves more than an episode, then it will get more."

"One episode."

"No."

Holly shoved at the hair slipping from her bun. She'd suspected this would be a sticking point for him, so she'd come prepared. "Three max."

"As many as necessary."

"Connor, I swear I'll walk right now if you don't agree."

He stared her down, his gray eyes unflinching. "Then walk."

Holly turned on her heel and reached for her raincoat. She had one arm in the sleeve when his palm slid around the bare skin of her other arm. He'd been entirely silent on the carpet, like a big cat in the jungle. The light touch of his warm palm sent goose bumps racing over her chilled skin.

He jerked his hand away, as if he hadn't meant to touch her and instantly regretted it. "Fine," he growled from the vicinity of her ear. "Three episodes max."

Holly faced him again. Even though he'd taken a step back, he was still much closer than he had been at the start of their negotiations. Despite the fact that she disliked almost everything about him, she was affected by the enormity of his presence. This was a man who could fill any room he occupied, and it wouldn't matter if it were a tiny motel room or a grand ballroom.

She finished pulling on the raincoat but didn't button it. "We want a disclaimer at the start of the episode that says it's for entertainment only."

"We already do that for legal purposes." His eyes slid over her face and down to her T-shirt. "Edward Jones High School track. You were a runner?"

"Sprints, and I sucked at it."

"Yeah, but at least you got a sweet T-shirt with a decade of wear out of it."

"Is that a fashion insult?" she asked in outrage.

His grin was disarming and lopsided, and did weird things to her stomach. "I like that you're wearing it. It's wholesome."

Holly didn't know if she was offended or oddly complimented. "I suppose you're used to women wearing designer labels, but around here we work, and we need clothes that we can work in."

His gaze returned to her face and mouth, and she had the strangest feeling that he was thinking about something else entirely.

"Anyway," Holly continued, "there's one more request, and then we'll be all squared. Actually, it's not so much a request as a nonnegotiable demand." She wiped her palms on the sides of her jeans. She wasn't happy about this one, but it was the only way she could see to protect her family. If Connor Grimm was let loose, he might dig around where he didn't belong. She didn't give two hoots if he wanted to scamper after some supposed ghost in the apple orchards—apart from the exposure it would bring—but he absolutely could not be allowed to discover the secret she and her ancestors had kept hidden for centuries. The only way to ensure her family was safe was to keep him on a tight leash. Winter had refused the task, and Holly didn't trust

Missy not to get distracted by Connor's annoyingly charming smile. That, unfortunately, left Holly as the sacrificial lamb. Feeling like a martyr she said, "I want an active partner role in your investigations."

His eyebrow winged upward in obvious surprise. "You want to investigate the haunting with me?"

No, she wanted to keep a close eye on his every move and thwart him if he got too close to things that were none of his business. "Yes. I insist on it." She'd known Connor would want to know why, so she'd practiced the next part in front of the mirror so that she would look earnest when she said it. "I'm the manager, and I want to have control of the narrative."

Connor hesitated for a moment. "I usually investigate with my brother, but he can't be on site this time. It's an unusual request—"

"Demand," she corrected.

Connor narrowed his eyes. "*Demand*, but it might benefit me to have your local expertise. Consider it done." He held out his hand, and Holly hesitated. She didn't want to seal the deal, but she had little other choice. She slid her hand into his, the rasp of his palm already familiar from the brief touch before, and his fingers closed around hers. Again, the heat of his body was in shocking contrast to the chill of hers. "You're cold," he said flatly, still holding onto her hand.

"I stood in the rain for twenty minutes trying to make myself come in."

"Am I that scary?"

"You're that smug."

He gave a bark of laughter and released her. "We have a deal, Holly Celeste. When do I move in?"

CHAPTER FIVE

Holly snorted. "Yeah, right. Good one."

"I'm dead serious. My crew will stay at the motel, but my assistant and I will need to be on the premises. I can't be running back and forth into town all the time. It's in the contract. Didn't you read it?"

Holly's jaw clenched. Her T-shirt was wet in patches, and her skin had been ice-cold each time he'd touched it. Connor was irritated to discover he was having a hard time focusing on the contract negotiations when all he wanted to do was warm her up a bit.

"You can't live with us for weeks at a time!" Holly cried, her face pale. "No way! Get a trailer!"

Connor sighed. It would have been so much easier if she were eager to have answers, like some of his previous clients. One couple had even offered him their own bed, which he'd politely declined. Access to the Celeste house would have also meant easy access to the basement and the attic, to possible hidden records or other clues. A trailer was better than nothing—at least he could stay on the premises as late as he needed—but it wasn't ideal.

"The house is huge," he said with as much reason as he could inject in his voice. "Surely there is a spare room."

Holly darted forward and snatched his hand, did a weird reverse shake, and pushed it away. "I take back my handshake. The deal is off."

"You can't take back a handshake. The hand has been shaken."

"Oh, I can, and I have. It's now unshaken."

"That's not a thing."

"It's a trailer or nothing, and you're lucky I'm agreeing to that. It's bad enough you're going to be snooping around our property at all hours. You can't be in our house too."

"Fine," Connor snapped, "but these negotiations are feeling very one-sided."

She shrugged, entirely unconcerned. If he hadn't wanted this gig so badly, he might have given up on her when she sent Kevin and Mark packing, but he *did* want this mystery, and damned if she wasn't already using that against him.

When she'd demanded that she take part in the investigation, he'd been knocked off kilter for a moment, but when she'd explained that she wanted to control the narrative, it had made sense. She was so protective over the farm that, now that he thought about it, he would have been surprised if she hadn't asked.

Sorry, *demanded*.

The agreement worked out perfectly for him. More time with Holly meant more opportunities to gently probe about the other odd happenings at Wicked Good Apples.

Someone rapped on the door, and a moment later Charlotte wedged her way into the room, forcing Holly forward so that she had to stand beside him. Connor caught a whiff of berries and mint in her dark hair. His last girlfriend had used salon-sanctioned shampoo that cost three hundred dollars a bottle, and wouldn't touch anything without a designer label—Holly had been right about that. And yet Holly, who used Christmas shampoo in May and wore a ten-year-old high school T-shirt, was somehow more intriguing than his ex had ever been.

"I heard shouting," Charlotte purred as she shook out her Hello Kitty umbrella and leaned it against the wall. She'd taken out her pigtails and had coiled her hair into a dozen tiny buns all over her head.

Bullshit, Connor thought. There was no way she'd heard them in her cabin through the thundering rain. She'd seen Holly enter and had been nosy was more like it.

Charlotte waved her hand, flashing a lime-green manicure. "Hi, I'm Charlotte Hernandez, Connor's assistant and right-hand woman. *Grimm Reality* wouldn't be a success without my tireless behind-the-scenes work, but do I get any credit for that?"

Connor snorted. "Yes, you do actually. You insisted your name go first on the end credits, *and* you named a show episode after yourself, *and* you made Charlotte's Pick an annual event." Charlotte was right when she said the show wouldn't be a success without her. It was one of the many reasons she brought home the same salary that he and Erikson did.

Charlotte grinned, her eyes twinkling. "Oh yeah." She returned her focus to Holly, who had a faint look of admiration on her face. "In case you're wondering, no, Connor and I aren't sleeping together. He's like a cranky big brother, and the idea of a sexual relationship with him is repulsive."

Holly gave an awkward laugh. "I wasn't going to ask that."

"Maybe not, but I would hate for anyone to think for even a moment that we were involved in *that way*." Charlotte shuddered.

Holly nodded solemnly. "I completely understand."

Good thing he was a confident man.

Charlotte propped a hand on her hip. "You must be Holly Celeste."

"I am."

"Well, Holly, Connor's a pretty busy guy, so if you ever have any questions about coordination, what part of the property is being used, what the filming schedule is, or anything else, I'm your girl. I know Connor's life better than he does. For example," she said, turning to him, "your ex called, and she wants a one-time emotional damage payment for the night she thought you were going to propose, but you broke up with her instead."

Connor briefly closed his eyes. "If Lisa wants to talk to me, she has my number."

"Oh, it wasn't Lisa. It was Juliette."

Holly gazed up at him with an unreadable look in her eye. She probably thought he was some shallow TV personality sleeping with and discarding women like a B-list actor, when the truth was he'd only had two girlfriends in the past five years, and neither relationship had lasted longer than six months. It seemed women didn't love coming in second to *Grimm Reality*.

Connor gave Charlotte a speaking glare. Charlotte pressed her finger to her lips. "Got it," she stage-whispered. She took out her phone and began typing into her notes app, speaking out loud as she did. "Do not talk about former girlfriends in front of cute new client."

Connor was going to kill her.

Holly edged around Charlotte. "Thanks for calling me cute, Charlotte, but don't worry about it. I have zero interest in Connor's private life. I'll see you both tomorrow."

Before Connor could say anything else, Holly had slipped out the door.

"What the hell, Charlotte?" he snarled the moment the latch clicked.

"I did it for your own good, Boss." She patted him on the shoulder. "I took one look at her and knew she was trouble, so I thought I'd head off anything before it had a chance to start. She's no Lisa or Juliette. She probably has feelings and shit."

Connor was offended. "*I* have feelings."

Charlotte scowled at a water stain on the front of the mini fridge. "No, you don't; you're in show business. Even if you did, it doesn't matter: you move every few weeks, and sometimes you're on location for a month or more. Until *Grimm Reality* is canceled, you are a relationship no-go. Besides, we still don't know what's going on in those orchards, and you don't want to mess that up by making questionable personal choices."

She was right, as usual.

Connor pushed aside thoughts of Holly's berry shampoo and strode to his laptop. "I'll send you the terms of the contract, and we need to get two trailers out to Wicked Good Apples pronto. It's time to find out what's really happening on that farm."

≈ ≈

Missy, Winter, and Holly stood on the porch and watched as a truck backed a second streamlined trailer onto the grassy lawn that separated the house and the Golden Delicious orchard.

"I can't believe he's actually staying on premises," Winter said. Her curly red hair was pulled into a low ponytail, and a pair of work gloves was tucked into the back pocket of her jeans. "That's some dedication. I would've bet serious money he was one of those hosts that only shows up for pretend interviews."

"No, he's the real deal." Holly's stomach sank as she watched Connor motion the truck farther back. He was wearing paint-stained jeans, worn work boots, and another plain T-shirt—this one forest green. The early dawn light cast a golden outline around his body, making him look far more angelic than Holly knew he was.

Missy sighed. "He's such a ten."

"Is that why you squeezed into that dress this morning?" Winter asked, eyeing the knitted violet dress Missy had wriggled into the moment she'd heard the trucks arrive.

"Um, duh, but also I'm going on Cherry and Derek's morning show to announce that we're *Grimm Reality*'s newest filming location. I thought I'd begin drumming up some publicity straight away."

Holly silently groaned. There was no restraining Missy now. Soon people would begin stopping by, not to buy apples or taste cider like the apple farm needed, but to gawk at the film crews. Holly hoped that was the only attention she and her sisters would draw.

Connor and the truck driver unhitched the trailer, and Connor waved at the sisters. Missy and Winter waved back, but Holly only glared.

"You're not usually so cranky," Winter commented when she noticed Holly's expression. "What's going on?"

"I don't trust him."

Missy ran her fingers through her moussed hair. "You worry too much. This kind of exposure is just what this old apple farm needs. I'm sick of living in the shadows."

"Those shadows have kept us alive."

"I don't know, Holly. *Are* we living?"

Before Holly could answer, Winter tugged her work gloves from her pocket and slapped them against her palm. "I need to prune the trees in the back orchard. I could use some help."

"Um, hello? I have an interview to do, remember? I can't get this dirty." Missy waved her hands over her tight plum dress and sky-high heels. She did look amazing. Of the three sisters, she was the only one who could really pull off an outfit like that.

"I'll help," Holly said. They all knew it was going to be her anyway. "I have to spend an hour with the accounts, but then I'll be out."

Winter nodded and clomped off the porch. Missy followed with a cute little run, her heels clipping on the weathered boards with quick taps. Holly pressed her fingers to her eyes and took two deep breaths. When she dropped them, Connor was watching her with a gaze that saw far too much.

Having him here was a mistake. He was an observer of human nature, and he was likely to learn just as much about the Celestes by watching them interact as he was the "ghost" in the orchards.

Trouble, trouble, on the double, Holly thought with a frown, and went inside.

CHAPTER SIX

Once the trailers were in place, Connor got straight to business. In addition to cohosting *Grimm Reality*, he also produced it, so he spent the morning canvassing the orchards with his lead cameraman and discussing lighting, angles, and locations. Wicked Good Apples wasn't as large as the apple farm across town, but the orchards were old and diverse and had a charming quality to them. The trees were gnarled and twisted, their blush-colored blossoms in striking contrast to the craggy branches. The grasses were tall between trees and the layout wasn't always intuitive, but the more Connor traversed the orchards, the more he understood why Holly felt so strongly about them. There was something special here, something ancient and gothic and handcrafted in a way the larger apple farms with their homogenous trees could never be.

The Celeste house was accessed by a winding dirt driveway lined with massive maple trees, and beside the house was an old gray barn with a wood-burned sign that read: "Wicked Good Apples—'Nuff Said." He hadn't been inside the barn yet, but he knew it was where visitors paid for their apples and bought cookie cutters and apple pie filling in the fall.

Apple trees completely surrounded the property. The orchards at the far back abutted a forest thick with birches, beeches, and firs. A clear babbling brook snaked between the trees, and a set of weathered boards had been slapped across it to function as a bridge.

Everywhere Connor explored there were secrets to be found. Across the brook there was a little cow path that wound through a patch of new-growth birches, their papery skins peeling like little bits of ash in a fire. There was a ladder of gray boards nailed to an ancient ash on the far eastern end of the property, and when Connor looked upward, he found an old tree house, the roof caved in and the unmistakable script of children on the door that, although faded by time, he could still read: "No Boys Allowed." There was an abandoned wagon in a wild barley field, and dirt patches beyond where he thought the women might grow pumpkins and gourds in the fall. The birds were out in full force, as was the sun, and by the time Connor returned to the trailer to consult with Charlotte, he found himself charmed stupid by the entire place.

Charmed *and* excited. It was the perfect setting for strange happenings.

After they discussed taking shots of the house and the Golden Delicious orchards first, Charlotte reminded him he had an appointment with Amy Gordon at three. Amy was a regular Wicked Good Apples customer and was eager to be interviewed about her weird experience at the orchards.

Connor glanced at his watch. He still had a couple hours before he had to head to Amy's house with the film crew, and he'd spotted Holly and her sister pruning the apple trees in one of the older, obviously less used orchards by the brook. While their hands were distracted, it might be a good time to chat them up. People often wove bits of interesting information into their everyday conversations, and Connor was a collector of bits of information. Besides, he'd promised Holly he'd involve her, and that meant asking her along to the interview.

He strode across the grass and breathed in the sweet scents of blossoming clover. He'd spent the past month in the muggy swamps of Louisiana, and there was something to be said for stepping outside in May and not immediately breaking into a sweat. Connor was from Boston, so he wasn't a newbie to New England, but he'd grown up in the city instead of in the fields, and sometimes when he was in a place like this, he wondered what he'd missed out on.

He found the sisters at the edge of the orchard, so close to the stream that he could hear the gurgle of water. He couldn't tell which sister was with Holly since the two redheads were twins, as were the aunts. It was fascinating how twins so often ran in families. He wondered if Holly's mother had been a twin or if she'd been an older singleton like Holly was.

Winter and Missy were both small, compact women with silky red curls and pixie-like noses, and he wouldn't have been all that surprised if they'd had pointed ears. In general terms they were attractive women, but the minute he entered the row Holly and her sister were working in, his eyes zeroed in on Holly.

Unlike her sisters, her hair was straight and dark, and the hazel of her eyes had green undertones. Holly was a bit taller than the twins too, and although she was still shorter than him, she had the impressive ability to look down on him as if he were two feet tall instead of over six. She had high cheekbones, a lush mouth, and a figure that filled out her jeans and tank top in a way that made Connor's blood heat. He thought women were beautiful in all shapes and sizes, but he personally preferred partners who had a little extra curve.

Holly bent over to clip a branch, and he gave a silent groan before forcing the visual from his head. Charlotte was right; he had zero business thinking about Holly in any way other than as a professional partner—not that he had to worry about mixing business with pleasure; Holly had made it clear where she stood on that when she'd left his motel room the night before.

The branch Holly severed drifted silently to the ground. Connor blinked. The branch had floated as if it were a leaf caught on the wind instead of tumbling to the grass with the force of gravity. He was almost sure of it, except he supposed it was possible it had caught on a lower branch and had only *appeared* to be suspended in the air in a way no object with mass should.

The sister lifted her head and stared at him, as if she'd been pinged by his presence. "Holly," she said sharply. The moment she opened her mouth, he knew it was Winter. Winter had a challenging voice that he remembered from his first visit. She seemed like the type of person that could be a formidable foe or an equally formidable friend.

Holly's shoulders stiffened, and with her next snip the branch dropped to the ground with a soft thud. The hairs on the back of Connor's arms stood as he strode over to them. He was ninety-five percent certain he'd witnessed something not quite natural. "Hello, ladies. How's it going?"

"Fine," Winter answered, leaning on one hip and crossing her arms. "Have you seen the entire property?"

"Yes. It's perfect," he said simply.

Holly finally gave him the time of day, lowering her clippers and turning to smile up at him with such radiance that his heart stopped in his chest. He hadn't seen her smile before, he realized—at least not like that. It was a smile filled with love and pride and joy for her orchards, and he had the sudden thought that if a woman ever smiled for *him* like that, he'd marry her on the spot.

Caught off guard by the unwelcome thought, he quickly added, "Perfect for filming."

Holly's smile faded along with the sparkle in her eye. "Right. Filming."

Connor glanced away. When he looked back, he focused on Winter. He gestured to the gnarled apple trees that were slighter and twistier than all the rest. "Is this the original orchard?"

"Yes. When our great-great-grandmother planted the orchards, she started back here. The grounds are hilly enough that you can see this orchard from the front porch." A sound trilled from Winter's back pocket, and she pulled out her phone to silence it. "I have to run to the house and make sure Aunt Daisy takes her meds."

"Oh, I'll do that," Holly offered, but Winter was already backing away, a mischievous glint in her eye.

"Nope, I got it. Besides, you know our family history better than anyone, Holly. You should be the one to tell it."

She plunged into the apple trees, ignoring Holly as she called after her.

Connor jammed his hands in his pockets and gave her his most disarming grin. "I guess you're stuck with me."

Holly glared at him before picking up Winter's clippers and thrusting them at him. "If you're going to make a nuisance of yourself, you might as well help."

He must be losing his touch, Connor thought as he took the clippers. That grin usually charmed even the most stubborn of his detractors. He watched Holly work for a few minutes. Her assessments were swift, her movements sure. It was obvious she'd done this thousands of times and could probably prune a tree in her sleep. "You're clipping away the smaller branches?"

"Yes, it allows for better growth of the larger branches." She gestured to the tree beside her. "You can do that one."

Connor circled the tree and severed a scraggly branch with a satisfying snip. The wood fell to the ground with a soft thump. "So, your great-great-grandmother planted this orchard first?" he prompted.

"Yes, Great-great-grandma Autumn started the orchards here, and generations after have added to it. It takes five to eight years for a new apple tree to bear fruit, so it requires time and patience to run an orchard. It's not a get-rich-quick operation."

Connor snipped another branch and swatted at a fly that was buzzing around his ear. "Did she intend for it to be open to the public?"

"I think you know the answer to that." Holly's greenish-gray eyes narrowed, unimpressed by his play at ignorance. "Two hundred years ago farms were mostly self-sufficient. She planted them for her family." Holly glanced away to work on the tree, but before she did, Connor thought he spotted a flash of disingenuity in her eyes. A half-truth, then. But why?

"Did she have a large family?"

"Three girls."

He let the shears lower. "An older girl and a set of twins?"

Snip. Snip. "Yes."

Well, that was interesting. It would be very rare for the same birth order to be repeated each generation. So rare, in fact, that it was almost impossible.

"Was your grandmother from here?" he asked casually.

"No. Switzerland. She immigrated alone, then she met a local farmer, fell in love, and started this place."

He wanted to ask about her mother, but he knew if he pried too much, she'd close down completely, so he stuck to history. She seemed more comfortable talking about that, and there was plenty to learn from the past, especially if there was a ghost haunting the place.

Holly walked over to him and pointed to a weak branch he'd missed. "That one," she said. She was close enough that he could see the perspiration beading along her hairline. He breathed deeply, annoyed by the effect her mint and berry shampoo seemed to have on him.

He clipped the growth and then rested his arm on a thick branch. "Your great-great-grandmother's name was Autumn. And your aunts are Daisy and Rose. What is your mother's name?"

"Her name was Lilac."

Was. That was right, he'd read an article about the car accident in the sheath of papers Charlotte had handed him. If he remembered right, the news clipping had been frustratingly vague about the cause of the wreck.

"Daisy, Rose, and Lilac—all spring flowers. And you and your sisters are named Holly, Winter, and Missy." He frowned when he got to Missy, which didn't fit in with the obvious winter theme. He didn't remember seeing any other name in his research. "Is that her real name?"

Holly's lips twitched. "She had it legally changed. She was named Mistletoe, but don't tell her I told you."

Connor grimaced and Holly laughed out loud. He liked her laugh: it was deep and throaty and genuine. "Poor girl."

"Yeah, I don't really know what our mom was thinking."

"Every generation of girls is named after a season?"

"Yes. When we've gone through all four seasons, we cycle through them again. Because our aunts and mother had spring names, my sisters and I should have had summer names, but our mother had a habit of doing what she wanted. Cutesy, isn't it?"

Cutesy was one explanation. Deeply spiritual and elemental was another.

Connor waved his hand to shoo the annoying fly off Holly's shoulder. When his fingertips accidentally grazed her skin, she inhaled quietly. His eyes involuntarily fell to her mouth before returning to her hazel gaze. "So you're just a cute family with generations of totally normal women running an apple farm?"

The fly landed on her forearm, and he brushed it away again, but this time he left his fingertips on her smooth skin, which was hot from the sun. Without thinking about what he was doing, he slid his hand up to cup her elbow.

Holly's eyes widened and she blurted, "Yup, that's us: totally normal."

They stood beneath the flowering apple trees, his palm cradling her elbow and his eyes searching hers as if he could read all of her secrets if only he looked deeply enough. He swore the air thickened around them like an atmospheric bubble.

"Good to know," he murmured. "For a minute there I thought you might be witches."

CHAPTER SEVEN

Holly was so distracted by the feel of his hand on her bare skin that it took a moment for his words to sink in. His charisma and sharp intelligence, along with a dose of lucky good looks, were what made him such an enchanting television host—and when that magnetism was turned full force on a person, it was almost impossible to ignore the spell he wove.

Unless he accused said person of being a witch.

Holly yanked her arm away. Had he seriously just put the charm on her in order to weasel some ridiculous confession out of her? There was low and then there was *low*. She was angry with him, but even angrier with herself. She didn't even like the man; how had she allowed herself to be drawn into the moment like that?

His gaze was inscrutable when he said, "That came out wrong."

"Oh, so you didn't mean to imply that I'm a witch?"

He didn't answer.

Holly scoffed and backed up a step. "You're unbelievable. I know you're looking for some juicy TV drama, but you're barking up the wrong tree, buddy. There aren't any witches on this apple farm, and there never have been." And still her skin crinkled with fear. He'd been there a single morning, and already he was edging toward a truth that *had* to stay hidden. Was this why he'd chosen Wicked Good Apples over any number of other haunted locations in the state? Did he suspect there was more than a ghost in their orchards?

Clouds began rolling in from the east, the blue sky darkening with the advent of an afternoon thunderstorm. Holly was so angry she barely noticed the encroaching pile of steely clouds. "Let me be clear, Connor Grimm: you can sit on your ass in the cold all night long looking for ghosts, but if you come after me or my family, I will bring you down with the wrath of fricking Zeus." She stabbed her finger in the air. "And don't you dare try the same tactics with my sisters, because Missy will definitely fall for it, and she's a lot more sensitive than people realize."

He frowned. "Tactics?"

"I know a play when I hear one. You thought you'd see if you could get the hick chick all flustered and then throw a comment like that at her."

He took a step forward, but she practically snarled, so he paused. "Listen, Holly, it wasn't the best timing, but I sure as hell wasn't playing you." He raked his hand through his hair and murmured, "I don't know what I was doing."

She might have believed him if she hadn't heard his own assistant mention his slew of unhappy exes.

"And I don't think you're some 'hick chick,'" he added. "I don't know anything about you really, but I'd like the chance to learn. For work purposes."

Holly gave a harsh laugh. "That's never going to happen. We're going to have the barest of professional relationships for the next few weeks, and then you can trot off and convince some other unsuspecting sap that his property is haunted."

His eyes flashed with anger. "I don't know if you're really so conceited that you think the thousands of people who have witnessed the supernatural are idiots, or if you're just trying to convince yourself it's not real so you can mock what I do, but either way you have loyal customers who will attest to something strange going on here. You claim to love your orchards deeply, and yet you're so quick to dismiss the accounts of the very people that butter your bread."

Holly's cheeks burned at the insult. "Really? Just who are these 'loyal customers' who claim to have all the answers you're looking for?"

Thunder rumbled overhead, and he lifted his face to the sky before he answered. She tried very hard not to picture a streak of lightning sizzling the ground at his feet. "Amy Gordon, for one. I'm scheduled to meet with her in half an hour. I actually came out here to invite you along."

"*HA!*"

"'*HA*' what?"

"'*HA*' as in Amy Gordon is a fraud. She's pissed at me because she stepped on Prickles the last time she was here and then tried to sue me, but no lawyer would take on her case." Amy was also dating Holly's ex-boyfriend, and Holly wouldn't put it past Amy to hold a grudge about that too.

His brows drew together. "Prickles?"

"Yes. He's my hedgehog." She crossed her arms, prepared to defend her choice of pet. A raindrop splattered on her cheek and she took a deep breath, trying to calm her emotions. The man had just accused her of being a witch; she didn't need to give him any more ammunition with ill-timed weather events. "He's adorbs, even though sometimes he gets loose and explores the barn. I should have sued *her* for almost crushing him with her big stupid feet."

Connor dismissed her excuse with a shake of his head. "She might have issues with you, but in her initial interview her account didn't sound fake."

"You're being misled," she insisted. "I can prove that any 'loyal customer' claiming to have seen strange things at Wicked Good Apples is only yanking your chain."

A soft rain began to fall, and Holly refused to notice how Connor's T-shirt stuck to his abs or how the water dripped down his strong chin.

"All right, let's make this fun," he said, a gleam in his eye. "If Amy can convince you of her story, you'll let me search your attic and basement for old letters, records, or ledgers. A house that's been inhabited by the same family for two hundred years has to have a treasure trove of documents stuffed in trunks and boxes, and I'm looking for a particular name."

She agreed instantly. The last time Amy had been at the farm was when she'd almost murdered Prickles with her ugly clogs, and there was no way Amy had seen a ghost in the middle of the day. Holly was already smug with the idea of rubbing Connor's mistake in his face. "If you're right I'll let you search the attic and basement *with* me. But if I'm right, you promise to shoot only one episode."

His jaw tensed as the rain came down harder, pelting the dirt and grass at their feet and jouncing the blossoms with fat drops. The fragrant scent of disturbed apple blossoms hung in the air even as a flash of lightning streaked across the sky. Connor held out his hand for the second time in so many days. "You have a deal, Celeste. Get dry and meet me at my truck in twenty minutes."

She shook his hand with more force than necessary. "Get ready to eat humble pie, Grimm."

He grinned. "Where did you learn your insults? The 1950s schoolyard bully's handbook?"

Holly burst out laughing and was instantly aggravated with herself. "Less talking and more walking. I have a bet to win."

❧ ❧

Holly slid into the leather seat of Connor's pickup truck, shook out her bright yellow umbrella, and slammed the door shut.

"Where did this rain come from?" Connor asked as he started the truck. It leaped to life with a sleek prowl. "I thought the forecast said it was supposed to be sunny skies all day."

"Welcome to Maine. If you don't like the weather, wait five minutes." She gestured out the windshield to a blue patch of sky on the horizon.

When she glanced over, she noticed he'd changed into his TV clothes, which consisted of dark jeans and the famous crisp white polo shirt with the words *Grimm Brother* embroidered on the pocket. She'd seen shirts exactly like it sold online for Halloween and cosplay. His hair was wet from the rain, and he smelled as if he'd applied a hint of fresh cologne—that same pine and spice scent that made her think of cool fall days creeping into winter. She owned an apple farm, which meant fall was one of her favorite times of the year, and she thought it was a little unfair that the man she disliked so much would smell so delicious.

Holly hadn't gone out of her way to dress in anything special since she wouldn't be on camera. She'd left her hair down to dry, and it fell over the shoulders of her T-shirt that proudly proclaimed her an Oxford comma lover. Her ensemble was complete with a pair of jeans that had a rip on the thigh, and tan work boots. She bit her lip. Maybe she should have at least found a pair of jeans that didn't have a tear.

"My film crew is already at Amy's." Connor's eyes darted to the time on the console. "We're a few minutes late. I've already preinterviewed Amy, and I'm going to follow a similar line of questioning for the cameras. If you have any questions, feel free to speak up, but no browbeating the witness."

"I don't want to be on camera."

"We'll edit out your voice if her answers are of any interest." He steered the truck down the rutted driveway and turned onto a back road, although to be fair, all the roads in that area were back roads. The windshield wipers swept away the last drops of rain as the sun began to peek from between gray clouds. "Should we set a time to investigate the attic?"

The smile he gave her was so mischievous that if her purse hadn't jittered on her lap at that moment, she might have embarrassed herself by staring too long. Holly discretely shifted the bag and hoped he hadn't seen it move, but his eyes were already back on the road.

"Don't get cocky. I bring the worst out in Amy Gordon. You'll see."

He arched a brow and turned at a mailbox painted with a bright red cardinal. "You have history other than the lawsuit?"

"Oh yeah. We graduated high school together. She slept with my boyfriend senior year, and now she's dating my ex."

Connor stifled a groan. "This is probably going to be a mistake."

Holly smiled innocently. "Don't be silly. She can have Jeremy; he's my ex for a reason. All I care about is exposing her for the fraud she is."

He parked the truck and turned to her, his slate-gray gaze assessing her from her loose hair down to her boots, his eyes returning to linger for a brief moment on the skin showing through the tear in her jeans. "Now I'm certain I'm going to regret this."

A big white van was already parked in Amy's driveway, its rear doors flung open now that the rain had stopped to reveal more camera equipment than Holly would ever know what to do with. She followed Connor to the front door, and even though it was cracked open, he still rang the doorbell. A moment later a camerawoman appeared and gestured him inside.

Holly gawked at Amy's living room, which had been transformed into a mini film set. A navy couch was positioned by a wall-to-wall bay window, the coffee table in front of it staged with a steaming mug of tea. All the other furniture had been pushed against the walls. Bright, white lights were positioned around the couch, and a big fuzzy microphone on a stick was propped against the wall, ready to hover over Amy's head while she spoke.

Amy stood in the center of the room, assessing the changes with delight. She was wearing a black-and-white-striped dress accessorized with a chunky ruby necklace. A bit too *Beetlejuice* for Holly's taste, but whatever. Amy's blonde locks were curled and hair-sprayed stiff, and she'd applied an enormous amount of makeup. So much, in fact, that Holly was genuinely worried it might start melting under the heat of the lights.

The moment Amy's eyes landed on Connor she beamed him a thousand-watt smile and strutted over with the swinging hips of a catwalk model. "Connor," she purred, holding out her hand. Holly thought she probably wanted him to kiss it, but he only gave her a brief shake and released her fingers.

"Amy, thank you again for letting us film in your home. I brought with me Holly Celeste from Wicked Good Apples. I thought she might like to observe the interview and filming process."

Amy's ultra-bright smile faded. "I'm not sure I feel comfortable having her in the room when I'm talking about such . . . *delicate* matters. I might feel censored."

Holly bared her teeth. "You won't even know I'm here." Before Amy could make a stink about her presence, she faded into the noisy background and claimed an empty wooden chair that had been pushed against the wall.

While Connor competently directed his team, Holly observed him with a pinched brow. He knew everyone's name and asked about their trips north, inquired about their families, made jokes about the weather, gave condolences about colicky babies, and generally seemed to command the adoration of the entire room.

Ugh. He was such a showman!

At last the team was ready and the cameras began rolling. Connor was in full investigative TV personality mode as he sat beside Amy on the couch and said, "Amy, you've been visiting Wicked Good Apples since you were a child—is that right?"

Amy nodded. "They've always had the best apples. Everyone in town knows it. It's a beautiful spot, even if the owners are strange."

Strange! That little . . .

Connor's gray eyes searched Amy's face. "But everything changed last year when you stopped by for your annual apple picking trip. It was a typical Saturday afternoon, but what happened wasn't normal at all, was it?"

Amy's carefully crafted smile faltered a bit. "No, Connor, it wasn't normal. We were in the far orchard, picking some of the heirloom apple varieties that you can't get anywhere else these days, when I felt a sudden chill at my back." She shivered. It wasn't a theatrical shiver meant to impress, but rather an involuntary chill. Holly cocked her head in interest. "I turned to speak to my husband, but he'd wandered into another row, so I was all alone." Amy swallowed and held out her hand.

Connor took her fingers without hesitation and squeezed comfortingly. Holly rolled her eyes.

"At least I thought I was alone until I saw the man. He was sitting on the ground underneath one of the apple trees, one knee bent, and he was whistling while he peeled an apple with a knife. He was dressed strangely, as if he'd just stepped out of the 1800s. He had on an old-fashioned gray coat with a vest and trousers. I could even see the silver chain of a pocket watch."

"Was there anything else odd about him?"

Amy nodded. "He was wearing a roundish black hat."

An assistant jumped forward and handed Connor a sheet of paper with the photograph of a black, bowler-type hat on it. He showed it to Amy. "Did it look like this?"

Amy nodded again and caught her bottom lip between her teeth. "Exactly like that. He had a waxed moustache, and one of his eyes was milky white. When he smiled up at me, his teeth were crooked."

Holly was so caught up in Amy's story that she set her purse on the ground, completely forgetting she'd unzipped it so air could circulate inside. Holly had scrolled the paranormal websites that had begun popping up a few years ago claiming Wicked Good Apples was haunted, but she and her sisters had never encountered a ghost on the farm. After a while Holly had concluded it was all conspiracy-theory nonsense, but then she'd never heard any person speak of the supposed ghost with a quiver in her voice the way Amy was doing right now.

"It was so chilly that my teeth were chattering, even though it was sunny and seventy degrees. I remember being startled, and I said something like, 'Oh, I didn't see you there.'"

"Did he answer you?" Connor's tone was coaxing, his entire body turned to her as if he were riveted by her tale.

She nodded and her fingers twisted together in her lap. "He held out the apple he was peeling and said, 'Care for a poisoned apple?' I got scared and backed away, and he gave this mocking sort of laugh and said, 'I wouldn't have eaten it either—if I'd known.'"

Chills raced over Holly's skin and her hands suddenly felt clammy. She wiped them on the thighs of her jeans, but she couldn't tear her gaze away from Amy. Amy was an uber bitch with a dramatic need for attention, but nothing about her story sounded fake. In fact, she seemed more scared and nervous than excited to share it.

Connor's assistant handed him another sheet of paper, this one a photograph of an oil portrait of a man Holly had never seen before. Connor passed Amy the paper. The moment her eyes fell on the portrait, she flinched and shoved the photograph back into his hands.

"Is that him?" Connor asked.

Amy nodded, her fingers visibly trembling.

Connor focused on the camera. "It's not just any ghost haunting Wicked Good Apples. The man Miss Gordon identified is none other than Councilman Jonathan Miller."

Holly felt as if she'd just been slapped. Her cheeks heated and her vision wavered. She knew that name. If Connor was right about the spirit being Councilman Miller, then the ghost was real. The foundation of her family's entire business had been built on Councilman Miller and what he'd done to her great-great-grandmother.

"What happened next?" Connor prompted Amy.

"I ran away screaming and found my husband. By the time we got back to the tree, the man was gone, but there was a peeled apple on the ground. My husband said anyone could have left it, but"—Amy forced her stiff hair behind her ears—"I knew it was his. My husband took me inside the barn to rest, and I was just getting over my terror when I stepped on this stupid hedgehog the owners had negligently left out."

Now *there* was the annoying and self-righteous Amy Holly knew.

Holly was so focused on her inner turmoil over learning the identity of the ghost that she almost didn't spot the dark patch of spines waddling toward the couch. When she saw them, she did a double take. *Oh no!* She snatched her purse off the ground and pulled it open. Prickles was gone. She zeroed in on the little hedgehog inching toward

Amy's spiky heels. If Amy stepped on him with those murder weapons on her feet . . .

Cursing her stupidity, Holly began to slink along the wall behind the cameras, stepping over cords as she crept closer to the front of the room. She'd brought Prickles with her to rattle Amy into showing her true colors. She hadn't expected Amy's story to strike her with such authenticity, and when she realized Amy *believed* what she was saying, Holly had decided against antagonizing the other woman with the hedgehog. Except then she'd forgotten her purse was unzipped and had set it down.

Connor was asking Amy a few follow-up questions, but Holly wasn't listening anymore. She slowly dropped to her knees and began to crawl forward, blushing when she realized multiple crewmembers had torn their gazes from the interview to watch her antics.

Amy was chatting more animatedly now that the scariest part of her story was over, and Holly thought she might be able to reach Prickles without either Connor or Amy noticing. That hope was dashed when Connor's gaze flickered from Amy's face down to her, and his expression faltered for a moment.

Holly pointed to Prickles, who was waddling toward Amy's delicately crossed ankles. What was it about this woman that Prickles loved so much? Maybe her feet smelled. Connor's gaze followed Holly's finger to the hedgehog, its tiny black nose twitching, and his eyes closed briefly in exasperation.

"Thank you so much, Amy. I know this has been difficult for you," he said. Funny, it sounded like he was speaking through a clenched jaw.

"It was sooooo scary." Amy scooted closer to him and rested her hand on his knee. "My husband never believed me. It's the reason we divorced." She pouted her heavily glossed lips, apparently forgetting she now had a boyfriend. "I was emotionally traumatized by Wicked Good Apples."

Holly stopped crawling and gaped up at Amy. That *bitch*! She was trying to set up groundwork to sue them!

Perfectly Wicked

Three things happened in rapid succession. First Holly sneezed, drawing Amy's attention to where she was on her hands and knees six feet away from the couch. As Amy blinked in confusion, Prickles then gently brushed against her foot, making her jump to her feet with an all-mighty scream. And at that exact moment, a storm-loosened branch crashed through the massive picture window that faced the forest, the glass exploding into the living room in a spray of sharp shards.

CHAPTER EIGHT

Holly dove for the hedgehog, shielding him with her body, and Connor pivoted off the couch and threw himself over Holly. His crewmembers cried out as chaos ensued, and through it all Amy stood in the center of the room shrieking like a banshee. Connor hunched over Holly, his head ducked close to hers and his arms braced on the floor. Glass rained down on them, pricking his skin and the back of his neck like annoying gnat bites.

After the tinkling glass had settled, Connor lifted his head. Shards of glass fell out of his hair and sprinkled onto the ground. He brushed aside the dark curtain of Holly's hair so he could see her face. Her eyes were tightly closed, but she popped one open when her cheek was exposed. "Is it over?"

"Yes." He stood and reached for her, pulling her to her feet while more glass tinkled to the floor. The hedgehog was rolled into a frightened ball on the hardwood. "Are you all right?"

She nodded shakily, and he scanned her body for signs of injury. Aside from her bloodless cheeks and trembling fingers, she appeared fine.

Holly's gaze fell to the little droplets of blood welling on his arms. "You're hurt!"

"Just a few cuts." Now that he knew she was all right, he was furious, even though he wasn't quite sure whom or what he was angry with. The shattered window wasn't Holly's fault—wasn't anyone's fault—but as he surveyed the room, it was clear there were a lot of people shaken up by the freak accident.

"Is anyone injured?" he called out.

There was a chorus of *nos* as his people shook glass out of their hair and brushed off the equipment, but there was one resounding *YES*!

It belonged to Amy. She was shaking with rage and had one long, fake nail pointed in accusation at Holly.

"This is your fault!" she shrieked, her cheeks and neck flushed. "You brought that stupid, ugly hedgehog to terrorize me. Wasn't it enough that you emotionally damaged me and broke up my marriage? Now you've shattered my window and sliced my arm!" She thrust her arm forward where the tiniest bead of blood sat on her skin. "I'm going to sue the shit out of you, you wicked witch. But first I'm going to stomp that little rodent into dust!"

Amy took an angry step toward the hedgehog, which had just begun to uncurl. Connor moved fast, but Holly was faster. She leaped in front of the hedgehog, her dark hair tumbling down her back and her eyes snapping. "If you touch that hedgehog I'll . . . I'll *curse* you."

Amy recoiled, the blood draining from her cheeks. "You're evil."

"No, I'm just a woman with a hedgehog." Holly pulled a work glove from her back pocket, tugged it on, and scooped up Prickles. "Let's get out of here, baby," she murmured to the creature, and she marched across the room, her boots crunching over the glass and her chin held high.

Connor's crew observed the spectacle with undisguised entertainment. Connor had spent the last ten years chasing oddities, and this was still one of his strangest days filming.

"Well," he said, swallowing the sudden desire to laugh, "if everyone's all right, let's sweep up. Karl, will you board up the window while I speak privately with Miss Gordon?"

His crew jumped into action while they speculated about the strange incident. "Bad omen," he heard whispered more than once. The crew was a superstitious lot—not entirely unexpected considering what they did for a living—but Connor wondered if they were right to worry. He thought of the photograph of smoke curling from Daisy's hands, the phone call warning him that the Celestes were wicked, the unpredictable bouts of bad weather, and now the shattered window. What exactly had he gotten them all into?

Amy was still standing in the middle of the room, her fists clenched and her makeup beginning to smudge under her eyes. "You had better watch your back," she spat before he could suggest they move somewhere more private to speak. "Holly's apple farm is wicked and haunted. Trust me, you'd be safer staying anywhere else. I have a spare room you're welcome to use. I know my boyfriend wouldn't mind. He's Holly's ex, and he knows all about how weird that family is." She smoothed her fingers over her hair-spray-hardened curls and gave him a seductive smile. Connor noticed she had lipstick on her teeth. They'd have to edit that out. Amy coyly tilted her head, and the gleam in her eye was similar to that of a vulture's about to descend on a meal. "My boyfriend doesn't stay over often. You could protect me at night when I get scared."

Connor ignored the unsubtle invitation to join her in the sack. "What happened today was an accident. I hope you realize that, Miss Gordon. Holly's apple farm might have a haunted past, but that doesn't mean she made that window shatter. You saw her crawling toward her hedgehog just as I did. The window was at least six feet away."

The flirtatious smile vanished. "She's responsible," Amy insisted. "Somehow, she's responsible. I've never trusted her or her sisters. Half the town is scared of them, and the other half only likes them because of their cider. You should hear some of the stories Jeremy tells. Holly was awkward and strange even in high school, and she still is. Who keeps a pet hedgehog for fuck's sake?"

Connor did his best to tamp down his anger. He was in a professional setting, and there were ears everywhere. "Despite your high school feelings about Holly, there are a number of witnesses to today's event. I suggest you think long and hard before filing any lawsuits. You wouldn't want to be exposed as a fool."

It took a moment for Amy to realize he wasn't flirting back and that he had no intention of heeding her warnings. She scoffed in disbelief.

Satisfied that she understood his warning, Connor was about to turn away when he added, "And by the way, Amy, I like strange and wicked. It's kind of my thing."

෨ ෬

An hour later Connor and his crew had finished cleaning Amy's house and had packed away their gear. Amy spent the entire time pacing back and forth in the living room, her heels clacking on the hardwood and her thumbs flying across her phone screen, only pausing long enough to throw the occasional vicious look his way. She was no doubt contacting every lawyer she knew, Connor thought with a sigh. Small-town dynamics were always fraught with complicated relationships, and it seemed Holly had her share of haters.

The entire time he worked, the words that had been angrily slung back and forth that afternoon rang in his ears.

"Holly Celeste, you wicked witch!"
"If you touch that hedgehog, I'll curse you!"
"You're evil."
"Holly's farm is wicked and haunted."

Connor had little experience with witches, and he'd never been able to prove they existed. He'd had brushes with what he swore were supernatural beings, but never before had he had so much evidence to go on. The language being used by the town to describe the Celestes wasn't an accident, and there was the not-so-small matter of someone sending him that photo—someone who was obviously familiar with the women. That feeling of *knowing* flooded his bloodstream, even if in the back of his mind he acknowledged that everything didn't fully fit. For example, if the Celestes were witches with the best apple cider in town, why was their apple farm on the verge of bankruptcy instead of thriving?

Holly's response to his ungraceful accusation in the orchards had been to deny she was a witch, but if she were a witch, that's exactly what he would expect her to do.

Connor was helping Tom load the last of the camera equipment into the van when he spotted Holly sitting in the cab of his truck. He was surprised she hadn't called one of her sisters to come pick her up, but then he looked down at his feet, where he'd set her purse. Oh, of course. She'd left her purse inside, and her phone was probably in it. She'd chosen to sit in the car and wait instead of reentering the viper's nest, and he couldn't blame her.

He waved off Tom, picked up Holly's purse, and carried it to the truck. When he opened the door, she didn't look at him, but continued petting the flat spikes of the little hedgehog napping in her lap. Connor set the purse on the console between them, buckled his seat belt, and started the ignition.

"So," he said, "that was interesting."

Holly groaned. "Sorry."

"For what? You didn't make that window shatter."

She glanced down at the tiny snoozing Prickles. "I shouldn't have brought him. I meant to taunt her with him, but I changed my mind, except by then he'd already escaped."

Connor thought of the vision she'd made creeping across the floor on her hands and knees to catch the hedgehog, and fought back a smile. Never in a million years would he forget the moment he realized she was chasing down a loose hedgehog in the middle of his interview.

"Was anyone hurt?"

He shook his head. "A few cuts, but nothing major. We're lucky no one was standing by the window, or it might have been a different story."

"Is Amy going to sue you?"

"I think Amy wants to sue everyone." He let a few minutes of silence pass and then said, "What did you think of her interview?"

Holly drummed her fingers on the handle of the door. "Although Amy Gordon is an attention-obsessed bitch, I thought she was telling the truth about the ghost." She shifted in her seat, the belt pressing between her breasts in a way Connor silently scolded himself for noticing. "You've heard her story before."

He nodded. "From more than one person. Run-ins with Councilman Miller are the most commonly cited incidents on your farm. Haven't you read any of the speculative sites associated with Wicked Good Apples?"

"I've browsed them," she admitted, "but I've never seen his name mentioned. People describe only a nineteenth-century man. How did you discover his identity?"

"Research." The instant he'd seen the photograph he'd become fully invested in the paranormal activities at Wicked Good Apples, and he'd devoted every spare moment over the past year working on identifying the ghost. He'd spent eye-watering hours narrowing down the time period in which the ghost had likely lived based on the apparition's clothing, and then even more time hunched over genealogy books and calling local historical societies. Eventually he'd discovered a birth announcement for a male child born with a blind eye, who'd later become a powerful town councilman. Connor had learned that the old building where the town's three-person council used to meet still stood, and he'd contacted the current owners. They'd enthusiastically sent him snapshots of several artifacts that had come with the house, and one of them had been an oil portrait of the council. The intensive effort had paid off in spades: almost immediately his interviewees had corroborated that Councilman Miller was the ghost.

"In the stories people share, sometimes the councilman is standing, sometimes he's seated under a tree. He's been seen peeling an apple and eating an apple, but it's almost always in the old orchard where we were pruning today. Amy is the first person who's claimed to have talked to him, though."

Holly chewed on her bottom lip. "Amy said the ghost offered her a poisoned apple and then implied that eating a poisoned apple was how he died. You think Councilman Miller was killed by one of our apples two hundred years ago, don't you? That that's why he's haunting our orchards."

He slowed behind a minivan. "I do. What I can't figure out is why now."

"What do you mean?"

"Where has he been the past two centuries? There aren't any records or indications of hauntings, and then—bam—four years ago he suddenly appears in your orchards, moaning about something that happened two hundred years ago and scaring off your customers."

From the corner of his eye, he spotted Holly's hand pause over the hedgehog's spikes and her breath catch. He pounced on it. "What happened four years ago?"

Holly resumed stroking the hedgehog and said with an even voice, "How would I know?"

He might have believed her if it weren't for the way her free hand fisted at her side.

"You think one of my ancestors gave him the poisoned apple," she accused.

He shrugged. "Maybe. Two hundred years ago your great-great-grandmother, Autumn, married a farmer named Thomas, but not everyone was pleased with the union. In particular, the head of the town council, Jonathan Miller, had a serious problem with her, although I haven't yet found any reputable records that explain what the dispute was over."

Her knuckles turned white with pressure along her thigh. "Why did you ask me about my family history in the orchard this morning if you already know more than I do?"

"I was curious what you would share."

"You were testing me."

He shook his head no. "I was corroborating the story with another source."

"You said you wanted to search the attic and cellar for a particular name. Is it Jonathan Miller's?"

"Yes. If I can find some mention of him in a letter or diary, I might be able to learn more about his relationship with your great-great-grandmother and her husband."

Holly glared at him, and he didn't miss the fire in her eyes. "You said this episode would be good for business, but I hardly think accusing one of my ancestors of murder via poisoned apple, on national TV, is going to entice people to visit our apple farm."

He'd hoped she wouldn't make that leap, but of course she had. It was true that backlash was a small possibility once the episode aired, but the greater likelihood was that the old story would inspire people to visit, whether out of morbid curiosity or simple perversity. He'd learned that humans liked to do what they were told they shouldn't. "You could rename the farm The Poisoned Apple," he joked. At her severe look he sighed and said, "Truthfully, I think it's going to draw customers, not repel them."

Prickles opened his eyes and yawned, and damned if he wasn't cute as hell.

"Any other secrets you want to share?" Holly asked, her knuckles still white.

Yeah, there were a few more things, but considering the day they'd had so far, he didn't think now was the best time to mention them.

He turned into her driveway without answering and let his eyes drift upward to the stretching branches of the budding maples. It would be absolutely gorgeous in the fall, when the leaves were a brilliant red against the crisp sky.

When he pulled to a stop in front of his trailer and climbed out, he spotted her Aunt Daisy sitting on the porch swing, her stark white hair drifting behind her with the gentle movement. She could have been a ghostly fixture of the house if it weren't for the hot-pink Daisy Duck sweatshirt she was wearing.

"Yoo-hoo!" Aunt Daisy called, waving them over with a black-gloved hand. He narrowed his eyes at the gloves as he waited for Holly, who hurried to his side with Prickles cupped in her palm. "There you are, Holly. Jeremy stopped by. He said he tried texting and calling but couldn't get a hold of you."

"Jeremy?" Connor murmured. "As in your ex-boyfriend and Amy Gordon's current boyfriend?"

Holly wrinkled her nose. "Yup, that's the one. He always knows the worst time to call. It's a freaking talent." Then to her aunt she said, "Thanks, Aunt Daisy."

They climbed the shallow, warped porch steps, and Connor made a mental note to shore them up the next day, telling himself it was because he couldn't risk any of his crew members falling through.

Daisy's eyes were milky white, and Connor frowned as they approached, realizing she'd called out to them as if she could see. Daisy had the same features as the younger twins: a sweet snub nose with freckles and snow-white hair that must've been as bright red as theirs when she was younger. The family resemblance between all the twins was remarkable. Holly, on the other hand, might as well have been born into a completely different family for all the similarities she had, with her dark hair and high cheekbones.

Aunt Daisy turned and looked at him as if she could see straight through him. "Connor, what are you and that assistant of yours doing for dinner tonight?"

"He's busy," Holly answered quickly. "And Charlotte's a vegan." She turned and started to push him back down the porch with her free hand. "There's a new Indian restaurant in Augusta, about twenty minutes south. You should try it."

Aunt Daisy tutted. "Nonsense! It wouldn't be right for our new neighbors to have to drive into town for supper when we have plenty ten feet away."

"Yes, it wouldn't be *right*, Holly," Connor taunted with a grin. And because he knew it would irk her if he accepted, he said, "We would *love* to eat with you."

60

CHAPTER NINE

"Oh my God, how hard would it have been to send a text that we have guests?" Missy howled as she burst into the kitchen. Holly, Winter, Aunt Daisy, Aunt Rose, Charlotte, and Connor were already passing around bowls of spaghetti and salad and a platter of breadsticks. Missy was still dressed in her sparkly plum dress and heels, and her irritation faded when she noticed the empty chair beside Connor. She strutted over and sank down beside him.

"How was the radio interview?" Winter asked, piling spaghetti on her plate. Holly caught Charlotte eyeing Winter in amazement as she added yet another scoop of spaghetti. A sad plate of lettuce and tomatoes sat before Charlotte, because along with being vegan, she also didn't eat gluten.

"The host was soooo sweet," Missy purred, filling her glass from a pale green decanter. "He was fascinated to hear that those little conspiracy sites could be right about a ghost in the orchards. I invited him over for a midnight séance." She took a sip and spit the amber liquid back into the glass. "Ugh, why isn't this alcohol?"

"The light green bottle is sparkling cider," Holly answered. "The dark green is the apple wine." The aunts had gone all out for their

61

guests, showcasing the best of Wicked Good Apples' products: apple jelly, sparkling cider, apple wine, and even apple cider vinegar—the only problem was that all the liquids were in similar bottles. "I hope he declined your offer to visit." Really! The last thing they needed was some overblown radio host camped out in their backyard. One too-large media personality was enough.

Missy smirked and downed the sparkling cider before making a "gimme" gesture for the wine bottle. "Oh, not that kind of séance."

Aunt Rose and Aunt Daisy were used to Missy's equal attitude toward sex, but Charlotte didn't know that and glanced nervously at them as she stuffed a romaine leaf into her mouth.

"How was *your* day?" Missy asked, turning in her seat and waggling her eyebrows at Connor and then Holly. "Amy Gordon is all over Facebook saying you two blew out her window."

"Amy Gordon is a big fat liar." Holly poured a second glass of sparkling cider. After the day she'd had, she knew a migraine was coming, and alcohol would only make it worse. Her head was already starting to ache over her left ear.

Holly glanced at Connor over the rim of her glass as she took a sip. She didn't know why she was so unnerved by the sight of him in her kitchen, fork and knife in hand as he ate and listened closely to every word. She was so used to their space being filled with feminine energy, and Connor's very big, very male presence was giving her the panicky feeling that everything was changing right beneath her nose.

She didn't want Connor Grimm in her house or in her life. He was too confident. Too determined. Too ruthless.

And yet he'd used his body to protect her from the shattered window today, taking the sting of glass so that she didn't have to. She knew he'd been on the verge of saving Prickles from Amy's rage too. As much as Holly wanted to hate him, so far he'd done nothing to earn her ire. Everyone loved Connor Grimm, from his crew to his fans, but that didn't mean she had to.

And it didn't mean she had to trust him.

"Holly's right," Charlotte said, examining a tomato with the scrutiny of a doctor. "A branch fell into the window. I saw it happen."

"That freak storm that blew through this morning must've loosened it. Holly couldn't have had anything to do with that," Missy said, blinking innocently at Holly. Holly slid her finger across her throat in response and Missy smothered her smile in her wine.

Aunt Rose clucked her tongue. "That Amy Gordon has always been a troublemaker. Holly's boyfriend slept with her in high school, didn't he, Daisy?"

"Yes, he did. Or was it the Lafebre girl?"

"Her too," Missy piped in helpfully. "Holly's boyfriend slept with pretty much everyone in high school. You were lucky you were using condoms. That dude probably had every STD known to science."

Holly's cheeks were flaming. "Thank you, everyone. Great recap of Holly's high school sex life. What are your plans now?" she asked Charlotte, deliberately redirecting the conversation. "Do you plan to film at night?"

Charlotte nodded, decided the tomato was acceptable, and popped it in her mouth. "The audiences expect it. You know, the whole shtick with the green night vision lens and the beeping electromagnetic field meter. We probably won't catch Miller on camera, though."

"Miller?" Winter asked.

Connor finally spoke, filling in the rest of the family on the history he'd shared with her in the car. To their credit, her family kept their expressions neutral when he told them the ghost's name. She wasn't sure her aunts and sisters were making all the connections: how Connor had narrowed the first sightings of Councilman Miller to four years ago, which just so happened to be when Aunt Rose's potion had stopped working. It also happened to be that four years ago was when the farm's finances had begun to nosedive. The Celestes had heard rumors of the ghost, but other than browsing a few websites, they'd never taken the gossip seriously because they'd never seen the ghost themselves. If the spirit of Councilman Miller actually existed and was haunting their property, was it possible he'd been scaring their customers more than they'd realized? She'd have to mention it to her family after Connor left.

"Have you heard of Councilman Jonathan Miller before?" he asked Aunt Rose and Aunt Daisy. "Or do you know of any dispute between him and Autumn in 1820?"

Aunt Daisy shook her head, but Rose considered and said, "Seems to me we may have heard a rumor or two about it, but these old brains don't work like they used to."

Holly caught her breath and dropped her eyes to the golden liquid in her glass. What an act, those two. They were as sharp as tacks and could remember the date of the last time they went roller skating forty-five years ago.

Connor leaned forward and clasped his hands together beneath his chin as he studied the aunts. "Is there anything you do recall?"

"Well, it seems to me," Aunt Rose began, "that mama once told us the orchards were planted by Autumn to spite a councilman."

Daisy nodded in agreement. "Yes, that sounds right. It was something to do with an apple seed she received as a gift. The gift angered the councilman, although we don't know why, and Autumn responded by growing an entire apple orchard."

Holly loved that part of the story. Autumn's reflex to grow an apple orchard out of spite had been a very Celeste thing to do.

"Very few people can out-stubborn a Celeste," Holly said, but maybe she'd been a little quieter than she'd intended, because she felt Connor's curious gaze on her face. She hadn't whispered, had she? Her head was beginning to throb.

"That is both a blessing and a curse." Aunt Rose looked sternly at Holly. "It wouldn't hurt the Celestes to learn a little give-and-take."

Excusez-moi? Holly knew how to be flexible! She was practically a rubber band. Okay, maybe she wasn't *that* flexible. She was more like a paperclip. She *could* bend if she had to, but she really preferred to stay in shape.

"Was there something special about the original apple seed?" Connor asked.

Holly shouldn't have been surprised that he zeroed in on the exact question to ask, but it was so uncannily on the nose that it caught her off guard. She wasn't the only one.

"That's the part we don't remember, if we ever knew," Rose said after a pause.

She lied smoothly, but Holly's family was underestimating the Grimm sitting at the table with them. The truth was the Celestes didn't know the full story behind the dispute between Autumn and Councilman Miller. Heck, Holly hadn't even known that the man had been murdered. Aunt Rose had basically shared all they did know—apart from why the apple seed was special.

Holly wished her aunts hadn't said a word. Connor Grimm didn't need any help ruining them.

Missy sighed. "I'm so bummed I've never seen the ghost before. Have you, Winter?"

Winter shook her head no, and while they discussed the Councilman Jonathan Miller ghost sightings, a foot nudged Holly's. She shifted but then felt it again. She looked up to find Connor staring at her from across the table.

"Are you all right?" he mouthed.

She gave him a thumbs-up, and those gray eyes narrowed as if he didn't believe her.

A robot text tone beeped from Holly's phone, which she'd left on the counter. "Did you ever call Jeremy back?" Aunt Daisy asked.

Holly sipped her sparkling cider. "Nope. I don't owe Jeremy anything."

The table went awkwardly silent, and an irritated voice said, "It's nice to know how you feel, Holly."

Holly lifted her eyes from her almost-empty glass and cringed at the sight of Jeremy standing at the swinging kitchen door. Jeremy was a tax lawyer with political ambitions, and he dressed the part: creased pants, shiny loafers, stuffy tan overcoat. His eyes bulged out of his sockets a little bit, and she thought he used so much gel in his hair to draw attention away from the fact. Jeremy blinked in annoyance as he moved farther into the room. "I stopped by again when I still didn't hear from you. Amy told me about the exploding window."

Holly picked up her fork and twirled it in the pasta without taking a bite. "Er—thanks for checking in." She had no idea why he'd felt it was necessary, unless Amy had sent him for some reason.

Jeremy's lips pinched when he noticed Connor at the table. He and Connor sized each other up in silence, and it was apparent by their stony expressions that each found the other lacking.

"You must be Connor Grimm," Jeremy said. Did he have a cold? Why was his voice so nasally? Had he *always* sounded like that? "I hope you're not taking advantage of these ladies while you're here. Perhaps they should retain legal counsel."

Missy rolled her eyes. "We're fine, Jeremy. And you're a *tax* lawyer."

He flushed. "I didn't mean me," he snapped. He'd always disliked Missy. He'd once told Holly she should speak to her sister about "toning down" her image because she was starting to get a reputation for being a slut. Holly had dumped him with her next breath.

After she'd broken up with him, Holly had made a grilled cheese sandwich, gone to bed, and forgotten all about him until two days later. That was how passionate their relationship had been. It wouldn't have been a stretch to say she'd had wilder sex in her dreams than with Jeremy.

"We don't need legal counsel," Holly said shortly, rubbing her temples. "I looked over the contract, and it's fairly standard."

"You're hardly a lawyer, Holly. You're just an apple farm manager."

Holly ground her teeth together.

"I have another reason for coming over," Jeremy continued, oblivious or uncaring that he'd just insulted her. "Amy wants to sue you."

Missy tightened the elastic on her ponytail. "Amy sucks. I guess I see why you two get along."

Burn.

Aunt Rose gestured to Jeremy. "Dear, take off your coat and join us. We have plenty of food."

"It *has* been a long day," Jeremy said. He peeled off the tan coat, revealing a suit and navy-striped tie that was still perfectly knotted even after his "long day," while Aunt Rose got him a plate from the cabinet. He pulled out the chair beside Winter, and she grudgingly scooted over. "Amy is excitable," he said, not bothering to defend his girlfriend. "She wants to sue both Holly *and* Grimm."

Connor arched a brow. "She can try, but she signed an iron-clad contract with Grimm Productions. What does she want to sue us for?"

"Emotional distress and physical harm."

"That bead of blood really did her in," Holly snickered, and Connor's lips twitched.

Jeremy's gaze darted from Connor to Holly. "What were you doing at Amy's house anyway, Hols? Especially with that disgusting rodent? I've told you time and again those things are riddled with salmonella."

Holly slammed her glass on the table, suddenly so very tired of Jeremy's unsolicited lectures. "He is *not* a rodent!" The outburst was satisfying, but it cost her. She flinched as her aching headache morphed into a full-blown migraine. She reached for the sparkling cider bottle, knowing from experience that hydration helped.

Jeremy shook his head with disapproval. "Don't you think you've had enough?"

Missy covered her eyes. "Oh *no* you didn't."

Aunt Daisy quickly tried to ask Jeremy about work, but it was too late. Holly stared at him with every ounce of menace she possessed. Outside a tree branch tapped on the glass as the wind picked up. "What did you just say to me?"

"You're clearly drunk. I'd say you've had enough." He plucked the sparkling cider bottle from her hand and set it out of reach.

Holly's mouth dropped open. The audacity! She could not imagine such a scenario in reverse, because men were allowed to have outbursts without it being assumed they were drunk and hysterical. How could Jeremy think he had the right to police *her* decisions in *her* house? What made him think he knew what was best for *her* body?

The whole table fell silent, and a muscle ticked in Connor's jaw. Holly stood, reached over Jeremy, and snagged the bottle. She sat back down and filled her glass to within a centimeter of the top. She wasn't going to bother telling him she hadn't had so much as a sip of alcohol or that it was cider rather than wine; it was none of his business either way. "You don't get to make decisions about my body."

Connor gave her a feral smile of approval just as the edges of her vision began to blur from the migraine.

Jeremy opened his mouth to retort but visibly flinched. Holly was pretty sure Missy had kicked him under the table.

Aunt Daisy broke the tension by asking Jeremy about work again, and while he yammered on about a new tax law, Holly leaned forward and whispered across her plate to Connor, "I think I know why Councilman Miller was murdered."

"Why's that?"

"He told Autumn she didn't need to drink another glass of wine."

Connor threw his head back and laughed, and Holly found herself responding to his merriment with a grin of her own. She only noticed that they'd become the center of attention when the table went quiet again. Charlotte was staring at Connor as if she'd never seen him crack a smile before, and Jeremy was glowering.

By then Holly's vision was almost completely gone. She suffered from ocular migraines when she overextended herself, which meant temporary blindness and a headache so splitting it made her want to scream.

"Excuse me," she said, pushing her chair out. She gripped the table edge with both hands and tried to picture the layout of the room. She could not, *would* not weave or bump into something in front of Jeremy and fuel his mistaken assumption that she was drunk.

"Holly, do you need your tonic?" Aunt Rose asked.

"Yes, please." There was no fooling her aunts; they were aware of all the freak weather changes lately and what the consequences would be for Holly. Besides, no one mixed a potion like Aunt Rose.

Holly cautiously walked out of the room and was somewhat amazed that she managed to do so without running into any furniture. She made it all the way to the living room before she crashed into the stair banister and stumbled backward. Warm hands caught her arms and steadied her. "Need some help?"

She was relieved to hear Connor's deep voice by her ear instead of Jeremy's know-it-all nasally one. She shivered at the whisper of warm breath on the back of her neck.

"I'm having a migraine," she admitted. "I can't see."

Connor made a noise in the back of his throat. "I thought there was something wrong. Can you make it up the stairs?"

"Probably, but maybe you could guide me so I don't knock over any vases in the hallway upstairs?"

"I'll do you one better."

She gave a little shriek as he scooped her into his arms. With one arm around her back and the other curved under her knees, Connor started up the stairs with surprising ease. Sightless, she was more aware than ever of his pine and spice scent, of his body heat warming his T-shirt, and the shifting muscles of his torso beneath the thin cotton. She tried to control her breathing, excruciatingly aware that her sort-of-nemesis was cradling her close to his chest and that his long fingers were splayed just above her knee, burning through the denim.

"Where to?" he asked, his chest rumbling.

"To the left. Mine is the last room on the right."

He followed her directions, his steps soundless on the runner, and pushed open the door to her room with his foot.

Holly bit her lip as she tried to imagine how her room appeared to him. There were books scattered everywhere because she'd been trying to find a particular romance the other night, and more than one pair of jeans had been tried on and tossed without being refolded. An entire wall was a collage of old-fashioned Polaroids and black-and-white photos of items on the farm: apples, sunsets, birds, and flowers. She'd left her window open, and the room smelled of fresh rain and apple blossoms.

Connor stepped over something lying on the floor and set her on the edge of her bed, her thigh brushing against his and his hand sliding across her shoulder blades as he released her. Holly spread her fingers on the rough, cream-colored quilt behind her. "Thanks."

A heartbeat passed before he said in a low voice, "Do you want me to take off your boots?"

"I can do that."

"Won't it hurt your head to bend over?"

It would, actually. She'd planned on swallowing ibuprofen and lying down as she was, or at least until Aunt Rose delivered her elixir. But the temptation of having her boots off and not touching her clean bed was too much to resist. "Yes. If you want to, that'd be great."

There was a heavy pause, and then his knee was brushing against her boot as he kneeled in front of her. He lifted her foot with one big hand wrapped around her ankle and set the sole on his hard thigh. She tried not to breathe, knowing that if she did she would draw in lungfuls of *him*. He tugged on the laces, the quiet rasp of cotton sliding over cotton filling the room as he released the bow, and then he was loosening the rest of the laces with steady, competent fingers. By the time he cupped his hand around her heel again to gently tug off the boot, her stomach was pitching with a feeling she was uninterested in acknowledging. Air hit her foot and she set it down, but it landed on his thigh, and this time she was wearing socks instead of boots and could feel every warm inch of him. She quickly jerked her foot away.

"Er—sorry."

"Don't worry about it." His voice was low and gravelly as he reached for her other foot, his arm grazing the inside of her thigh. She hated her lungs for going breathless simply because this charismatic ghost hunter was kneeling at her feet, taking off her shoes. If she admitted to herself how much he was affecting her, she'd have to hide in her room for the rest of eternity, reading books about how to develop common sense. Connor Grimm probably slept with a new woman at every filming location, and here she was breathing hard from having her boots unlaced. It was pathetic. Clearly, she'd gone too long without intimacy.

He deftly unlaced and pulled off her second boot and set it to the side. She waited for him to stand, but he didn't. She could almost feel the heat radiating from him and wondered what he was thinking, wondered why he hadn't moved. "Need help taking anything else off?"

"Um, nope. I'm good."

He laughed quietly and pushed to his feet.

"Before you leave, will you put the bottle of ibuprofen in my hand? It's on my nightstand."

The air shifted and he returned a moment later, the pills rattling in the bottle. He pressed a water glass into her hand, which he must've also found on her nightstand, and then asked her how many pills before shaking them into her palm.

Holly swallowed the tablets and then crawled over her bed and gingerly laid her head on the pillow.

"Your aunt asked if you needed a tonic?"

"Oh, it's just a folk remedy for headaches." She pressed her fingertips to her temples, and they pulsed with her own heartbeat. "Like Alka-Seltzer and stuff." *Or not.*

He made a humming noise in the back of his throat. "I see. Are you going to sleep in your jeans?"

Her fingers drifted to the top button of her jeans. She'd chosen a much snugger pair than usual, and they *were* digging into her belly. "Cover me and I'll take them off myself."

A moment later the blankets underneath her feet tugged and Connor draped them over her body, concealing her from view. "You don't need help?"

"I've been undressing myself for a long time." She exhaled with relief when she popped the button and dragged the zipper down. She swore the sound of the teeth peeling apart was louder than usual.

Connor's voice was strained when he said, "I want to search the attic tomorrow if you're up for it. These old cellars are usually damp, so I think the attic is our best shot at finding letters or other paperwork in decent condition."

"Okay." Holly shoved the waistband of the jeans down her hips, and they caught around her thighs. She wriggled, but that was a mistake—her head instantly exploded with pain from the jerky movement. She hissed between her teeth and paused, lying completely still.

Connor's voice was blessedly low and—concerned?—when he asked, "What?"

"Nothing."

"Your pants are stuck, aren't they?"

"Fuck off, Grimm."

He laughed. "Let me help you. I won't look, I promise. I'll stare at the wall and reach under the blanket."

"Like a gyno exam?"

He cleared his throat. "Um . . ."

Holly flushed, horrified. "No, not like that! I just meant how at the gynecologist you have the sheet on you and the doctor goes under and . . . never mind. It's not like you'd know. Please leave before I die of mortification."

"Holly, I'm a grown-ass adult. I can hear about a gynecology exam without fainting. Now if you want me to leave, I will. But if you want me to take off your pants, I'll do that too, and I promise we'll never talk about it again."

"Fine," she moaned. "This is already shaping up to be one of the most humiliating days of my life. You might as well."

The end of the mattress depressed when Connor kneeled on it, and then the air from the opened window slid over her bare skin when he lifted the blanket. The waist band of her jeans was stuck around the thick part of her thighs, and her cheeks heated further when his calloused, warm fingers slipped between the denim and her skin. Without a word, or even an unsteady breath, he efficiently peeled them down her legs and discarded them.

The blanket settled over her legs again, and she felt somewhat worse by how unaffected he was. Not that she wanted him to be interested in her, but she also didn't want him *not* to be—for the sake of her ego.

She heard him moving around the room, and then from the doorway he said, "Feel better, Holly. I'll see you tomorrow." A few seconds later the door clicked shut.

Holly groaned and pulled the covers over her face.

CHAPTER TEN

Connor blew dust off a bundle of sheet music and tried to pay attention to the items he was searching through, but every few minutes his eyes involuntarily sought out Holly, who was kneeling by a trunk and rifling through mildewed and moth-eaten clothing from God-knows-what century.

Unsurprisingly, he hadn't slept well the night before. He'd tossed and turned well into the early morning hours, his thoughts bouncing from how soft and warm Holly had felt in his arms when he'd carried her upstairs, to questions about the councilman, and then wondering what the hell Holly had ever seen in that dickbag Jeremy.

He tried to focus on the task at hand, but moments later he was remembering the pretty flush on Holly's cheeks as he'd unlaced her boots, and how her breathing had hitched slightly when he'd kneeled between her thighs. She wasn't interested in him that way, he reminded himself as he flipped through the sheets of music. He had to respect that boundary, and the truth was he shouldn't have been wanting to toe it anyway. Despite Holly's dislike of him and the fact that she was keeping some serious secrets, Connor was beginning to admire her. She was tough and funny, and some day she would find a partner who'd actually stick around. With his lifestyle, what did Connor have to offer any woman other than a quick fling?

It was for the best that she wished he'd disappear along with the ghost.

He flipped to the last sheet of music. There weren't any hidden letters or annotations—they were just plain sheets of music for a piano.

Holly wiggled her butt as she reached deeper into the trunk and Connor dropped his head to take three deep breaths. He'd never experienced this curious mixture of laughing with a woman one minute, being exasperated by her the next, and then wanting to slowly peel off her jeans for real five seconds later. It was an emotional roller coaster that was making him feel like a teenager. Connor was usually very good about separating his private life and his professional life, so this *crush* he was beginning to have on Holly—because a teenage word was the most appropriate—was starting to get under his skin.

Charlotte's warning echoed in his ears: *"You are a relationship no-go. Besides, we still don't know what's going on in those orchards, and you don't want to mess that up by making questionable personal choices."*

Right. So it was time he reined in his wayward hormones and suffocated them under work. It was a foolproof plan.

Connor tossed the sheet music into the hatbox and closed the lid. Part of the cardboard disintegrated in his hand. The Celestes' walk-in attic was large and roomy, which made it the perfect spot to stash generations of junk. There were trunks and sheet-draped furniture, coatracks and music stands, a tuba and a broken bicycle, apple crates upon apple crates, empty glass bottles, and more. The place was a veritable treasure trove of Celeste history, and his heart had beat excitedly in his chest the moment Holly had opened the door.

That had been an hour ago, and still he'd found absolutely nothing relevant. They'd stirred the dust so that motes floated in the morning sunlight slanting through the high half windows, and it was starting to grow hazy and warm in the attic as the morning wore on.

Holly sneezed and slammed the lid to the trunk shut. "Nothing here," she said. "Although I had no idea my ancestors liked mink so much."

Her hair was pulled into a bun, leaving the long length of her neck bare. Connor wondered if she liked to be kissed there, and if anyone had taken the time to explore all the secret spots that made her sigh. When he realized what he was thinking, he firmly pushed the inappropriate fantasy from his head and dragged his focus from the tight jeans that showcased her ass perfectly every time she bent over. Shit, it was going to be a long few weeks if he couldn't stop salivating over Holly every time she wore a pair of jeans, which was every day.

Feeling like a jerk for even looking at her ass, he cleared his throat. "Nothing here either. We're digging for Autumn's belongings in particular. Would those be farther in the back?"

She wiped her hands on the thighs of her jeans and grimaced. "Maybe? There's so much junk in here that we'd have to shift everything to make a path. It would take forever."

"I can call Charlotte to help me. You've done enough."

Holly checked the time on her phone. "I'll give you another hour. We can at least get started on it."

They assessed what lay between them and the rafters. She was right: the floor was so jammed tight with boxes and trunks and all sorts of discarded materials that it would take a full day's work to reach whatever might be stashed in the back.

Fortunately Connor wasn't afraid of a little hard work. He hefted a crumbling box of books on top of the junk beside it. Holly joined him, and together they began moving items out of the way.

They worked in silence for a while, each of them lost in their own thoughts. Holly struggled to move a doll cradle because one of the rockers was stuck beneath a heavy trunk, so Connor lifted the trunk while she pulled. They were both sweating and so tightly enclosed in the small path they were making that it was impossible not to bump into each other. Every time they accidentally brushed—a bare arm against another arm, a hip against a thigh, a shoulder grazing a belly, his blood heated until he wasn't sure what was making him sweat more: the attic or all the little touches.

Holly studied the cradle for a minute before pushing it over the mound of junk toward the eaves. "Do you have children?"

Connor sneezed and reached for a crate of old-fashioned irons. "No."

"Do you want them? Actually that's kind of personal—you don't have to answer if you don't want to."

He'd always assumed he would have children, but he was in his thirties now and still single. "Maybe someday. You?"

"Same." She swiped her arm across her brow, smearing grime by her eye.

He gestured to her face. "You have dirt on your temple."

She rubbed her temple, but only succeeded in spreading the grime further. "Better?"

"Worse. May I?"

When she nodded, he lifted the hem of his shirt and carefully wiped the smudge away. When he lowered the fabric, he found her gaze glued to his abs, and suddenly every minute he'd spent in the gym sweating over weights while working through mysteries in his mind was worth it.

She cleared her throat. "Thanks." She nudged aside a box of doll clothes, which were most likely moldy. After several minutes of moving items in thick silence, she returned to their previous vein of conversation. "Have you been married before?"

"No. You?"

"No, although I'm pretty sure Jeremy was thinking about proposing."

That dick? Connor couldn't imagine Holly kissing the guy, much less marrying him. The very thought of it made his skin crawl. "When did you two break up?" And did she know the wanker still thought he had a claim on her even though he was dating Amy?

"Six months ago."

"Did he lock your wine away?"

"Oh my God, that was awful, right?" She stood from where she was crouching and shook her head. "He was stuffy when we were dating, but it's a small town, and most of the guys my age are already married, so it's either give a few odd relationships a chance or wait until everyone else starts getting divorced. He's gotten worse since we broke up, though. That was too much last night."

"I can't imagine why it didn't work out with him."

She huffed. "Yeah, turns out 'condescending pig' isn't my type after all."

"And just when I thought I had a shot."

Her lips curved. "You're a lot of things, Grimm, but you're not a condescending pig."

Connor tried to sound casual when he shifted some records and said, "So what *is* your type then?"

"I guess I still don't know. I'm in my late twenties, and all I've learned so far is what I *don't* like."

"That's a start. What don't you like?"

Holly propped her hip on the corner of an old dresser and started ticking things off on her fingers. "Misogynists, idiots, men who think they're smarter than me when they're not, men who try to tell me how to run the apple farm, men who hate hedgehogs, men in love with hotdogs, men who think—"

"Wait a minute—did you say 'men in love with hotdogs'?"

Holly nodded sadly. "It was the date from hell. Missy set me up, and when I got to the restaurant, the guy had already ordered and eaten three hotdogs—the wrappers were sitting right in front of him. When the waitress came over, he ordered six more. I wanted a hamburger, but he insisted I have a hotdog. Then he went on to tell me all the disturbing ways a hotdog can be used . . . er . . . *romantically.*"

Connor gawked at her. "No way."

"Way. Then it got worse."

"How?"

"He slipped an uneaten hotdog in his pocket, and when we left, he touched my ear with it."

Connor didn't know if he wanted to laugh or cry. "That's terrible."

"You have no idea what it's like for women out there. How about you? I imagine you don't have any problem with the pool of available women."

A bird chirped and they met each other's eyes in surprise. There must've been a nest farther back in the rafters. "I date some," he admitted, "but less than you might think."

"Oh? Why's that?"

Too many strings. Too many expectations. Too much effort. He didn't think any of those answers would endear him to her, but they were the truth. "I haven't found anyone worth the effort. I'm busy and I have limited time. I move around a lot and I'm away more than I'm home. I've been in my apartment exactly twelve days this year."

"Ah." She nodded sagely as she stood and lifted a crate of empty bottles. "So you're married to *Grimm Reality*."

He'd never thought of it that way, but he supposed she was right. *Grimm Reality* was both his wife and his baby, and he'd never been the two-timing type.

"Which means you only have the time and energy for easy, no-strings flings," she added, and blinked sweetly. "Must be tough for you."

"I've tried relationships," he said, not liking how she was making him sound. "I'm willing to put in the effort if it's worth it."

She arched a brow and shoved the crate between the bones of an old ironing board and a box. "But no one has been worth it?" Before he could respond, she changed the topic. "How did you get started in this line of work, anyway? Did you wake up one morning and say, 'Hey, Mom, I'm going to study ghosts'?"

He plastered on the smile he reserved for this exact question. "How did you know? Actually, I think it's just in my blood. My father was a journalist, my grandfather was an author, and my great-grandfather wrote down other people's stories. When it was time to decide what to do with my life, I figured I couldn't go wrong doing the thing I loved. Erikson and I actually started out as a YouTube channel before we got picked up by a major network."

She studied him with hazel eyes that seemed to pierce straight through the fake smile. Dust motes danced around her head, and in their small space he could smell the dust and mold mixing with her sweet Christmas scent. "No," she said finally, "that's not the whole story."

"You can look online. That's the story."

"Our blood legacy can guide us, but we have to choose it too. I should know. This apple farm has been in my family for two hundred years, and yet I would have walked away and left it to my sisters if I hadn't had a personal connection to it. What's your personal connection?"

Connor wiped his brow with his shirt and sat down on one of the boxes. He'd never had anyone question his story before. His standard bio gave the whole spiel about his grandfather, and it was half the truth, but not the most important half. After all this time, how was Holly the first person to want to dig deeper?

Holly followed his lead and perched on a half-caved-in dollhouse across from him, a bead of sweat sliding from her neck to between her breasts. Her green tank top was dampened with perspiration, and for the fortieth time Connor found his thoughts wandering toward forbidden territory. Well, if work wasn't suppressing his wayward thoughts, maybe telling her the truth would. If she looked at him with even half the wariness he thought she would after hearing his origin story, he'd finally be able to put his unwelcome attraction to her to rest. He could close himself off completely. Connor *never* exposed this particular vulnerability—not to anyone—and the fact that he was planning to do so now in the hopes that it would push her away and extinguish his desire was kind of desperate.

And still he found his mouth opening and the words spilling out. "It's hard to talk about it with someone who doesn't believe in the supernatural." Her gaze darted away. Connor leaned forward, his eyebrows lifting. "Wait a second, you don't believe in the supernatural, *right*?"

"I don't think I ever said that."

"You said the first day I met you, and I quote, 'The supernatural isn't real, and these orchards aren't haunted.'"

"Well, I didn't want you here."

His pulse kicked up a notch, and his instincts whispered to him. "So then you knew there was a ghost? Have you seen it?"

"No, I haven't. Until Amy's story, I honestly didn't believe the ghost sightings were real. But I may have fibbed about not believing in the supernatural." She polished her thumbnail on the hem of her tank top. "I suppose there are things out there that other people don't know about."

She lifted her hazel eyes and met his. They held each other's gaze for a moment, and every one of those whispering instincts began to scream. "Are *you* supernatural, Holly?"

She didn't laugh. "Are you avoiding my question about your origin as a ghost hunter, Connor?"

Someone was avoiding questions, and it wasn't him. His suspicions about the Celeste family had continued to crystalize over the past few days. Although he still hadn't seen actual proof beyond the photograph, which still could have been staged, his ancient storyteller blood was stirring, and he knew he was walking parallel to the truth. He had circumstantial evidence, and if he bided his time, he was certain he'd get what he'd come for. Either someone would slip and say something they shouldn't, or he'd witness the impossible.

When he'd arrived, he'd been operating under the assumption that Aunt Daisy would be his main focus, but the moment he'd walked into the Celeste kitchen, the hair on his arms had lifted, and he'd known there were more secrets to be revealed than he'd first thought.

Holly Celeste was a witch, and he was going to prove it.

CHAPTER ELEVEN

Holly watched Connor as his brilliant mind sizzled behind intense granite eyes. She'd worried that he was there for more than the ghost, and his taunt in the apple orchard and now this supernatural question all but confirmed it. What else had he discovered in the short time he'd been there? What had made him so certain that she and her family were more than just unlucky Mainers with a haunted apple orchard? Had someone in town said something to make him suspicious?

No one knew for certain what they were, but it was no secret that the Celeste name was divisive. They had their supporters—a staunch core of folks in the community who loved their heirloom apple farm and the quirky women who owned it, and who were die-hard devotees of Wicked Good Apples cider. Holly had an entire box of drawings of Prickles that kids had given her over the years, and he was practically a celebrity during the apple season. Many of those customers had become friends and were people Holly knew she and her sisters could count on if they ever needed help, and vice versa.

But there were others who were not so friendly, who downright hated the Celestes. They were the people who thought the rambling Celeste house was creepy, the sisters reclusive—or, in Missy's case, trouble. They were the people who avoided the Celeste house on Halloween and told their kids to stay far away. They snubbed Holly and her sisters in the grocery store and whispered behind their backs—but the gossip always reached them. Holly was certain they were the folks who would have accused her of witchcraft two hundred years ago and thrown her into the lake to drown.

Deep down Holly knew that even though she and her family were good people, the instincts of their haters weren't wrong. Some folks could just *feel* that the Celestes were different—perhaps it was a protective reflex that had evolved over time. Or maybe, since Aunt Rose and Aunt Daisy didn't usually inspire the same reactions of terror and repulsion, it was an unintended consequence of the wells of power that seethed beneath Holly and her sisters' skin.

Holly couldn't fault people for their fear, but she did fault them for how they treated her and her family. The Celestes had been good community members for hundreds of years, and yet some people acted like they were monsters. Could one of *those* people have said something to Connor to make him so confident that the Celestes were hiding a supernatural secret? Or could he feel the difference too?

No matter how he had come to his conclusions, it frightened her that he was circling around the thing she wanted kept most quiet. *"Are you supernatural, Holly?"*

She mentally rolled her eyes. He probably still thought she was a witch.

"I'll tell you why I really became a ghost hunter," he said, "for a trade."

"What do you want?"

"You decide what's fair."

"Deal."

Connor's sweat-darkened T-shirt was filthy with dust, his dark brown hair was mussed, and there was a streak of grime down his cheek that disappeared along his jawline, where he hadn't shaved in several days. His tanned hands were clasped loosely together between jean-clad knees as he leaned on his forearms. Everything about this man rubbed her the wrong way, and yet her traitorous body only seemed to want more of that friction, even as he sat in her filthy attic accusing her of hiding secrets.

You have heat stroke, she told herself. It was the only explanation for the unreasonable stirring in her belly.

Connor rubbed his palm over his chin and said, "I was haunted as a child." His expression was blank, as if he were expecting her to mock him. She kept her face neutral and waited for him to expound. "It was the ghost of a man who once lived in our apartment. He'd killed himself. When I was nine and Erikson was seven, we were both . . . *visited* by him. We were terrified and told our parents, but they just laughed it off. Except it kept happening. Every night, month after month, we'd lie in our beds, so frightened that our bodies were stiff. And then the room would suddenly chill until we could see our breath, and we'd know what was coming.

"He'd slip through the wall, his neck bent at an angle and his eyes wild, and he would stare at us hiding in our beds, and he would just cry, sob as if his heart were breaking. Eventually, he would stretch his ghostly pale fingers toward us, trying to touch us. That was when we'd run into our parents' room, screaming.

"At their wit's end, our parents eventually took us to see a psychologist, and then for more mental health evaluations. We stopped eating. We weren't sleeping. No one could figure out what was wrong with us, and no one was willing to believe us when we flat-out told them we were being haunted. We missed so much school, either from sleeping in the day because we were up all night, or because we were at appointments, that half our education ended up being pieced together from books and Google."

Without thinking, Holly reached over and grasped his hand. "I'm sorry no one believed you."

He shrugged. "Why *would* they believe us? For most of the world, the supernatural doesn't exist. When Erikson and I were old enough, we decided we were going to expose the supernatural, normalize it, so that people like us wouldn't be shunned any longer." He turned his hand over and laced his fingers with hers. His thumb idly traced over her own, sending chills straight up her arm even in the sweltering heat. She should pull away. And she would . . . in a moment.

"Whatever happened to your childhood ghost?"

"I don't know. Eventually our family moved out of the apartment—a last-ditch effort to get Erikson and me to sleep and eat again. It worked, but the damage was already done. Our parents divorced a year later, and Erikson and I never once forgot that we were responsible for destroying our family. I haven't gone back to the old apartment. I haven't . . . faced that yet."

"Why do you keep your haunting a secret? It seems like something your audience would accept."

He shook his head. "I need to appear 'normal' so that I can be convincing to those just on the edge of belief. No one will believe a dude who cried ghost as a kid, but a man who's skeptical and yet keeps proving the supernatural could exist? Now that introduces doubt, and it makes people wonder."

It was a clever tactic, but she was sorry he had to keep such an important part of his past hidden away.

"Your turn," he said.

Holly bit her lip as she considered. She'd been planning to say something stupid or silly, but he'd shared a painful secret with her, and it wouldn't be a fair exchange if she repaid his vulnerability with a flippant comment.

Dammit.

"I was not popular in high school," she started, "which you've probably already gathered after meeting Amy. I wasn't particularly welcome either." Was she really going to tell this famous TV personality one of her most shameful memories? It was something Holly never talked about, not even with her own sisters. She didn't know why this was the incident that had come to mind after he'd told her about his childhood haunting. Holly rubbed the toe of her boot on the floor, creating a little circle in the dust.

"Stop," Connor barked, releasing her hand and rising abruptly. "I don't want to know."

Holly blinked in confusion. "Why not? You shared your story, now it's my turn. A deal's a deal."

"I shouldn't have asked for anything in return," he growled. "It was my choice to share. I wasn't coerced and I won't coerce you. You'll tell me some other time. Or maybe you won't. Whatever—it's your choice."

Holly stood too, the space between them inches at best. She lightly touched his arm. "I want to share it with you." She was surprised to find that was true. Maybe it was because Connor had dedicated his life to believing the unbelievable, to validating the fears and tragedies of others. Whatever the reason, she felt safe sharing this memory with him, the last person she'd ever expected to show vulnerability to. "Maybe it needs to be said."

Connor studied her face for a moment, nodded, and sank back down. Holly leaned against the edge of the dollhouse and crossed her arms over her chest. "When I was in eighth grade, I killed my mom."

To his credit, Connor hid most of his shock. Only the slightest widening of his eyes gave away his surprise. "How did you kill her?"

Holly focused over his shoulder on a faded oil portrait of her great-aunt propped against a box. "My sisters were at school, but I was home. I told my mom I was sick, but the truth was that a rumor was going around school that I didn't wash my clothes and only had one pair of jeans. You know how cruel middle school kids can be. They called me a dirty scrub. They said since my dad had left, we'd gone broke and my mom couldn't afford to buy us clothes. That maybe she shouldn't have been such a bitch to him. They were repeating what they overheard at home, but none of them had the facts. My father didn't leave; my mom kicked him out for being a dickwad. They never know the truth when they're dragging your name through the mud."

Connor nodded in understanding. "In middle school Erikson told his best friend we were visited by a ghost and had to move because of it. His 'friend' told everyone. I think I would have chosen another year of being haunted over those two years of merciless teasing and snubbing."

She grimaced. "Middle school is brutal. I definitely didn't handle the rumors well. I couldn't bear to go to school, so I stayed home the day she died, and cried and cried and cried. It started storming out when my mom was driving home from the grocery store, and she lost control of the car. By the time the paramedics arrived, she was dead."

"Oh, Holly," Connor breathed. He stretched out his hand as if to touch and comfort her, but halted midair and dropped it. "You couldn't have stopped that."

Holly rubbed her hands over her arms, feeling oddly chilled even though it was sweltering in the attic. "I could have. If I hadn't stayed home, she wouldn't have gone to the grocery store to buy me soup and crackers. If I hadn't lost control of my emotions . . . if I hadn't let those stupid kids rile me up so much, she'd still be alive today." She turned her head away. She couldn't say more, couldn't make him understand how it *had* been her fault, without giving away her secret. The storm had killed her mother, and Holly had *been* the storm. After the funeral no one in her family had ever brought up the car accident again. Their silence was meant to ease her conscience, but nothing would ever erase her guilt.

"Did your father raise you after that?"

Holly scoffed. "No. He was a drunk, and the only things he was generous with were his fists. He had no interest in his children beyond what he could use us for. Aunt Rose and Aunt Daisy got custody of us. They gave up their independent lives so they could watch over us. They sacrificed to keep us safe."

Holly knew now the extent of what her aunts had done for her and her sisters. When Lilac had died, they'd left careers they'd loved without a second thought, and had moved to the apple farm. They'd been cautious people, unlike their boisterous sister, whom Missy took after, and they'd instituted a number of new rules to keep the girls' powers under wraps. At the time, Holly had thought they were being strict or that maybe they were punishing her for what she'd done. As an adult, she saw their rules for what they'd really been: a way to keep the girls safe. Sometimes Holly wondered if the tight faces and silent looks she remembered from that time weren't so much their grief, but a deep and chilling fear.

She blew out a breath. "My aunts gave up everything, and my father didn't even have to pay child support. I'll never understand what my mother saw in him. It makes me worry that I've inherited some sort of flawed gene where I'm drawn to all the wrong men. Jeremy is the most recent example of that."

"I think it's the opposite. You're single because you refuse to settle for what your mom had."

Holly gave him a half smile. Somehow he'd managed to put a nice twist on her tragic dating history. "After my mother's accident the rumors at school got worse. I swear my tormentors smelled the complicity on me. They whispered that I was wicked, a devil worshipper, a murderer. They terrorized me, and that trickled down to my sisters. I kind of ruined high school for Winter and Missy."

"*They*—not you—ruined high school for your sisters."

"That's technically true, but I was responsible for letting it bother me in the first place. My mother's death taught me that I was never again going to let the opinions of a few ignorant people dictate how I felt."

It had also taught her what happened when she lost control. She'd been experiencing strong emotions lately, which was dangerous for more than one reason. Her mother's death was a reminder of how important it was that she keep a lid on her feelings.

That, and the fact that displays of power could get her noticed by dangerous people.

"You can't hold yourself responsible for an accident, Holly." Connor unfolded his large body and stood so that she was forced to tilt her chin to keep eye contact. "You were just a girl who stayed home sick one day."

Holly blinked away sudden tears and turned her face, embarrassed by emotions that still hovered close to the surface even after all these years.

"Holly." Connor's voice was deep, low, gentle. She lifted her gaze, drawn to the shades of his voice like a sailor to a siren. They held eye contact, the air thickening around them. She checked to make sure it wasn't her—but no, it was something else, something created by the way he was looking down at her, not with pity or disgust, but with tenderness and understanding.

A tear slid from the corner of her eye, trailing down her cheek. Connor lifted his hand slowly, as if waiting for her to move away. When she didn't, he gently dragged his thumb across her cheek, wiping away the wet track.

Holly inhaled, conscious that less than half a foot separated them in the narrow pathway they'd cleared. For the past half hour, they'd brushed against each other, bumping and jouncing and exchanging murmured apologies, until Holly was flustered and overwhelmed by her body's response to him.

She didn't *want* to like Connor Grimm. She didn't want to feel sympathy for his past or understand his mission to validate those with the same experiences. She didn't want to feel seen by those intense gray eyes. She was supposed to want him gone. She was supposed to be the smart one, the steady one who took over protecting their family now that Aunt Daisy and Aunt Rose no longer could.

And yet she felt frozen there, the wall of heat from his body and his scent wrapping around her like tethers keeping her in place. She should turn away and keep working, forget all about this heart-to-heart that had widened what had previously been only a tiny vulnerability when it came to Connor Grimm.

Because now he wasn't just the sexy paranormal ghost hunter sniffing around her family. He was a man who'd once been a traumatized boy, a person with the desire to do good in the world, even if he couldn't see how his actions might harm people like her.

Hesitantly, she lifted her hand and pressed her palm to his chest. His T-shirt was slightly damp and dusty to her touch. The air in the attic was oppressive, their skin slick with sweat. "Do you want . . . ?"

His heart kicked beneath her palm, and his voice was thick when he asked, "Do I want what?"

She didn't know what she was going to say, and felt stupid having even started the sentence. She started to remove her hand, but he caught her wrist in a light grasp. "Say it."

Holly licked her lips. She wasn't good at this, never had been. She didn't know what she wanted with Connor past this one moment, although she certainly knew what she *shouldn't* want. But right now, in defiance of all good sense, what she wanted was to press her mouth to his. Just once. Just to get it out of her system. If she did, maybe she could walk away and feel pleased to have discovered it was no big deal. She would have banished this ghost of attraction hanging over her head, muddling all her decisions. She would be able to remind herself why he was the absolute worst person for her to be attracted to, and then comfortably put it behind her.

"Do you want to kiss me?"

His lips parted slightly, and his eyes darkened. "*Yes.*"

There was zero hesitation in his voice, and it made her stomach tighten with anticipation. He lifted his palms to cradle her face on both sides, tilting her so that she was staring into those stormy irises. Time slowed; nothing stood between them but humid air and dust motes. He dipped his head and hovered a few centimeters over her lips, but he didn't kiss her.

She realized he wasn't going to, that even now he was going to wait for her to make the first move. Holly pushed up on her toes and pressed her mouth to his.

The moment their lips touched, something strange happened to her power. It flared without her consent, wind lifting strands of loose hair off the back of her neck and swooping around them in a gentle whirlwind. She barely noticed, and thankfully neither did Connor. His lips were soft and skilled, one hand sliding from her face to the side of her neck so that he could angle her better for him. He slanted his mouth, deepening the kiss by painstaking degrees until he touched his tongue to her bottom lip. Holly parted her lips to the request and his tongue swept inside, mingling with her own, tasting her with the single-mindedness he usually reserved for his show.

She settled her hands on his hips, the wind fluttering her shirt and brushing across the small of her back. Connor was big and warm, and he dominated the space, his large hands handling her with both care and command. His thumb stroked down the front of her throat and settled against the hollow at the base, the entire touch so unintentionally possessive that she burned.

"Hello!" Winter hollered. "Is anyone up here? Holly? Grimm?"

They froze, and in a split second Holly became fully aware of her power playing and leashed it so that the gentle breeze died down. The reality of what they were doing spilled over her like a bucket of cold water. She had been kissing Connor Grimm, the man who was determined to out her family, and not only that, but she'd nearly done the work for him by exposing her power.

Had she really just justified that kiss by hoping it would get him out of her system? Had a person ever been so reckless or stupid?

Connor's eyes met hers as he slowly withdrew his hands. Her cheeks were burning from embarrassment, the heat of the attic, and a kiss so mind-blowing she was still reeling from it. The first thing he said was, "Where did that breeze come from?"

Holly gulped and took a hasty step backward, bumping into a tower of boxes behind her. "I opened a window earlier," she stammered.

He frowned but didn't question her further.

Holly pressed her fingers to her lips, stunned by what she'd done and painfully aware that if she kept living in denial like this, she was going to do even more damage. She had to acknowledge the facts: despite all rational reason, she was attracted to Connor. Everything about him was wrong. He was addicted to his work, he traveled ceaselessly, and he was a threat to her family, so it shouldn't have surprised her that she was drawn to him. That was what she did: she picked the wrong men.

No, this could be salvaged, she told herself desperately. Yes, she'd lost her senses for a moment, but it wasn't like it meant anything. It was just a kiss. She could totally come back from this. Holly Celeste was going to turn her narrative around and make a wise decision about a man for once.

"Holly? Grimm?"

"We're back here!" Connor called out.

Holly quickly fixed her bun and tugged on the hem of her tank top. Connor rubbed his hand over his mouth and said, so that only she could hear, "I'm not sure that will help. Your lips are swollen."

"What I hear you saying is that it looks like we've been kissing."

"It's kind of sexy. I like that the woman I've been kissing is all rumpled and marked by me."

Holly wiped a bead of sweat from her temple. "I wouldn't have pegged you for the primal, mate-marking kind of guy."

At her comment his eyes flickered with some emotion she couldn't identify, but before he could reply, a box was knocked over, and a plume of dust rose into the air. Winter kicked the rotted cardboard in frustration. "What are you guys doing back here? This place is a junk pit. I say throw it all out."

Holly bent over a box and pretended to be looking through it. "We're making a path to the back of the attic. We're hoping to find some of Autumn's possessions."

Holly peeked over her shoulder, but Winter's attention had been caught by a crate of records. "Yeah, well, we have a little bit of a situation downstairs, and I could really use Queen Naysayer on my side." Winter was a music junkie and couldn't help flipping through the records. "You know how it goes: Aunt Rose and Aunt Daisy and Missy get caught up in all these wild, romantic schemes, and you and I always have to—" She paused, as if just remembering Connor's presence. "Well, anyway, I could use your help."

"Okay, I'll be down in a few minutes."

Winter nodded, and not having found anything worth salvaging from the record crate, started back down the path. Halfway there she paused and looked back. "You'd better not be using her for some ulterior agenda, Grimm. Holly is one of a kind, and she deserves the best."

After she left, Holly dropped her head into her hands.

"How the hell?" Connor seemed mystified. "You barely even looked up. I thought for sure we'd gotten away with it."

"Nothing gets past Winter." Holly stood and edged around him, determined not to be drawn into his arms like some kind of predictable magnet. She backed down the crooked pathway and said to his narrow-eyed expression, "You should keep that in mind."

CHAPTER TWELVE

Connor and Charlotte worked in the attic until late afternoon. They didn't speak much, which was fine with Connor because his mind was fully occupied with thoughts of Holly and the Celeste family.

The kiss had been staggering. He'd been completely unprepared for the layers of passion, tenderness, and lust that had ridden on a single touch of Holly's lips. Connor adored women; he loved kissing them and finding mutual pleasure with them, but the kiss with Holly—that had been something entirely different. The problem was he wasn't sure *what* it had been. What had transpired between them had felt intensely right, as if she'd always been meant to be in his arms.

Connor blanched at the unexpectedly sappy thought. Thank God no one could read his mind, because although he believed in ghosts and witches and all manner of things that went bump in the night, the concept of soul mates was a bit too far-fetched even for him. Ghosts had been acknowledged for centuries. Soul mates were a greeting card and Hollywood invention.

While he shifted furniture and sneezed through dust clouds, Winter's warning played over and over in his head. *"Holly is one of a kind. She deserves the best."* Had there been hidden meaning in her words? Was it an allusion to Holly being a *kind* of something, or had it just been a sisterly threat?

Then there was the truth of the statement. Holly *was* unique—he wasn't sure how unique yet—but interacting with her was like taking a breath of fresh air after a lifetime of living underground. When had he ever met a woman with a pet hedgehog, an ass that could make a man cry, a penchant for Christmas shampoo in May, and a fierce commitment to her family legacy?

Never.

"She deserves the best." Was Connor the best? Hell, no. Connor was married to his show, as Holly had established; he'd never had a relationship that lasted longer than six months; and he moved around frequently. He wasn't an asshole, or at least he liked to think he wasn't. He didn't cheat or make promises he didn't intend to keep, and he did his best never to lead his partner on. Things with Holly had spiraled out of control, but if this was a road they were going to go down—and God it was a road he really wanted to go down—then they'd have to have a discussion about expectations. Because when it came down to it, he might not be the best long-term boyfriend for Holly, but he could be her best fling.

Connor frowned and kicked an iron shoe. For some reason, the thought of being Holly's fling irritated him.

By dinnertime Charlotte was sneezing continuously, and the lighting in the attic was too dim to get any more work done. After hours of backbreaking labor, they'd finally reached the rafters, and tomorrow when it was light again he'd go through any items he found there.

"You owe me dinner," Charlotte said hoarsely as he dropped her off at her trailer.

"I'll get you in half an hour," he promised.

Connor showered and dressed in clothes that weren't grimy, then spent fifteen minutes catching Erikson up on the progress they'd made so far at Wicked Good Apples. Erikson was in Montana, hunting down leads on reported hauntings in an old gold mining town where a famous mine had collapsed on a dozen men in the 1800s.

"Do you need my help?" Erikson asked. "It sounds like you're getting in pretty deep over there."

Connor frowned and pinched the bridge of his nose. What had he said that suggested he was getting personal to the case? Maybe it was just that he and Erikson were so close it was hard to keep secrets from each other. Their shared ghost trauma had cemented their relationship at a young age. Connor was two years older, but they'd been equals since their first psych eval.

"No, I'm fine. I'm almost certain I know what they are. I just need to prove it."

"What about Holly? You've mentioned her more than anyone else. You think you can get her to open up to you?"

Connor drummed his fingers on the cover of a research book. "I don't know. They're a tight-knit family, so I need to tread lightly."

"You still think they're witches?"

"Yes." Connor rubbed his eyes. "No. I don't know. A lot of things that have happened on the farm seem witchy: the rain during droughts, avoiding the apple disease that wiped out the neighboring orchard a decade ago, the photograph of Daisy's hands over the barrel, and even the fact that they've never visited a doctor. Not one of them, ever. They don't exist in a single medical database that Charlotte could find, Erikson. That's bizarre, right? And yet it doesn't feel like a perfect fit. It feels like I'm missing something important."

Erikson sounded worried when he said, "We've come in contact with some supernatural things before, but we mostly deal with ghosts, Con. Be careful. This is pretty new territory for us."

"You be careful too. Don't go climbing into any old gold mine shafts."

"Who would be that stupid?"

"You would."

Erikson laughed. "Well, I won't this time. Text you later."

Connor hung up and left his trailer to knock on Charlotte's door. When she opened it, she was dressed in a bathrobe, and her eyes were so red and swollen that he flinched. "Christ Charlotte, what happened to you?"

"You!" she snapped. "*You* happened to me. I have allergies, and hours in that stupid dusty attic have done me in."

"Char, I had no idea. Why didn't you say something?"

"Because I'm an idiot." She pressed a baggie of ice to her eye. "I'm going to lie down. Bring me back a salad." She turned away, muttering about being rail thin by the time she left this vegan-hating town, and Connor quietly closed the door.

He was striding toward his pickup truck when he noticed the black sedan parked behind Holly's ancient Kia. He instantly recognized it as belonging to Jeremy. What was that jerk doing back here? Connor thought of Winter's plea for Holly's calm head hours ago, and he turned on his heel and walked straight to the Celeste house.

It was none of his business. He should turn around, find a diner, and leave the family to their affairs.

He knocked on the door. A moment later Winter opened it with a flat expression that gave away nothing about how she felt at seeing him on her doorstep. "I was expecting you."

Strange. He hadn't said anything about stopping by. Maybe she'd assumed he'd come to see Holly after what she'd nearly caught them doing in the attic today.

Connor tucked his hands in his pockets and rocked back on his heels. "I see Jeremy's car is here."

"Yeah, he and his girlfriend have been invited by the aunts and Missy."

"Is that so?"

"Yup."

It was a standoff. She wasn't moving aside to let him in, and she wasn't divulging any extra information, but she wasn't shutting the door in his face either. Winter was an enigma. Connor still didn't have a solid read on the woman, but he had the very distinct feeling that if she'd been born a few centuries earlier, she'd have wielded a battleax, and he would have been rightfully afraid of her wrath.

He was considering his best course of action when the door opened wider, and Holly appeared. Happiness flickered in her eyes when she saw him standing there, but she quickly hid it. Interesting. "What are you doing hanging around outside?"

"I saw Jeremy's truck and wanted to make sure everything was all right."

Holly threw up her hands in exasperation. "Who knows? Missy has been very secretive. Want to come in?"

Connor was stepping over the threshold before he'd even made the conscious decision to join her.

Winter had disappeared, so it was just him following Holly down the wallpapered hallway that led to the living room. Her jeans were faded and skintight, her feet bare, and her silky black hair was curling down her back. Connor battled the urge to slide his palm against her waist and pull her flush to him so that he could taste the side of her neck.

Holly halted outside the living room door and faced him, her lips parting slightly when she caught sight of his expression. "You can still turn around."

Connor couldn't tear his gaze from her mouth. "Why would I want to?"

"I have a feeling that whatever's about to happen is going to be ugly. Missy was purposely vague this morning when she was trying to convince us to attend her grand pitch, but if her scheme involves Jeremy and Amy, it can't be good."

"I want to stay."

"For now, anyway."

What was that supposed to mean? Before he could ask, she pushed open the living room door.

The two aunts were sitting beside each other on a long floral couch, their white braided hair wrapped around their heads in identical hairstyles, the only difference being the type of flower tucked in each braid. Rose wore a fabric rose, and Daisy wore a fabric daisy. Connor's eyes flickered to Daisy's hands. Where Rose's hands were sprinkled with rings, Daisy's were encased in thin black gloves even though it was warm inside. Every time he'd seen her—apart from in the photograph—she'd been wearing them. What could it mean?

Missy paced near an unlit brick fireplace, twisting her fingers in either excitement or agitation; he wasn't sure. Prickles was curled in a snoozing ball on the multihued rag rug, safely sheltered underneath the antique walnut coffee table that separated the aunts from a loveseat positioned in front of an entire wall of books. Sitting on that loveseat were Jeremy and Amy. Jeremy's dress shirt was buttoned so tightly that it looked like some of his blood was being retained in his head.

When Holly entered, Amy placed her hand possessively on Jeremy's leg. After glaring at Holly, she shot Connor a look filled with jilted vengeance. "Who invited the ghost hunter?"

"I did," Holly said. Connor liked that she didn't justify her decision.

Jeremy scowled when Connor's hand accidentally brushed against Holly's. It was so obvious the guy wasn't over her that Connor couldn't believe Holly didn't see it. Connor might have felt bad for him if he weren't such a dickhead.

"This doesn't have anything to do with Grimm Productions," Jeremy said in his nasally voice.

"Doesn't matter," Holly replied. "My house, my rules. You seem to have a hard time understanding that."

Aunt Rose tsked. "Now, now, Holly. You and Winter seem to have already made up your minds, and you promised Missy this morning that you'd consider her proposal. Let's hear her, Jeremy, and Amy out."

Holly crossed her arms over her chest, and the air shifted at Connor's back as Winter slipped into the room.

"Great, now everyone is here." Missy clapped her hands once. "Are you ready for this bit of genius? Jeremy and Amy called me this morning with a proposition that I think is worth serious consideration."

Connor studied Amy's expression as she waited for Missy to reveal this grand plan of theirs. She was so smug he almost couldn't look.

"This was Amy's idea," Jeremy said immediately. For some reason Connor doubted that. He didn't know what Jeremy's end game was, but Connor had trusted ghosts more than he trusted Dickbag. Jeremy tightened the already tight knot on his tie, and Connor didn't know how he was still breathing. "She was emotionally wrought by the window incident yesterday, and by Holly bringing her—"

"Uninvited rodent into my house!" Amy cut in shrilly, eyeing said "rodent" sleeping underneath the coffee table with disgust.

"He is *not* a rodent," Holly snarled.

Jeremy patted Amy's knee. "As you can see, Amy is still very much disturbed by the assault."

Assault? These two were out of their minds. Connor had seen petty and selfish come out of the woodwork more times than he could count: when fame and money were on the table, good neighbors and loving family members could change in ways that were hard to fathom. He understood that Amy and Holly's feud went back to high school and that Jeremy's part in it only complicated feelings, but assault by hedgehog was a new low, even in his line of work.

"But eventually Amy calmed down like a good girl—"

Condescending jerk.

"—and in the interest of being decent people, we're willing to drop the lawsuit in exchange for something that could be mutually beneficial to us all."

Missy was bouncing on the balls of her feet, as if she couldn't stand to wait any longer. "Dating with a ghost!" she shrieked.

Holly and Winter exchanged a confused look.

If Missy noticed, she was undeterred. "After the *Grimm Reality* episode airs, we'll be hot for a minute, and we need to take full advantage. Amy came up with the idea, so she'll be credited as the creator when we pitch the idea to a few TV networks. The concept is simple: the cameras will follow around one of the owners of Wicked Good Apples as she and her boyfriend contend with an intrusive third party—Wicked Good Apples' very own ghost."

Missy did a half curtsy as Daisy and Rose slowly clapped, appearing torn between wanting to support the idea and worrying about the consequences of it. Holly was frowning, and Winter was, typically, blank-faced.

"What's your part in it?" Holly asked Jeremy.

He grinned at her. "I'd be the boyfriend, Hols."

"If you think I'm going to let Amy pretend to be an owner of this apple farm, then you—"

"No, no," he chuckled. "Amy would stay behind the scenes. *You* would be the girlfriend, Holly. We already have a history together. It would be easy to act like we were a couple again."

Holly stiffened beside him, and Connor felt his own body go cold. Jeremy wanted her to do *what*? Play girlfriend on national television with him and some ghost? Riding the coattails of Connor's show was one thing, and Connor would never begrudge Holly the business, but this was something else entirely. Jeremy no doubt hoped the close proximity and media exposure would endear him to Holly again. Was Connor the only one able to see the other man's endgame? Was Amy too blinded by potential dollar signs to see how her boyfriend pined for his ex?

Connor crossed his arms and leaned against the wall and said absolutely nothing.

"You told me you had a reality show idea to pitch in the wake of the *Grimm Reality* episode airing," Holly said, directing her anger toward Missy. "You didn't mention you wanted me—or *him*—to star in it."

Missy opened her palms. "That's because I knew you wouldn't hear me out."

Jeremy walked over to Holly, his expression soft and pleading. He took her hands in his and said so quietly that Connor could barely hear, "Give it some thought, Hols. You and I were so good together. It would be completely believable. We'd make enough money so that when the show was over we could support the orchards without worry, and the exposure would make me a shoo-in for the town council. It would be a win–win for both of us."

Holy God, did Connor want to punch this guy in his face. Connor hadn't missed the *we* that Jeremy had slipped in there. Jeremy and Holly had broken up six months ago, and Jeremy had moved on with a woman who treated Holly like dirt. Now, all of a sudden, when her orchards were going to be on national TV, he realized he wasn't over her?

Connor had thought Jeremy's longing for Holly was a case of the other man finally smartening up to what he'd lost, but in actuality his motives were pure selfishness. Jeremy didn't want Holly because she was incredible and complex; he wanted her because she could boost his social currency.

Connor was seething, and it took him a full thirty seconds to realize he wasn't just pissed at Jeremy for being a shitty human being—he was *jealous*. Connor didn't do the jealousy thing—especially not over a woman he wasn't even dating. For frigs sake, he and Holly had only *kissed*. He took a deep breath and focused on Holly's reaction.

Holly was trembling when she pulled her hands from Jeremy's, and her eyes were flashing with rage. At that moment thunder rumbled overhead—another evening storm. It must've been the daytime heat that was causing them. He'd rarely seen such volatile weather as he had over the past few days.

"Oh shit, Holly. Seriously?" Missy planted her hands on her hips. "This is a killer idea."

"She doesn't like it because *I* came up with it," Amy said sulkily. "It's not like it would be real. Jeremy is completely over her." But the expression on her face said she wasn't so sure about that.

Holly ignored Amy. "Missy, if you want to do the show so badly, *you* shack up with him."

Raindrops appeared on the window and dribbled down the glass. The apple trees, which were in view out the window, waved in a long roll down the hill.

"Wait a minute." Jeremy grabbed Holly's hands again, and Connor fought the urge to knock them away. "I want *you*, Holly. We're perfect for TV. We even have built-in conflict for the story arc: couples therapy! We'll work on some of the problems you mentioned when we broke up for real. I could work on making you happier with . . . you know." He waggled his eyebrows suggestively.

Amy glared at them from across the room, her eyes reflecting an open battle between greed and jealousy. She wanted the show and what it could do for her, but she hated that it meant her boyfriend would be spending so much time with his ex.

Jeremy continued, oblivious to the lancing stare of his girlfriend. "And you could work on not being so emotional. You could take a class!"

Connor thought Jeremy might be the dumbest man on earth.

Holly ripped her hands out of Jeremy's for a second time. "The answer is *no*. No way, not ever, not in any universe. If this family wants to pitch a reality show, have at it. I've been outvoted about everything else, so you all might as well do this too. But I will *not* be taking part in it."

Jeremy's face darkened into something embarrassed and ugly. "Is it because of him?" he spat, jerking his chin in Connor's direction. Connor gave him a wolfish smile, and that only made Jeremy's cheeks redden further. "Are you worried he'd be jealous? Are you already fucking him?"

Connor's smile faded.

Winter stiffened, and even Missy narrowed her eyes.

Everyone waited with bated breath to see what Holly would do. Damned if she didn't surprise him when she very calmly said, "What I do or don't do is none of your business any longer." She strode to the living room door and shoved it open. "Sue me, Amy. I'd rather that than see the two of you ever again. Bye."

Jeremy's cheeks were puce when his eyes darted to Missy. "I'll call you, Missy."

Missy's face could have been carved from stone. "Don't bother."

"Now wait just a minute! You can't be angry with me. I have every right to know if she's sleeping around like some slut."

The windows rattled in their frames with a strong gust of wind at the same moment that Connor realized he'd had enough. He grabbed Jeremy by the front of his shirt and dragged him through the door. "She said *bye*," he growled as he shoved the stunned man down the hallway. He heard Amy's heels clapping after them. "If she has to say it a second time, it's going to be bad for you."

Jeremy stumbled to a stop at the front door and straightened his tie while Amy squeezed past Connor to his side, her chin jutting with indignation. "You think you've won, Grimm," Jeremy snarled, "but in a few weeks you'll move on and I'll still be here, biding my time. Eventually she'll come around." He glanced down at Amy and lamely added, "To doing the show."

"Holly will make her own choices, but if I had to bet, I'd say you won't be one of them." Connor leaned forward so that only Jeremy could hear his next words. "And if you ever call her a slut again, I'll knock your fucking teeth out."

Connor took great satisfaction in slamming the door in Jeremy's shocked face.

CHAPTER THIRTEEN

Holly was very, very angry, and she was having a hard time even looking at her family while Connor ushered her asshole ex down the hallway, with Amy trotting after them. Most of her anger was directed toward Missy.

"Holly, I'm—"

"How could you do this?" Holly interrupted. The wind shrieked around the house, and she knew some of the blossoms would be blown off the trees in the orchards. She needed to get her temper in check, but she felt betrayed.

"Holly," Aunt Rose warned.

"I know," Holly said through gritted teeth. She took three deep breaths and forced herself to reel in some of the power she'd unleashed. It felt good to release some buildup from her depthless well of contained power, but she'd been doing it too much lately and it wasn't safe.

Winter's arms were crossed over her chest as she glared at Missy.

Missy lifted her hands and let them drop. "I don't have an excuse. I didn't realize you and Jeremy were on such bad terms. He told me you'd been texting him and that you were still good friends. I mean, I knew he was a dick last night, but Jeremy's *always* been kind of a dick, so it didn't seem like anything out of the ordinary." She swallowed hard. "I'm sorry, Holly. Even with all that, I still knew you wouldn't like to be on TV. I shouldn't have done it."

Holly continued to take several steadying breaths while she absorbed Missy's apology. *Had* Jeremy always been a jerk? Had her family known it the entire time they were together? Why hadn't Holly seen it?

"Listen," Holly said, "the reality show isn't a terrible idea. I know I said you all outvoted me, and it's true that the media attention around the apple farm really worries me, but it doesn't mean it's the wrong thing to do. Just leave me out of it."

"No." Missy shook her head, and a red curl tumbled from her clip. "We'll find another way. Honestly, I didn't love the idea of working with Amy and Jeremy anyway."

"We'll figure it out." Holly glanced at her aunts. "Sorry. Amy's definitely going to sue us again."

Aunt Rose sniffed. "Let her try."

Despite the residual icky feeling in her gut, Holly was smiling when she left the living room and almost ran into Connor, who was returning from bouncer duty. "Are they gone?"

"Yup. Left a cloud of dust behind them."

"Thanks for showing them the way out. I was about to lose it."

"And yet you so very calmly invited them to sue you," he said as he fell in step beside her.

She led him through the dining room into the kitchen, where she turned on the tap and filled the teakettle with water. Another migraine was on the way, and mint tea was at least comforting, if not helpful. She tried to be sparing with how much of Aunt Rose's elixir she used; there was always a price, and she wasn't the one who had to pay it. "That's because I wanted to strangle him with my bare hands, and I was afraid if I loosened the reins even a tiny bit, I might actually do it. Tea?"

"Sure."

While Holly rummaged in the tea box, he took two mugs from the cabinet overhead and set them on the counter. "Everything all right with your family?"

"We cleared things up." She was angrier with Jeremy than with Missy. That bastard had had a lot of nerve to lie to Missy and then call Holly a slut when he didn't get his way.

Connor leaned against the counter as she set the kettle on the stove and started the burner. "What happened between you and Jeremy anyway?"

"He wasn't my type."

"So you've said."

Holly absently swung the teabags from their strings. "Okay, there may have been a few reasons for our breakup beyond him being a jerk."

Connor was leaning against the counter, his tanned arms crossed, his eyes ever patient and always seeing too much. It made it hard for her to concentrate on what she was saying because all she could think about was how it had felt when he'd curled his hand around the side of her neck and stroked his tongue across her bottom lip.

No—bad Holly! She must not forget she was taking control of her narrative. No more picking the wrong guy.

"Things like bad sex and too many emotions?"

Holly huffed. "Yeah, pretty much. By the end of our relationship, I'd learned he was boring, controlling—and not in the fun way—and selfish in bed. Like, so selfish he was terrible."

Amusement flickered in his eyes. "How terrible?"

"You're loving this, aren't you?"

"I totally am."

She couldn't help smiling. "So terrible that he always finished and never thought about, um, *my* finish."

The amusement on his face disappeared. "What the hell?"

"Looking back, I'm not sure he thought a woman's pleasure was important."

Connor scowled as the water in the kettle began to roil. "That's someone who doesn't deserve to have sex."

"Yes, well." Steam poured from the spout of the teapot, and she dropped the mint bags into the mugs. "We had many exhaustive talks about it, and I tried to show him what I liked, but it just didn't seem to stick. Sometimes, by the time I was finished instructing him, I was too tired to enjoy it."

Connor lifted the kettle and poured water into the mugs. "You showed him what you liked?" He handed her a steaming mug, fragrant with mint, and his burning gaze met hers.

"I did."

"You know," he murmured, "I've been told I'm a quick study."

Holly's cheeks flushed, and she wrapped both hands around the mug, finding steadiness in its warmth. Was he . . . was he implying that he'd be interested in learning what made her feel good?

Aunt Rose saved her from having to fish a response from the whirlpool of emotions that was currently her brain when she pushed through the kitchen door and patted Connor all over the arm to thank him for escorting Jeremy from the house. Not long afterward, Holly told Connor she needed to lie down before the migraine got worse.

"I'm finishing with the attic tomorrow morning, if you want to join me," Connor told her when he walked her to the bottom of the stairs. "Could be fun."

"If I'm feeling better I'll come up for a bit."

"Need help getting upstairs?"

"No," she said a little too quickly. She wasn't sure she could handle any more mortifying stuck-jeans incidents, or even just having Connor in her room. She might've been willing to entertain her aggravating feelings of attraction to him under normal circumstances, but these weren't normal circumstances, and he wasn't a normal man. If Connor Grimm ever figured out what her family was hiding, he'd broadcast it to the world, and Holly couldn't be romantically entangled with a man who was two steps shy of ruining her family.

She'd keep on top of Connor's discoveries, but she absolutely would not, *could not*, find herself in his arms again. As long as he kept his investigation focused on the ghost and the supposed murder of the councilman, they'd be dandy. He'd shoot his episode and he'd leave, and Holly would be able to breathe once more.

"I'm fine," she said, lifting her chin with resolve. "I'll see you tomorrow."

He'd been watching her thoughts flit across her face, and he hesitated as if he wanted to say more, but he only nodded and said, "See you then."

CHAPTER FOURTEEN

The following morning Connor was already going through a hatbox of thimbles and other sewing bits when Holly made her way through the precarious pathway of junk to the back of the attic. She was wearing a pair of sunglasses because the light still hurt her eyes, but she was feeling much better overall.

When Connor looked up, she handed him a ceramic cup of coffee. "I don't know what you like, so it just has milk."

"Perfect," he said, scanning her from sunglasses to jeans. "How are you feeling?"

"Better."

"Do you get migraines often?"

She shrugged as she toed aside a half-sewn doll dress that he'd piled with the thimbles and spools. "Sometimes I have a lot; sometimes I go months without them. They're unpredictable." *Liar, liar.* They were as predictable as the sun rising in the east.

He nodded at the lid of the wooden sewing box. "The initials are *A.C.* I think we've found Autumn's stuff."

"I can't believe her possessions are actually here." Holly knelt beside him and reverently ran her hands over the sewing box. "It's two hundred years old. That's wild."

His eyes twinkled. "It's cool, right?"

"What are we looking for?"

"Journals and documents, first and foremost. Letters would be great, jotted notes, handwritten receipts—all of that. But really anything that will give us clues about Autumn's life will be helpful."

Holly scanned the narrow space under the eaves and spotted a dark navy trunk that had been pushed so far back and forgotten for so long that mice had nested on top of it. She dragged it forward, dust spitting into the air, and flipped open the tarnished brass latches. When she lifted the lid, the old mouse nest and droppings slid to the floor, and she tried not to gag. Holly had a thing with mice, and that thing was she hated them. It was part of the reason Prickles being labeled a rodent made her so pissy.

She clicked on the flashlight she'd brought with her and shined it inside. "Holy shit," she whispered. "Connor, take a look at this."

He kneeled beside her and gave a low whistle.

The trunk was stacked with dozens of thin books with leather covers, and they looked a lot like journals.

Holly lifted out the book on top and gingerly peeled back the cover, aware that she was probably the first person to handle it in over two hundred years. On the front page, in faded ink it read:

Autumn Celeste
1820

Her heart thumping with a mixture of fear and excitement, Holly pushed her sunglasses on top of her head and gently turned the page. She caught her breath, prepared to read Autumn Celeste's deepest secrets, but instead her brows pinched together in confusion. The page was blank. She turned to the next page and then the next. All of them were blank.

Connor frowned and lifted out the next volume. It was labeled *1819*, and it too was blank inside.

"This is weird, right?" Holly said as she opened the book for 1818, only to find more empty pages.

"I would say it's weird," he agreed. "If they were a stack of blank books that would be one thing, but why write out the date for every year only to leave the journal empty?" He pointed to the ink on the first book and then compared it to the ink on the second. "Different ink. She didn't write them all at the same time."

They took out the remainder of the books—a total of twenty—and at the very bottom they found a bundle of correspondence tied with a faded black ribbon.

Their eyes met in excitement. Holly was surprisingly eager to discover more about the woman who'd left them her apple legacy. Holly should have taken the time to learn about her family history before now, but she'd always let duty and chores get in the way. It shouldn't have taken Connor coming here for her to slow down and give proper attention to the past.

Connor nodded to Holly, and she slid the first letter off the top of the stack, grateful that she was here for this discovery. If there was anything sensitive in the letters, she'd have a chance to either make explanations or skip over it entirely.

There was no address on the letter and Holly wondered if it had been hand delivered. She unfolded the paper, which was dry and fragile with age. The writing was slanted and difficult to read, the ink severely faded. She shined the flashlight on it and stumbled over the words as she read aloud.

Councilman—

I must ask that you do not write to my husband again. The claims you made in your last correspondence angered him greatly, and I fear further provocation will not bode well for you. Out of concern for my husband and what he may do if you continue, I insist you cease your baseless accusations. You cannot blame a man for defending his wife, and Thomas is a devoted husband and dedicated citizen of our town. What you claim to have seen that night was a simple misunderstanding. You must know that your campaign against me will not change Thomas's mind about the station. You stand only to hurt a good man.

Take care with your words, Councilman. Accusations have consequences.

Autumn

"Holy shit," Holly whispered again. Half tales of how their orchard had come to be had filtered through the generations, but she'd never had proof until now. She'd known only that Autumn had planted the orchards out of spite and that the seeds had been special indeed, but there was a greater story here, perhaps one that would explain Councilman Miller's ghostly presence in their orchards.

Maybe this would be enough to satisfy Connor.

Connor's eyes were gleaming with excitement. "This proves she and the councilman were not only in contact but also on poor terms. The threat is implicit: back off, or you'll be in trouble."

Holly nodded. "It sounds like he accused her of something and then tattled on her to her husband. Apparently, her husband didn't appreciate it."

If fit with what she and her sisters had been told. Autumn Celeste had been the only remaining child after her mother and sisters were burned in Switzerland for being witches in what Aunt Rose liked to call *gendercide*. Autumn had eventually escaped to America, where she'd met her farmer husband and fallen in love, only to be accused of being a witch by the local councilman.

Connor pieced together the story far too quickly for Holly's liking. "I bet he accused her of witchcraft. He must've 'seen' something in the middle of the night and thought to confront her husband. There were more than enough spiteful and gullible husbands who would listen to anything spewed by a man as powerful and wealthy as Councilman Miller, even if it meant persecuting his own wife."

Holly's skin prickled as it did every time she thought of how fifty thousand "witches" had been executed in Europe, the vast majority of them women. "Men fear powerful women."

Connor nodded. "Some do. Thankfully, it seems Autumn's husband wasn't one of them." He gently extracted the letter from her hand

and let his eyes roam over the text. "She wrote this letter out of fear that the councilman would push her husband too far. She wanted to protect her husband, except she never sent it." He rubbed his palm over his chin as he thought. "She wrote at the bottom that the councilman's witch hunt wouldn't change her husband's mind about the station. Do you know anything about that?"

Holly shook her head no.

"I'll have Charlotte dig into any local records involving police, fire, and train stations at the time."

"If the ghost in our orchards is real, I don't think Councilman Miller backed off."

Connor leaned on his heels. "So who killed the councilman? Autumn, her husband, or someone else entirely?"

"Men are statistically more likely to commit murder, but I'm going to guess you go with the witch poisoning the apple," she said tartly. She tried not to be angry about yet another woman, her *ancestor*, being accused of doing evil simply because she was powerful.

Connor laid a warm hand on her wrist, and when she lifted her eyes, she saw that a line had appeared between his brows.

"Well?" she asked when he didn't say anything.

"I was going to reassure you that it isn't like that, but maybe it is. Maybe I *am* witch hunting. Maybe in more ways than one," he muttered softly, so softly that she wasn't sure she'd heard him right. He raked a hand through his hair and gazed into the distance. "If witches do exist," he said at last, "I get why they want to stay hidden. History has not been on their side." When his eyes met hers again, they were so penetrating that Holly's breath caught. "I want to normalize the paranormal, not hurt people."

"Autumn Celeste was not a witch." Holly took the letter from his hand and folded it again. The air between them was saturated with suspicion. "But she was persecuted all the same."

"I'm not here to persecute anyone."

"Then leave her out of it." What she meant was, leave *us* out of it.

Connor drummed his fingers on the edge of the trunk. "I'm not going to accuse Autumn of anything unless I have solid proof."

Holly was frustrated, but she'd done all she could for now. She opened the next letter, a missive to a woman at church about donating shawls to the needy. They combed through the remaining letters, but none of them mentioned Councilman Miller again.

Holly spent the next half hour working silently beside Connor, sweating in the hazy golden light of the attic, until they'd gone through all of Autumn's meager belongings. Aside from her sewing box and the trunk of blank journals and letters, they'd discovered a keepsake box containing the moth-eaten baby clothes of her three daughters and locks of their hair, several hatboxes with the crushed hats still inside, and a few poetry books.

Connor stood and stretched, lifting his arms over his head. The hem of his T-shirt rode up enough that Holly got an eyeful of abs and a dark, happy trail. She gulped and turned her head away, and when Connor wasn't looking, she grabbed the blank journal from 1820 that she'd stashed behind the trunk when they were repacking it. She tucked it into the back of her jeans and smiled brightly at him before she followed him out of the attic.

CHAPTER FIFTEEN

Connor considered himself a pretty decent lie detector, and when Holly had told him Autumn wasn't a witch, she'd had all the trademark tells of someone speaking the truth.

But not the whole truth.

Their discussion nagged at him. In between consultations with his camera crew and meetings with Charlotte about the next set of interviews, he thought about what Holly had said. Had Autumn murdered the councilman, or was Connor targeting her unfairly? As Holly's ancestor, it was entirely possible Autumn had also been different, but if she'd been anything like Holly, there was no way she'd been evil. So if Autumn hadn't been a witch, then what *had* she been? What was *Holly*? Why did he still feel like he was missing something that was right in front of him?

Connor rubbed his eyes and returned his focus to the book he'd finally tracked down at a German antiques dealer two months before. The volume was fragile, at least three hundred years old, and written in Old High German. He'd paid for expedited translation, but even so the book had only arrived with the English notes the day before. The author of the eighteenth-century volume claimed to be an expert on "the devil's creatures." So far Connor had read about gigantic spiders and bulls with three eyes. Not exactly helpful for his situation at Wicked Good Apples.

"When are we spending the night in the orchard?" Charlotte asked, snapping her gum and breaking his concentration again. She had her tablet in front of her and was tapping on the screen with brightly colored nails.

"It's forecasted to rain tonight so I was thinking tomorrow." Connor closed the book and picked up his phone. He'd sent Erikson a screenshot of the letter Autumn had never sent, and his brother had been feverish with excitement and hadn't stopped texting him since.

Connor should have been excited too, but there was something bothering him. He couldn't help but feel he was nosing around where he wasn't wanted. He'd had that feeling in the past, and it usually meant he was onto something. The supernatural didn't like to be messed with. So why was it getting under his skin this time?

"Hello, Earth to Connor, did you hear what I said?"

He blinked. "No."

"Our private detective got back to me about the number that called to warn you away from the Celestes when we first got here."

Connor was suddenly all ears. "And?"

"He was able to trace it to a trailer park in town. The guy used 'star' sixty-seven to disable Caller ID, but he called from his regular phone. You'll never believe the name associated with the account." Charlotte paused for dramatic effect. She even stacked her hands behind her head and put her neon-green high-heeled boots on the table between them. His trailer was small, and the table even smaller, so it took some amusing maneuvering before she managed.

Connor tried not to smile. "Don't keep me in suspense, Char."

She was slightly out of breath when she answered, "Ryan Miller."

Connor sat forward. "Don't tell me . . ."

"Oh, I'm telling you. We ran his family tree. Descendent of *the* Councilman Jonathan Miller."

Connor was already snatching his keys off the counter.

༼ ༽

Shady Oaks was a nicely maintained trailer park on the outskirts of town. The roads through the park were dirt, and the trailers ranged from doublewide to 1950s aluminum. As Connor drove along one of the dirt lanes with his window down, his cab was filled with a cacophony of barking. A few kids were playing with a red dodgeball on one of the lawns and didn't so much as spare them a glance as they passed through.

Number twenty-eight was wedged between two trailers with neat flower beds and freshly painted porch steps, and *man* how the neighbors must've hated twenty-eight because it was the polar opposite. Ryan Miller's lawn hadn't been mowed yet that year, and weeds were knee high around his lot. His mailbox looked like a bat had been taken to it and Ryan hadn't bothered fixing it.

Connor pulled in behind a dented Toyota that was a shade between rust and puce.

"My best friend grew up in a trailer park," Charlotte said, popping a bubble. "In a place this nice they must hate this dude."

Connor threw the truck in park and studied the sticker of a middle finger plastered to Ryan's front door. "It's a long way from uptight witch-hating councilman."

They climbed the porch steps and Charlotte said, "I wouldn't be so sure. I have a feeling this guy hates a lot of things."

Connor went to ring the doorbell, but it was broken, so he knocked. While they waited, he peeked through the window, but it was completely sealed off by a thick black curtain.

After a minute the door opened halfway, and Ryan Miller stared suspiciously through the gap. He was in his early fifties, with gray-threaded hair and a hooked nose. His eyes were small and close together, and he was so scrawny that Connor instantly pegged him for an addict. The scent of marijuana and litter boxes drifted from inside the trailer, and a cigarette was clasped between his yellowed fingers.

"Are you Ryan Miller?" Connor asked.

Ryan sucked on the cigarette and squinted. "Depends who wants to know." His gaze darted to Charlotte, and recognition dawned in his eyes. "Holy shit, I know you two. You're the ghost-hunter people from that show."

"We are. You and I spoke on the phone a few days ago."

Ryan's thin lips curled. "I knew that Caller ID blocking shit didn't work."

"We have a few questions for you. Can we come in?"

Ryan took another drag on the cigarette. "I don't know about that. I ain't got much to say."

Connor pulled two twenties from his pocket and held them up. "Still don't have anything to say?"

Ryan snatched the bills and stuffed them in his pocket. "Come in."

Inside the trailer dirty clothes were piled on every possible surface. Empty Cheez-It and pizza boxes were stacked on a counter that had more crumbs than the bottom of a chip bag, and everywhere Connor looked there were ashtrays overflowing with cigarette butts and charred roaches. Cat boxes lined an entire wall of the living room—Connor counted six—although he didn't spot any of the little fur balls.

There was no place to sit, and Ryan didn't make any effort to shift the junk, so instead they stood awkwardly between the living room and the kitchen. "Why'd you call me, Ryan? You said you knew more about the Celeste family history than most. You told me I was going to have bad luck if I didn't stay away."

Ryan shrugged and pulled on the cigarette. He blew the smoke in their direction like a giant asshole. "I was trying to help you out, man. My granddad always said those Celeste bitches were witches. Swore it up and down. Said they stole our future from us when they murdered my great-great-grandfather, except they never had to pay for what they did because bad shit happened to anyone who ever investigated them."

"Who was your great-great-grandfather?"

"Some rich town founder. He inherited a buttload of money from his father but went into politics like some fucking idiot. When he was murdered, his son spent every last penny trying to prove it was the Celestes, but before he could get justice, he died too. Some shady shit if you ask me. Bastard left the rest of us broke. I coulda been a millionaire if it weren't for the Celestes."

Connor shoved his hands in his pockets and tried to relax his posture into easygoing-buddy stance. "Any idea why your ancestors thought the Celestes were responsible? Or why they thought they were witches?"

"They didn't think they were witches; they *knew.*"

Charlotte said, "Do you have any proof?"

Ryan laughed. "Proof they're witches? Gimmie a break, babe."

Charlotte stiffened beside Connor, but she remained professional when she said, "I meant do you have any letters or diaries—anything that corroborates your grandfather's stories?"

"Are you calling me a liar? You know, I didn't have to warn you. I was doing you guys a favor, and then you show up here acting like some fucking movie stars when—"

"She's not calling you a liar," Connor interrupted in a soothing voice, "but we have asshole bosses at the network who demand proof of everything so we don't get sued. Trust me, if it was up to us, this would be in the next show."

Appeased, Ryan stubbed out his cigarette and said, "I might have something, but it'll cost you a little extra."

Connor fished out another twenty and handed it over.

"I'll be back in a minute." Ryan stuffed the bill with the rest in his dirty jeans pocket. "Don't snoop around my shit."

As soon as he retreated into the bowels of the trailer, Charlotte opened her mouth to say something, but Connor shook his head. She closed it again but mouthed, "He's an asshole." She'd get no argument from him there.

Charlotte hitched her purse higher on her shoulder and wandered around the living room, studying the photos on the walls. From where he stood Connor spotted several photos of Ryan holding large fish against icy-white backdrops. Charlotte paused before a framed photo of two men, and her eyes widened as she beckoned Connor over.

Connor glanced at the hallway where Ryan had disappeared, and strode toward her. The photograph was slightly out of focus, but when he saw who was in it, he sucked in a breath.

"What are you gawking at?" Ryan appeared at the entrance to the living room, a worn Bible in one hand. "I thought I told you not to snoop."

Connor gestured to the photo where Ryan had his arm slung around another man's shoulders. "We know him. That's Jeremy O'Toole."

"So fucking what?"

"You guys friends?"

Ryan squinted. "Cousins. His dad and my dad are brothers."

"But you don't have the same last name?" Charlotte asked.

"His dad was already married but fuckin' around when he got his side chick pregnant, so Jeremy got his mom's name. Why do you care so much?" he asked, suddenly suspicious.

"We don't," Connor answered, but his mind was racing. Ryan claimed to know the Celestes were witches, which meant Jeremy would have heard the story too. Was that one of the strange things about Holly that Jeremy had mentioned to Amy? Had Jeremy dated Holly despite the rumors or because of them? Exactly how much was he like his great-great-grandfather, Councilman Miller? Jeremy wanted to go into politics like his ancestor, but did the similarities end there? Or did he have some ulterior agenda with the Celestes?

Ryan turned away from the photo and peeled open the cover of the centuries-old family Bible. He pointed to the name *Jonathan Miller* written inside. "That was the guy they murdered. This belonged to my great-great-grandfather."

Connor pulled his phone from his pocket and asked if he could take photos. Ryan stared him down until he handed over another twenty. Once the money disappeared, Ryan nodded, and Connor started snapping.

Ryan flipped to the back of the Bible, where a few pieces of paper had been tucked away. He took one out, unfolded it, and handed it to Connor. It was faded and yellowed, and the paper was so creased it was barely in one sheet anymore. Connor's eyes ran over it. It appeared to be a town tax proposal, but it cut out halfway through, and at the bottom someone had jotted a few notes, almost like a modern-day to-do list. Connor recognized the writing from the town records he and Charlotte had already studied. It belonged to Miller.

- *Ask Mary to write down what she saw through her window that night.*
- *Mail our accounts to the newspaper. Will it be enough? It will be their word against ours.*
- *Cut down the apple tree for proof.*
- *Suggest to Thomas that I may be willing to forget what I saw in exchange for his signature.*

Connor took another picture and tried to stifle his excitement. "Would you be willing to sign a release saying we can show these photos on television?"

"Welllll," Ryan said, rubbing his jaw and drawing out the word, "that would cost you."

Connor produced another twenty, and Charlotte produced a release form from her giant purse.

A few minutes later they were back in the cab of the truck, and Connor was reversing out of the driveway. "Who is Mary?" Charlotte asked. "What did the councilman see that night? Both he and Autumn have referenced a particular night where he supposedly saw *something*. Autumn claimed it was a misunderstanding, but now we have this Mary as a witness."

"Whatever happened that night, it convinced Miller that Autumn Celeste was a witch. He thought exposing her would give him the ammunition he needed to force Thomas's signature."

Charlotte blew out a frustrated breath. "What did he need the signature for?"

"I'm guessing it had something to do with the station Autumn mentioned in her letter." Connor flipped on his blinker and exited the trailer park. "The most intriguing part to me was the note about cutting down the apple tree for proof. What the hell was that about? Proof of what? Was the tree related to what he saw that night?"

Charlotte tugged on one of her pigtails. "I don't know. We haven't had a case this mysterious in a long time. When we get back, I'm going to start looking into all the Marys who lived in town in 1820. I'm starting to think the Celeste/Miller mystery is going to take more than one episode to get through."

Connor was thinking the same thing, and he was pretty sure he knew how Holly was going to feel about that.

CHAPTER SIXTEEN

Rain pattered softly on the roof as Holly tugged on the neckline of her dress and frowned into the mirror.

"Stop that," Missy chided, slapping Holly's hands away. "You're going to stretch out the fabric. You look amazing. You're going to be the hit of the party tonight."

Holly had made the mistake of agreeing to go to Missy's friend's birthday party on Great Pond, and Holly's bad choices had only spiraled from there. She'd then allowed Missy to dress her in a black wrap dress with a sexy silhouette and a bare back. Missy had wanted to do her hair and makeup, and since Holly had already given up any semblance of good decision-making, she'd let her. The results were cascading curls, which were actually pretty, and enough dark makeup that Holly wasn't sure if she was looking at a person in the mirror or a raccoon.

"Take some off," she said, pointing to her eyes.

"No, that's a smoky eye. Poor thing, you don't even know what a smoky eye is. Good thing Missy is here to take care of you."

Holly stared into the mirror with regret. Why had she agreed to this? She had a spicy romance novel on her Kindle; she'd made apple-scented candles with Aunt Rose earlier that day; and the gentle rain made for a perfect night in.

Because of Connor, her inner voice chirped. Oh, right. She'd convinced herself at some point while pouring wax that all she needed was a fun night out with a few hot guys, and then she'd be able to put her attraction to Connor in perspective. It had been a long time since she'd seen anyone socially who wasn't either a customer or Jeremy. Clearly, this reclusion was responsible for making Connor appear more enticing than he was. Once she mingled with other attractive, intelligent men, she would see that Connor was sadly average, and then she wouldn't have to worry about throwing herself at the only person hellbent on ruining her family.

Perfect reasoning, she told herself as she pulled on the hem of her dress. Nothing wrong with it at all.

"I already called an Uber. Let's go." Missy gripped her arm and dragged her downstairs. "Bye everyone! Don't wait up!" she howled as she pushed Holly through the front door and toward the waiting car.

"I can drive," Holly protested.

"Um, no you can't. Didn't I tell you this was a rum-themed party?"

"What? No! How do you even theme a party after an alcohol?"

Holly slid onto the seat and Missy followed behind. She was stunning in a white leather skirt and a soft pink top that should have clashed with her hair but somehow didn't. "Rum cake, rum ice cream, rum punch, rum cigars . . ."

"All right, all right. I wish I'd known; I can't stand rum." Not since she'd vomited a fifth of it back in college.

"Don't worry." Missy withdrew a slender flask from her purse and waggled it in front of Holly. "Your girl has you covered."

"I can't believe I let you talk me into this."

"I can't believe you agreed to do it," Missy said as they hit the main route. "I've never known you to do anything fun."

"Hey! I'm super fun. I'm the funnest."

Missy snorted. "You're not anywhere near the funnest. You've always been so worried about protecting the family that I think you've forgotten to live."

"That's not true!" Was it?

A wicked gleam entered Missy's eye. "You can make up for it tonight. This is the hottest party of the spring. It's basically a college party with class, because, you know, we're older now."

Yes, a rum party on the lake sounded very classy. And very safe.

By the time they reached the lake house, Holly's stomach was cramping with nerves. The property was beautiful, with a dark wood-shingled house and weathered steps that led down a steep embankment to a dock on the lake. Fairy lights were strung along the deck railing, and the moment Holly stepped out of the car, she smelled cigarette smoke and weed. The rain had temporarily ceased, and bodies spilled from the house onto the deck, the damp green grass, and the dock below. Everyone was dressed as if they were at a cocktail party instead of a rum rager.

"See, they're all holding real glasses instead of red Solo cups," Missy said, nudging Holly with her shoulder. "Classy."

Until someone had too much and shattered one, Holly thought. *Okay, that was not a fun thought. Fun thoughts only. Must prove Missy wrong.*

Once inside, Missy took her hand and towed her through the crush of bodies to the kitchen, where Missy's friend and owner of the house was presiding behind a temporary bar.

"Missy!" Mike cried, pulling her into a tight hug. "Glad you could make it." He turned his blue eyes on Holly and grinned. "Holly, I'm happy Missy could drag you out."

Mike had graduated in Holly's class, but she barely remembered him from school, which meant he hadn't been one of her tormenters. *Their* faces she'd never forget. In college Mike and Missy had become friends and stayed in touch over the years. He was a chiropractor now, with a body chiseled in the gym. He was exactly what Holly was looking for: smart and handsome.

Maybe this had been a good idea after all.

Mike gestured to the table, which was crowded with an assortment of bottles, all of them filled with amber liquid in varying hues. "We have rum, rum, dark rum, light rum, and rum," he said. He pointed to a set of white bowls heaped with different garnishes like lemon and pineapple. Beyond them were bottles of Coke and other mixers. "Help yourselves, ladies." He grinned at them with a movie-star white smile. Holly should ask him what whitening agent he used or if he was just brushing with a good toothpaste.

Oh God, she *was* boring.

Mike handed Holly a glass, and his fingers brushed against hers. She waited for the butterflies, but none came. Maybe she needed to flirt more for the zing. Holly examined the display of rum bottles and discretely watched Mike until he turned to greet an arriving couple, then filled her glass with Coke.

"I saw that," Missy whispered at her side. "Let me get my flask." Before she could move, two of her friends squealed from the other side of the kitchen and ran over.

"Don't worry about it. I'm going to mingle," Holly said. "I'll catch up with you in a bit."

Missy nodded, and she and her two friends poured generous glasses of rum while exclaiming about how adorable the house was and how the party theme was *so* clever and classy.

Holly wandered the deer-and-plaid-themed rooms, stopping to exchange awkward pleasantries with classmates from high school who probably didn't even remember whispering behind her back, and waved with genuine happiness to various customers she knew from the apple farm.

She was passing a bookshelf crammed with hunting magazines when a wave of nausea swept over her. Holly pressed her palm to her belly and scanned the room a second time until her gaze fell on one of only three people who could be responsible for such a reaction. Stacy's dark eyes met hers, two manicured fingers rubbing her temple. Holly forced a half smile, and Stacy made her way over.

"Holly, I didn't know you and Mike were friends."

"We aren't. He's Missy's friend, and she dragged me along."

Stacy nodded and pivoted to stand shoulder to shoulder with Holly so they could study the room together.

Holly wasn't sure why Stacy was sticking around. It wasn't like they were friends, and being this close to each other was extremely uncomfortable. "I hate half the people here," Holly blurted. She and Stacy had gone to the same high school, graduated in the same class, and knew the same people.

Stacy lifted her glass halfway to lips that gleamed with perfectly applied gloss. "Because half of them were evil dicks to you in high school?"

Holly gave a surprised squawk. "Uh, yeah. You noticed?"

Stacy didn't remove her gaze from the crowd when she said, "I noticed, and I should have done something about it."

Holly was so stunned that a single flick could have knocked her over. *Stacy*—her nemesis dictated by nature—was admitting a wrong-doing to *her*? "No. You would have just made a target of yourself. Nothing was going to stop them."

Stacy did look at her then, her eyes reflecting the lights of the overhead antler chandelier. "I should have anyway. People like us should stick together."

"We're nothing alike."

Stacy smirked, even as the grooves in her forehead deepened with pain. "Maybe not, but we at least have more in common with each other than we do with them."

That was true. "Where are your brothers?" Holly leaned forward to look for the handsome set of twins who'd graduated the same year as her own twin sisters.

"Demetrius is here somewhere, but Kai is home."

Holly's stomach was trying to crawl up her throat, so she eased a few inches away from Stacy. "Well, have fun, I guess. Tell Demetrius I say hi."

"Holly, before you go, I just want to remind you of our offer."

"Right. Your offer. I haven't forgotten."

"And . . . I want to tell you to be careful." Stacy pulled her lip between her teeth. "There's something strange in the air."

A warning from Stacy wasn't to be taken lightly. Like she'd said, she and Holly, although opposites, still had measurable talents that most people didn't. For Stacy, that meant having a far more informed grasp of the magical than Holly, whose family lived in shadows and denial. "Thanks."

Stacy returned to her friends across the room, and Holly's cramping stomach immediately relaxed some.

It was hot and stuffy inside, even with the windows open, and Holly knew she would feel better with more distance from Stacy, so she made her way onto the back patio, running the conversation with Stacy through her mind. She and Stacy had always kept an antagonistic distance, as much from necessity as from the nature of what they were. But this maturity on Stacy's part was new, and Holly wondered if maybe the other woman was onto something when she said that people like them should stick together. Holly and her family didn't have community the way Stacy did, and for the first time Holly wondered if they were missing out on more than they'd realized.

Holly was headed toward the dock for a glimpse of the water, when someone stopped her with a hand on her wrist.

"Holly, I haven't seen you in a while."

Holly smiled automatically, but it took her a moment to recognize Blake Stephenson. When she did, the smile turned genuine. She'd gone to high school with Blake; he'd been one of the few people who hadn't made her feel like a freak. "Blake, how are you?"

He grinned, showcasing an adorably crooked eyetooth, and ran a hand through his sandy-brown hair. "Same old, same old. Working remotely for ESPN. How about you? I hear Wicked Good Apples is doing well. You're going to be on TV, right? Some ghost-hunting show?"

"*Grimm Reality*," Holly said. The breeze ruffled her skirt and rocked the dock on the water below. It was going to start drizzling soon. "Supposedly we have a ghost."

"Never liked ghosts much myself." Blake nodded to her drink. "Can I top you off?"

"No, I'm fine, thanks."

"I was headed to the dock. Want to come with me, and we can catch up? I only ever see Missy on social media. I have no idea what's going on in *your* life."

Since she'd been going that way too, Holly nodded. Blake casually placed his hand on the small of her back as he guided her down the steps, and she waited for the tingle. Again, there was nothing. *What the hell!* All Connor had to do was look at her and she got zings and tingles all over. This was more serious than she'd thought. Her plan was going to backfire if she couldn't prove to herself that there were other men out there who could make her react the same way Connor did.

The boards shifted when they stepped on the floating dock. Several other couples were already clustered together, drinking and talking over a black pond shrouded in wispy fog.

Blake told her a bit about his job, and Holly found herself laughing more than once. He was in the middle of reenacting a football goof that had gone viral when a shitfaced partier fell heavily on the dock, bouncing their end upward. Blake, who was already off balance, stumbled backward and spilled his drink down the front of his polo shirt.

"Ah shit," he said, ineffectively wiping at the dark stain.

Holly grimaced. "Are you attached to that shirt? Because that stain is going to need bleach."

"No, but I was really attached to my drink. I'm going to grab another one. You want anything?" When she declined but offered to go with him, he said, "Don't worry about it. Stay here and save our spot. I'll be back in a few minutes."

Holly waited, breathing in the rain-scented night and the smells of the pond. It was cool enough that she wished for a sweater, but too nice to bother going inside to get one. She rubbed her hands over her bare arms and was enjoying the view of the house lights sparkling on the water so much that she barely noticed the time passing and the couples gradually moving inside. Blake still hadn't returned, and she figured he'd either been held up or he'd ditched her. She tried to care either way but couldn't seem to. The truth was she'd rather spend the evening alone under the cloudy night sky than socialize. Her experiment was a failure. There was not a single man in attendance who intrigued her, attracted her, or infuriated her like Connor Grimm.

It began to mist, and she reluctantly decided it was time to head inside. She was turning away from the water when she thought she heard a whimper. Holly paused and strained to listen through the thumping bass coming from the house. The fog had gradually thickened over the pond, shortening visibility to ten feet at best. She was about to chalk it up to her imagination when she heard the whimper again. It didn't sound human, but animal.

Holly walked to the end of the dock and scanned the water. Sometimes fog distorted noise, so it was possible the whimper was coming from shore . . . except there! It came again! This time the fog shifted enough for her to spot a large rock protruding from the water ten feet from the dock. Sitting atop it and shivering violently was a puppy. *How on earth?* The poor thing must've swum out and climbed onto the rock and been too scared or exhausted to swim back to shore. It was the only explanation for how he could have ended up in such a precarious situation.

Holly chewed on her lip as she considered how best to reach the dog. The water wasn't too deep, but even at ten feet out, it would likely go up to her chest. It would be cold and murky, and she wasn't thrilled at the idea of swimming alone, in the dark, with a thunderstorm brewing overhead. But what other choice did she have?

Well, there was *one* other way. Holly looked over her shoulder. The increasing rain had driven everyone indoors. Warm squares of light spilled onto the darkened lawn, and she could hear muted laughter and music from within.

Not a soul was in sight, and still she hesitated. Cell phone cameras and security cameras were everywhere, even when you didn't think they were. What if Blake came out to check on her now that it had begun raining? There were simply too many people here for her to risk it.

Holly heaved a sigh as she slipped off her shoes and left them with her cell phone and purse on the dock. She sat on the cold boards and let one toe touch the water. It was icy and so dark it almost looked black.

"This is your lucky day, you know that, dog?" she called out.

The dog whimpered in response.

Holly slowly dropped into the water. Her soles squished into silt, and freezing water closed around the tops of her thighs, soaking her dress. She shivered as she began wading toward the quaking dog, trying not to gag at the thought of what she was stepping in.

"This isn't scary at all," she whispered. Mist coated her face and beaded in her hair. She was going to have to leave the party after this; there was no way she could walk around looking like a muddy, drowned rat. Plus all the makeup Missy had slapped on her eyes was probably dripping in inky rivers down her cheeks.

Something brushed softly against Holly's ankle, and she blanched. "It's just a fish," she assured the dog, as if he cared. "This isn't creepy. Who *doesn't* wade in cold, dark water at midnight? I mean, worst-case scenario is leeches, right?" The water had risen to her belly button. Only a few more feet to go and she'd reach the puppy.

"I hope this teaches you a lesson," she said sternly. The little white terrier puppy yapped and blinked shaggy hair out of his eyes. "I don't want to catch you swimming without proper supervision again." Holly held out her hand and let the dog sniff and lick her knuckles before she reached for him. He was wet and smelly and shaking so hard she had to tuck him close to her chest to keep him from jittering out of her grasp.

Holly turned toward dry land with the wet dog curled in her arms. She'd only taken one step when thunder rolled directly overhead and lightning split the sky, briefly illuminating the dock. "Not good, not good, not good," she chanted. Her foot slipped on a rock and she stumbled, catching her balance, but only after she'd submerged the dog up to his nose. She lifted him back out of the water, and he shook his head, dispersing droplets all over her face.

Thunder rumbled with such force that the water vibrated. "Screw this." She was risking both of their lives when there wasn't a soul outside. With two hands Holly held the dog out from her chest. A hurricane-strength gust of wind roared down the lake, lifting the puppy's light body from her grasp and carrying him the last ten feet to shore, where it deposited him gently on the grass.

Lightning flashed again, casting light over the pup on the bank and the man standing beside him.

Holly met Connor's eyes, and a barrage of emotions struck her one after the other: disbelief, fear, anger. She didn't have a chance to settle on one, because at that moment a bolt of lightning struck the post of the dock with a sizzling *CRACK*! The air filled with the acrid scent of burning wood, and the post snapped in half. Holly saw it falling, but she couldn't move fast enough in the water to get out of the way. She threw her hands up to shield her face as it struck her on the shoulder and dragged her under.

CHAPTER SEVENTEEN

Connor's interview of Lionel Hardy had been a bust. The man had been vague in his recollections of the ghost at Wicked Good Apples, and every time Connor had asked him a deeper question, he'd deflected so that the footage had been all but useless.

Charlotte had chosen to ride back with the van crew so she could look over some of the video, and Connor was following behind in his truck when his phone lit up with an unknown Maine number.

"Hello?"

"Connor!" a woman shouted. It was noisy wherever she was, music and voices crowding together in the background. "It's Missy!"

"Hey, Missy." He switched the phone to Bluetooth and rested one hand on top of the wheel. He'd given all the Celeste women his number, but Missy was the first to use it. "Is everything all right?"

"Better than all right!" she yelled. She sounded drunk as hell. "I'm at a party with someone who has the *best* ghost story about my orchards. Jenny—what's your name?" A voice mumbled and Missy said, "Jenny Cole! Never met her before, but she seems nice and she's sooooo pretty. I bet she'd look amazing on camera! I texted Winter and told her all about it, and she was like, 'You should call Connor *right now*,' and so I was like, 'Okay!'"

Connor grinned. "That's great, Missy. It's pretty late, though. How about you text me Jenny's number, and I'll get in touch with her tomorrow."

"Ugh, Connor, you're missing out *now*!" Missy whined. "What?" Her voice faded as she talked to someone next to her. "No, I don't . . . I don't know where Holly is. She went outside a while ago." Her voice returned to the receiver, louder this time. "Connor, are you still there?"

Holly was at the party? For some reason he was surprised. In the short time he'd known her, she'd seemed like a content-at-home sort of person, but for all he knew she could be attending weekly bong bashes. Missy's other comment, not meant for him, stuck in his head. Holly had gone outside "a while ago" in this weather? Alone? Rain dribbled down his windshield, and the branches of the trees lining the road bounced up and down in the wind.

"Give me the address."

Ten minutes later he pulled into the dirt driveway of a fancy house decorated with white lights and packed with cars pulled onto the lawn. This was definitely the place.

He jumped out of his truck as thunder rumbled overhead and lightning flashed across the sky, momentarily illuminating the dock down an embankment. When Connor spotted the abandoned pair of heels and purse, his heart twisted with savage fear. He sprinted toward the embankment and slid down, coating his jeans and boots with mud.

Where was she? Had she fallen in the water? Had someone hurt her?

Connor scanned the water and spotted a woman half submerged in the black liquid. Not just any woman—Holly. She was carrying something small and trembling in her arms; her wet hair was clinging to her neck, and her eyes were round with fear as thunder vibrated the very air.

Connor shouted for her, but she didn't hear over the thunder and what sounded like a freight train of wind tunneling down the center of the pond. His skin prickled when she held out her arms and the wind lifted the dog from her hands and carried him to shore, setting him gently on the grass near Connor's feet.

Buzzing awareness zipped through his bloodstream as he dragged his stunned gaze from the dog to Holly. Carefully controlled hurricane-force winds simply didn't exist—at least not in the natural word.

Their eyes met and held. Emotions swirled in her gaze, but before he could get a solid read on her expression, lighting struck with frightening violence, searing through the post of the dock as if it were slicing through butter.

The scent of burnt wood stung his nose as the post toppled straight onto Holly.

"HOLLY!" he roared, and plunged into the icy water. Silt sucked at his boots as he splashed up to his waist, inhaled, and dived under.

Panic. Pure, vein-freezing panic. Connor had never felt anything like it as his hands pushed against the velvety water, searching and seeking and not finding her body. His lungs were burning, and he was going to have to lift his head for air when his fingers brushed against the skin of her bare arm.

He grabbed her above her elbow and hauled her upward, her wet hair gliding across his arm until they broke through the surface. She started coughing immediately, and he lifted her into his arms and cradled her to his chest, water dripping in streams from her saturated dress.

Their exit from the water was treacherous and slow as his boots slipped on rocks and sank into the muddy bottom of the pond. It felt as if the pond had wet, grasping fingers that were reluctant to let them leave. At last he managed to carry her out of the water and onto the slick grass slope of the embankment.

He gently laid her on the ground and knelt over her, brushing her hair aside. She was coughing and retching up water, but after a moment she rolled to her back and opened her eyes. "Bad timing for a swim?"

"You scared the shit out of me, Holly! Are you all right?" He probed her temple with his fingertips, feeling for a wound. "Where were you hit?"

"My shoulder," she said hoarsely. His hand dropped lower, and she flinched when he found the spot, but to the best of his quick assessment, it didn't look like anything was bleeding or broken, only tender. "The post dragged me under for a few seconds."

"You almost drowned." He knew he sounded angry, but there was no helping it. His heart was still hammering against his ribcage like a mallet. "What were you doing out there in the middle of a frigging thunderstorm?"

She struggled to sit, and Connor helped her up. She wrapped her arms around her knees and pointed her chin down to the dog. Connor had completely forgotten about the little fur ball. The puppy had inched closer, still shivering, and was now sitting curled into her side. Her hand moved to rest protectively on his head. "He was stuck on a rock in the water."

She refused to meet his gaze as they both silently remembered what he'd seen.

"We need to get you to the hospital."

"No. Honestly, Connor, I'm fine. I just want to go home."

Right. Because the Celestes had never seen a doctor. Never been to a hospital. What magical cure waited for her at home?

A myriad of emotions fought for space in his brain: worry that she'd been hit too hard, utter relief that he'd been there to drag her out of the water, confusion about what he'd witnessed, and pure gratitude that he'd been driving close by when Missy called.

"What are you doing here?" she asked.

The sky continued to weep, the rain dribbling down her cheeks and dripping off the ends of her hair. She was shivering nonstop, so Connor pulled her into his chest and wrapped his arms around her. Her skin was ice-cold, and she smelled of pond water and Christmas.

"We'll talk when you're dry. Come on. I have clothes in my truck—a benefit to always being on the road."

She pulled out of his arms and scooped up the puppy. "We can't leave him."

"No, we can't."

When they reached his truck, he opened the passenger door, and she gratefully slid inside. He rounded the hood, started the ignition, and turned the heat on high. Once the air was blowing full force, he rummaged in the rear seat for the backpack he always had on hand. In his line of work, he never knew when he was going to need a change of clothes, a toothbrush, or a flashlight.

He fished out a T-shirt and a pair of sweatpants that, although too big for her, were infinitely better than the sopping wet dress plastered to her body. He handed them to her and said gruffly, "I'll look away."

Holly situated the dog on the leather seat beside her and took the dry clothes from him. "I need you to unzip my dress."

He silently groaned. Of course she did.

She turned her back to him and pulled her hair over one shoulder, baring a smooth, braless back in a little black dress that didn't leave a lot to the imagination.

Connor tugged on the zipper tab that ran from her lower back to the top of her ass, the black fabric parting to reveal a lacy pair of panties.

He was being tortured, he thought. It was the only explanation.

"Thank you," Holly said through chattering teeth. "You're soaking wet too. I'll be fine. You should take the dry clothes."

Connor glared at her. "That's not happening. Do you need help taking your dress off?" He half hoped she did, half hoped she didn't.

She shook her head, and he turned away to stare out the window. There was a wet slap as her dress hit the floor, and he tried not to imagine how she looked right then: full breasts, tight nipples, a soft belly and curvy hips—all of her bare and a mere two feet away from him. Connor pressed his forehead to the cool glass. He wasn't doing a very good job of not picturing her.

After a minute she said, "You're safe."

Not by a long shot. He turned and felt a stab of satisfaction at seeing her dressed in *his* clothes. The black T-shirt practically hung off her, as did the navy sweats, but she'd rolled the waistband to make them fit somewhat better. She'd rubbed off the smudged makeup, and her hair hung in ropes over her shoulders, wetting patches of the T-shirt. Even though she was wearing dry clothes, she was still shivering, and her cheeks were nearly bloodless.

Connor took her hands between his and rubbed them to warm them up.

"I think the dog has an owner," she said. "I felt a collar."

He brought her hands to his mouth and blew on them. "I'll look in a minute." The blue dashboard lights illuminated the frown line that had formed between her brows when he accidentally grazed her palms with his lips. "Want me to take you home?"

"Yes, but let me text Missy first so she doesn't worry." She withdrew her hands and patted the pockets of the sweatpants, only to realize her phone and whatever else she'd brought with her were still on the dock. "Shit."

"I'll text her, and then I'll grab your stuff."

By the time he returned, Missy was standing outside the truck, her head stuck through the window while she talked to Holly and rubbed the dog's head. They were exchanging furious whispers, and Connor was one hundred percent certain they were discussing what he'd seen at the pond.

When he approached, Missy gave him a bright smile and pulled the pup through the window. "His collar says he belongs to Mike, my friend who owns the house. I'm taking this puppy inside and finding him a warm bed and ripping Mike a new one for not keeping an eye on him."

"Do you want to come home with us after?" Holly asked, somewhat desperately he thought.

Missy gave Holly a long look. Connor could smell the rum on her breath from where he stood. "No, I don't think I should."

Holly glared at her, but Missy was already backing away with the puppy curled on her chest. "Text me if you need me," she said to Holly in a singsong voice.

Connor climbed behind the wheel, and once Missy was safely inside the house with the puppy, he put the truck in reverse and backed out of the driveway onto the road.

The only sounds were the pattering of rain, the swipe of windshield wipers, and the low hum of the engine. After several minutes Connor said, "I was headed home from an interview when Missy called. She said there was a woman at the party who'd seen the ghost at Wicked Good Apples."

"Oh."

Silence.

As casually as he could manage he said, "That hurricane gust of wind that carried the dog to shore was pretty strange, wouldn't you say?"

"So freakish. The weather guy did say that strong gusts of wind were likely this evening."

He glanced at her in the glow of the dashboard lights, and she smiled at him as if he hadn't just witnessed magic.

CHAPTER EIGHTEEN

Holly gave Connor her most innocent smile, but his gaze was hard, and she knew he wasn't going to let her get away with flippant avoidance. He'd witnessed her secret, and not just any secret, but the world-shattering kind that could end the simplicity of the lives she and her ancestors had built and fiercely guarded over generations.

He had confirmation now that she wasn't normal, but he still didn't know *what* she was. Not yet. Hopefully, not ever.

Her gaze fell to her hands in her lap. Her fingers were still cold, and her pond-soaked hair was keeping her shoulders damp. When the post struck her, it had been horrifying, the weight of it dragging her beneath the surface before she could catch her breath. She'd swallowed water, and then the dark, frigid liquid had slithered over her skin and swallowed *her*. She'd been disoriented and frightened, and then a strong hand had wrapped around her arm, and she'd thought: *Connor*. And she'd just known she was going to be okay.

He'd saved her life. He'd dragged her from the silted bottom of the pond and then scooped her up like he had the night she'd had a migraine. When he'd laid her on the grass and hovered over her, panicked and brushing hair from her face, she'd nearly lost her breath again.

She was balancing on a dangerous precipice: she wanted Connor Grimm in a way that defied all sense. She knew how dangerous he was to her family, how dog determined he was to uncover the truth about them, and how temporarily he would be in her life.

And yet this inconvenient attraction wasn't going away. Her mission tonight had been a bust. There had been several cute, accomplished men at the party, and not a single one had made her heart beat faster or her stomach flutter. No one's gray eyes had looked at her as if they could slip beneath her skin and see straight into her soul. No one had intrigued her with single-minded intensity or intelligent, open curiosity. Why did it have to be him? Why did he have to be the one who invaded her every thought and made her break out in chills by simply being near?

More importantly, what was she going to do about it?

Was it possible to sleep with Connor Grimm and still keep her deepest self hidden? She wasn't worried about falling in love with him—she'd have to be an idiot to fall in love with a man who was leaving in a few weeks, and Holly liked to think she wasn't an idiot. She *was* worried she might reveal more of her family secret than she intended, like she had tonight.

He'd seen her. He knew she was something *more*. He knew, on a very minimal level, what she could do.

If history had it right, that should scare the shit out of him. Maybe she'd already solved her attraction problem by frightening him off.

They drove in silence, the tension between them thickening with every turn of the wheel, and when he pulled into her driveway, Holly sighed with relief.

The truck had barely come to a stop when Holly released her seat belt and shoved open the door. "Thanks, Connor!" she yelled as she sprinted to the porch.

She was about to twist the doorknob when he spun her around to face him, his broad silhouette backlit by the porch light. Rain pelted behind him, dripping off the eaves and battering the blue hydrangeas.

"What are you, Holly?" He was so close she could feel the heat of his body and smell the pond water and pine on him. He pressed his palm against the door over her head, caging her in a way that made her knees weak.

Holly's heart was pounding so hard it almost drowned out the sounds of the rain. She licked her lips nervously. This man would see through a lie, and so she said the only thing she could. "I'm different."

His eyes narrowed. "A witch."

"No."

"You control the weather."

Holly struggled with what to tell him. He wasn't stupid; he'd seen what he'd seen, but that didn't mean she had to admit to more than necessary. She took a deep breath, and for the first time in her life shared a sliver of her secret with another person. "Some."

He was silent, his gaze so intent, so probing, that she nearly quailed beneath it.

"I, um, I understand if that frightens you—"

"Shut up." His lips met hers with all the pent-up frustration they'd both been feeling, his tongue running over the seam of her mouth and demanding entrance. She obliged, and their tongues tangled with such desperation, such depth, that it was hard to tell where she ended and he began.

He pulled back for the barest moment. *"Yes!"* she breathed.

Then his mouth was on hers again, and when he pushed her against the door, she thrilled to her toes. His thigh wedged between her legs, and he deliberately pressed up against her, drawing a moan from her that he swallowed with his mouth. She ran her fingers through the silky strands at the back of his head and dragged her palm to his cheek, the rough stubble of his unshaven beard scraping her skin. How would that rough rasp feel in more sensitive areas?

She trembled with need at the thought, but he must've mistaken it for a chill because he reluctantly drew back and said, "We need to get you warm."

"I thought that's what you were doing?"

His fingers flexed around her waist, and she could tell he was battling the desire to push her through the door and strip her down on the couch. She cupped the side of his neck, and before she could issue an invitation to do just that, he said, "You need a hot shower."

She felt for the knob behind her and opened the door with one hand while reaching for him with the other. She tugged him over the threshold and said quietly, "So do you."

He followed her upstairs to the shared bathroom, and when she would have pulled him in with her, he braced his hands on the doorframe and shook his head slowly, his eyes raking over her in a way that made her feel like he had X-ray vision, and he was seeing her naked beneath the bagging shirt and sweatpants. Her body hummed in response.

"If I get in that shower with you," he said through clenched teeth, "I have a pretty good idea of what we're going to do, and I'm *not* going to do those things with your aunts sleeping two doors down."

Holly tilted her head, drinking in the way his eyes darkened as they ran over the T-shirt clinging to her breasts. "Why not?"

He leaned in and said softly by her temple, "Because when we do those things—*if* we do those things—I plan on making you noisy."

Holly clenched her thighs together and was saved from having to respond by the gentle closing of the door.

She showered quickly, washing the pond water out of her hair and off her skin with her berry-and-mint-scented shampoo. The water was scalding, but the chill she felt was bone-deep. She didn't want to take too long, though, because at least *she* had been in dry clothes. Connor had been soaking wet the entire way back, and still was.

She dried off with a fluffy pink towel and wrapped it around her breasts, leaving his sweatpants in the bathroom for him. When she stepped into the hallway, it was empty. She found him in her room, studying the collage of black-and-white photos of the farm over the years.

"You have a whole history here," he said as she entered. His eyes swept over her, from her wet hair to the towel tucked around her body, and then down to her bare toes.

Holly stood beside him and traced her fingertip over one of the photos. It was a snapshot of a woman holding an apple in her palm. She'd lifted it so that it blocked out the low sun, allowing the rays to bend around the apple as if it were a gift from the angels. "Sometimes you're just born into the right life."

He inhaled but didn't speak.

"I left your clothes in the bathroom. The T-shirt is a little damp from my hair, but you can't put that back on," she said, gesturing to his wet shirt. "There's a fresh towel on the sink."

He turned and strode out without saying another word, and Holly quickly dressed in a pair of leggings and a thin tank top. She didn't bother with a bra, and she didn't particularly mind that the peaks of her nipples were showing through the fabric. Connor struggling with his self-control was one of the sexiest things she'd ever seen. It made her feel powerful in a way that had nothing to do with what she was, and that was a new and intoxicating feeling.

Holly pressed her palms to her cheeks. So much for writing a new narrative. She was seriously in lust with the man, and there was no point in denying it any longer.

Connor returned with warp speed—it always amazed her how quickly men showered and dressed—and the minute he entered, his eyes fell to her chest.

"You're trying to kill me."

"It's a sin to wear a bra past seven PM."

"I fully agree. I hung my wet clothes in the bathroom to dry. I'll take them with me when I leave. I don't want you to have to answer questions from your aunts and sisters in the morning."

Holly shrugged. "They're going to ask questions anyway the moment Missy wakes up and starts yapping. Thank you, by the way. For showing up at the right time. For . . . for everything."

For not being afraid of her.

He paced in her small room, running his hands over her things and filling her space with his presence. "I don't know if I believe in that."

"Believe in what?"

He pulled out her desk chair and sat, dwarfing the white-painted furniture with his size. "Right place, right time. It happens occasionally, but I didn't plan on interviewing my witness tonight. He called and said he had to work tomorrow, so it had to be tonight."

"Lucky for me."

Connor scrubbed his hand down his face. "What are we doing, Holly?"

She sat on the bed across from him, their knees nearly touching. "What do you mean?"

His gaze was so intense that she squirmed. "What do you want from me?"

"I want you stop investigating my family."

He turned away for a moment, avoiding her eyes. "I don't mean professionally. I mean what do you want from *me*? I'm not boyfriend material, but I think you know that. I'm leaving in a few weeks, and I won't be back."

She hated the way her heart sank at those words. In a very short time, she'd grown accustomed to running into him at every turn, to seeing him each morning. Of course he was leaving. She had never once doubted that. So why did it feel so shitty to hear it?

Many women in her position would protect their hearts and avoid further entanglement, but what was the point of living if you *didn't* live because you were always afraid of being hurt?

If only he weren't on that dammed TV show! If she slept with him and he exposed her family's greatest secret, could she live with herself after? Especially if she was responsible for giving him that knowledge? He'd confirmed tonight that she and her family were different—or supernatural, as he would put it—and she was terrified that he wouldn't rest until he knew everything.

Holly nibbled on her lower lip as she weighed her intense desire for this man against the primal need to protect her family. The smart choice was to walk away. The Celestes had a contract with Connor's production company, so he was there to stay regardless, but if she avoided him, froze him out, she *might* stand a chance at keeping herself in check. Because Holly knew Connor hadn't chosen this location for just a ghost story. He was at their apple farm for more.

He was there for *them*.

She took a fortifying breath. "I don't want anything from you. I think we should cool it."

His expression was flat. "Because of what I saw tonight?"

"Like you said, you're leaving in a few weeks. We have to work with each other in that time, so it's best if we keep things professional. That way there won't be any hard feelings when you go."

"You're pulling away because you're afraid of what you'll reveal about yourself."

She rubbed her temples. "You don't understand."

"Help me understand."

"Some things are best kept secret."

"I disagree."

"Then we're at an impasse."

Connor stood. "It's not what I want, but I respect your decision."

The next words were out of her mouth before she could stop them. "What do *you* want?"

He answered without hesitation. "I want to strip you out of your clothes and kiss every inch of your skin." His gaze fell to her thighs. "I want to taste you. I want to hear you when you come. I want to learn what makes you hot, and I want to see how fast I can get you there, and after that I want to see how long I can take getting you there. I want to know your body like I know my own, and then I want to spread your legs and bury myself inside you until I forget my own fucking name."

Holly's jaw dropped, and she thought she might have gone completely liquid inside. Every nerve ending felt sensitive and tingly, as if he'd stroked her with his hands instead of his words.

Connor strode to the door. He turned at the frame and said softly, "If you change your mind, you should know that when it comes to you and me, I don't give a shit what you are, Holly; I only care *who* you are."

CHAPTER NINETEEN

When had things become so damned complicated?

Connor had come to Wicked Good Apples knowing that at worst he would leave with a killer episode on the councilman, and at best he would shoot his show into the next echelon by proving the paranormal existed beyond ghosts.

Now that he knew his suspicions about Holly and her family were right and that the photo he'd been sent of Aunt Daisy was almost certainly real, he should have been chomping at the bit to tear their secret wide open.

So why was he suddenly unsure if it was the right thing to do?

Connor had chosen this place to make a splash, to prove once and for all that the paranormal was real, and everyone who'd ever experienced it was not only normal but *vindicated*. Was he really going to throw away the chance to change so many lives over vague guilt about sharing a secret that wasn't his? Since when had he ever let that stop him?

Connor was a storyteller at heart. That was what he'd come here to do, and damn it all, that was what he was going to do.

As for his relationship with Holly—she'd told him she wanted to cool things down, and he couldn't really blame her. Like Charlotte had said, he was a relationship no-go. He was completely fine with keeping it professional from here on out.

Okay, so he might have lain awake thinking of the terror he'd felt when he saw her slip under that murky water, and then later he might have tossed and turned remembering how she'd looked in his clothes with all those soft, sweet curves hidden underneath, but all that proved was that it had been a while since he'd had sex, not that he had *feelings* or anything.

Everything was good. Everything was on track. She was right to pull back; it would make it easier for him to do what needed to be done.

"I don't think I've ever seen you this distracted," Charlotte said, waving a stack of papers in front of his face.

Connor jerked to attention. "Did you say something?"

"Yeah, I asked if you got the shots you wanted."

He'd spent the morning with his film crew taking video footage of the apple farm that would later be spliced into the program. He'd even brought them up to the attic, with Holly's permission, where he'd filmed a monologue as he sorted through the old journals. One of the journals had been missing, and he suspected he knew who'd taken it. But why remove a blank journal?

"Yeah, I did," he said.

After he'd finished filming, he'd spent the early afternoon compiling research and coordinating interviews. His crew was coming back at eight to set up lighting and cameras for the night portion with the electromagnetic field detector. The EMF reader was mostly for show—he doubted the councilman would appear on demand—but the apple orchards would be the perfect spooky backdrop for the theatrics. It was supposed to be a clear night with a full moon.

Restless and needing to stretch his legs, Connor dropped his notes on the small table in the trailer and stood. "I'm going to head over to the house and invite the Celestes to the filming tonight."

Charlotte was chewing on a pen cap as she rifled through unofficial records of birth and genealogy charts dating from the 1800s, compiling all the Marys that had lived near Autumn and in the surrounding towns. She waved him away, and Connor escaped the confines of the trailer, relieved to breathe in the flower-drenched May air. The sky overhead was a rare seamless blue, leading him to believe the weather reports promising a clear night. Most of the apple trees were flush with shades of green, the leaves tender and new, the buds beginning to form into juicy fruit. Wicked Good Apples was truly a hidden gem.

A light breeze ruffled his hair as he took the steps to the porch. One of the boards gave, and he halted, remembering that he'd planned to fix them, and turned back to his truck. He lifted a toolbox from the truck bed and got to work shoring up the steps. He had a nail in his mouth and was kneeling on the ground, hammering a second nail into the board, when a prickling sensation on the back of his neck told him he wasn't alone. He glanced up and found Holly leaning her forearms on the porch railing, watching him. Her hands were clasped together, the sunlight glinting off multiple rings on her fingers. She was in her usual uniform of jeans and a tank top, but she'd layered a blue plaid on top to combat the slight chill.

Connor brushed the hair out of his eyes and spit out the nail. "How are you feeling? Does your shoulder hurt?"

"It's a little tender, but otherwise I'm fine. Fixing the steps was on Winter's list," she said, nodding to the boards.

"Well, now she can cross it off."

Holly studied him, her expression pensive, but she didn't say anything else while he worked. He finished hammering in the last nail and stood and stretched. "Anything on your mind?"

"Maybe."

"Want to talk?" Connor ascended the steps and prowled toward her. She smelled like her usual Christmas scent and something sweeter beneath it, like cocoa-scented lotion.

"Why are you looking at me like that?"

He halted before he reached her and forced himself to cross his arms over his chest and lean against the railing when what he really wanted to do was tug her close and taste her mouth again. "You smell nice."

"You smell like sweat. And spice."

"Is that bad?"

"I wish it was," she muttered.

He reached forward and traced the thin gold chain around her neck. A crystal pendant hung at the end, snug between her breasts, as dark as midnight and polished to a shine. He hooked his finger under the chain and lifted it so that the pendant dangled from his fingers. "What is this?"

"Onyx," she answered, her gaze falling to the gem. "It represents strength and self-control."

"It must work, because you have boatloads of those."

She gently pulled the chain from his grasp. "How so?"

"You keep this farm going and the family together, and you protect everyone. You never relax, never let go."

"You don't know that," she said, tucking the stone back into her shirt.

"I know more about you than you realize."

"You only think you do."

"Oh yeah?" He arched a brow. "I know you love animals and books and apples. I know you'd sacrifice anything for this apple farm and your family. I know that you drink a ton of coffee, and you have vicious migraines after you control the weather."

The color drained from Holly's cheeks, and he knew he'd hit a nerve. After he'd tossed and turned into the wee hours of the morning fantasizing about her curves, his thoughts had turned to what he'd seen at the dock. Then he'd remembered the sudden rainstorms and freak gusts of wind that had hit the apple farm over the last few days, and he'd jumped out of bed to chart each instance of unpredictable weather and what Holly had been doing at the time.

It had been pouring the day she'd unhappily signed the contract, but he had no way of knowing if she'd suffered a migraine that night.

There had been a freak rainstorm the first day they'd been together in the orchard and he'd called her a witch. Later she'd had a migraine.

The wind had been wild enough to blow apple blossoms off trees and rattle the windows the day Jeremy had suggested the couple reality show. Again, she'd had a migraine.

She'd moved the puppy last night and had been rubbing her temples before he left her room. Based on the evidence, he'd concluded that somehow her power made her ill.

He'd been writing his list by the white light of a camping lamp when he'd thought of the secrets they'd shared in the attic before their first kiss. Holly had told him she'd been home crying and wildly upset the day her mother had died in a car accident after a storm tore through and her mother lost control of the car. Holly had claimed to have killed her mother, and now he understood what she meant. At the terrible realization, his heart had broken for the little girl Holly had been and what had clearly been an accident. He'd wanted to climb into bed with her and wrap her in his arms and comfort her for what she'd been through, for the guilt she'd held onto her entire life. But he hadn't.

Instead, he'd found his notes about the strange happenings at Wicked Good Apples. There had been accounts of rain during dry summers and then dry grounds during floods. Was that because of Holly? What about the rest of the odd occurrences? The disease-free apples? The cider so good it was almost sinful? Did Aunt Daisy have anything to do with that, with her black smoke over the barrel of apples?

Holly didn't say a word to him. She simply turned on her heel and walked inside, letting the screen door slam behind her.

Connor cursed and let her go. This was for the best. He'd been getting too close to her, so close that he'd begun to question his judgment. His show came first. It had always come first and it always would.

The trailer door banged open in the distance, and Charlotte stuck her head out and howled, "I think I found Mary!"

CHAPTER TWENTY

"He knows," Holly said. She'd called a family meeting in the library, which was a former sitting room that had become so overtaken with books that at some point over the decades it had transformed into a library. The two aunts were seated together on an old-fashioned settee upholstered in crushed velvet, while Missy, egregiously hungover and still wearing her pajamas and a pair of sunglasses, slumped in a stuffed armchair. Winter leaned against a bookshelf, dirt on the knees of her jeans and work gloves tucked in her pockets. Someone had lit a cranberry candle, and Prickles was curled on Aunt Daisy's lap, her black gloves stroking his tiny head.

"Who knows what, dear?" Aunt Rose asked.

"Connor thinks she's a witch," Winter said in a flat voice.

Holly turned on her. "You knew this would happen!" she accused. "Why would you ever push us to sign the contract?"

Winter glared at her. "Believe it or not, I don't know everything."

Holly didn't back down. "Do you know what this could mean for our family? I knew he wasn't here for some stupid ghost story. I knew he had to be here for some other reason because there are a hundred haunted houses in Maine. He's here to expose *us*."

"He won't be able to." Winter gave an unconcerned shrug. "He doesn't know what we are, and even if he did, no one would believe him because he doesn't have any proof."

"She used power in front of him," Missy said, and took a swig of Gatorade.

Aunt Daisy and Aunt Rose paled.

"It was an accident!" Holly yelped.

Missy flinched. "Oh my God, keep it down, will you? Some of us are still rum-ified right now."

Aunt Rose tutted in sympathy. "Dear, you know I can make a potion to fix that. I wish you girls would let me help more."

"So your hands can cramp up for a full day afterward in karmic retaliation for helping someone? I think not. I pickled myself, and pickled I'll stay."

"What happened, Holly?" Aunt Daisy asked. Prickles lifted his head; looked around the room; and, content with his position in life, immediately fell back asleep.

Holly briefly explained the incident at the pond, and when she finished, her family sat in thoughtful silence.

"Well, it's not ideal," Aunt Rose finally admitted.

Holly plunked onto a footstool and dropped her head into her hands. "That's a generous way of telling me I messed up and we're screwed." She lifted her head again. "He's already putting together the pieces. He correlated my migraines with usages of power. He'll be watching us like a hawk, even more so than before. I wish we could break the contract and get him out of here."

Aunt Daisy patted her shoulder with her gloved hand. "We'll just need to be extra careful. I don't have to remind you what happens to women like us when others discover what we are."

No, she didn't. History had made sure that families like theirs stayed hidden.

"Or what will happen if you girls draw too much attention to yourselves," Aunt Rose added solemnly. "Daisy and I can't protect you any longer. You *must* moderate yourself, Holly. You haven't been in control lately."

Aunt Daisy was right, and Holly burned with embarrassment. Everything had been so much easier four years ago, when Aunt Rose had been able to dilute the strength of their powers with her potions, but even their experienced aunts could no longer mask what Holly and her sisters had become. Their power had outstripped even the most potent of Aunt Daisy's concoctions. It was up to Holly and her sisters to master and harness their powers now, which were unnaturally strong even among their kind. The sisters would have gladly traded what nature had given them for normal lives, but there were those among their kind who coveted the level of power they had. Dangerous people.

And all of Holly's uncontrolled incidents lately might as well have been a beacon flashing for their attention.

"He can't know," Missy said confidently. Her hair was a frizzy riot around her head, and Holly was pretty sure she was still wearing makeup from last night underneath the sunglasses. "Like Winter said, almost no one knows about us. Besides, I don't think he's a threat. You should see the way he looks at Holly. His gray eyes get all love swoony and alpha wolfy. I think he wants to bang her brains out."

"No, he doesn't," Holly muttered, hoping to hell she wasn't blushing because that was *exactly* what Connor had said he wanted to do last night.

"Alpha wolfy?" Winter asked with a smirk.

"Yeah." Missy swallowed another mouthful of Gatorade. "Like he wants to punch out a bunch of guys and then make Holly scream his name in bed."

"Missy!" Holly hissed.

Missy grinned at their aunts. "They read romance. They know." She pointed finger guns at the aunts and shot them off. "Love bullets."

"Oh my God, meeting dismissed," Holly said. "I just wanted to warn you all to be careful around him."

While Missy launched into a detailed recap of a show she was watching, Winter exited the library into the hallway, where Holly quickly caught up with her.

"Hold on, Win. Do you know how this is going to end?"

Winter shook her head. "It's all foggy until suddenly it's not. I don't get to choose what visions I see, and nothing is already decided."

Holly searched her sister's eyes. Winter was hardworking and fierce, and she kept her guard up even around her family. "I don't give a damn about your no-meddling rule. If you see something, you let me know."

"I'll think about it." Winter stomped off to tend to the grounds.

෨ ෴

By dinnertime, Connor had done all the prep work necessary for that evening's filming and found himself wandering the grounds in hopes that he would run into Holly. Pathetic.

He went back to his trailer and tried to read more of the old Germanic text about evil beings, but his thoughts kept returning to Holly. Since they were keeping it professional, he had a contractual obligation to tell her about the filming in the orchard that night and invite her to take part.

Relieved to have an acceptable reason to find her, Connor jogged to the front door of the house and raised his hand to knock. Before he could, Winter opened the door. She'd obviously just come in from the orchards because her nose was sunburned, her jeans were dirty, and she was holding a sweating bottle of water in one hand. "She's in the barn," Winter said, and closed the door in his face.

How did she *do* that?

Connor took the dirt path that cut between the house and the weathered barn. When he reached the barn, he found the side door cracked. It was dim inside when he entered, but light glowed faintly from the stairwell at the back.

Connor wound his way between empty crates, shelves covered with dust cloths, and spinning trays of postcards. When he reached the stairs, he took them slowly, his heartbeat accelerating with each step. What was she doing in the hayloft? Was it something not quite witchy?

At the top of the stairs there was another door, this one also slightly ajar. When he pushed it open, his lips parted in shock at what he saw.

Holly was wearing a pair of paint-splattered leggings and a paint-covered shirt tied in a knot above her belly button. She was kneeling over a canvas that lay on top of a drop cloth, her dark hair falling from her bun and framing her face as she swept a paintbrush in long, sure strokes. The hayloft was brightly lit by the late afternoon sun, and there was a long worktable at the back of the room, covered in jars, brushes, and powdery pigments. There were finished canvases propped against the walls, stacked on the floor, or resting on easels. A few were hanging from nails, but most were tossed aside as if they were garbage.

Connor had been hunting ghosts most of his life, and these paintings still made the hair rise on his arms.

Holly turned as the door bumped into the wall and leaned back on her heels, paintbrush in hand. She swiped at her hair, leaving a blue streak along the side of her face.

"Can I come in?" Connor asked.

"Winter must've sent you," Holly muttered. He couldn't tell if that pleased her or annoyed her. "God forbid she share her reasons with anyone else. If you think *I'm* closed off, then Winter is sealed tighter than Fort Knox."

Connor eased into the room and shut the door behind him. He glanced at the first painting in a stack against the wall. It was four feet by four feet of pure despair: a frothy ocean and ravenous sky devouring a man as his wife helplessly screamed. Her mouth was gaping, as was the void in her chest. Connor shivered and turned to the next painting. A storm, wild and ruthless, devastating a town down to its foundations. "Do you sell these?"

"Do you think anyone would want them?" she asked bleakly.

Everywhere he turned there were violent weather scenes: tornadoes, hurricanes, driving rains and terrifying floods, thunderous clouds, and bodies decaying in the relentless desert sun. He wandered along the wall, pausing when he reached a painting that was nothing but a child's mitten in the center of the white canvas, and he *felt* more than saw that it was a fatal avalanche.

"What is all this?"

She tracked him with her eyes, her bottom lip caught between her teeth. "It's horrible, isn't it?"

"Why do you paint them?" He traced his finger along sand granules that she'd added to the taupe paint of a desert so dry he needed a glass of water just looking at it.

"They're my nightmares."

Connor flinched. Her nightmares? Was she really plagued with these horrors every night?

"Not literally," she said, as if reading his mind. She dipped the paintbrush in a glass of water and swished it around. The blue paint swirled and then gradually diluted, turning the liquid midnight blue. The brush handle clinked against the glass before she pulled it out and dabbed the bristles on the cloth floor covering. "It's complicated."

"Try me."

"Do they freak you out?"

He imagined they would some people, but Connor had experienced more damaged hearts and broken souls than most. He'd seen terror, loss, longing, and unrelenting love that had endured even after death. What Holly had created was a visual gallery of the emotions he'd witnessed but could never quite put into words. It was as if she'd taken his experiences and given them form.

He felt . . . relieved that someone else understood.

Connor sat on an overturned crate next to her and clasped his hands over his knee. "No, they don't freak me out. They're from the furthest end of the spectrum of emotions. They're the transcendent emotions—the ones that are so powerful they can exist across planes: hatred, terror, devastating loss."

Holly nodded and set the brush down. "That's an interesting way of seeing it. These are the reminders of the devastation great power can cause. Once I've painted them, I can let them go. They don't take up space in my head anymore. They're like . . . a picture journal."

Connor searched her eyes and said softly, "They haunt you, these images?"

She shrugged and stood to stretch, lifting her arms over her head and turning her face to the ceiling. Her shirt shifted higher up her torso, and Connor's mouth went dry. "They come to me, and they won't leave until they're executed, so I create them with paint and canvas."

He filed away her comments. They didn't make sense now, but he was certain they would with time.

"Are you scared of me now that you've seen my secret chamber of horrors?"

Connor reached for the knot on her shirt and tugged her closer, until she was standing in between his thighs. "I've been scared of a lot of things, but never you."

She glanced away at that and he took note, but for the first time in a long time he wanted something more than the story.

Connor splayed his hands on her hips, feeling the heat of her through the thin fabric of her leggings. He flexed his fingers but didn't make another move. She'd put the brakes on, and she'd have to be the one to take them off.

Holly's fingers speared into his hair, and his breath caught. He was supposed to be inviting her to the night filming. He should have been hounding her for answers about what secrets her family was hiding. Instead, all he could think about was touching her, tasting her. He didn't delve too deeply into the emotions that hovered in the back of his consciousness: the ones that urged him to connect with this person who understood horror as surely as he did. He ignored the faint warning that they were close to crossing a line that couldn't be uncrossed. He pushed away the guilt about exposing her family.

This was where Holly came to chase oblivion, and he wanted to find that with her.

The air swelled between them, growing heavy with tension. A breeze rifled his hair, and he was almost certain there weren't any windows open this time, if there ever had been, in the attic.

She tilted his head with one soft hand under his chin, so that he was looking up at her from where he sat on the overturned crate. Her eyes were thoughtful, her plush lower lip tugged between her teeth. "Are you sure about wanting more now that you know I'm different?"

"It has never been a question of whether I want you."

She pushed on his shoulders until he got the hint and came off the crate to kneel in front of her, his hands on her hips and his breath on her belly. "I know I said I wanted to cool it," she whispered, "but can we pretend, just this one time, that you're not leaving and that we don't have opposite agendas?"

"Yeah," he rasped, his fingers hooking into her waistband. "If this is what you want, right now, we can be just Holly and Connor."

She laid her hands over his, encouraging him to tug down the fabric an inch. "This is what I want. Just you and me."

He kissed the exposed flesh, rubbing his lips and beard scruff lightly over her skin, and then repeated the process, inch by agonizing inch, until the top of her black lace panties appeared. Connor ran his tongue over the edge of them before dipping underneath the elastic to repeat the action. "More?"

"Take my pants off."

Connor never complied with any instruction faster. Within seconds he'd dragged her leggings down and tossed them aside, leaving her in lace panties that made him heavy with desire. Conner blew hot air across the lace before kissing her through them. "Now what?"

"Now," she said firmly, "I want you to give the orders. I have a feeling you can be bossy in bed, and I think I would like that with you."

Connor's blood raged in his veins. He slid his finger inside the leg hole of her panties and said with deep command, "Spread your legs."

She immediately widened her stance and he pulled the thin fabric aside, exposing her to the cool attic air.

God, she was beautiful. Connor figured every time a man tugged aside a woman's panties he thought it was the most beautiful sight in the world, but there was something about Holly that made this moment deeper, sexier, and more dangerous than any he'd had before.

He parted her and leaned forward to slide his tongue over her, one long drag that ended at her clitoris. Holly moaned and flexed her fingers in his hair as he gently sucked her into his mouth. He released her after a moment and then ran his tongue over her again, rubbing and licking and enjoying her until her legs began to tremble.

No longer content with holding her panties to the side, Connor peeled them down her legs and threw them to the side. Finally free of the fabric, he lifted her thigh and hooked it over his shoulder.

With her fully opened and exposed to him, he buried his face in her, tasting her and lapping at her until her hips undulated under his mouth. He inserted a finger inside her, and with a "come hither" gesture began stroking that sweet spot that made her fingers dig into his shoulders.

"Connor," she moaned. "Connor, Connor, Connor."

Every chant of his name on her lips bound him tighter to her. His thoughts were primal and completely devoid of rational thought. This was *his* woman. He was going to make her scream *his* name and melt like wax in *his* hands.

He stood, lifting her in his arms and carrying her to the table with the paints on it. He set her bottom on the edge and nudged her back. Glass clinked together and containers fell; a jar of black paint tipped over and spilled, but he didn't notice until he accidentally put his hand in it.

Uncaring about the paint, Connor gripped her thighs with his hands, opening her to him like a feast. The sight of his black paint handprint on the inside of her thigh was so hot that his inner wolf growled with satisfaction. She'd said before she didn't know he was into mate marking, and until that minute neither had he.

Not that she was his mate.

But he sure as hell enjoyed marking her.

Connor returned to the center of her pleasure and drove her relentlessly upward until Holly's thighs squeezed around his head and she came with a cry that had him feral with need, the windowpanes rattling with a burst of wind that came from within the attic rather than out.

She was still trembling from her release when Connor stood and looked down at her, his blood on fire. "Take your shirt and bra off."

Holly shimmied out of her shirt, and his breath caught at the sight of her matching black lace bra. As her bra fell away, he was unable to tear his gaze from her.

She was entirely naked on the table, a black handprint on her thigh, her dark hair having come loose and curling around her shoulders. The pink nipples of her full breasts were already tightening in the chilly air of the hayloft, and her hazel and green eyes were so smoky with desire that his chest squeezed at the wonder of being able to experience her like this.

Jesus, she was fucking amazing.

Connor smoothed his finger over the raised skin of her collarbone. Holly's eyes fell to the handprint on her thigh, and a little wrinkle appeared between her brows before she noted the spilled black paint at her side.

"A fortunate accident," Connor said thickly as he leaned forward and kissed the top of her breast, "because now I'm thinking I want to paint you all over."

Holly grinned. "Only if I get to paint you after."

CHAPTER TWENTY-ONE

Holly was still reeling from the most carnal and satisfying orgasm she'd ever had when Connor traced a black paint-tipped finger down and around her breast. She'd escaped to the hayloft to clear her mind of her most recent nightmare and to forget about Connor for a few hours. When he'd walked through the door, her heart had turned leaden in her chest. It truly was a studio of horrors—any normal person would have backed out with their hands raised and called the police. But Connor had understood. In his line of work, he'd witnessed eternal grief, rage that was so potent it was a shackle, and desperation that could withstand time. Instead of the paintings scaring him away, somehow they'd drawn him closer.

He leaned forward and kissed inside the painted line, dragging his tongue over the sensitive skin until he reached her nipple, but he didn't take her into his mouth. Instead, he focused on her other breast, painting another circle around it and then mimicking the stroke with his tongue.

"I can't get enough of you," he growled. "Why are you so addictive? From the moment I saw you, I haven't been able to get you out of my head."

Her stomach dipped even as her shoulders fell back, granting him further access. She knew exactly what he meant. A breeze played with her hair, and she was vaguely aware that she was venting a thin stream of power. She'd never before lost control of her power during intimacy. What was it about Connor that made her break through all her self-restraint and rules?

He continued kissing her breasts until she was desperate for more, for *him*, and only then did he take one peak into his mouth. He released her and murmured encouragingly into her skin, "I think you can come again for me, can't you, Holly?" He brought his hand up to cup her other breast before remembering it was covered in paint. He growled in frustration. "I didn't think this through."

Holly flexed her legs around his waist as his lips found her neck instead, kissing the column of her throat, then her ear, and finally her mouth. She placed her hands on either side of his head and held him to her as they made out with the wild passion of teenagers, his painted hands sliding over her skin and smudging her with color.

She was entirely naked while he still wore jeans and a T-shirt, and although she enjoyed the vulnerable and sexy feeling, she was ready to even the score. She yanked his T-shirt over his head and tried not to let her jaw drop. Connor Grimm was seriously cut. She'd caught a glimpse of his abs before in the attic, but with his shirt off she was finally able to drink in the sight of him with a throaty noise of feminine approval. He had defined arms and shoulders that his *Grimm Reality* white polo didn't do justice to, and his broad chest was dusted with hair. A pentagram was tattooed on his right pectoral, the ink freshly black, as if he'd just had it touched up. His waist was thick with muscle, each one delineated in a way she hadn't ever seen on an actual human before.

Connor's hooded gaze took in her unashamed appreciation until Holly finally tore her eyes away. She laid her palm in the spilled black ink, and heat flared in his eyes when she pressed her hand flat to his chest, covering his heart. When she pulled away, she stared at her mark on him and swallowed, irrationally moved by the stupid, accidental symbolism.

Because she was far more affected than she should have been, then she *wanted* to be, she smeared the handprint into a black streak, cupped her painted hand around his neck, and pulled his mouth to hers again.

After that they were a blur of paint and hands, mouths and tongues and teeth. She was giggling as she tried to unbuckle his belt without getting paint on it when she heard heels clacking on the stairs that led to the hayloft.

Her panicked eyes met his. She was entirely nude, and he was stripped down to the waist, both of them covered in paint, their play literally written all over their bodies.

Connor yanked her off the table and shoved her behind him, concealing her with his body just as the door burst open and Missy stomped into the room.

"There you are!" she shouted to Connor. "Your crew needs you, and they've been looking for you all over the damned property. Wait . . . why are you covered in paint? Is that . . . is that *Holly* behind you?"

Holly groaned and pressed her forehead into his back. "I'm going to die," she whispered.

Connor squeezed her arm once before clearing his throat and saying, "If you could give us a few minutes, Missy. Tell my crew I'll be out when I can."

Missy didn't say anything, and Holly didn't dare peek around Connor to view her expression, but a moment later the door closed.

Connor spun around and they looked at each other—splattered in painted handprints and caught by her younger sister—and burst into laughter.

෨ ෪

Holly was lying on her bed after showering, her face pressed into her pillow as she vacillated between the extreme humiliation of being caught sans panties with the one man she should *not* be fooling around with, and reliving the memory of the hottest climax of her life.

Connor Grimm had given her oral, and she would never be the same. She was destroyed for eternity.

Jeremy couldn't even bother reciprocating, while Connor had blown her mind without a single thought to his own pleasure, aside from the fact that it had seemed like he'd really enjoyed making her come, and hell if that hadn't made it even sexier.

Someone knocked on the door, and a moment later Missy poked her face in. Holly buried her head under the pillow and mumbled, "*Now* you knock?"

"How was I supposed to know you were banging Connor Grimm?" Missy asked, depressing the edge of the bed as she sat down. "It must've been those alpha-wolfy eyes. I cannot imagine any other reason my very stern and uptight older sister would be entirely covered in paint and looking like she was having hotter sex than even *I've* had, and that's saying something."

"We haven't *had* sex thanks to you."

Missy yanked the pillow off Holly's head, her smile wide. "This is kind of fun. Mature Holly, so *entirely* sure she was immune to the charms of the big bad ghost hunter."

"I hate you. Why are you here?"

"To torture you, of course," Missy said, glancing at her nails and frowning. "I need a manicure. Oh, also the aunts want to tell you something about that journal of Autumn's you gave them."

After Holly had pilfered the journal, which was a silly way to think of it considering it was *her* house and therefore *her* journal, she'd told her aunts about the oddity of Autumn's journals all being blank, even though each one was carefully labeled with the year. The aunts had agreed that it was strange and had promised to look into it.

Holly finally peeled her face off the mattress. "What did they say?"

"I don't know. I wasn't paying attention because I've been answering nonstop emails about the show. Hey, do you think I should ask Mike out on a date? He was devastated about his little puppy, and that really redeemed him in my eyes."

"Ugh, Missy!" Holly rolled off the bed and grabbed the hoodie hanging from the back of her desk chair.

"I know, right? Should I really ruin a friendship on the off chance I can stand him longer than a few weeks?"

"No! That's not why I said *ugh*."

"Wait," Missy cried, catching her arm. "Before you go, I think you need to have the Big Sister Talk."

"What do you mean?"

"Well, you've never had a big sister, so I've designated myself the deliverer of the Big Sister Talk—you know, like the talk you gave me in high school, where you told me to be careful with my heart and always have on lip gloss."

"I'm pretty sure lip gloss did not factor into the talk."

She waved her hand. "Close enough. The thing is, I know you, Holly, and you're not really someone who enjoys sex."

"I do too!"

Missy blew out a stream of air that made a strand of red hair dance across her forehead. "That's not what I meant. This Big Sister Talk stuff is hard. What I meant is that for you sex is intertwined with feelings, so I think you can understand why I might be worried that you're fooling around with Connor. I mean God, the man is so hot he could make candles smoke with a look, but he's bouncing when the episodes wrap up, and I don't want you to get hurt when he leaves."

Holly pulled Missy into a hug. "Thanks, Missy. It's kind of nice to be worried over."

"Yes, well, it's not very fun doing the worrying. I don't know how you manage it all the time."

"You can rest easy. I know Connor is leaving. Even though I never meant for anything to happen with him, I'm beginning to think I need to live a little more freely and go after what I want, like you do."

Missy preened. "I *am* excellent at living freely."

"Please don't tell anyone else about Connor," Holly begged. "I'm not prepared for that. And when he leaves, I don't want to be asked about it by everyone and coddled. I just want to be able to move on."

Missy crossed her heart, but as Holly left the room she shouted down the hallway, *"Make sure you use condoms!"*

Holly closed her eyes in exasperation. Missy had been loud enough that Holly would be surprised if Connor hadn't heard her all the way out in his trailer.

CHAPTER TWENTY-TWO

Holly found the aunts in the little herb and vegetable patch behind the house. Aunt Rose was kneeling in the dirt with a giant straw hat on her head, digging out old plants and preparing to seed for the summer. Daisy was swaying on a wooden swing that had peeling paint and faded cushions, sipping an iced tea and contentedly watching her sister putter in the approaching twilight.

"Missy found me," Holly said, kneeling beside Aunt Rose and yanking out a particularly tough stalk. "She said you have news about the blank journal?" Holly tossed the vegetation to the side, the scent of fresh dirt still clinging to its roots.

"We think we do," corrected Aunt Daisy from the swing. A chilly wind swept around the corner of the house, and she zipped her hot-pink sweatshirt up to her chin. Aunt Daisy had lost most of her vision decades ago, but it had only sharpened her hearing. Holly's cheeks reddened as she thought of Missy hollering about condoms. Aunt Daisy had definitely heard.

Aunt Rose sat on her heels and adjusted the brim of her hat. "We don't think they're blank."

Holly stared at her in confusion. Aunt Rose and Aunt Daisy were in their early sixties and were as sharp as tacks; but the journals *were* blank. "I don't follow."

"We aren't sure about anything," Aunt Rose admitted. "Our family line has chosen to live quietly. One of the consequences of that is a loss of knowledge over time."

It seemed there were a lot of consequences for the way the Celestes had chosen to live. At some point in history their family had decided to "live quietly," which was a fancy way of saying they'd agreed to use their power as little as possible. Maybe they thought it was safer, or maybe they were ashamed of what they were. Holly didn't know the reason, but she did know that all of that stifled energy didn't just disappear. Generation after generation, it built in the Celeste bloodline, until it could no longer be contained and had found an outlet in three little girls, infusing them with all the pent-up power of generations. As a result, Aunt Rose and Aunt Daisy suspected Holly and her sisters were some of the most powerful of their kind to exist in centuries.

From an early age the girls had been taught how dangerous the world was for them and how imperative it was that they learn to blend in. That meant denying a lot of who they were and what they could do while still allowing enough of an outlet for their powers that history didn't repeat itself.

"We think Autumn cursed the books," Aunt Daisy piped in, the swing hinges rhythmically punctuating every third word, "so that only her descendants could read it."

Holly sat back, thunderstruck. "Cursing is *real*?"

Aunt Daisy and Aunt Rose were quiet for the same length of time, and Holly swore for the millionth time that the twins could communicate telepathically.

"With our family line's choice to live quietly, we have lost centuries of oral knowledge," Aunt Rose finally answered. "What would have been passed down—the history of our kind, information about how to control our powers, and all the tips and tricks that would have come with hundreds of years of knowledge—was instead silenced and forgotten."

And there was another consequence of her family's choices: it seemed life was nothing but a series of consequences and unpleasant corrections.

"And in some ways, because we've lost that knowledge and history, we've also lost our identity." Aunt Rose reached for another plant and tugged it free. "We have power, but not the proper knowledge to use it. But we *do* have some very old texts that Daisy and I are going to look through to see if we can find answers."

If the answers were written down somewhere, Rose and Daisy would find them. They'd both been librarians before her mother died. The Celestes *really* liked their books. The problem was that in the past, what they'd needed to know hadn't been preserved in the written word. It wasn't like their existence was common knowledge. And unlike Stacy's community, Holly and her kind were largely solitary and had very few others they could ask for help.

"Okay." Holly yanked out a weed. "I want to solve the mystery with Autumn and Councilman Miller before Connor does, in case the truth implicates our family."

Holly helped clear a few more plants while chatting about what herbs Rose wanted to plant for the summer. Aunt Rose was an expert in herbs, and she carefully tended them during the warmer months and dried them for winter use.

"Oh, Aunt Daisy, Winter said something about needing you for cider tomorrow," Holly said after a bit, stretching her arms over her head.

Aunt Daisy nodded, and Holly patted her on the shoulder as she walked back into the kitchen. She was pouring a glass of water when her phone buzzed. She pulled it from her back pocket and grinned stupidly when she saw that the text was from Connor.

Connor: *Did you get all the paint off?*
Holly: *Yes. You?*

Connor: *The best I could. Charlotte caught me when I was walking back to my trailer. I told her I tripped over a bucket of paint. I don't think she believed me. The handprints probably gave me away.*
Holly: *At least SHE didn't walk in on us.*
Connor: *Before I got so delightfully distracted, I meant to ask if you want to watch the filming in the orchard tonight. It's a full moon.*
Holly: *I can't. We celebrate June 1st.*
Connor: *Why?*

Holly could practically sense his curiosity through the text.

Holly: *It's just a silly tradition. We have a bonfire to clear away the waste from pruning. It's not like we dance naked under the moonlight.*

Three dots popped up as he typed, and then they disappeared again. The process repeated multiple times until finally a text came through.

Connor: *Now that's a shame. I'd really like to see you dancing naked around a fire.*

She typed back that maybe someday he would and then quickly erased it. No, someday he wouldn't, because whatever they were doing was temporary. They had a limited number of tomorrows together, and she was pretty sure none of them would involve full-moon fantasies.

❧ ❦

Connor shined a flashlight beneath his chin and spoke into the camera. "We're here in the old Gala orchard, which was planted two hundred years ago by Autumn Celeste. This is where most of the sightings of the councilman have taken place. It was under this apple tree that Amy Gordon spoke to the councilman, and this is where she later found the rotten apple core that he left behind."

Connor backed up to the tree and gestured to its gnarled and knotted trunk. The camera followed his movements and then panned upward to capture a perfect shot of the moon and stars through the black, twisted branches.

When the camera turned back to him, Connor held the flashlight beam over the EMF detector. "If this red bulb lights up, it means the machine is detecting high levels of electromagnetic energy."

While the cameras filmed, he asked the ghost to talk to him. He was dramatic for the cameras, but the EMF wasn't going off, and he didn't see the councilman anywhere. He was unsurprised. Most of his brushes with the paranormal happened when he was alone or with his brother, not when an entire film crew was hanging around.

Other ghost-hunting shows had rigged EMFs that would go off so they could claim a ghostly presence. Connor was happy to cultivate drama on *Grimm Reality*—it was a necessity for any successful show—but he didn't deal in lies. If the EMF went off, which it did occasionally, it went off for real. When it didn't, he liked to think it only built his audience's trust in him.

He wandered through the old orchard waving the EMF meter in front of him, his mind only half on what he was doing. To the west he could see the glow of the Celeste bonfire, could hear echoes of laughter and the sounds of someone playing the violin. He didn't know which sister was playing it, and he was dying to find out. Was it Holly? Winter? What other delightful secrets was their family hiding?

When Holly had told him her family celebrated June 1st, he'd been both intrigued and confounded. Witches and pagans had celebrated the solstices for thousands of years, but the solstice wasn't for another twenty days. He'd spent half an hour scrolling the internet, looking for any reason that someone might celebrate June 1st each year, and had come up with nothing other than it was International Dinosaur Day and National Go Barefoot Day.

For the first time ever, Connor would rather be somewhere else than hosting his show. His show was his life—had been his life for a decade—but at that moment he wanted nothing more than to sit on a log in front of a bonfire and hold Holly's hand. He wanted to watch her throw her head back and laugh, the flames dancing in her eyes, and the navy canvas of stars overhead.

If they were alone, he'd slowly unbutton her plaid and kiss her soft skin, breathe in her scent, and make love to her with the shifting glow of flames and shadow inking their skin.

Shit, what was the matter with him? Maybe Charlotte was right. Maybe he was getting so close that he was losing perspective. He'd gone from convincing himself it was best to keep it professional with Holly so that he wouldn't compromise the integrity of his show, to stripping her out of her clothes literally the first chance he had.

And hell, he'd choose bringing Holly to orgasm while hearing her chant his name *every* time. That was what worried him. He'd never before prioritized anything over his show, but with Holly, things were starting to feel complicated. He was making choices that weren't necessarily in the best interest of his business.

Charlotte walked toward him, her own flashlight sweeping over the trees. Sometimes when Erikson wasn't available, Charlotte stepped in as cohost. She brought an entirely new energy to the show that Connor appreciated more and more. Charlotte was the most proficient assistant he'd ever had, but he was beginning to think her talents were wasted behind the camera. It was something to consider.

"Dozens of witnesses claim to have seen the councilman wandering the orchards, apple in hand. Much like this one," Charlotte said, pulling an apple from her jacket pocket. There weren't any apples on the trees yet, but the Celestes had plenty in storage. She took a dramatic bite out of its flesh, and the sound mic hovered overhead, making sure to capture each crunch. "Is it possible a man died here two hundred years ago, poisoned by the fruit from one of these very trees?"

"If so," Connor added, shining his light up and down the tree, "who poisoned the apple, and why?"

They would insert dramatic music there, along with a commercial break that would nicely pad their pockets.

"Good work," his cameraman said.

Connor nodded. "Let's get a few more shots of us wandering through the trees and sharing all of our hypotheses."

They spent the next half hour filming, he and Charlotte pulling out all the dramatic stops and scanning with the EMF sensor. Charlotte *thought* she saw the EMF sensor light up, and Connor thought that would make another good commercial break.

Connor was in the middle of orchestrating a specific shot of the moon when the green light on the EMF reader flashed. He signaled his cameraman, and the lens zoomed in on the machine. The green lightbulb represented the lowest level of EMF, followed by light green, yellow, orange, and then red. Connor watched the steady green bulb and carefully waved the machine around, expecting the light to blink off. It didn't. Suddenly all the bulbs lit up in such a blazing rainbow of light that Connor was stunned.

"Oh my God," Charlotte said when the lights stayed steady. "Are you seeing this?"

He'd never seen anything like it, actually.

A sharp, piercing scream came from the direction of the Celeste fire.

He whipped his head around, every hair on his body standing straight up. He knew his crew was just as spooked, because a hush fell over them. A second scream rang through the orchard. Connor dropped the EMF reader and took off at a sprint.

CHAPTER TWENTY-THREE

The bonfire was in full blaze under the heavy orb of the full moon. Holly sat on an old log, the heat of the flames warming her cheeks and the orange glow pushing back the darkness in a perfect radius around them. Winter transitioned from a lively jig to a slow, heart-breaking melody that sounded as if she were wrenching the notes from the depths of her soul. Winter had been playing the violin since she'd discovered their grandmother's old fiddle in the attic. When she wasn't fixing things on the farm or beating the weight bag behind the barn, she was pouring her demons into music.

Missy had woven buttercup and lilac crowns for Aunt Rose and Aunt Daisy, who were sitting in more comfortable camping chairs. The twin aunts looked like fairies with their braided white hair and flower crowns, the flickering light and shadow smoothing over the age on their faces. Holly thought briefly of her mother, who should have been sitting there with them, blossoms bright in her dark hair.

Missy, Winter, and Holly were wearing winter crowns fashioned of dark green ivy leaves and plump holly berries coated with glittery fake frost. The crowns were used year after year, but Missy made real ones for the December 1st celebrations.

Missy added another branch to the fire, and the flames jumped, bright sparks scattering into the sky while Winter played as if her heart were rendering in two. Not for the first time Holly wondered if Winter was good enough to play in an orchestra and whether Winter had chosen to stay on the farm because of what they were instead of what she could be.

"What a beautiful celebration," Aunt Rose said. She wrapped her crocheted shawl tighter around her shoulders and smiled softly at her twin. "Each one left is a treasure."

Holly zipped her sweatshirt to her chin and swirled the liquid in the blown glass goblet in her hand. "You two talk like you're a hundred years old when you're not a day over sixty."

Missy lifted a matching goblet filled with Wicked Good Apple cider and said, "Here, here!" She drank deeply and made a face. "Ugh, I forgot this wasn't wine."

"Missy, you're not supposed to drink that yet," Holly scolded, refilling Missy's glass. "That's for the ceremony."

Missy pouted. "Can we get this ceremony going then?"

The quarterly bonfire wasn't exactly the silly tradition Holly had led Connor to believe. For two centuries the Celeste women had celebrated the seasons based not on the sun or length of day, but by the way the Book of Valleys was divided. At each celebration they made offerings for their farmlands to prosper. Holly wasn't sure it actually *did* anything, but it was tradition, and she knew how powerful tradition could be. She certainly wouldn't be the first to break it. Besides, it was something special they did as a family, just as any other family might celebrate Christmas or Chanukah.

Winter drew out the last note on her violin, and the fire popped in the sudden silence. She sat down and propped the violin on the log, her expression closed off. Holly worried about Winter more than she did Missy. Missy was social and bubbly and irrepressible. Winter was still water: deep and contained.

"Your turn to start," Missy said to Winter. Winter nodded, and grabbing the salt shaker from beside the log, she sprinkled a ring around the them. Then she pulled a square of newspaper from her sweatshirt pocket and unfolded it. Holly spotted the black-and-white photograph of Wicked Good Apples with the headline: *"Local Apple Farm Goes on TV."*

Winter gave thanks for the apple farm's new chance at breaking even and tossed the paper into the flames. The aunts followed, with Aunt Rose throwing in a dried apple blossom and Aunt Daisy dropping in a crocheted apple. Was it Holly's imagination, or did the fire flare higher with each thanksgiving?

Missy offered the pair of earrings that "Jason complimented and told me made me look like a bad bitch," which had nothing to do with the apple farm, but then Missy never *did* give offerings that had anything to do with the orchards. It was finally Holly's turn. She stood and tilted her face to the stars before she reached into her pocket.

Movement from the corner of her eye caught her attention, and she squinted through the smoke and flames into the darkened orchard. Was that the figure of a man? Was Connor skulking around, spying on them? Was his crew filming them? She'd kill him!

A strange chill swept over the clearing. She began to shiver and her teeth chattered as if it were twenty degrees rather than sixty. She skirted the fire, her gaze probing the darkness. "Connor?"

Winter vaulted to her feet, her hazel eyes wide and her stance battle ready. "No," she hissed. "Something that shouldn't be here."

The form drifted closer, as if its feet were somehow gliding across the ground, and as it neared the salt circle, its features, although still hazy, sharpened enough that Holly gasped. It *couldn't* be.

A man dressed in dark trousers, a finely tailored coat, and a bowler hat swayed before them. His features were translucent, but Holly could see the blunt nose and a dark eye that burned with hatred. His hair was combed flat while his moustache had been waxed into points. He had narrow shoulders and reedy legs, but there was nothing frail about the spirit itself. It looked as if it existed from an excess of sheer spite alone.

Aunt Rose and Aunt Daisy stood to close ranks with the sisters. "Who are you?" Aunt Rose demanded.

The spirit's eyes bore into Aunt Rose with the passion of a brimstone minister staring down evil itself. "Where is the witch?"

The ghost's voice was thin and muffled, as if he were shouting through an invisible curtain between worlds.

Holly exchanged glances with Winter, who was coiled as tightly as a spring beside her.

Councilman Miller reached into his bulging coat pocket and withdrew an apple. He rubbed it across his sleeve before taking an enormous bite with tobacco-stained teeth. One of his eyes was milky white, just as Amy had described. Holly wasn't imagining it: she heard the snap of apple skin as his teeth sank into the white flesh.

"Witch," he hissed again once he'd chewed and swallowed. "Where is the witch who took everything from me?"

"Begone," Aunt Rose ordered. Holly felt a soft buzz along her skin coming from Aunt Rose's direction. "You don't belong here. Go to your afterworld and let us be."

"I cannot rest, cannot find peace," the councilman moaned. "She stole it from me. I could have had everything. I could have been great. Then I saw the truth, and I knew." He drifted closer but screamed when he reached the line of salt and undulated backward like a mirage. "The poisoned apple," he spat. "She poisoned it. She murdered me."

His haunting, hateful eyes roamed over each woman until they landed on Holly. She felt his stare as if it were burning all the way through her flesh and into her soul. "*You!* You did this!"

Holly pointed her thumb to her chest. "Me?"

"*Witch! It is your turn to suffer!*" The councilman's howl was a piercing, whistling shriek that made Holly's flesh creep.

"You have the wrong person," Holly said, drawing herself to her full height. No way was she going to be cowed by a woman-hating councilman, dead or alive. "You are a ghost, and you've been caught between worlds for hundreds of years. Let go of your hate and you'll be free." She didn't actually know if that was true, but wasn't that the premise of every haunting? Unresolved business?

"Not until you die a most gruesome death, Autumn Celeste. Not until your flesh rots from your bones, and the acid in your stomach turns inside out, crawling up your throat and scalding your mouth and blistering your tongue. Not until you suffer the way you made me suffer."

Holly blinked, finally realizing that he'd mistaken her for Autumn. She'd never seen a likeness of Autumn—there weren't any photographs or renderings of the woman—but it was possible Holly strongly resembled her ancestor, especially if Autumn had had dark hair as the firstborn in the family.

Missy rolled her eyes. "Blah blah, you hate women, you're so scorned—we get it. Find a new lie to tell yourself, ghostie."

The councilman hissed at Missy, but there was no shutting Missy up once she was on a roll.

"You wouldn't believe it, but your creepy ass has snagged us a film crew, and they're here right now. They'd *love* to blast your ugly mug all over the TV, not that you know what that is. Let me give them a shout."

Before the councilman could respond, Missy threw her head back and let out a blood-curdling scream. Councilman Miller shot backward as if she were cursing him.

"I don't know if they heard me," Missy said, encouraged by his reaction, and screamed again.

Councilman Miller retreated another few feet and tossed Holly a look so filled with malice that fingers of dread tapped down her spine. "You will die, Autumn Celeste. You will die a horrible, torturous death." An instant later he vanished. The chill in the air evaporated, and Holly once again felt the heat of the fire on her back.

"I guess ghosts are real," Winter said flatly.

"No wonder Autumn despised him," Holly said, irritated with the tremble in her voice. It was never pleasant to have your death promised by something so filled with hatred that it had managed to defy the natural order of things for two hundred years.

A moment later Connor burst into the clearing, his eyes wild. The moment he spotted her, he ran over and grabbed her by the shoulders. "I heard screaming. Are you all right? You're shaking."

"That fucking ghost was here," Missy answered for her, "and he was a giant dick. I think Holly's right: I think he's been scaring off our customers ever since he started showing up. Oh good, your camera guy is here. I want to expose this jerk for what he is. I'm going to turn this around on him and get every woman in America buying our apples just to spite his sexist ass."

Connor glared at the cameraman. "Shut it off," he snarled.

His cameraman seemed taken aback but dropped the camera without comment.

Connor turned back to Holly, the warmth of his hands comforting after the chilly encounter. "Tell me what happened."

Holly had known it was possible ghosts existed, had even believed Amy's story about seeing one in their orchards. She'd trusted Connor when he'd told her he was haunted as a child. But admitting there *might* be a ghost on their property was a far cry from actually interacting with one. Amy's fear had been palpable when she'd described her encounter with the councilman, and now Holly understood why. Councilman Miller was an overwhelmingly vile man in death; she shuddered to think how amplified that would have been in life.

Holly suspected she knew the exact event that had drawn Councilman Miller back to the physical plane four years ago. She'd shared her theory with her sisters and aunts after the disastrous spaghetti dinner. *They* were responsible—Holly and her sisters. They must've unleashed the ghost when Aunt Rose could no longer contain their power. She didn't know how, but the timing was just too coincidental. Holly shivered to think what else they might *still* be drawing to them simply by existing.

Councilman Miller now clung to this world with nothing but a thirst for revenge, and he wouldn't rest until he'd destroyed the Celestes' apple farm.

Until he'd destroyed *her*.

In his immaterial form, the councilman was confused about time and believed her to be Autumn. Or at least that's what Holly thought was happening; she didn't know much about ghosts. She lifted her face and met Connor's worried eyes. Fortunately, she knew an expert on the subject.

"No, no, no, turn the camera back on," Missy ordered with a stamp of her foot. Her voice was so authoritative that the cameraman actually lifted the camera before he glanced at Connor and quickly lowered it again. Missy spun around to face Holly and crossed her arms over her chest. "Come on, Holly. This is perfect footage. I want to be on TV, and I think I can leverage this. I have a degree in publicity that you never let me use." She shifted her focus past Holly to Connor. "I give consent to interview. I saw the bastard, and I'm willing to talk about him."

"It's in your contract that no Celeste will interview on camera," Connor said, rubbing his palms up and down Holly's arms.

He was probably dying to have Missy's account on tape, so the fact that he insisted on sticking to the terms of their bargain made Holly a little weak in the knees. She was a sucker for a man with honor.

Missy was pouting prettily. She'd always been adorable when she was in a snit, even as a young girl. "You don't trust me," she accused.

Surprised, Holly stepped away from Connor. Was that how it seemed to Missy? Holly was only trying to protect the family by keeping them clear of more paranormal associations than necessary; she wasn't trying to stifle Missy or become a Celeste dictator. Although, when she made decisions for all of them, she supposed it could be construed that way.

Was she the proverbial hand crushing the butterfly? She didn't want any of their faces on national TV, especially not in connection with ghost hauntings, but since when did she get to make decisions for everyone else? Besides, *she* was the one putting their family in danger by pursuing Connor when she knew he was out to expose them. She didn't have any right to tell the others what to do or what not to do. It was time she learned to let go and trust.

"I do trust you," Holly said on a deep breath. To Connor she added, "I'll waive the clause in the contract." She knew Missy wouldn't be stupid enough to mention the witch part of their conversation with

Councilman Miller on national TV, and she should have trusted her sister to make her own decisions long before now.

"Are you sure?" Connor asked. He was practically vibrating with anticipation, but he waited for her reassurance.

"Yeah, I'm sure."

A minute later the camera was rolling as the light crew arrived and set up around Missy. Missy checked her reflection in the lens, primping her curls and wiping away eyeliner from her cheek. She tried to get Winter to stand in the frame next to her, but Winter resolutely crossed her arms and refused.

While Connor began interviewing Missy, Holly walked over to Aunt Daisy and hooked her arm through her aunt's. In a low voice she said, "This ghost business is a disaster waiting to happen."

Aunt Daisy patted her hand. "Dear, when *aren't* we flirting with disaster?"

CHAPTER TWENTY-FOUR

Missy had been absolutely brilliant. She'd been stunning, perky, and a natural on camera. She'd known just how to play up each dramatic moment, and by the time she'd finished relaying what had happened, Connor had had chills on his arms. The councilman had been here, with the women, while he'd been chasing his tail in the old orchard.

It was the first time the ghost had ever made an appearance in front of the Celestes. Why now? Was he rattled by Connor's presence? Was there some other shift that Connor wasn't yet aware of?

They'd wrapped up filming at nearly one in the morning. By then, Holly and her aunts had disappeared. Usually he was so focused on interviews that a hurricane could blow through and he wouldn't notice, but he'd been vaguely aware of Holly's presence the entire time and he'd instantly noticed when he'd no longer felt it.

Connor had offered to walk Missy and Winter back to the house, to which Missy had scoffed and replied, "I ain't afraid of no ghost."

"Like I haven't heard that one before, Ghostbuster."

After they'd disappeared into the orchards, he'd spent the next hour wrapping up with his crew before hitting the hay. He'd *wanted* to sneak into the house and find Holly, to hear what had happened from her own lips, because he suspected Missy was leaving out a few key moments, but he wasn't sure he should be prowling around their house in the middle of the night after the scare they'd all had. So he'd lain awake in bed for hours before finally drifting off at dawn.

At noon the next day, he was buried in paperwork at the small table in his trailer when someone gave a rap on the door and pushed it open.

"Char, did you find any other articles on the microfiche?" he asked.

"Nope," Holly answered.

Connor started, then removed his black-framed glasses and tossed them aside. "Holly."

She shut the door behind her and wandered in, looking around at the laminate counter and the yellow chintz curtains that framed the tiny window over the miniscule sink. The "dining" area consisted of a bench seat, a square table, and a folding chair—all of which were stacked with papers and books, his laptop, his charging cords, a tablet, and legal pads. At the rear of the trailer, long yellow curtains separated the sleeping area—a full-sized bed and closet with a three-foot rod—from the kitchen.

"Don't take your glasses off for me," she said, running her fingertips over an embossed book of fairy tales. "I think they're sexy."

Connor leaned back and stretched out his legs. "I'll remember that. How are you doing after last night?"

She shrugged and propped a hip against the counter. She'd left her hair loose and curling around her shoulders. Come to think of it, she looked different all around: tight black jeans, a gray shirt with flirty sleeves, and sandals. This was not her usual work attire.

"I'm doing all right. I don't love that we *actually* have a ghost. How was Missy's interview? She's been talking nonstop about it and has taken to wearing sunglasses indoors. She thinks she's a star."

"Oh, she was definitely a star. She could be an actress if she wanted. Even with her amazing acting skills, I'm wondering if she may have left out a few key details for the cameras." He watched her expression closely, but there was no attempt at artifice. She simply nodded in agreement.

"The councilman said a couple things about Autumn being a witch, and I already told you I don't want this turned into a witch hunt, so Missy didn't mention anything."

"Come sit. Tell me about it."

"There's nowhere to sit."

He patted his lap, and she looked down her nose at him. He laughed and got up so that she could take his seat, and then he moved the stack of papers and books off the folding chair and set them on the counter. "So what *really* happened last night?"

When she finished telling him how the councilman had mistaken her for Autumn and promised she'd die, Connor sat in thoughtful silence, his fingers steepled under his chin.

"You look worried," she joked.

"I am, Holly. Ghosts can physically hurt people."

She seemed gobsmacked. "He was *translucent*."

"It doesn't matter. No one knows for sure how it works, but just as spirits can take physical form, alter temperatures, and speak, they can also touch. Not all, but some are able to. From what we've already observed the councilman do, I'd say he has the ability."

Holly bit her bottom lip, and Connor's gaze fell to her mouth. Her perfectly kissable mouth.

"Connor!" Holly snapped her fingers in front of his face. "Stop looking at me like I'm a snack. You just told me this ghost can hurt me."

"Right." He cleared his throat. *Priorities, Grimm.* "His hatred is what has tethered him to this world."

"He thinks Autumn poisoned him with an apple like he's in some stupid fairy tale." She gestured to the fairy-tale book on the counter.

"We don't know what happened," he said cautiously, because he thought it was just as likely that Autumn *had* poisoned him as she hadn't. The Celeste women were strong and loyal. If someone they loved was threatened, he had no doubt they'd be fearsome defenders. Autumn had clearly felt concern over what her husband would do if

Councilman Miller didn't stop his witch hunt. It was possible she'd taken matters into her own hands to protect her husband.

It was also possible she was being unfairly blamed, as so many women had been over the centuries. He wasn't going to speculate on air about her part in the murder until he had proof—he owed Autumn that much.

"We might never know," Holly said in exasperation. "In the meantime, I can't have this guy haunting our orchards, scaring our customers, and threatening to kill me. Going along with the haunting for business reasons is one thing; having a *real* malicious spook on the property is another. How do I get rid of him?"

"He's stuck in a loop." Connor shifted in the uncomfortable chair and knocked over a stack of newspapers. He gathered them up and shoved them behind the phone charging pad. "He shows up in the same place over and over again. Your bonfire was the first time he appeared elsewhere, the first time he conversed with anyone apart from Amy, that we know of. Something has shifted—there's been a catalyst of some sort. It could be my presence here; it could be that you've finally given validity to his existence." Connor shrugged. "We'll likely never know. What I do know is that the encounters tend to escalate after the catalyst. He believes you are Autumn, and there is no point in trying to reason with a ghost."

Holly lifted her hands, which sparkled with a number of silver rings. "So what now? I have to live with this nut? Isn't it bad enough that he tortured my great-great-grandmother? Why does he get to harass another whole generation of Celeste women?"

It really was disgusting that a man like Miller could continue his hateful, sexist agenda, Connor thought, but it wasn't like they could put a restraining order on a ghost.

"The most effective way to get rid of a ghost is to break the cycle it's stuck in. Usually this means helping it find the closure it was denied in life. In the past ghosts have disappeared after their murder was solved, after their loved one was safe, after they saw whatever perceived injustice was rectified. In Councilman Miller's case, he likely won't leave until he thinks Autumn has paid for what she's done for him."

Holly shook her head slowly, the black onyx necklace shifting across her shirt. "No, I don't think so. Men like him won't be satisfied so long as any of the Celestes exist. He won't tolerate difference. He won't tolerate powerful women."

The hairs stood on the back of his arms. He knew she was right. "We'll find a way," he said at last.

"No, *we* won't. After you finish filming, you're leaving. Unless you also evict ghosts."

"It's not generally in my job description."

She shrugged. "So then it's my problem. I just thought I'd get your opinion on it."

He hated that she was shutting him out of her life, even as he knew she was right. It could take years to exorcise a ghost, and he was leaving in a few weeks at most. They already had enough material for one episode, and they were working on a second. With a three-show max per their contract, that didn't leave him a lot of wiggle room. That indeed made the vengeful ghost Holly's problem, and he didn't like that one bit.

"We found Mary," he said, searching for the photocopies of the property deeds and the newspaper articles Charlotte had assembled.

Holly tilted her head. "Mary?"

Connor filled her in on his visit to his mystery caller, Ryan Miller, and although she was annoyed he'd gone without her, she was visibly excited when she looked at the photo of Councilman Miller's list.

- *Ask Mary to write down what she saw through her window that night.*
- *Mail our accounts to the newspaper. Will it be enough? It will be their word against ours.*
- *Cut down the apple tree for proof.*
- *Suggest to Thomas that I may be willing to forget what I saw in exchange for his signature.*

"This is the Mary you found?" she asked, handing his phone back. Outside, a lawnmower started up.

"Charlotte did. She's spent a lot of time at the historical society and the town office. In 1820, a man named Thomas Tukey owned the property next to yours, and he was married to Mary Tukey. Mary Tukey was also a member of St. John's congregation, which was also Autumn and Councilman Miller's church." He passed her the stack of photocopies.

Holly scanned the newspaper article on top, her eyebrows pinching together. "The paper printed a complaint from Mary Tukey about the Celeste cows getting into her corn."

"Yeah, they used to publish stuff like that. Look at the next page."

The next several pages were photocopies of various newspaper clippings: the wedding of Autumn Celeste, a notice of a church fair where both Autumn and Mary were mentioned as the women who'd knitted the most shawls, and the death of Councilman Miller by "unexplained circumstances but suspected convulsions due to the foam about his mouth." The second to last sheet of paper was a survey done on the Celeste farm and the adjoining property.

"What's this?" Holly asked, holding up the rough map.

"In 1820, the massive grove of pines and oaks that separate your property from the former Tukey residence wouldn't have existed. And if they didn't exist . . ."

" . . . then anyone looking out from the Tukey house would have been able to see the Celeste property," Holly finished for him, "which means Mary really did see whatever it was Miller also claimed to have seen on the night in question."

Connor grinned at her. "Bingo."

Holly flipped to the final sheet and squinted. She turned it sideways, and he knew she recognized the significance of it when she inhaled sharply. "It's a proposal for a railway station!"

Connor nodded. "It took a lot of searching, but we finally found record of the station Autumn made reference to in her letter. In 1818, Councilman Miller introduced a proposal to build a railway branch through town. It would have connected this town to the farming town north of here, eventually hooking into what would later become the Maine–Massachusetts line."

Holly studied the schematics with her lip caught between her teeth. Then she flipped back to the old survey of her property. "Oh!" When she lifted her eyes, they were flashing with anger. "He wanted to buy Autumn's property and build the railway station there!"

"Your apple farm just so happens to be smack-dab in between the two towns, and there are a number of other geographic advantages, such as running water on the property, which would have aided in building the station and tracks."

"So he wanted the town to buy the property from Autumn and her husband, except they put up a fight." She absently held out her hand for Connor's phone, and he suppressed a smile when he placed it in her palm. She pulled up the photo of Councilman Miller's list. *"'Suggest to Thomas that I may be willing to forget what I saw in exchange for his signature.'"*

"Whatever Miller and Mary saw that night," Connor said, "it was enough to convince Miller that Autumn was a witch. He saw an opportunity to turn the town and church against her. Either his accusations of witchcraft would force Thomas into signing over his property in an attempt to quell the rumors, or the attacks would ruin Autumn's reputation and satiate Miller's appetite for revenge, because how dare a woman thwart his grand plans? Either way, he won."

Holly lowered the papers and phone in disgust. "What a snake."

Connor agreed, but was unsurprised by Miller's scheming. Men with political ambitions and money rarely cared about the lives they ruined so long as they continued amassing power. He strongly suspected the railway deal would have somehow lined Miller's pockets or otherwise furthered his political agenda. Although the town council had been comprised of three men, through various documents Connor had gleaned that Miller had essentially owned the other councilmen. As a one-man council, Miller would have been unstoppable. Except Autumn *had* stopped him.

"I'm impressed," Holly said. "You guys are pretty good at this research thing. Do you have a date for the night Miller and Mary saw something?"

Connor shook his head. "No. Miller's ghost claims he was poisoned by an apple, and the article we found states he died with froth on his mouth—so poison fits. His death was printed at the end of October, when apples were readily available. My best guess is that whatever he saw, it happened either that summer or that spring." Connor hesitated a moment, then said, "There's one more thing."

Holly lifted a brow as she waited. Connor wasn't eager to tell her the next bit, but he couldn't imagine keeping something so important from her. "Ryan Miller is Jeremy's cousin."

Holly's jaw dropped. *"What?"*

"Jeremy never shared that with you?"

She shook her head, her earrings glittering in the light streaming through the tiny window. "You're saying Jeremy is a descendent of Councilman Miller?" She gave a bark of disparaging laughter. *"Of course* he is. Why wouldn't I date the rotten relation of the man who persecuted my family? That's my MO."

"Don't do that, Holly."

"Why not? History is literally repeating itself. Councilman Miller tried to manipulate Autumn to advance his political agenda, and Jeremy is trying to use me to lift his visibility so he can secure a seat on the same town council two hundred years later. At least Autumn had the good sense not to date *her* Miller."

Before Connor could respond, Holly's phone chirped, and she pulled it from her pocket, startling when she noted the time. "Eek! I'm going to be late."

"Where are you going?" Connor asked as he followed her outside. The sun was bright in contrast to the dim light in the trailer, and the smell of fresh-cut grass brought him straight back to summers visiting his aunt in upstate Massachusetts.

"Apple Blossom Festival," Holly said, gesturing to a pickup truck parked beside his in the driveway. It was so old that the hubs of the wheels were coated in rust, and he suspected it wasn't inspected. Packed into the back were crates, a folding table, a few signs that he couldn't read, and chairs. "It's our local hello to spring. You might not have noticed, but apples are kind of a big deal around here. Wicked Good Apples always signs up for a table." Holly tucked her hair behind her ears and glanced up at him, her hazel eyes rimmed with green behind her thick lashes. "Want to come? It promises to be a long four hours of handing out free samples of cider, collecting cash, and chatting with locals."

Connor had a thousand things he had to do for the show. There were clips to be sorted, interviews to be conducted, research to be filed, and he needed to prep for a call with his network later that night—but not a single one of those things sounded as appealing as spending the next four hours hanging out with Holly and giving away cider.

"Hell yeah, I do."

CHAPTER TWENTY-FIVE

"You should sell this commercially, dear," Mrs. Delancy said as she held out a folded bill. "It's the best apple cider in the state."

Holly tucked the cash in a zippered pouch and offered Mrs. Delancy a bag with handles. The older lady shook her head and wedged the bottle in her already stuffed canvas tote. Mrs. Delancy had been a loyal customer of Wicked Good Apples for a decade, and she hadn't changed a smidge over the years. Her hair was still gray and curled tightly to her scalp, her shoulders were still stooped, and her praise was still effusive. Whenever she visited the apple farm, she always reminded Holly that there were people in town who loved them, and when she drove away, she left behind a warm feeling in Holly's chest.

Mrs. Delancy winked at Connor before saying to Holly, "I see you have yourself a nice man this year."

Holly flashed Connor a grin. "He's okay."

Mrs. Delancy chuckled. "Have fun, you kids. I'm off to find a candied apple that is guaranteed to pull out my dentures."

Holly waved goodbye to Mrs. Delancy, who tottered toward the candy apple table. The Wicked Good Apples table wasn't as elaborate as some at the festival, with its dark purple tablecloth and uninspired display of glass cider bottles, but they'd done a brisk business since the festival had begun at two.

Connor thanked a couple that had just bought six half gallons, and wiped the back of his hand over his brow. "Whew, you weren't kidding. Your cider is the most popular one here."

The sun slid behind a cloud, giving them a much-needed respite from its relentless rays. Holly hadn't bothered packing the canopy since most years the heat was tolerable, but for once she was regretting her laziness. Across the parking lot, The Apple Dream had of course brought theirs, the edges strung with little apple-shaped twinkle lights. They also had a big apple cutout with a hole for a face so kids could stand behind it and get their picture taken, and a professionally printed banner with gold lettering. Stacy and one of her workers staffed a table decorated with vases of apple blossoms and cutesy apple-themed merchandise.

"Not popular enough to pay the bills anymore," she muttered.

Connor sat on the tailgate of the truck and crossed his booted ankles. "Well, it's not like you try."

"Excusez-moi?"

"Your presentation could use some help, babe."

Holly zipped the cash purse and sniffed. "We're not showy, unlike *some* people."

"Hmm," was all Connor said. She didn't know what that meant, but she suspected he saw more than she wished he did. She knew Wicked Good Apples could do a hell of a lot better than its break-even model if she let Missy do her job properly, but even Missy knew it was crucial for them to maintain balance; that it was too dangerous to draw attention to themselves. Their lives were an exercise in frustration.

The ghost, however, was not part of the plan. He was messing with their delicate balance and bleeding the farm dry by scaring off more customers than they'd realized. He had to go.

"I'll admit our booth has been a tiny bit busier than usual, since it seems everyone wants to meet the star of *Grimm Reality*. It was brilliant of you to start autographing Wicked Good Apples cider bottles."

"Come rest for a minute while there's a lull," Connor said, grabbing her hand and tugging her to sit next to him on the open tailgate of the truck. Her thigh pressed along his, and she itched to interlace their fingers, but whatever was going on between them was not for the town to see. The Celestes were already too often the center of gossip, so she reluctantly slipped her hand free and laid it on top of her thigh.

Connor's gaze was unwavering as he searched her face. "Stay with me tonight?"

Holly knew there were a hundred reasons to say no, to pump the brakes again, to protect her heart. But she was tired of always being the responsible one. For once she wanted to enjoy her life as it was happening; she wanted to sink into an experience without analyzing how it would affect her family and her future seven ways to Sunday. She wanted to enjoy Connor Grimm for as long as she could.

"Yes."

She walked her fingers up his arm and pushed the sleeve of his T-shirt higher so that she could see his tattoo. The last time he'd been shirtless, she'd been far too focused on other things to pay attention to his ink. Now, as she studied it, she realized it wasn't a ghost, but five conjoined circles all overlapping one another. "What is this?"

"Early New Englanders believed symbols like these could protect them from demons and witches."

"You think you need protection from witches?" She *almost* smiled. The irony was too much.

"Not exactly. Erikson and I used fake IDs to get them when we were teens. They were meant to protect us from being haunted again."

"Did it work?"

His lips brushed so lightly across her temple that she wasn't sure if it was an accident or if he'd done it on purpose. "No. We continue to see ghosts." He slid his palm behind her, splaying it on the corrugated metal, with his fingertips brushing her jeans.

Holly's stomach recoiled just as she heard a woman clear her throat across the table. "Ahem."

Holly jumped up and met Stacy's amused eyes. Over Stacy's shoulder she thought she spotted two people who looked an awful lot like Jeremy and Amy, but before she could confirm it, they disappeared into the crowd.

"Hi, Stacy," Holly said, pressing her hand to her stomach. A line appeared between Connor's brows as he caught the action from the corner of his eye. As usual, Stacy was immaculately outfitted in a cute little The Apple Dream T-shirt knotted at the side, designer jeans, and designer ankle boots.

"Holly," Stacy said, blinking as if the sun were too bright. "I see you're moving a good amount of merchandise today."

She smiled, uncertain where she stood with Stacy. Had they called a truce at the rum party? Were they still enemies? They'd never be friends—but maybe they could be on the same side. "Yes. I think my guest has helped."

Stacy turned her attention to Connor, her curls bouncing like they were in a hair commercial. She stuck out a slender hand, her nails now manicured with tiny apple blossoms. "I'm Stacy of The Apple Dream," she said, flashing him a blinding smile. "I'm sure you've heard of us. We're the most successful apple farm in the state and supply cider to over two hundred Maine and New Hampshire locations."

Holly rolled her eyes.

Connor's voice was cool and professional when he said, "No, I've never heard of you. What did you say the name of your farm was? The Apple Mirage?"

Holly's lips twitched. She was almost positive Connor *had* heard of Stacy's farm, but she appreciated the allegiance.

Stacy's eyes widened with shock as he dropped her hand. "It's The Apple *Dream*. I'm surprised Holly didn't tell you. We made an offer for her cider recipe and farm right before she signed the TV contract." Stacy pressed her lips together. She was wearing the perfect shade of plum lipstick. Holly always felt ridiculous when she wore lipstick, and she was jealous, but unsurprised, that Stacy pulled it off beautifully. "We're looking to expand our business. We're hiring on a new manager who would oversee operations at the Celeste farm if we acquired it, considering we—" She abruptly cut herself off and Holly winced. Stacy had been way too close to telling Connor she and her family couldn't physically stand to be so close to the Celestes. "Well, I can't blame you for picking the TV show," she said instead, turning to Holly. "It should help your business. For a while."

For a while, meaning Stacy thought that after the initial bump in business, Wicked Good Apples would soon be back in the red. If they couldn't get rid of the ghost, she might be right, Holly thought grimly.

"You two know each other well?" Connor asked, his all too perceptive gaze darting between the women.

Holly brushed him off with a quick "We were in the same high school class." She wished Stacy would go back to her table before she gave away any secrets—and before Holly lost her lunch all over the ground.

"And Holly's sisters were in the same class as my twin brothers," Stacy added, even as the lines radiating from her eyes showed physical pain.

Connor's brows lifted. "You have twin brothers born the same year as Holly's twin sisters?"

"Funny, isn't it?" Stacy shifted her hip. "My family has been here as long as Holly's too."

Holly wanted to hiss at her to shut up. Stacy knew Connor Grimm was a ghost hunter and a TV star, but she had no idea what he was really after, and she was giving him way too much information.

As if she sensed Holly's anxiety, Stacy glanced over her shoulder to check on her table and found a line beginning to form. "I have to head back, but I wanted to extend my congratulations, Holly, and remind you again that when things cool down a bit, our offer still stands."

"Why do you want her cider recipe if yours is so successful?" Connor asked.

Stacy stared at him. "Have you tried it?"

He nodded.

"That's your answer," she said simply. "The Celestes have a secret recipe that no one can replicate." She winked at Holly. "If I didn't know better, I'd say it was magic."

Holly's breath caught as Stacy spun on her heel and returned to her table. She was going to *murder* her! She could feel Connor's speculative gaze on her hot cheeks, but she refused to meet his eyes while she helped three customers in a row.

The Blossom Band began tuning their instruments at the far end of the parking lot, and the scent of fried apple donuts traveled on the air. The moment the customers turned away from the table, Connor, who was standing behind her, brushed her hair to the side and leaned forward to whisper in her ear, "Is your cider recipe magical, Holly?"

"You know what they say," she answered blithely, moving out of his reach. "Love is the secret ingredient."

By the expression on his face, she knew he wasn't buying it. "Are you feeling better?"

"What do you mean?"

"You seemed a little green around the gills when Stacy was here."

"Oh. Yeah, that woman is so perfect she makes me sick."

"Does it happen often?"

"Stacy making me feel nauseated? All the time," she answered flippantly.

Again, he looked at her as if he could see through her avoidance and straight into her thoughts, but he didn't say anything else because more customers had approached the table, and he and Holly were soon swept into two steady hours of exchanging goods and making small talk. Connor signed almost every cider bottle they sold and graciously took selfie after selfie with the customers. Holly appreciated how warmly he interacted with all of his fans, never tiring of the same questions or the demands on his attention. So many people wanted to share their own ghost experiences with him, and the way he paid attention to each one as if it were the most riveting thing he'd ever heard must've been exhausting, but he was unflagging in his kindness.

He was a good listener, Holly thought as she made change for a pregnant mother. For the past half hour, an elderly man had been talking Connor's ear off about his barn, which he claimed was haunted by a bull, and Connor had been nodding along and listening to the man as if he were sharing the secret to immortality.

His generosity spoke so strongly to his character that Holly's heart blipped lovingly in her chest. Her smile faltered as the change left her hand. No, no, no, no, *no*. *No* blipping. No gooey thoughts. Only an extraordinary idiot would let her heart blip for a man who was leaving in a few weeks.

An *idiot*.

Holly wasn't an idiot, was she? No, she was not. Therefore, the blipping heart clearly had to do with something else. That bag, she thought desperately, her eyes landing on the canvas tote a woman carried that proclaimed "Reading Romance Is My Drug." Yes, she *loved* that bag.

Holly was still raving about the bag in her mind as she and Connor packed up the table at the end of the afternoon and drove home with the wind whistling through the opened windows, as if she loved the bag hard enough then she would forget that all-consuming, heart-stopping moment when she had felt something for Connor that went beyond words, beyond emotions, and settled squarely in territory that was serious trouble.

"Did you see that lady's bag?" Holly asked after they'd unloaded the truck and were walking toward his trailer. Her thoughts were like panicked mice in her head. "It was *amazing*. A real hell of a bag."

"It must've been," he said, giving her a strange look as he opened the door and gestured her inside. "You've been talking about it nonstop."

"Yes, well, you can never have too many great canvas totes."

Connor shifted some of the books and paperwork off the table so they could have the apple cider donuts and apple pie they'd picked up at the festival. He set a stack on the counter, and Holly's gaze was drawn to an opened book on top of the pile.

Her entire body flushed hot, and a ringing sound began in her ears. She knew that book; they had a copy in their house. Only a handful had ever been printed, and it was written entirely in Old High German so it was a pain to translate, but she'd read it all the same. They'd all read it. It was one of the few books in existence that had correctly identified what they were.

And it was lying open to that very page.

Holly's vision began to blacken at the edges. Where the hell had he gotten that book? Had he been able to translate it? Had he made the connection yet, or had it just fallen open to that page on a stroke of bad luck?

Apple donuts followed by mind-blowing sex were the last things Holly wanted now. What she wanted was to get away from this man who had relentlessly dug into their past and who now stood on the precipice of exposing them to the world.

"I . . . I have to go," Holly stammered.

"Are you all right? You're white as a sheet." He reached for her, but Holly stumbled backward, feeling for the knob behind her.

"I'm sick. Too much cider—it's upset my stomach."

The door swung open behind her, and she climbed down the trailer steps with wobbling legs. The moment her feet hit the ground, she started to run.

CHAPTER TWENTY-SIX

Connor stood in the open doorway and watched Holly sprint to her house, his brows pinched in confusion. She'd been acting strange ever since they'd left the Apple Blossom Festival, and he'd wondered if she was having doubts about agreeing to spend the night with him. He'd planned to tell her he was happy just hanging out and watching a movie on the iPad if that was what she wanted, but before he could get the words out, she'd bolted as if something had spooked her.

He glanced around the small space, retracing their steps when they'd entered. What had happened to freak her out? She'd been fine one minute, and then the next her cheeks had drained of color. She'd had the same look of terror on her face as someone who'd just encountered a ghost.

The table had been covered with his books, notes, and files, so he'd shifted some to the counter, and when he'd spun back around with another armful, she'd acted as if she'd just spotted a body in his sink. He scanned the sideboard, his gaze falling on the opened pages of the old German book he'd been looking through that morning. Intuition whispered along his spine as he focused on the text. The pages in question were about the devil's creature known as the Wicked

Witch. Holly had made it clear she wasn't a witch. If this was what had upset her, why?

Connor paced the trailer and chewed on his thumbnail, occasionally glancing back at the book. He rummaged through his stacks of papers for the book's translation. He hadn't paid much attention when he'd read it because he'd believed her when she said she wasn't a witch, but now he looked more closely at the translation that corresponded with the two opened pages. His eyes bounced from the computer printout to the ancient text and back.

In the book, the word *Wicked* was written on the left page and the word *Witch* was written on the right page, the term spread across the layout. In the left margin the author had illustrated a woman with a vile hooked nose and a cauldron—basically the template for every drawing of a wicked witch. On the right, the author had sketched an herb garden and the sun.

In the center of the pages the author had described the Wicked Witch. Connor grabbed his glasses from where they'd slipped to the floor among a sheaf of papers and slid them onto his nose. He began to reread what had been translated into English.

The Wicked has powers born of evil, and she uses them to cast disease and despair among the peoples. The Wicked has been known to poison children and curse fields to lie fallow, women to lie barren, and illness to sweep the land. Evil speaks to her in whispers, and she is compelled to destroy all that is good.

The Witch casts spells and makes potions, and one must tread warily lest she deceives one into loving a person with a poor disposition and manner. She charms and heals, but she must not be trusted, for she is a woman and cannot help but meddle where only God should. Beware the good Witch.

Connor read them again and again. He was missing something; he *had* to be. He drummed his fingers on the notebook and distractedly glanced at the white bakery bag of cider donuts, the cinnamon scent no longer appetizing.

Wicked Good Apples was the name of Holly's farm—a nod to the local tendency to say *wicked* in lieu of *very*. He'd been warned by both Ryan Miller and Amy Gordon that Holly and her sisters were wicked.

Holly and her sisters celebrated the seasons with a quarterly ritual. Holly controlled the weather, at least to some extent.

There was a secret ingredient in their apple cider that was possibly magical. *Everything* led him back to witch.

"That can't be right," he snarled, raking his hand through his hair. He slumped in the bench seat and stared at the ugly yellow chintz curtains over the sink.

His phone rang and he lunged for it, hoping it was Holly. "Hello?"

"Hey, bro."

"Oh. Hi."

"Don't sound so happy to talk to me." Erikson laughed.

Connor stretched out his legs and settled in to talk to his brother. "It's not that."

"Then what is it?"

Connor checked the time. It was almost seven PM, which was five PM Montana time. "Aren't you supposed to be in a dark mine filming ghosts right now?"

Erikson hedged the question. "Is everything going all right? You sound stressed."

"Not stressed. Stupid. I'm missing something right under my nose."

"Does it have to do with the Celeste women?"

Connor rubbed his chin. He needed to shave before he went on camera again. "Yeah, it does."

"You still haven't figured out what they are?" Erikson asked. Connor could have sworn he heard the sound of a speaker in the background.

"Not yet, but I'm so close I can taste it."

"Ah shit. I was hoping she was wrong, but you definitely sound obsessed."

"She?"

"Charlotte. She called yesterday. She said things are getting weird out there, and she's worried about you. She thinks you're too close to one of the Celeste women—Holly."

Connor fisted his free hand. "That's no one's business but mine and Holly's."

"Geez, you don't have to bite my head off. And don't get mad at Charlotte either—you can't blame her for being worried. You've never made a case personal before. For frig's sake, Connor, she said she caught you coming out of the barn with painted handprints all over your body."

"Again, that's no one else's business."

A momentary pause fell between them.

"It's not about the sex," Erikson finally said. "Charlotte thinks you're pulling your punches. She thinks . . . and I can't even believe I'm saying this to *you* of all people . . . she thinks you're falling for the woman."

Connor gave a bark of laughter. "Nope. Charlotte's completely misreading the situation. Holly and I are—" What? What were they? They hadn't slept together. They hadn't had any exclusivity talks or thrown around the word *relationship*. They were two people who'd flirted together—that was all.

He smiled as he thought of the painted handprints. Okay, flirted with some very sexy paint activities thrown in.

As for falling in love with Holly? That was absurd. Connor had never loved a woman, and as long as he was married to his show, he never would.

"You're what?" Erikson asked.

"We're friends," he finished lamely.

Erikson clucked his tongue. "Delusional, dude."

"What's the point of this conversation besides annoying the shit out of me?" Connor snapped. "I'm trying to produce the best damned episode we've ever had, and I have stuff to do that doesn't involve hanging around my trailer sharing feelings with my brother."

Now that was *definitely* a loudspeaker in the background. Since when did they have loudspeakers in abandoned gold mines?

"The point is I'm coming out there," Erikson said. "They're calling my flight now."

"Don't you dare!"

"Too late. I don't know what's happening at Wicked Good Apples, but Charlotte thinks you need me, and I think you do too. See you tomorrow."

Before Connor could reply, the phone went dead in his ear. He dropped it to the table and stood, ready to give Charlotte a piece of his mind, when his eyes fell on the opened pages of the book.

His heart stopped.

Suddenly he saw with stunning clarity what he'd been missing. It had been there all along, but like most people, he simply hadn't seen it.

"Holy shit," he whispered. He grabbed his phone again and shot off a text.

Connor: *I know what you are.*

A few minutes later three dots appeared. Connor held his breath until Holly's message came through.

Holly: *Meet me in the old orchard at eleven.*

CHAPTER TWENTY-SEVEN

Holly walked slowly into the old orchard. On a good day she could travel from the house to the orchard in ten minutes flat. Tonight it had taken her twenty, and it wasn't because it was dark. The moon was bright enough that she was easily able to navigate the silver-blanketed terrain, but despite her internal pep talk about how everything was going to be all right, she was terrified of what she was about to face.

Never before had anyone known what Holly and her family truly were—and she wasn't fully convinced Connor did either. Her doubt was the reason she hadn't told any of her family about the text that had made her heart drop straight to her feet, and why she hadn't told them she was meeting him in the orchard. It was possible she was wrong, and she would have alarmed everyone for no reason.

The apple blossoms were morphing into tiny green fruit, but their sweet scent was still in the air. Grasshoppers chirped and a few lone fireflies circulated over the grass, blinking in tandem as they signaled for a mate. Normally, Holly would have basked in these simple spring gifts, but tonight she was so consumed with dread that she was barely able to appreciate her surroundings.

She was deathly afraid that if Connor was right, he was going to expose them on national TV. And a tiny, far more selfish part of her was worried how he would treat her now. It was possible he wouldn't want to come within ten feet of her, much less bang her brains out, as Missy had so eloquently put it.

Holly swallowed as she entered the last row of the old orchard. She swore if she saw Councilman Miller's ghost right then, she'd punch his damned face. She could *not* handle that ghoul on top of this disaster.

Connor was already waiting for her. He'd brought a quilt and spread it on the ground and was lying on his back, his hands stacked behind his head as he stared up at the stars. Holly batted at a mosquito and dragged her feet as she approached him, until at last she stood at the edge of the quilt. She took a deep breath and said, "Hi."

She still wasn't sure what she was going to do if he had figured it out. Beg him to keep it quiet? Threaten to sic Winter on him? Cry?

Connor turned his head and ran his eyes over her. "Come sit down."

Holly dropped onto the blanket and sat with her legs crossed, her hands loosely clasped in her lap. Connor rolled to a sitting position and faced her. She studied his face, trying to discern from his expression what he was feeling, but he was predictably stoic, with nothing but those keen gray eyes returning her searching gaze.

"No small talk," Holly blurted. "Let's get this over with."

He nodded. "Okay. I finally know what you are, Holly."

She lifted both brows.

"You're Wicked."

"Like that's original," she snorted. But inside she quailed.

His lips curved. "You know that's not what I mean. You're *Wicked*, as in the supernatural creature. I didn't see it for so long because, like the rest of society, I think of wicked witches, but that was never the case, was it? They were always two separate things. Two separate pages in the book. Two separate supernatural beings mistakenly conflated into one."

Holly ran her tongue around the dry inside of her mouth but didn't speak. Couldn't speak.

"The book I have explains the difference. Witches were seen as having good magic. They healed, made love potions, and were creatures of the sun. Wickeds were known for being evil. They incited plagues and disease." He looked her directly in the eye. "They caused floods and rainstorms that ruined villages, and they brought on droughts that withered crops."

Holly's heart was pounding so hard she almost couldn't hear his words over the roar of blood.

"Wickeds are evil and do evil," Connor continued, "or at least that's what the book says. But you know what, Holly? I know you. I know your family. You're *not* evil. So either I'm wrong or that book is wrong." He leaned back on his hands, his granite eyes never leaving her face. "I'm willing to bet history got it wrong."

Holly was appalled when moisture appeared in her eyes, and she quickly blinked it away. She had doubted him, but she should have known that Connor Grimm would look deeper than the surface. This was a man who didn't stop until he reached the truth—the *real* truth.

In that moment Holly made a choice: for the first time in her life she was going to be brave enough, reckless enough, to trust someone else with her secret.

She took a deep breath. "History got a little wrong, a little right."

Connor leaned forward with laser-like focus. "Tell me about it."

Holly wanted to reach for his hand, but she still didn't dare touch him. Just because he wanted to learn about Wickeds didn't mean he wanted one to touch him, and she knew if he pulled away it would crush her. "Not until you give me your word that you won't expose my family to the world."

Seconds ticked by, one after another. Connor said quietly, "You have my word. I've been trying to convince myself that it would compromise the integrity of my show if I discovered something paranormal and didn't share it, but I think I knew all along I couldn't do it. Because you're not just some*thing*, Holly, you're some*one*, and I don't think the world is ready for what you're about to tell me."

Relief pulsed through Holly until she felt electrified. She'd feared that out of a misguided desire to help others, this ruthless story hunter would lay her and her family bare for strangers to ridicule and hate, not understanding how it would destroy them. Again, she should have known better.

If anyone knew how the paranormal could ruin a life, it was Connor Grimm.

"You're right about the book," she said, her newfound freedom loosening the words from her tongue. "It's one of very few written volumes that correctly recorded our species. A long, long time ago Mother Mage, or the Creator—whatever you want to call her—loved humanity so much that she gave them Witches. And they were good and had 'good' magic and did good things. But the laws of this universe require balance, and so she was compelled to also make Wickeds, who had 'bad' powers and were meant to do evil. Mother Mage truly did care for humans, though, so she gave them another gift: she made the Wickeds women."

Connor's intensity was almost overwhelming, as if he were focusing so hard on her that he could hear the very blood pumping through her wrists. "There are no male Wickeds?"

Holly shook her head. "It's only passed to women. Mother Mage was confident that women were smart enough, strong enough, and resilient enough to bear the burden. She trusted that they would find a way to use their 'bad' powers *for* humanity instead of against it."

Connor wrapped his hands around one knee. "Smart," he said after a moment. "My sex has many attributes, but the ability to handle that kind of power without burning down the Earth in dick-measuring contests isn't one of them."

Holly smiled at him with such gratitude for his understanding that he seemed momentarily stunned. "Each Wicked has a particular power that calls to her. For me, it's manipulating weather events: the better to flood, cause droughts, start hurricanes, and the like."

"Let me guess: Winter can see the future."

Holly's eyebrows flew upward. Clever, clever ghost hunter. "Yes, to thwart good things from happening of course."

"And Missy?"

"Missy can cause illness." Holly rubbed her palm over her thigh. "Over time Wickeds learned to do exactly as Mother Mage had wished. My family and I use our powers for limited good. I say 'limited' because we've discovered the less we meddle with the natural order of things, the less karmic rebound and unintended consequences there are. And the more we stay off the map."

Connor was quickly piecing together how they used their powers for good. "So you do things like water the orchards and drain the dirt when it pours."

She nodded. "Occasionally I get involved in bigger things, but I really try not to. Oftentimes my emotions manifest as power. I don't always succeed in separating the two, but I am much better than I was when I was younger." After she'd started a thunderstorm and killed her mother with a middle school tantrum. "Winter uses her visions to foresee things like shipping cost increases and what the winter will be like, but her visions are spotty, and she can't control them."

Connor gave a low whistle. "You do realize you guys could be millionaires with that kind of ability to see into the future, right?"

Holly laughed. "Yeah, but that would be pretty evil, wouldn't it?"

"Okay, so Mother Mage was definitely smart to limit this to women. How does Missy manipulate something like creating illnesses into a good thing?"

"Remember that apple tree plague that never touched us?" When he nodded she said, "Missy created an illness that killed it off at our borders. She uses her abilities like an antibiotic."

His eyes widened. "That's *brilliant*. So she makes illnesses that kill diseases."

This was more fun than Holly had expected. She'd never had the chance to explain what they did, to someone who didn't already know. "Aunt Daisy has a death touch, and so she uses her power to decay and ferment the apples for our cider. That's our secret ingredient."

Connor closed his eyes and smiled as if he'd just been given knowledge of how the universe started. "*That's* why she always wears the gloves."

Holly nodded. "There may have been a time when Wickeds with a death touch could control themselves without gloves, but my family has lost that knowledge. Aunt Rose can make potions. My mother"—she inhaled deeply—"she could fly."

He processed that for a moment. "What about the nightmares? Your paintings?"

"Well, the powers aren't fun like Witch magic. They're a burden. A curse. You know how the capable person at work gets more and more projects just because the boss knows it'll get done, but the slacker has it easy? It's sort of like that. Mother Mage knew we could handle the curse, and so we do, but it takes a toll. We feel compelled to use our power for evil. Images appear and they haunt us until they're manifested. I guess it was the universe's way of ensuring we complied. We've all found ways around it. I manifest my visions into paintings and then they go away. Winter pours hers into violin music."

Connor took her hand in his, and some of the tension in her shoulders eased at his touch. "I'm sorry, Holly. That's a massive burden to bear."

It really was, but she'd never had sympathy before because the only other people who'd known were people who had to carry the same load.

"How did it all get mixed together?" Connor asked. "How did Wickeds and Witches become Wicked Witches?"

"The story is that a long time ago Wickeds and Witches worked in harmony with humanity. Wickeds cleared diseased fields and brought rain when it was dry, while Witches made potions and cast charms." She paused and added, "You should know that Witches can be male or female. That's an important distinction, and it explains why over time the male elders of the communities became angry and jealous of the Wickeds. The men hated that they had no influence over the Wickeds, that women alone had so much power that no male could control.

They began to grumble that if the Wickeds could cause a drought, who was to say they weren't responsible for all droughts? When a field lay fallow, they whispered that it was because of the Wickeds' death touch. When illness took a child, they reminded people that Wickeds could cause sickness. The elders had found a marginalized group to blame for everyone's problems, and in doing so they solidified their own power and importance.

"Eventually humans grew to distrust anything supernatural, be it Wicked power or Witch magic. Over time the two became one and the same in people's minds: Wicked Witches. The following persecution was ruthless.

"The majority of people massacred during the witch hunts were women, and very few were actually Witches or Wickeds. After the witch hunts, Wickeds let themselves be erased from history for their own safety. As a species, we've lived in the shadows ever since. My family even more than others."

Connor stood suddenly and began to pace back and forth behind the blanket. "Exactly how powerful are you?"

Holly's breath caught in her throat. "Why would you ask me that?"

Connor paused mid-stride. "I meant you in the general sense of all Wickeds, but exactly how powerful are *you*, Holly?"

Holly's fingertips tingled. "I—I'm powerful. So are my sisters. Our family line has been more temperate than others, eager to downplay what we are, but it had an unintended consequence: generation after generation, the restrained powers built until the three of us were born."

"The stifled powers spilled into you and your sisters."

Holly nodded. "The universe demands balance."

"If your kind let loose and did all the evil they were capable of, what could they do?"

"We could destroy the world," Holly said simply. "Humanity is doing it well enough on their own, but we could end it in a fraction of the time."

Connor rubbed his palm over his chin and assessed her. "What happened four years ago?"

Holly knew not to underestimate him, and yet he still managed to surprise her when he made connections that shouldn't have been so obvious. "Aunt Rose was able to hide the strength of our powers for a long time by giving us a potion. Four years ago it stopped working; our powers outstripped even the strongest of her concoctions. Maybe if we hadn't turned our backs on our culture, we could have found another way, but she'd reached her limit of knowledge, and what we needed couldn't be found in any book."

"When you stopped taking the potion, there must've been a surge of power. That was what drew Councilman Miller to your plane," Connor said. "That's when the sightings began."

"That's what I now believe, yes."

"Why did you need to hide the strength of your powers? Humans don't know of your existence, so why does it matter?"

"Humans may not, but there are other, scarier Wickeds out there. Specifically the Shadow Council. Wickeds don't have a formal government, unlike the—" she bit her tongue.

"We'll come back to that. What's the Shadow Council?"

"It's an organization that functions as a check on any Wicked who gives into her impulses too much and jeopardizes the secrecy of our identity."

"So a hit squad."

Holly gave a strangled laugh. "I guess so. Aunt Rose and Aunt Daisy tried to hide my sisters and me so that our unusual level of power wouldn't draw the council's attention. It's been four years since the potion stopped working." She shrugged. "Maybe we've escaped their notice."

Connor studied her with his piercing gray gaze. "Who *does* have a working government?" Even as he asked the question, realization dawned in his eyes, and he went utterly still. *"Witches."*

She nodded in confirmation.

His focus drifted to an apple tree in the distance. "You keep talking about balance," he said slowly. "Wickeds balance Witches and vice versa. In order to do that effectively, they must need to live in the same vicinity. That's why they used to work in harmony with humanity all those thousands of years ago, and it's how they were eventually conflated into one: they were always near one another."

Holly felt as if she were watching a master piece together a ten-thousand-piece puzzle.

Connor's intense scrutiny returned to her face. "Stacy is a Witch," he said.

Shit. Holly was suddenly grateful this man was on her side. "Stacy's family was likely drawn here by Autumn's presence. Stacy and her brothers were born to balance out me and my sisters, or maybe the opposite is true. Stacy's family knows what we are but very little about what we can do. Wickeds are an enigma, even to ourselves. We've lived in the shadows too long. My family especially."

"You feel nauseated around Stacy."

"Yes, and I think I give her a headache." Holly chewed on her bottom lip. "That's why when I say her perfectionism makes me ill, I'm only half joking. It's an unpleasant feeling, and we separate as quickly as we can. I'm not certain, but I think in close quarters we may nullify each other. The truth is Witches get the fun magic. They have a strong network and government, and they can sparkle without having to battle personal demons and stress about balance. When it comes to equilibrium, the world is always going to need more good than bad. That's partly why Witches can practice without restraint and why there are more of them. It's also one of the reasons The Apple Dream does so well and Wicked Good Apples does not. For Wickeds, maintaining balance isn't just a crappy mission assigned to us at birth; it's a key component of our sanity."

"Damn, Holly. So you're telling me Wickeds suffer on a daily basis denying their powers and evil impulses, bearing this curse for centuries and secretly keeping the world together through sheer cleverness—all while humanity, and men in particular, have persecuted them out of ignorance, jealousy, and fear?"

"That about sums it up."

"*Screw* that." Connor dropped to his knees in front of her and framed her face between his palms. "We don't deserve you." His lips touched hers with such tenderness that it felt like a physical thank-you, a gift of gratitude for what she and the other Wickeds did.

Holly's heart blipped again.

CHAPTER TWENTY-EIGHT

Holly tentatively wrapped her arms around Connor's neck, reveling in the feel of his rough cheek against hers and admiring the soft glow of the moon on his hair and skin. "You're not afraid of me?" she murmured.

Connor kissed the corner of her mouth. "Do I seem afraid?"

"No," she breathed, her heart beating wildly in her chest.

"Do you still want to spend the night with me, Holly?"

"More than anything."

He growled, pleased with her answer, and his hand drifted to her breast, cupping her over her shirt and bra. His touch was like a spark igniting all of the fear and worry, terror and stress, and burning them away until nothing was left but blazing lust.

Then his mouth was everywhere, on her face, her neck, her lips. He pushed the plaid off her shoulders and nudged her onto the blanket. Holly lay on her back, looking at his dark silhouette against the star-studded sky, and it felt like they were the only two people in the universe.

She tugged on the hem of his shirt and he helped, sitting up to reach behind him and pull it over his head. She drank in the sight of his muscled chest and the pentagram tattoo, tracing her fingers over the ink before he lowered himself and began inching her tank top up her belly.

"I've had a hard time thinking about anything else but how you taste," he said in a thick voice. He pressed his lips to her belly button and slid the shirt up with both hands, his palms roughly gliding across her skin as the shirt bunched over the backs of his hands, his mouth following with heated, wet kisses. When he came to her breasts he pressed his face between them and then pulled her tank top over her head.

Holly reached behind her, unclasped her bra, and threw it aside, loving the way his eyes darkened as he drank in the sight of her bare breasts in the silver moonlight. She decided there was nothing more flattering than moonlight, although she suspected Connor would look at her in the same way whether she were under the glare of interrogation lights or in a candle-lit room. He had a way of focusing on her as if absolutely nothing else in the world existed.

She pulled him to her, kissing him with slow, dreamlike kisses. The orchards felt truly otherworldly, so soft and glowing and private, as if they were in their own intimate bubble of sighs and pleasure.

His bare skin slid over hers, his chest hair brushing across the peaks of her nipples only to be replaced by his nimble fingers and then his clever lips a moment later. He drew her into his mouth, the tug sending streaks of pleasure straight between her legs. He gently pinched and rolled and palmed her other breast and then switched, making sure to give them both equal treatment.

Holly lifted her hips against his, grinding into him, desperate for more. He read her needy body movements and traveled downward, unbuttoning her jeans with deft fingers. He pulled the jeans off her legs and Holly wiggled out of her panties. Then he was spreading her knees apart and dipping his head, kissing her and using his lips and tongue with such expert skill that she was already on the precipice before she even realized it.

She nudged his head back before she could crest. Connor seemed confused for a moment but she moved quickly, pushing him down to the blanket and straddling his belly. "Not this time, Grimm. This time we come together."

She pressed a kiss to his chest, her silky hair draping in a curtain around her and trailing across his skin. Goose bumps broke out on his flesh as she navigated downward, slowly unbuckling his belt and "accidentally" brushing the bulge in his jeans as she pretended to fumble with it.

"You really *are* wicked," he hissed.

She laughed as she finally separated the belt and then went to work on his zipper, freeing the length of him to the night air and her admiring gaze. She licked her palm and wrapped it around him, stroking upward in one long sweep. Connor's face went taut, his eyes glittering with desire as he watched her handle him.

Holly tugged his jeans off and returned, exploring him as thoroughly as he'd explored her in the hayloft. She traced him with her hands, cupped him, stroked him, and then she bent her head and took him into her mouth.

"Holly," he groaned as she ran the flat of her tongue over his length and followed it with her curled fist. She increased her speed until at last he lifted her away as she had done to him. "You're going to finish this before it begins."

She smiled at him, feeling like a nude moonlight goddess, her breasts heavy and her nipples tight. She knew Connor was thinking of her in the same way because she'd never seen a man look at her with such awe.

He reached for his discarded jeans and pulled out a condom. Holly took it from him and ripped the foil open with her teeth, pulled out the latex, and rolled it on him—which was far more difficult than it should have been because Connor's mouth and hands were *everywhere*.

She laughed, nudging him back as she straddled him once again and slowly, slowly took him inside her. Her eyes were closed as she adjusted to his size, her breathing shallow with the intense feeling of fullness.

Connor grasped her hips in his hands and waited for her to move when she was ready. Holly began to rock over him with dreamlike fluidity. She laid her palms on his thighs behind her and tilted her head back, letting the moon slide over her face as she slid over him. Perspiration began to form on her skin as Connor's fingers found where they joined and began to circle.

"You're the most beautiful thing I've seen," he ground out.

"Connor, I'm going to—"

He lifted her off as if she weighed nothing and gave her a playful slap on the butt. "Not yet. Remember, we come together this time." With that he pressed her onto her back and she wrapped her legs around him as he sank into her.

Holly was used to being on top—Jeremy had been lazy and it had been the only way it had felt good, even if she'd never come and had always had to take care of herself afterward. So she was shocked and then thrilled when Connor started hitting angles that made her see stars.

"Why are you watching my face?" she asked on a moan, rolling her head to the side out of embarrassment.

Connor palmed her cheek so she was facing him again. "I want to see what you like. I haven't had the benefit of your lessons, so it looks like I'm going to have to learn on my own. Unless you want to show me what you like?" He scraped his teeth across the cord of her neck as he ground himself over her in a way that made her clench around him. "What do you like, Holly?"

"This is good," she panted. "I also like . . ." her cheeks flamed and she pressed her lips together. How was she supposed to share her most secret fantasies out loud?

"Nope, now I *need* to know. Don't get shy on me." He reached around and squeezed her ass cheek, opening her more to him, and dropped his mouth to her ear so he could whisper, "I'll share my secret—I like all kinds of sex. If you want, I'll do things to you that are so dirty you can't even look me in the eye the next day. Or we'll keep doing this." He kissed her mouth, stroking her open with his tongue. "As long as it's with you," he murmured, "it's what I want."

He'd do *anything*? Holly's mind wandered to all the different things she'd come across online. She hadn't experimented with most of it, but it would be terribly fun to try some of it with Connor. Maybe she'd start with something small.

"From behind," she gasped as he slid his entire length into her.

Connor flipped her over with big, gentle hands and her gaze locked on the apple tree ahead as he entered her. It only took three thrusts before she was nearly undone. "Connor," she warned.

"I got you, babe. Together." He cupped her hip with one hand and reached around with the other to rub her clitoris as he thrust forward. A few strokes later and Holly was crashing into the best orgasm of her life while Connor pulsed behind her with his own release, breathing heavily.

They collapsed onto the quilt, and he rolled the edges around them so that they were cocooned together, her nose pressed against his throat. He swept his hand up and down her back, occasionally fondling her butt.

"Are you an ass man?" Holly asked on a yawn.

"I'm an everything man. I wasn't kidding when I said that."

She leaned on her elbow and smiled down at him, her dark hair falling over her shoulder and onto his chest. The crickets were loud around them, but she was snug and satisfied, tucked into his strong, warm embrace. "Can we stay out here for a while?"

He lifted the ends of her hair and brushed them lightly across the top of her breast. "My Wicked woman, we can stay out here for as long as you like."

CHAPTER TWENTY-NINE

Connor was fucked in multiple senses of the word. First, literally. Holly was soft and curvy, and she knew how to lean into her pleasure in a way that made him desperate to spend the next few weeks doing nothing but hearing her hoarse cry while she came around him. Maybe a few months. Or a lifetime.

He was already getting hard again as he thought about how it had felt to have her legs wrapped around his waist. Her head was nestled into his chest as he stroked down her spine, cupped her butt, and then stroked upward again. It had been a while since Connor had slept with anyone, but that alone couldn't account for how good it had felt to join with his Wicked. She'd been enchanting as she'd ridden him in the moonlight, her breasts pushed forward and her hair cascading down her back, her eyes closed in utter pleasure.

"You're getting hard again," she murmured, her palm drifting over his erection.

"Are you cold?"

"No."

"Good." He rolled on top of her, kissing down her body and nuzzling her belly before dipping lower, his head disappearing beneath the quilt. He opened her to him, tasting her and coating his fingers with her wetness as he slowly began to pleasure her again. She writhed against his mouth with a hypnotic rhythm that made him heavy and swollen with desire.

The second way he was fucked, he thought as her hands wove into his hair, was that he adored absolutely everything about this woman. He loved her spirit, her fierceness, and her incredible strength in holding herself together against what she'd been cursed with.

Holly's thighs squeezed around his head, and he thought he might come just from hearing her gasp and moan.

The flat of Connor's tongue was pressed against her when his eyes flew open with a shockingly unwelcome thought. Wait, did he *love* her? Was Charlotte right? Had he fallen in love with Holly Celeste without even knowing it?

Holly's hips bucked against his still mouth, using his tongue for her own pleasure, and he rumbled with approval. He slid another finger inside her and suspected there were a lot of fun things he and Holly could try together. She was a little hedonist at heart, and her satisfaction only multiplied his.

Connor drove her upward, losing control of his thoughts as he sank into the feeling of pleasuring her, and when she shattered, he rolled on another condom and pushed inside her, stroking hard and fast and pushing her over the edge a second time. That time she screamed, giving him a savage sense of male satisfaction. Connor wasn't usually a possessive lover, but just the thought of any other man pleasuring those noises out of her made him go cold with jealousy.

"Are you sore?" he asked before taking her breast into his mouth. "We can stop."

"Never stop," she breathed, lazily looping her arms around his neck, her hazel and green-rimmed eyes glazed.

Connor kept eye contact with her as he gentled his thrusts. He felt primal and possessive, tender and blessed. He felt . . . completed.

That didn't make any sense, he thought vaguely as they moved together. If she completed him, then that would mean they were meant for each other. It would mean that when separated they were two parts of the same puzzle, their picture incomplete.

It would mean he loved her.

That was crazy. He didn't love Holly.

She came again, and he watched the joy spread across her face before he followed.

༜ ๏

An hour later, Connor reluctantly helped Holly dress.

"You're spending a lot of time back there," she said, looking over her shoulder. He was kneeling behind her, his jeans unzipped, as he positioned her panties on her ass.

"Skyclad," he said. "Witches call being in the nude 'skyclad.'"

"I'm not a Witch."

"Yeah, but I'm thinking there are some practices you could adopt, like being skyclad all the time."

Holly laughed as she yanked her shirt over her head, covering her beautiful back. She pulled her hair out of the neck hole, and it fell in dark contrast over the light-colored tank top. "I *do* like the way you worship my body."

Connor gave her ass a smack and stood to pull on his own shirt while she tugged on her jeans. "You're aware that for the rest of the time we're filming here, I'm not going to be able to walk into this orchard without thinking of you riding me with the moon over your head."

Holly ducked her chin, and if he had to bet on it, he'd say she was blushing. "Yeah, well, *you* don't have to live here," she muttered.

Connor frowned as she bent to tie her boots. What did she mean by that? He was about to ask, but before he could, she smiled brightly up at him and said, "Does this mean we're fuck buddies?"

He scowled. "No, we are *not* 'fuck buddies.' A fuck buddy is someone you call at three AM and don't care if you see again."

"Right, and since this is my farm, you *have* to see me."

"Are you being deliberately obtuse?"

She finished tying her boots and stood. "I'm trying to keep things light, Connor. You're leaving, remember? You're not boyfriend material—you said so yourself."

Her words did nothing to diminish his suddenly foul mood as he shook out the quilt and stuffed it under his arm. "I don't have to see you every day. I *want* to see you."

"Aw, that's sweet." She patted him gently on the cheek, which only made him clench his teeth together.

They started toward the trailer and the house, both of which stood dark and still in the distance. He was thinking over their exchange when a text came through. Erikson had landed in Portland and was getting a hotel for the remainder of the night before driving up early the next morning.

Connor loved his brother more than anyone else on the planet. They were close in the way only two people with shared trauma could be. As children they'd defended each other to their parents, and they'd stood up to each other's bullies at school. Now that they were adults, they spent a lot of time apart, especially as their show had grown and they needed to split their time between locations, but they texted daily and called at least once a week. Connor had vaguely missed Erikson the way he always did when his brother wasn't around . . . but for the first time in his life he wasn't excited to see him.

He pondered why that was as he walked over the grass, the quilt under one arm and his hand on Holly's lower back. Maybe it was that he was perfectly happy with how things were going with Holly and he didn't want Erikson barging in and messing it up.

Maybe it was that he knew Holly's secret, and he wouldn't be sharing it with his brother or on national television.

It most definitely was *not* that Charlotte and Erikson were right and he was falling for her.

"My brother is coming tomorrow," he said after a few minutes of silence. Holly looked up at him with a question in her eyes. "He . . . um . . ." Connor cleared his throat. "He knows that I suspect your family of being supernatural."

Holly rubbed her finger over her lip as she thought. "Does he know we're Wickeds?"

Connor shook his head. "No."

"Are you going to tell him?"

Connor stopped and tugged her close. He dropped a light kiss on her mouth and said, "That's not up to me."

She seemed surprised. "Are you saying you wouldn't tell him if I didn't want you to? I thought you two were practically twins."

Connor laughed as they began walking again. "We're really close—but it's not my secret to share, Holly. Not with the world, and not with my brother."

"Shit."

"What?" They were almost to her house now, and he climbed the porch steps after her, pleased when the stairs remained solid under their feet.

"I'm a sucker for honorable men."

Connor pressed her to the door with his body and gave her a long, lingering kiss that ignited his blood again. Damn, how could he still want her after having her multiple times in the orchard? If he wasn't careful, he could see his desire for her developing into an addiction. "Funny, I'm a sucker for women with pet hedgehogs."

Holly breathed him in and reached for the doorknob.

He didn't want to see her go. "Come sleep in the trailer with me."

"I'm not sure I'm ready for everyone to know about us. I'm not sure I ever want them to know."

"Kind of late for that, isn't it? Both your sisters have walked in on us kissing, and Charlotte caught me with painted handprints on my body and told my brother."

Holly groaned. "Okay, so everyone knows. I'll think about it."

"No pressure. We probably wouldn't get much sleep if you did stay over." When had he ever *wanted* a woman to sleep over? His ex-girlfriends obviously had before, but he couldn't recall ever feeling like he didn't want to part with them. If they'd gone home at the end of the night, he didn't think he'd have minded.

Holly pushed the door opened and whispered, "See you tomorrow, Ghost Hunter."

"Tomorrow, Wicked."

CHAPTER THIRTY

Despite her late night, Holly awoke early the next morning and showered, aching in all sorts of sexy places and already eager to see Connor. She almost felt high from unburdening her secret and the following multiple orgasms. The greatest perk of sharing her secret was that she no longer had to worry about Connor exposing her family to the world. He was leaving in a few weeks, but now that everything was in the open, she could relax and fully enjoy her time with him. Connor Grimm knew exactly what she was and what she was capable of, and he'd wanted her anyway.

It was enough to make her toes curl.

She blushed as she remembered all the ways he *had* made her toes curl the night before. She could barely wait for a repeat performance.

When she was dressed, she entered the kitchen for her first cup of coffee. Aunt Rose and Aunt Daisy were sitting at the table, reading the newspaper and drinking tea, both of them dressed in the same brand of fuzzy sweater but in different color combinations: one soft pink, one apple red.

Holly was dropping a frozen waffle in the toaster when Missy stumbled in, bleary-eyed and her hair a riotous red mane around her face. "Coffee . . . need coffee." She blindly poured herself a cup and drank it black, hissing when it burned her tongue.

"Connor knows we're Wickeds, and he's promised not to expose us," Holly blurted.

No one reacted.

"Um, hello? Did you not hear me?" Holly asked.

Missy took another sip and hissed again when the coffee burned her tongue a second time. "Old news. Winter told us last night."

"That's not fair!" Holly jabbed the toaster lever down. "She can't go around sharing other people's important information just because she can sometimes see the future. Does she also know Connor's brother is arriving this morning?"

Aunt Rose lowered the sports section. "No, she hasn't said anything about that."

"Ooh yes!" Missy cried, reaching for the creamer. "Erikson is just as hot as his brother, and way more fun."

"What makes you think that?" Holly asked indignantly. She'd watched Erikson on the show, and Missy wasn't wrong about his looks. He was as tall and broad as his brother, but that was where the comparison ended. They each must've taken after a different parent, because where Connor had sexy mussed hair and granite eyes, Erikson was pure Viking, with blond hair and piercing blue eyes. It was true that on the show Connor was usually the more serious of the two, but that didn't mean he wasn't fun. It meant, typically, that he was the oldest. From experience Holly knew being the oldest sibling came with certain responsibilities.

"It's his lightning-quick smile and those crinkly blue eyes. You just know a guy like that knows how to play."

Holly's waffle popped, and she tossed it from hand to hand before nibbling on it without syrup. "Connor said he won't tell his brother we're Wickeds."

Missy poured half the creamer in her mug. "That's good."

"Is it? Those two are as close as we are. It won't feel right for him to keep a secret like that from his brother. The supernatural has been their whole life. For Connor to know something like this and not share it—it sort of feels like I'd be asking him to betray Erikson."

"Did you ask him to keep it from his brother?" Aunt Daisy lowered the paper, which she read with the use of a magnifying glass, and peered at Holly.

"No. But I didn't give him permission to tell him either. I didn't want to do that until I talked it over with the rest of you."

"Don't do it," Missy said promptly. She set her mug on the counter with a click. "Witches Be Bitches" was printed in pink cursive lettering on the ceramic. "Men suck and they can't be trusted."

Holly frowned. "That's not true. There are good men out there, good *people* out there, and Connor is one of them. I know he would never share our secret with someone he didn't trust."

Aunt Daisy smiled, the paper crinkling as she lifted it again. "I'd say you answered your own question, Holly."

She was right. Holly believed Connor Grimm's word to be as reliable as the sun, which meant if Connor trusted Erikson to keep it quiet, she could too. "Thanks. Where's Winter?"

Before anyone could answer, they heard the engine of a truck pulling to a short stop in front of the house, and two doors slammed. Holly exchanged a look with Missy and hurried to the front porch, opening it in time to see Winter stalk away from the passenger side of a rented pickup truck. A tall blond Viking of a man stood at the driver's side door with his arms crossed over his chest as he glared after her. They were both covered head to toe in mud.

Connor stepped out of his trailer, the door slapping shut behind him. His eyes met Holly's, and a secret acknowledgement of their night passed between them before his attention returned to what Holly presumed was his brother. "What the hell happened?" he demanded, jogging over.

Winter blazed toward the porch, her blue eyes flashing with fury and her shoulders stiff. "I need a shower," she muttered, brushing past a stunned Holly and Missy and leaving muddy footprints in her wake.

They turned to gape at Erikson, whose expression was equally livid. Connor looked him up and down. A blob of mud dripped off his shirt and splattered onto his work boot. "There's a hose behind the barn," Connor said, unsuccessfully trying to smother a smile. "Welcome to Wicked Good Apples."

CHAPTER THIRTY-ONE

Connor took more pleasure in pointing the hose at his brother than he should have.

"Sadist," Erikson growled as freezing cold water dripped down his face. "You're a sadist and these women are sadists."

"What happened, anyway?" Connor asked, shutting the spigot off when enough mud had been washed away that Erikson was once again recognizable. He crossed his arms and grinned at his brother. Erikson was hard to work into a snit, so it was an interesting change of pace to see his carefree and charismatic younger brother sputtering and raging.

"What happened is I should have stayed in Montana."

"Agreed. Like I told you on the phone, I have this handled."

"Is that so?" Erikson pulled his shirt over his head and wrung it out. "Is that why I saw you looking at the dark-haired woman on the porch like she was Helen of fricking Troy?"

"That dark-haired woman is Holly," Connor said through clenched teeth, "and you'll watch your mouth when you talk about her."

Erikson's head jerked up, and they stared at each other in astonishment. Connor had never, ever threatened his brother over a woman before. He hadn't meant to now, but the words had come out of their own volition when he'd heard the scorn in Erikson's voice.

"Damn." Erikson gave a low whistle. "I can't wait to meet *Holly* now."

"Don't do that," Connor snapped.

"Do what?"

"Be a dick."

They rounded the barn, Erikson squelching with every step, and nearly ran into Charlotte. She was wearing neon green from head to toe and clashed with, well, everything.

"Erik!" she cried happily, but when she spotted his bare chest and wet jeans, she wrinkled her nose. "What happened to you?"

"One of the Celeste sisters, that's what. I stopped to help her rescue a fawn caught in the mud, and neither of them was grateful. Do the trailers have showers?"

"Sad little streams of water dribble from sad little showerheads if that's what you mean."

"Good enough." He slapped Connor on the shoulder. "See you in ten."

Charlotte watched him go and then warily turned back to Connor. "Don't be mad."

"Mad that you went behind my back and called my brother? Why would that make me angry?"

She sighed. "Okay, fine, it wasn't cool—I get it. I just thought you needed him out here, that's all. Things are starting to feel . . . complicated. You missed the network call last night. You *never* miss a call."

"Nothing is complicated, Char. At least nothing that concerns the show. We're almost done with the second episode, and we have a third in the wings. Another week or so and we'll be out of here." It didn't mean anything that his stomach clenched at the thought, and some small part of him rebelled at the idea of leaving Holly.

"If you say so."

"I say so."

While Erikson showered and Charlotte returned to the trailer to look over the dialogue they'd written for the final Wicked Good

Apples episode, Connor ignored the thousands of tasks waiting for him, and went to find Holly.

He eventually discovered her in the apple cellar, sorting through crates of apples for the next batch of cider. Connor wrapped his arms around her from behind and kissed the side of her neck, breathing in her unique Christmas scent. He knew their . . . whatever this was . . . was still new, and they were in the infatuation stage, but he couldn't imagine *not* wanting to spend time with her, not wanting to kiss her soft mouth, not wanting to watch her wear those sexy jeans while she did chores around the farm.

Holly tilted her head back, smiled, and nuzzled into him. "Good morning."

Connor turned her around and drew her in for a hug. "At least an interesting one, if not a good one. How are you feeling?"

"About?"

"Everything. About me knowing what you are. About us."

He released her, and Holly brushed a strand of hair behind her ear and shrugged. "I feel fine." She waited a beat. "Okay, I feel freaking great. I've never shared our secret with anyone before, and it felt cathartic. And the sex wasn't bad."

"Wasn't bad!" Connor growled in mock offense. He grabbed the edge of her plaid and tugged her close again until her body was pressed into his.

Holly peeled off her work gloves and set them on top of a crate before she wrapped her arms around his neck. Why was it such a turn-on watching her take off work gloves? He had it bad.

"It's just that it was so dark, and it all happened so fast."

"We were out there for hours."

She bit her lip, her eyes dancing. "All I'm saying is that it seems like something we should do again so we can really lean into the experience."

"Now you're talking," he said just before his mouth landed on hers.

Where the sex they'd had in the apple orchard had been dreamy and then carnal, their coupling in the apple cellar was frantic and fun. They laughed almost as much as they moaned, peeling off clothes and shucking boots. Connor used the apple crates for some creative angles and was rewarded with expressions of pure pleasure on Holly's face.

He loved that she loved her body. He couldn't tear his eyes from her voluptuous figure, from the way her dark hair contrasted with her skin and how green her hazel eyes turned when they went unfocused with lust. She was open to trying anything, even if it was goofy. Even if it meant both of them toppling off an apple crate and laughing hysterically in a tangle of naked limbs until they began kissing in earnest, and then it wasn't so funny any longer.

Connor had had passionate sex before, and he'd even tried to make love with his ex when she'd complained that he barely looked at her during sex, but he'd never had fun in a way that went beyond physical pleasure. It wasn't just Holly's sweet, clenching body that he enjoyed; it was everything: her smile, the way she tucked her hair behind her ear, her throaty laugh, how her eyes looked up at him when her mouth was full.

Holly wasn't only a dynamo in bed—she was someone he could one day call his best friend. He admired her strength, respected her opinions, and hell if she didn't make him laugh more in a day than he usually did in a week.

He was filled with unexpected sadness when he realized it was a friendship that would never progress.

An hour, several knocked-over apple crates, and multiple orgasms later, they were rebuttoning their shirts, their cheeks glowing with satisfaction.

"Are you happy now that your brother is here?" Holly asked as she crouched to collect apples that had rolled out of a tipped-over crate.

Connor joined her, fitting three of the small apples in the palm of his hand. "I'm always happy to see Erikson."

"But?"

"Who said there was a *but*?"

"That line between your brows."

He sighed and gently laid the apples in the crate. "He thinks I've become distracted from the focus of the show."

"Distracted by me?" she asked, gesturing to herself with wide, innocent eyes.

Connor scooped up another handful of apples. "Yeah, you."

"Connor, it's okay to tell him what we are."

If Connor had been holding the apples, he would have dropped them again. He couldn't believe his ears. Holly had devoted her life to keeping her family secret quiet. In a literal sense their lives depended on that secrecy. It sickened Connor to imagine the hysteria and persecution that would follow if the world knew Wickeds existed. The fact that she was willing to let him share the secret with his brother was an incredible gift of trust.

Connor studied her, this woman who had given him everything, and felt humbled by how little he deserved it. What had he done for her in return? He'd brought attention to her apple farm when she'd had good reason to avoid the spotlight, and he'd hounded her until she'd had no choice but to share her secret.

Holly laid her hand on his arm. "I know Erikson will take good care of our secret. You wouldn't trust him otherwise."

Connor nodded and something twisted in his gut. He didn't know what it was, but it felt a lot like those feelings Charlotte had claimed he didn't have.

CHAPTER THIRTY-TWO

Erikson had showered and was sitting at the little table in the trailer shuffling through paperwork when Connor finally returned. His brother glanced up, looked away, and then whipped his head back. "What's the matter?"

Connor walked to the sink and filled a plastic cup with water, avoiding his brother's gaze. "What do you mean?"

"You have this look on you," Erikson said, setting the papers down. Connor turned around and leaned against the sink. "Like you're . . . happy."

Connor snorted. "I've been happy before."

"Not like this. This isn't our-show-hit-top-ratings happy. It's something else, like I'm-completed happy." Erikson's blue eyes widened. "Holy shit, it's Holly, isn't it?"

Connor didn't answer. He drained the cup and set it next to the sink.

"Are you in love with her?" Erikson pressed.

"I don't know," Connor admitted. "I don't think I deserve her."

Erikson stretched out his legs. "Don't be an idiot. You're not only a rich TV star, but you're actually a pretty decent guy."

"You don't know her. She's one of a kind."

"Hot sex?"

"I don't mean that way." The answer was yes, but hell if he was sharing that with his brother. It had never bothered him to talk sex with Erikson in the past, but if he shared details of his sex life with Holly it would feel like a betrayal. That was for him and Holly alone. "She's extraordinary. She manages this farm while watching out for her entire family. I've never met anyone like her. And neither have you."

Erikson's head lifted as if he were a dog on a scent. "Elaborate."

Connor took a seat across from him and said, "Buckle your seat belt, bro. I'm about to take you on a wild ride."

Twenty minutes later Erikson was pacing the trailer and practically vibrating with energy. "I can't believe it," he kept saying over and over. "Wickeds. Not Witches. Do you know what this means, Connor? It means there could be so much more out there that we don't know about."

It was a thought that had crossed Connor's mind more than once.

"This could pivot the entire show." At the look on Connor's face, Erikson said quickly, "Don't get me wrong. I understand why this has to be kept a secret. They'd be persecuted, possibly to death. But it doesn't mean we can't shift the focus of the show from ghosts and yetis and the Loch Ness monster to discovering other supernatural beings."

Again, Connor had entertained a similar idea before eventually dismissing it. "So that we can put other supernatural beings in a compromising position?"

"Damn," Erikson muttered, crossing his arms. "I know you're right, but *damn*. This is so extraordinary. And you've seen her power with your own eyes? It wasn't a trick or an illusion?"

"Trust me."

"Always," Erikson answered automatically. "This means the photo of the aunt was real, even though we still don't know who sent it."

"No, and that bothers me because it means someone else knows what the Celestes are. I need to tell Holly about it. Maybe she'll have some insight, maybe not, but she should know either way."

Erikson nodded in agreement. "So Holly can manipulate weather events, but what about the others? What about the curly-haired elf with the bad attitude?"

"You mean Winter? The one you got all muddy with?"

"Yeah. Winter."

"She glimpses the future." Connor described the rest of the family's "gifts"—or curses, as Holly put it.

"I get it now," Erikson finally said, sitting back down. "I get why Charlotte called me out here. You *are* hiding something; you *are* putting something ahead of the show, and I agree that it's the right thing to do. But it's not just that, Con. You're different here. I can feel your attention slipping from the show in other ways."

Connor raked his hand through his hair. He felt it too, but he was sure his passion and drive for the show would return as soon as he left. It was his wife and baby all rolled into one.

Involuntarily, a vision of Holly as his wife flashed in his mind. Connor immediately shut it down. *No.* He'd worked too hard for his show and come too far. He wouldn't let down his brother, Charlotte, or his crew. He couldn't have both Holly and *Grimm Reality*. He chose *Grimm Reality*, just as he always did.

"I'll be fine," Connor said. "In fact, I wanted to get your opinion on the shots for this last episode."

They chatted logistics for a few minutes until Connor became aware of raised voices. He glanced toward the trailer door, which was slightly ajar, and frowned. He could have sworn he'd shut it.

He pushed the door open wider and looked toward the house, spotting Jeremy's big SUV parked behind Holly's car. Holly was standing on the porch with Winter at her side, gesticulating wildly, her hair blowing around her shoulders as she said something to Jeremy, who was standing two steps down. Winter's arms were crossed over her chest, and she had a murderous expression on her face. Overhead clouds rolled in from the west.

Shit.

Connor jumped down the steps and walked toward them with deliberate calm, trying to convince himself that punching Jeremy in the face wouldn't be worth the jail time. He felt Erikson at his back as he approached the heated trio.

"Jeremy," he said, not bothering with niceties, "why are you here?"

"None of your business," Jeremy snapped. He was dressed in ironed slacks and was carrying a briefcase, as if he were on his way to a client meeting.

Erikson eyed the sky as dark clouds approached with unusual speed, his expression one of awe and excitement.

"Jeremy stopped by to threaten me," Holly said icily. Her hazel eyes were stormy with anger, and Connor knew just by looking at her that she was struggling to keep her rage in check.

"Is that so?" Connor felt his own temper heating with a very primal drive to defend his partner.

"Why do you twist my words, Holly?" Jeremy accused. "I'm trying to help you. Amy found a big-shot lawyer out of Boston who's willing to take on her case. You could lose your farm if she wins. She's going after you for emotional damage and assault."

The *hell* Holly was going to lose the apple farm. The minute Jeremy left, Connor was calling in his personal law team.

"Don't forget the last part, Jeremy. You'll convince her to drop the suit only if I reconsider the show."

"I care about you, Holly." Jeremy's voice was nasally as he snatched her hand. The sight of him touching her nearly pushed Connor over the edge. Thunder boomed overhead, a sure sign Holly was feeling similarly pissed. "I don't want to see you hurt, but you will be if you don't take me up on this offer. Trust me, if you know what's good for you, you'll hear me out."

"Leave." Holly's voice was so stony that a chill raced down Connor's spine.

Jeremy studied her face, and he finally must've realized she wasn't going to budge. The pleading expression of devotion morphed into something uglier and rejected. "You'll regret this," he promised, his hands shaking. "I know more than you think I do. I can ruin your life, and if I do, you'll have no one to blame but yourself. I paid my dues. I put my time in with you and your freaky sisters, and I deserve some of the recognition and fame coming your way. You *owe* me. I have ambitions, and you, Holly, are going to help me achieve them whether you want to or not."

The guy was fucking losing it, Connor thought with fury. Connor wasn't even surprised by Jeremy's unhinged entitlement—like creepy ghost; like descendant—but if Jeremy thought he was going to harass and harangue Holly into submission, then the man didn't yet understand the concept of regret.

Holly's tone was strikingly calm in contrast to the thunderous clouds overhead. "If you come here again, I'll file a restraining order."

Jeremy's face turned mottled red, and he jerked his palm back as if to strike her. Connor lunged for him, but before he could reach him, Jeremy went flying backward, his hands clutching his nose. He landed ass-first in the dirt, and his briefcase fell open, the papers scattering to the wind. Jeremy screamed in agony, his tears mingling with the blood dripping between his fingers. Winter stood in front of Holly, her fist still curled and a look of such fierceness on her face that Connor wouldn't have been surprised to see her standing in that exact same position with a sword instead of a killer cross-jab.

Connor and Erikson hauled a sputtering and crying Jeremy to his feet and forcibly walked him to his car. Connor wrenched open the driver's side door and jammed Jeremy inside.

"Don't ever come back," he snarled.

"That bicked bitch bill be sorry," Jeremy blubbered, his hands smeared red as he failed to staunch the bleeding.

Connor leaned in close enough that Erikson couldn't hear. "Let me make myself crystal clear, Jeremy: if you bother Holly again, I will destroy you, and I don't just mean physically. I'll drive you out of business, I'll shred your reputation, and I'll sic my impressively large and well-paid legal team on you. I'll beat you down so low you'll start to feel like the scum you are. And that's not even *half* of what Holly will do to you."

"Buck you, Brimm. Bolly still lubs me. You'll see."

Connor lowered his voice further and said savagely, "Holly is *mine*. Do you understand that? *Mine*. I take care of what's mine. Don't ever forget it."

Erikson tossed the briefcase on Jeremy's lap, and Connor slammed the door shut. A moment later the SUV backed out of the driveway with reckless speed, leaving a plume of dust in its wake.

"What'd you say to make him go all pale?" Erikson asked in amusement.

Connor watched the truck until it disappeared out of view. "I told him Winter was walking over."

CHAPTER THIRTY-THREE

Holly fussed over Winter's knuckles, even though Winter had repeatedly assured her she was fine. The entire Celeste kitchen was in an uproar over the scene that had transpired outside. Missy was furious she'd missed it; Aunt Rose was trying to convince Holly to file a restraining order while Aunt Daisy made tea; Erikson was texting on his phone and occasionally casting inscrutable looks in Winter's direction; and Connor's attention was entirely focused on her. Holly could feel the intensity of his gaze from where he leaned against the counter, silently stewing about something. She glanced up at him and gave him a smile, and he smiled back, but it didn't touch his eyes.

He'd said something to Jeremy at his truck, and she would have paid good money to know what it was because Jeremy's face had paled to a sickly color, and he'd driven away so fast he'd left dust flying in the air behind him.

Holly returned her attention to Winter just as Winter's eyes went vacant and her expression blanked. Holly waited while Winter fought off the vision, her sister's hand still grasped in hers, until finally Winter blinked again.

"Anything important?" Holly asked quietly.

Winter stood abruptly. "I need to think." She left the room without a word to anyone else. Erikson's eyes followed her, a little line between his brows.

Missy sidled up to the big blond Viking and gave him a flirty smile. "I'm Missy."

Erikson flashed her one of those trademark panty-melting smiles. "Erikson."

"Oh, I know who you are." Missy hopped on the counter and crossed her bare legs. "Have you come to wrap up the show? Are you a closer?"

Erikson appeared amused by the double entendre, but unaffected. "Something like that."

"Oh Holly!" Missy cried, forgetting all about her flirtatious efforts, her eyes widening in excitement. "In all the hoopla, the aunts and I forgot to tell you something exciting! You ghost hunters are going to love this. I mean, assuming he knows all about . . ." Missy tilted her head sideways at Erikson and waggled her eyebrows at Holly.

In turn, Holly looked toward Connor, who gave her a nod.

"Yep," Holly said. "He knows we're Wickeds."

"Oh goody," Missy squealed, jumping off the counter. "Come on, come on. Let's go, Aunties," she said, grabbing one of Erikson's hands and one of Aunt Rose's as she hauled them from the room.

Holly met Connor's eyes and shrugged. Something was definitely bothering him, because although he put his hand on her lower back as they followed the others into the living room, he didn't say a single word.

Holly and Connor sat in the love seat while Aunt Daisy and Aunt Rose took the couch. Erikson stood against the unlit fireplace and scanned the floor-to-ceiling wall of books with something like delight on his face. Prickles waddled over and stopped to sniff Erikson's boot before curling into a ball at his feet and promptly falling asleep.

Missy lifted Autumn Celeste's blank journal from the coffee table and reverently carried it to their aunts, presenting it as if it were made of gold leaf. "While you guys were off punching Holly's smarmy ex, the aunties were working their little Wicked asses off."

Aunt Rose sighed. There was no point in reprimanding Missy's language. She was completely incorrigible.

"Shouldn't we wait for your other sister?" Erikson interrupted.

Missy looked around as if surprised that Winter wasn't there, then shrugged. "Nah, she disappears all the time." At Erikson's unsure expression, Missy flipped her curly hair over her shoulder and said, "No, Wickeds can't literally disappear. I meant it in the normal sense. At least, I don't think Wickeds can disappear." She turned to the aunts. "Can some? No, never mind—let's get to the good stuff." Missy held out her arms with a flourish. "Commence, Aunts."

"Well, now." Aunt Rose fished for her reading glasses in the pocket of her sweater and set them on her nose. "Daisy and I suspected that Autumn cursed her journals so that no one but another Wicked could read them."

Connor shot Holly a surprised look, and she winked at him.

"Autumn was more familiar with her powers than we are these hundreds of years later. It took Rose and me quite a while to figure out how she could have done it."

"We even had to call old Gerta," Aunt Daisy said with a scowl, "and now we owe her Holly's firstborn child."

"*What!*" Holly screeched.

Aunt Daisy giggled. "I'm joking, Holly. A bit of ghoulish humor for our guests."

Holly's heart was still pounding. "You can't say stuff like that. You know I don't understand how all this Wicked stuff works."

"That's a failing on our part," Aunt Rose reflected. "Our family line decided to live quietly, and Daisy and I accepted the choice of our ancestors without questioning it. Ultimately, all it did was isolate the family from other Wickeds and burden you girls with rebound powers."

"Who is Gerta?" Connor asked.

"Like, the only other Wicked we know," Missy said. She made a hurry-up gesture. "Can we get on with the good stuff?"

Aunt Daisy sniffed. "You could use some patience, young lady."

"I could use a lot of things," Missy replied solemnly.

Aunt Rose fanned the book open so they could see the blank pages from where they sat. "With Gerta's help, we figured out that Autumn cursed the ink—we believe she had the same power as you, Missy. She decayed the pigment so that only a reversal of the decay would reveal the words."

Holly's eyebrows flew upward. "Can Missy *reverse* illness?"

Missy seemed flabbergasted. "I don't think so."

"No." Aunt Daisy shook her head, her white braid beginning to fall from its snug coil. "She can't. It took us a while to find a work-around, and the answer was rather simple. She'll need to decay Autumn's curse instead."

It took Holly a moment to wrap her brain around that. "So essentially Missy needs to attack Autumn's curse, not reverse it."

"Cool," Missy said, bounding over and kneeling by the book. "Let's give it a whirl."

Holly glanced over at Connor and then Erikson, who were so riveted by what they were watching that Holly thought the house could have collapsed on top of their heads and they wouldn't have noticed until the rubble blocked their view of the journal. It was kind of cute, she thought. It would be like if someone had spent their entire life trying to prove basketball existed, and now someone was about to play a real live basketball game right in front of them.

Missy dramatically rubbed her hands together and laid them flat on the pages and closed her eyes. The two Grimm brothers caught their breath as a dark mist skated over the blank pages of the book, and like magic, words began to appear.

"Holy shit," Erikson breathed.

After a minute of concentration, Missy removed her hands. The vibrant, taunting Missy was gone, her cheeks drained of color and her body limp. Holly stood to help her onto the couch between the aunts, where she slumped on Aunt Daisy's shoulder and closed her eyes.

There was always a price to be paid for thwarting the natural intent of the powers. When the power wasn't used for its intended purpose of chaos and destruction, the practicing Wicked suffered instead. It was yet another check on them, another way the universe ensured compliance. Holly had to bear migraines when she used power that didn't hurt anyone. Missy suffered burnouts where she looked like she'd just gone two rounds with cholera. When Aunt Rose mixed an elixir to help and heal rather than harm, her hands cramped with excruciating pain for a full day afterward. It was why Holly was so sparing with the migraine tonics, why Missy had refused the hangover cure, and why Aunt Rose had spent their childhood with lines of pain radiating from her eyes. She'd given the girls tonics to mute their powers and keep them hidden from the Shadow Council, and in return she'd suffered nearly every day for years.

"Will you read it, Holly?" Aunt Daisy asked. "I can't, and Aunt Rose doesn't see as well as she used to."

Holly nodded and lifted the book from her aunt's gloved hands. Her own hands trembled slightly as she read the date aloud. "'January 2, 1820. Yesterday was the first day of the new year, and I have many hopes and dreams for the coming months.'" Holly quickly scanned the entry, which was a boring account of how much wood was left and whether Thomas had actually liked the knitted socks Autumn had gifted him or if he'd only said he did. "It's just a normal journal entry," she said, fanning the pages as she searched for spring or summer entries that might have coincided with the night Councilman Miller saw something.

Holly flipped past a page and spotted the name Miller and thumbed back. When she saw the dates on the pages, she swallowed hard. June 1st—one of their nights of celebration—and June 2nd. She looked up and met Connor's eyes. Then she took a deep breath and began to read.

June 1, 1820

Thomas is terribly ill, and I fret day and night. His fever has not broken, his hands are so dry, and his body so hot that I live in

eternal fear that he will die and leave me on this cursed earth with-
out him. If I knew a Witch, I would commission a healing potion,
but I know of none that do not live far away in my homeland.

Tonight is the first, and I shall make an offering for his life. I
am but a curse, and what my husband needs is a blessing.

The silence in the room was all encompassing—not a single person shifted or spoke. Holly read the next page, dated June 2, 1820.

Last night was, as life often is, both a curse and a blessing. Whilst
I gazed into the fire and made my offering, I peered through the
smoke and saw the form of Councilman Miller watching me, his
lips twisted with sick satisfaction. He had come late into the night
to inquire about Thomas's welfare, or so he claimed, but I do not
believe that was his true intent, for in his hand he held the paper-
work for the sale of our land. I believe he wished to coerce Thomas
into signing away our property in the midst of his delirium.
Miller stoops so low, I wonder that he can straighten his back at
the end of the day.

Chills raced down her arms. Councilman Miller's ghost had visited on the same offering night more than two hundred years later,
appearing through the smoke of the fire in a similar manner.

He prayed aloud to God and demanded I heal those in the village
that I had made ill with my witchcraft. I tried to explain that I
did not harm anyone and that even my own husband was ill, but
his smile only widened. That was when I understood his inten-
tion. Miller has not thought well of me since he learned I did not
take my husband's name, and he blames me for Thomas's resis-
tance to selling. He does not understand how Thomas could love
someone like me.

This morning as I walked the fields by the small babbling
brook, I saw it: an apple tree. We have not had any luck planting

them here, but there it was, fully formed and grown overnight, a single fat, juicy apple hanging from its branches, even though it is only spring and far too early for such fruit. I knew my offering had been answered.

Holly met Missy's alarmed gaze. Her sister had roused enough to whisper, "Oh shit. I've been asking for some really wonky stuff at the offerings. I just thought they were tradition. I didn't know they were *real*."

"Me neither," Holly said, feeling a bit lied to. What had they been messing with all this time that they knew nothing about?

I plucked the apple, and later that morning I was inspired to curse it with a disease that would kill whatever illness was slowly taking my husband's life. He was too weak to eat the apple, so I mashed it finely and spoon-fed it to him. To my immense relief, he got well rapidly—so rapidly that by dinnertime the fever had broken, and he sat and took his supper with much more strength.

I love my Thomas, but he does not know what I am. I fear Councilman Miller shall tell him.

Holly flipped to the next page, dated a week later.

June 9, 1820

I saved the seeds from the miraculous apple and planted one in the ground by the front of the house. The next day it had sprouted into a fully formed tree. My husband was astonished, but he thought it was a blessing from God. Maybe it was.

Councilman Miller returned tonight. I had not heard from him and had foolishly hoped he had reconsidered, although I should have known better. He despises me. I believe he despises all women. If we were in my home country, he would lead the crusade to burn me alive.

He had heard Thomas was well and had come to convince him to sign the papers. He immediately noticed the apple tree, which had not been there the week previous, and tried to use it as proof that I am a Witch, but Thomas has a good heart, and he would not hear of it and sent him away.

I do not think that is the last we will hear from him.

Winter had slipped into the room and perched on the arm of the couch beside Holly, reading over her shoulder as Holly turned to the next page to continue the saga. Holly was almost afraid to discover how it ended. She knew something would result in Councilman Miller's death. Would this journal implicate Autumn or exonerate her?

Autumn had only been trying to live her life in peace, as Holly and her sisters did. Holly ached for the woman who'd been persecuted across two different countries for being different, who'd lost her family to that very hatred, only to find more of it at her new home.

Holly scanned the next few entries, and her cheeks paled. "This is it," she whispered. "This is what we've been looking for."

CHAPTER THIRTY-FOUR

In all his years of ghost hunting, Connor had never been so committed to discovering the truth about a ghost's past. He sat angled on the antique brocade love seat, his hands clasped between his knees and his focus riveted on Holly as she read the diary of a woman who'd been dead a hundred and fifty years. Her hair was falling over half her face, and he thought she was the most beautiful and bewitching (bewicked-ing?) woman he'd ever laid eyes on. How the hell was he supposed to move on to his next show and leave her behind?

It didn't matter how—the point was he *would*, and if her ghost problem was solved it would help ease his conscience.

Holly cleared her throat and continued reading.

June 12, 1820

> *Thomas caught Councilman Miller sawing down the apple tree in the middle of the night. 'Twas an ugly scene. Councilman Miller wished to take the tree to the council to "prove" that it was unnatural and so was I. He promised Thomas that if we did not*

*sell the land, he would see me burn, and my dear, dear Thomas
nearly murdered him on the spot.*

*After Councilman Miller left, I sat down and wrote him
a letter, begging him to cease his witch hunt. He has drawn in
my neighbor, Mary, and she has vouched that I am a witch in a
letter to the newspaper, but the editor is Thomas's cousin, and he
refused to publish it. I fear what my husband will do if Councilman Miller does not halt his crusade against me. In the end I did
not send the letter, simply because I do not think it will make a
difference.*

June 13, 1820

*After much thought, I have planted the remaining seeds from the
apple that cured my husband, this time by the babbling brook
near the original tree. Once grown, the trees present as any other,
so I do not think Councilman Miller will be able to use them
against us. Besides, it is none of Councilman Miller's business
what we do on our land—which will remain our land. I will not
be cowed into silence because of a hateful man's threats. I almost
wish to see the look on his face when they grow overnight.*

September 20, 1820

*Councilman Miller has been trying to turn the town against
me. He is rich, powerful, and without conscience, so he has been
successful in many ways, and I have become ostracized, as has
Thomas. Thomas does not care. He looks upon those who avoid us
with scorn and disgust. I have never loved him more.*

*In other ways Councilman Miller's mission has failed. He
has accused me of witchcraft and has pointed to the apples and
my husband's recovery as evidence. He has even blamed the torrential rains in May on me (I could not move the weather if I*

tried; that power belonged to my sister). So while many have turned their backs, there are other, more despairing souls who have begun visiting on the sly, asking me to heal their illnesses.

It began with a woman who was desperate for relief from a burden she could not carry without dying herself. I cursed one of the apples and gave it to her against my better judgment—for kindness from people like me is never appreciated or returned. After that, news spread among the women, and slowly more and more have come to me.

I think Thomas knows, but he does not say anything to me. I am not sure he wants to know the truth of what I am and what I do.

October 15, 1820

Councilman Miller is dead, and his son claims it was me who killed him. In fact, it was the evil in his own heart.

Holly's eyes met Connor's over the top of the book, her cheeks flushed with excitement and her hands trembling so finely the pages quivered. Connor wanted to hold her, but he wasn't sure if she would appreciate the gesture in front of her family, so instead he gave her an encouraging smile, because in truth he was trembling a little himself.

A young woman, Anne, came to see me for a mysterious illness. I did not know what ailed her, so I cursed an apple to kill whatever evil resided in her body. I believed it harmless to Anne because she has the purest soul I have ever met.

I had the apple in a basket with a little white cloth covering it and was about to walk to Anne's house when my husband called for me. I set the basket on the steps in the dooryard and went to him. By the time I returned, nearly an hour had passed. I opened the front door and found Councilman Miller standing at the bottom of the steps, wearing his calling hat and fine coat. I presume he'd come to attempt to blackmail us again but instead had seen the apple and eaten it! He, a councilman who holds the public opinion that women are second-class citizens because a woman could not resist the forbidden fruit!

I gasped in horror as he finished the apple and held the core in his hand, his clear eye glaring evilly at me, and I knew in that moment he would die. Councilman Miller is evil inside and out, more rotten to the core than any apple that falls from a tree. Indeed, a moment later he began to tremble and then shake. His eyes widened, and his body stiffened and he said, "Y-y-you poisoned me, Witch! I shall have my vengeance." And then he could speak no longer.

Oh, it was such a hideous sight! I despise Councilman Miller, but I do not wish to harm others, and as his body convulsed and foam collected on his bluish lips, all I could think was that I had interfered too much. If I have children, I vow that I will teach them to live small lives and use small power. The cost otherwise is simply too great.

When Councilman Miller was dead on the ground, I kicked away the apple core and called for Thomas. Councilman Miller's son blames me, but the evidence of seizure on the body is clear enough that I have been vindicated by the doctor.

Even though Councilman Miller is gone, I still feel his presence in the orchards, malevolent and hateful. I will attempt to banish him to the other side, but I fear his spirit may find its way back. He is not a man who will ever attain peace.

๛ ๛

The entire room sat in silence for several moments before Missy broke it by saying, "Well, damn."

"Yeah, damn," Connor agreed. As was the case more often than not, the truth was far more complicated than a simple guilty verdict. Yes, Autumn had cursed the apple to kill, but it had been intended to help another woman, not meant for the councilman. The councilman had stolen the apple and eaten what was not his, and because he was so bitter and hateful, it had killed him. Neither he nor Autumn was completely in the clear, but if Connor had to lay the blame at one person's feet, it would definitely be the councilman's. Autumn had been operating with a good heart; the councilman had acted with greed and spite.

"What do we do?" Holly asked him as she gently closed the journal. "Is this enough to release Councilman Miller's spirit?"

Connor rubbed his temples. "We can try. The truth might be enough to set him free."

"It's not a truth you can share on your show."

"No," Connor agreed. "We will have to reenact it for the camera, with altered facts."

Missy had recovered some from the exertion of revealing the text of the journal, and was now sitting between the aunts, her knee bouncing with impatience. "How do we get the ghostly apple gobbler to show up again? It will be so scary if he does. I might need someone big and strong to be at my side." She blinked innocently across the room at Erikson.

Yeah, right. Missy could hold her own against a ghost as well, if not better, than either he or Erikson. Her ancestor had proven that when it came to true evil, Wickeds were more than a match.

Connor studied his brother to see how he'd react to the obvious come-on. Erikson was a ladies man to the core. While Connor had had a few stilted relationships over the years, Erikson was all about whirlwind fun. Except Missy was *not* someone Connor wanted Erikson sleeping with. Connor did not need that kind of complication coming between him and Holly.

To his surprise, Erikson was smiling at Missy, but without any of his usual flirtatious heat. "Good thing you have Winter," he said, his gaze turning to the fierce redhead sitting on the arm of the couch. "I just watched her knock out a full-grown man without breaking a sweat. A ghost will be nothing."

In typical fashion, Winter's expression was difficult to read. Connor could not imagine a set of twins with more opposite personalities than Missy and Winter.

Missy sighed. "It's true. If Win can scare all her teachers into giving her A's, then she can scare Councilman Miller back to hell."

Aunt Rose's mouth dropped open. "You didn't do that, did you, Winter?"

Winter glared at Missy before muttering, "I couldn't help it if some of the teachers felt intimidated by my presence."

Erikson gave a bark of laughter, and Holly grinned fondly at her sister before returning her focus to Councilman Miller. "So how *do* we get him to come back around so we can tell him the truth? You Grimm brothers are the resident ghost hunters. Surely you have some ideas?"

"What made him show up the first time?" Erikson asked.

Connor shook his head. "I don't know. He's been on the property since the power surge—"

"Power surge?"

Holly nodded. "Connor figured out that the ghost sightings started four years ago, after Aunt Rose's masking potion stopped working. He and I think the sudden surge of power was enough to allow Miller back into our plane."

Erikson glanced between Connor and Holly. "Potion?"

They spent the next few minutes catching Erikson up, and when they finished, he was fidgeting with excitement. "Your theory isn't half bad. A burst of supernatural power could provide a temporary pathway for the ghost to slip between planes, like a blast of air pushing aside the curtains between worlds."

"Well, how do we get him back to where he belongs?" Missy asked. "Power-burst his ass again?"

Connor's gaze fell on Holly's mouth, where she was worrying her bottom lip with her teeth. "I think Holly is the key."

"Me?" Holly squeaked.

"He thinks you're Autumn. Ghosts don't live the same linear timeline as the rest of us. To him it may feel like a matter of days since he died, and it's possible you look enough like Autumn that he believes you *are* her. When he saw you at the fire, just as he first saw her the night of June first, 1820, it triggered him."

"Ooh, so Holly can be bait!" Missy cried. "Shall we reenact the fire? Dance around a cauldron? Gallop in circles on broomsticks?"

She was joking, but it wasn't the worst idea. "Miller was convinced Autumn truly was a witch," Connor said, sharing a look with Erikson and shrugging. "Playing into his misconceptions might actually draw him out."

Winter scowled. "You have to be kidding."

Erikson seemed to enjoy the idea of the women dressing in Halloween-store witch costumes and holding broomsticks more than he should have. "Got any pointy hats?"

"This is offensive to our kind," Holly said with a sniff, "and offensive to Witches too. However, if pandering to his stereotypes and hate will get us an audience and a chance to boot this loser back to where he belongs, I'll do it."

That's my girl, Connor thought. Always stepping up to the plate and doing what needed to be done.

And hell if those three words didn't resonate with him the rest of the day.

CHAPTER THIRTY-FIVE

Holly glared at her reflection in the mirror. "Why is it that every time you walk into my room with an armful of clothing, I know I'm going to hate the end result? And why is this skirt so damned short?"

"It's called a *sexy* witch costume, Holly. Don't you know anything?"

Holly looked over the cheap black costume with the jagged, thigh-high hem and long, draping sleeves. Missy had planted a large purple hat with a plastic spider on the brim on top of Holly's head. "Why do you have so many witch costumes?"

Missy was wearing a pair of black fishnet stockings with knee-high boots and a similar Halloween store costume and hat. "Because I know how to have fun on Halloween," she answered, leaning past Holly to check her black lipstick in the mirror. "Where's Winter? I have another costume for her on the bed."

"Yeah, she walked by and took one look and beat it."

"That girl! We're twins and I still don't understand her. Come on—let's see how the aunts are getting along. I spotted Aunt Rose pulling fake spider webs out of the Halloween decoration box down in the cellar."

Holly felt ridiculous as she followed Missy downstairs, where her two aunts stood chatting with Connor and Erikson in the living room. The aunts were dressed head to toe in black and had stretched fake spider webbing over their shoulders and into their hair. A plastic cauldron that they used for Halloween candy was tucked underneath Aunt Daisy's arm.

While the two Grimm brothers were occupied, Holly had an uninterrupted moment to study them. Erikson was broad shouldered, with sun-touched hair and lake-blue eyes that occasionally probed the room as if he were a treasure hunter and knew there was gold hidden somewhere. He must've been a Viking in another life, Holly thought. Other than their strong chins and the way they could focus with unnerving intensity, Holly found very little resemblance between Connor and his brother.

Connor was listening to Aunt Rose talk with the single-minded concentration that made the recipient of his attention feel like the only person in the world. His eyes were on Aunt Rose's face, his body turned toward hers as he absorbed every single word. His hair was mussed, and he hadn't shaved in two days—the result being enough dark scruff to make Holly's mouth water. He'd pulled on a black North Face sweatshirt to combat the evening chill, and Holly was jealous of his jeans and work boots. She glanced down at her skimpy "witch" outfit and scowled again.

Charismatic and intense, Connor was unlike any man Holly had ever known. She thought she could spend years with him and never tire of his insatiable curiosity and even more insatiable appetite in bed. He was unfailingly kind and thoughtful, but perhaps more than anything else, he'd accepted her for exactly who she was. There had been no hesitation, no period of time where he had to convince himself he wanted to be with her *despite* her being Wicked. He'd accepted the news without a bat of the eye and then had proceeded to show her how little it bothered him by making love to her. Holly suspected there were very few men like Connor Grimm in the world.

Aunt Rose finished her story and Connor turned to her, although she had the feeling he'd sensed her there all along. The moment his eyes met hers, she felt a burst of belonging so strong it took her breath away.

Shit. This guy was going to break her heart after all.

This was *exactly* why she never threw caution to the wind. Because then big, sexy, intense ghost hunters came along and made you fall in love with them right before they left you forever to go chase spirits.

The blood drained from Holly's cheeks. In love? Had she just thought herself in love with Connor Grimm? No. That was impossible, because she would never fall for a man she couldn't have, because that would be stupid, and Holly had already established that she was not stupid.

Connor grinned at her, his teeth a flash of white against the darkness of his scruff, and Holly almost collapsed in dismay. She *was* stupid! Somehow, despite all of her reassurances that she was perfectly capable of keeping things between them casual, she'd fallen in love with Connor Grimm.

In full panic mode, Holly plastered a wide smile on her face and shouted, "Are we ready?"

She and Connor left the room last. As soon as the others' backs were through the door, Connor wrapped an arm around her waist and nuzzled into her neck. "What's the matter?"

"Nothing!" she said cheerfully. Too cheerfully. Holly was never that peppy.

He planted a soft kiss just below her ear. "Liar."

"Maybe I'm worried this won't work and Councilman Miller won't show his face."

"Maybe. But you aren't."

Holly shut the door behind them and said, "What makes you think you know me so well?" It came out a little pissier than she'd intended, and Connor's brows lifted in surprise. Holly pushed off his arm. "Whatever. Let's get this over with."

He bounded down the steps after her, easily catching up with her urgent stride. "What's the matter with you?"

"With me?" she asked, whirling around on him. "What's the matter with me? I don't know, Connor. Maybe it's the fact that I'm sleeping with a guy who's leaving as soon as his filming wraps up."

His eyes narrowed. "What are you saying?"

"I'm saying I'm an idiot, that's all. I'm an idiot."

"For sleeping with me?"

No. For loving him.

Holly sighed, the wild panic slowly bleeding into resignation. "Let's go." She wasn't truly angry with him. He'd been nothing but honest about his show being the most important thing in his life. She'd known that, and she'd still decided to be reckless with her heart. She had only herself to blame.

They continued into the orchard, both lost in their own thoughts. The sun had sunk behind the horizon, leaving soft red streaks in the otherwise darkening sky. The first few stars had popped into view, and the mosquitoes were buzzing in delight at the banquet of human flesh. Fresh-cut grass and hay mingled in the air and Holly breathed in deeply. A mosquito went up her nose.

"Gahh! Missy, can't you kill the mosquitoes," Holly complained when they'd caught up with the group. "We'll be lucky if we aren't bloodless corpses by the time we get the fire going."

"Winter yelled at me last time I did that, and said I was depriving dragonflies of food. She also said a bunch of stuff about collapsing ecosystems and doomsday, but it was kind of boring so I didn't pay attention." Missy shifted the armful of brooms so she could see Holly better. "Where is Win, anyway?"

"I don't know. Use your twin intuition."

"Snippy, snippy. You know that's not a thing we have."

They reached the small clearing where they'd had their summer celebration, and while the brothers tossed brush from the pile into the pit and started the fire, Missy handed out broomsticks to Holly and the aunts.

"Remember, we're going to say, 'Hocus-pocus, I'm a witch; stew that frog and curse that bitch.'"

"I am *not* saying that." Aunt Daisy sniffed as she settled into the camping chair Connor had set up for her before tending to the fire.

"No one in this family is any fun," Missy complained. She stuck the broomstick between her legs and began galloping around the

Grimms as if she were a child with a horsehead stick. She threw her head back and cackled in her best imitation of a wicked witch, and Holly couldn't help but laugh. Missy was good for them. They'd be a sorry lot of stern Wickeds without her. She supposed she should tell her that some time.

By the time the fire was roaring and popping and licking at the night sky, it was nearly black out, and even the fireflies had settled into stillness. The smoke cleared away most of the mosquitoes, but Holly was already itching like crazy from dozens of earlier bites. She and Connor hadn't spoken much, but she felt his thoughtful gaze on her more often than not. She knew if they were alone, he'd weasel the confession out of her, and she didn't think her ego could handle telling him she loved him, only to watch him walk away.

"Well, we can't wait forever for Winter," Missy finally declared. Her head cocked. "Oh, maybe I *do* have twin intuition. I sense she's coming."

"Or you heard that branch snap just as I did," Holly said dryly.

A moment later Winter appeared in the small radius of light. She was wearing black jeans, a black sweatshirt, and a black baseball cap.

"Baseball cap does not say 'Witch.'" Missy plucked a witch hat out of the jumbled supplies on the ground and held it out to Winter. "Can you imagine Stacy wearing that ugly baseball hat?"

"Stacy wouldn't be caught dead in any of this," Holly pointed out.

Missy scowled. "It's true. That stupid Witch is a clothing designer's wet dream. Even her brothers walk around like fashion gods. Next time, I want to be born a Witch. They have all the fun." Missy shoved the hat toward Winter. "It's the least you can do since you decided to dress like a burglar."

Winter grumbled but removed the baseball cap, allowing her red hair to tumble down her shoulders and back. Holly noticed Erikson's eyes on Winter as she jammed the witch hat on top of her head, scowling.

"Okay, time to start the show," Missy cried, clapping her hands. "Boys, sit back and watch how it's done. Wickeds, it's time to be wicked witches. Everyone grab a broom. Oh my God, Winter, don't look at me like that. I'm not going to make you pretend to ride it. Are we all set? Right, now Holly and I are going to dance around the fire while I play spooky Halloween music on my phone."

Holly chose the broom they used in the barn, the paint worn away in the center where it was often handled. She peered into the darkness. Nothing was there yet but . . . she met Connor's eyes and gave him a slight nod. This might work after all.

Missy pulled a flask from the spider-printed garter around her thigh and took a swig. "Who else wants some fortifying brandy?"

Connor, Erikson, and Aunt Rose took her up on the offer, and then Missy pressed "Play" on the Halloween music, which consisted of a lot of spooky noises and TV-show variety *woooooooos*. Missy took another gulp of brandy and passed it to Holly. Holly shrugged and tilted the flask to her lips, the liquid burning all the way to her belly.

"Let's play 'Witch's Brew!'" Missy squealed, thumbing through the music on her phone. "Do you remember hearing that in elementary music class? We had to remember all the things the witch put in her brew."

Holly did remember, but it wasn't as fond a memory as it clearly was for Missy. Halloween had always made her slightly uncomfortable as the holiday where people celebrated the very Wickeds and Witches their ancestors had relentlessly persecuted centuries before.

A moment later the song began blaring, and maybe it was the shot of brandy or maybe it was Missy's enthusiasm, but soon Holly was dancing around the fire with Missy and breathlessly belting out the song.

Holly threw her head back and laughed when Missy grabbed Aunt Rose and tugged her toward the fire, swinging their aunt around as she joined in with singing the lyrics of the children's song. Holly was having so much fun she almost forgot why they were there. It took her a moment to recognize what was happening when a frigid January chill swept the clearing.

Connor was suddenly beside her, his hand on her arm as he stared into the darkness where a form had materialized.

"He's here."

CHAPTER THIRTY-SIX

Connor hadn't been able to concentrate on anything other than Holly's earlier declaration that she was an idiot for sleeping with him. What had she meant by it? Did she regret their time together? Had he done something to upset her?

While sitting on a log and breathing in the crisp air, he'd watched Missy gradually draw Holly out of her shell until she was giggling and dancing around the fire, her little witch skirt clinging to her thighs and her dark hair flying around her back as she screamed the lyrics to a children's Halloween song. The orange glow of the fire had draped around her, and she'd looked like a pagan goddess from another time. He could easily imagine her dancing around this very fire a thousand years earlier.

His heart fisted when she threw her head back and laughed, her eyes sparkling with joy and her throat bare to the night.

"Your Wicked is sexy," Erikson said in his ear.

Connor turned on him with murder in his eyes, and Erikson threw up his hands and chuckled softly. "Yeah, that's what I thought. You need to reevaluate your life, brother. It's not every day you meet a woman who makes you look like a kicked puppy."

Connor scoffed. "I don't look like a kicked puppy."

"You're practically whimpering, and I can't blame you. Like you said, she's one of a kind."

"We have three days of filming left, and then we're packing up and moving on." Connor couldn't tear his eyes from her, even as he talked to Erikson. "It was never going to last."

"Have you asked yourself why that is?"

Connor finally looked away from the Wickeds dancing in the moonlight. "What do you mean? Relationships don't work for us. We're constantly on the move."

"True." Erikson reached for a stray apple branch on the ground and began twirling it between his hands. "We've built an awesome show. We've accomplished everything we've ever dreamed of, and we haven't stopped traveling since we were old enough to escape our parents. Have you ever wondered why we push ourselves so hard, never resting, never setting down roots?"

"I know why *I* do. I want to normalize the paranormal so kids like us have a shot at a regular life. So that their parents look at them with love instead of disappointment and fear. So that when they're adults, they actually *have* a relationship with their parents."

"Yeah, that's the noble thing we keep telling ourselves." Erikson leaned back and let the stick fall to the ground. "It's probably how it started, but that's not the reason we keep moving from location to location, constantly filming and refusing to grow. Refusing to let go. Refusing to see what's right in front of us." Erikson let his eyes touch on Holly for a moment. "When it comes down to it, Con, we're still scared nine-year-olds running from the ghosts of our past."

"No, we aren't! We're not running from shit. We *chase* ghosts. We go where no one else will."

"We never confronted the ghost at our childhood home," Erikson said flatly. "We've been avoiding our past for years, trying so hard to prove that we're normal instead of embracing the fact that we're different. Look at them." He nodded toward Holly and Missy and Rose dancing around the fire. "They've at least accepted who they are, and it's a lot fucking scarier than what we are. Maybe it's time we do the same."

"What are you saying?"

Erikson rested his elbows on his knees, his eyes passionate as they bored into Connor's. "I'm saying maybe it's time we stop chasing everyone else's ghosts. Maybe it's time we accept what happened to us and move on. *Grow.*"

Connor didn't have a chance to respond because a chill swept over the clearing. The air plummeted to a temperature so bone cold that he instantly recognized it as spectral.

He jumped to his feet and was at Holly's side in a moment. "He's here."

She nodded, her eyes probing the darkness.

"Do you know what you're going to say?"

Again she nodded. "How will he know I'm telling the truth?" They'd agreed that Holly, acting as Autumn, would share the story of the apple mix-up. There was a chance the truth would dissolve Miller's tether of rage, although Connor wasn't going to hold his breath.

Connor hesitated. "It's hard to explain, but I believe he'll just know. There's a frequency to truth we can't recognize on this plane. Whether it sets him free is another story."

A shape materialized in the darkness, and Councilman Miller drifted toward the fire. No matter how many times Connor saw a ghost, he was always struck with the same cold dread. Every hair on his body stood as if he were being electrocuted. It was a distinct sensation, and the power of it was a crude barometer of the ghost's strength. Councilman Miller was an usually powerful specter, his energy tinged with such hatred that Connor tasted iron in his mouth.

Jonathan Miller looked as all Connor's interviewees had described him, wearing a sharp hat and finely tailored coat. The spirit had no substance—light passed straight through him—and still Connor swore flames from the fire flickered in the man's eyes. This was someone who'd wielded an enormous amount of power over others during his lifetime. He'd used his status and wealth to manipulate and oppress—and he'd gotten away with it until Autumn Celeste. The strength of Miller's greed and entitlement had allowed him to continue his reign of terror even after death, but Connor knew the ghost was once again going to meet his match in a Celeste woman.

"Witch," the councilman hissed, his voice seeming to come from every direction around them.

Connor's fists flexed. It was a pretty parlor trick, but he was unimpressed.

Councilman Miller floated closer to Holly, his ghostly eyes burning with animosity. "You dare to dance about in wickedness in *my* town, clothed to tempt men into sin. I should have brought charges of indecency and witchcraft against you. Thomas would not have scorned my deal if he weren't bespelled."

"Ugh, gag." Missy made a retching noise from the other side of the fire. "You're a piece of work, pal. This is *our* town now, and you're floating around like some old-timey weirdo pretending to be a big shot, when everyone knows you're nothing but a sexist pig and rapist excuser." She turned to Winter. "Did I miss anything?"

"Probably a lot," Winter said stonily, "but we don't have all night."

Holly stood strong and sure, Councilman Miller's rage never wavering from her face despite Missy's excellent character recital. Holly must've truly resembled Autumn Celeste to command the spirit's focus while women he would consider inferior raked him over the coals. Holly lifted her chin and faced him down. "You killed yourself."

Councilman Miller blinked, confused by her assertion and the truth he heard in it. "I would never."

"You stole the apple off Autumn's porch, the one wrapped in the white cloth in the basket."

"I didn't steal anything."

"Stealing is taking something that is not yours. I know people like you think laws and morals only apply to the less fortunate, but that doesn't change reality. You *stole* her apple and ate it. She had cursed the apple so that it would destroy evil, and when you ate the apple, it did its job." Her voice was strong and pure, the truth of her words ringing in the clearing. "Autumn Celeste had no intention of ending your life. You killed yourself through your own greed."

The ghost appeared thunderstruck as her words penetrated the consciousness that hovered between worlds. Connor watched expressions flit across his face. First there was vindication, for he believed himself to be right about Autumn being a wicked witch. Then there was confusion and a struggle to accept the truth. Connor held his breath. This could go one of two ways. Either Councilman Miller would embrace denial and blatantly twist the truth to suit his own needs, or he would accept the words for the fact they were. Knowing the kind of man Councilman Miller was, Connor was unsurprised when he chose the former.

"You still poisoned the apple, and whether you meant to murder me or not, you did."

"Big surprise, the jerk can't take responsibility for his own actions." Missy heaved a dramatic sigh. "I'm getting really sick of him. Grimms, how do we kick his ass back to hell?"

Exorcisms rarely worked, but then again, they rarely had five women with untold power in their midst.

"Agreed," Connor said. "It's time for this guy to go home."

CHAPTER THIRTY-SEVEN

If there was one thing Holly had learned over the years, it was that bullies rarely possessed the courage and bravery to go along with their posturing. Autumn Celeste and her husband had probably been the only people to ever stand up to the councilman. The other townspeople would have bowed to his will, either out of self-preservation or because they believed him respectable. Holly suspected Miller's perception of his own masculinity and importance was also his greatest weakness.

She took a step closer, and the ghost wavered backward, no doubt used to people quailing in his presence rather than approaching. "If you do not leave this world, I will hunt down the male heirs that carry your name, for I am not Autumn Celeste, but her descendent, and two hundred years have passed while you have been caught between worlds. When I have found these male descendants of yours, I will curse them all."

Councilman Miller's eyes narrowed into slits. "I'll see you burn first."

She ignored him. "I will curse your descendants so that they are poor and . . ." Holly tried to think of something else that would piss off a man like Councilman Miller, who believed men were the only worthy sex. "I will curse them to fall in love with Witches and only have daughters!" she exclaimed triumphantly.

Councilman Miller sucked in a breath. "You would not."

Holly glanced at her two sisters. "Would we?"

Missy blew the ghost a kiss. "I already have my eye on a gem named Ryan Miller. I would consider it an honor to destroy your genetic legacy."

Councilman Miller threw his head back and howled with rage. The sound was so full of anger and fury and bitter resentment that it bent the air around them, causing the blazing fire to die down. Holly threw up an invisible buffer of air and the fire instantly sprang back to life while the world outside their bubble quaked.

"Holly, the disturbance is causing the fabric between planes to thin," Connor said in her ear.

He was right. Holly's eyes widened as the air behind the councilman wavered as if being viewed through the heat of a grill. Beyond the haze, Holly glimpsed darkness, cool, beckoning, and seductive: a place where magic was the norm rather than an anomaly.

"Can you push him through?"

Holly tore her eyes from the warped curtain and focused on the grounding familiarity of Connor's face. "I don't know," she answered honestly. Autumn had tried to force Miller to the other side but hadn't fully succeeded, and *she'd* known what she was doing.

"Together," Missy said confidently as she took Holly's hand. Winter's compact body appeared on her other side, and she gripped Holly's free palm.

"Come on, aunts," Missy ordered. Rose held Missy's other hand while Winter rested her palm on Daisy's bare arm. All five Wickeds stared down the howling, twisted form of Councilman Miller.

"We'll feed you energy," Missy said, giving Holly's fingers a squeeze.

"Do you know how to do that?"

"Nope, but now seems like a good time to try."

Holly took a deep breath, and after one last look into Connor's steady, gray eyes, she focused on Councilman Miller. For the first time in her life, she was going to give her powers free rein.

She only hoped they wouldn't gallop away with her.

As she had with the dog, Holly channeled hurricane force winds at the councilman, forcing him to bend backward toward the splitting curtain between worlds. The ghost laughed mockingly as he rippled with the pressure, his presence holding firm in their world.

Holly exhaled and everything around her muted. She could no longer hear the flames flickering or the ghost's howls or the grasshoppers' song. Terrified of what she would find after so many years of leashing her power, she breathed in again and finally, fully opened herself to what lurked within.

Power instantly flooded her veins, and it tasted of balance: love and blinding hatred, determination and acquiescence, kindness and callousness. She felt the tenderness of her family sing in her blood and tasted the syrupy darkness of Wickedness as it coated her tongue. She felt whole in a way she'd never experienced before. It was as if two parts of herself had finally been united after decades of separation, and she could walk and breathe as a completed human being once more.

All these years she'd spent suppressing her power, locking herself down, suffering the consequences. And now . . . now she was finally, entirely, completely Holly.

She rejoiced in the feeling even as a new rush of power crashed into her. The energy drawn from her family mingled with her own, stoking hers higher and higher, until she blazed like an out-of-control forest fire. She began to feel intoxicated. High.

Unstoppable.

Councilman Miller didn't stand a chance. With laughable ease she dislodged his hold on their plane. Miller's anguished shriek ripped through the clearing before she slammed him through the curtain with enough force that she wouldn't have been surprised if she'd knocked him into yet another plane. An echo boomed across the orchards as Miller disappeared.

The enticing darkness of the other side vanished, but the wind still roared around Holly, whipping her hair across her face. She felt invincible, as if she could rip a mountain from its base or drag the sun from the sky.

Her power dimmed when her sisters withdrew their hands, but not enough to bring her back to reality. Why had she always fought this side of herself? Why did Wickeds hide away when they had more power in their little fingers than most humans had in their entire bodies? She had been *born* for this, and she was never going to let anything get in her way again.

Not her family.

Not a man.

No one.

Connor's hand gripped hers harshly. She was aware of the roughness of his palm on her skin, and a small part of her resurfaced. She wanted to go to him; these weren't her *real* thoughts, but the Wickedness inside her cells had been imprisoned for too long.

Holly turned toward the fire, and when Aunt Rose saw her, she gasped and pressed her fist to her mouth. It was time Holly fulfilled her birthright and—

Nausea struck her with sickening force. Holly staggered and ripped her hand out of Connor's to press it to her belly. She fought the debilitating twisting in her stomach as Stacy appeared in the clearing, flanked by her twin brothers. All three of them were dressed as if they'd just escaped a *GQ* party, their expensive scents layering over the smoke and pine.

"Get out of here," Holly hissed, and her voice didn't sound like her own, but something colder. Something . . . not fully human.

Stacy threw up her palms, and a shimmering, waving wall of light encircled the clearing, a barrier between the power inside and the innocent world that lay beyond. Even basking in her own whirlwind of power, Holly could recognize how beautiful Stacy's magic was. It sparkled with a rainbow of colors, and the pressure of it felt warm and light in a way her own powers never did—but was no less potent for it.

Stacy strode past the fire with all the confidence of a supermodel. Holly watched her approach, the out-of-control part of her simmering with challenge. She'd never witnessed Stacy's magic before today, had never been in a position where they both might be acting exactly as nature had intended them to act. This was uncharted territory.

Stacy didn't waver or pause when Holly's winds buffeted against her. Testing. Sampling.

Stacy shimmered like her wall, the shield of magic she'd pulled around herself allowing her to move through Holly's storm. Holly considered fully letting loose. Was Stacy a match for her? Could she truly stop her?

Before Holly could decide if she wanted to go there, Stacy was in front of her. To Holly's utter shock, instead of wielding her own magic like a weapon, Stacy threw her arms around Holly's shoulders and hugged her tightly.

They both cried out at the jarring, blunting contact, but Stacy only clung to Holly harder. They began shaking so violently that they sank to their knees. Holly felt her powers begin to dim and soften, and then drain away like water in a bathtub, a slow, inexorable draw that she was terrified would leave her dead and empty inside. Stacy's protective wall collapsed, her face haggard and absent of its healthy glow, her magic temporarily muted along with all of Holly's Wicked power.

And in the silent darkness of the night, there was once again balance.

Holly held onto Stacy for several long moments, trembling with the whiplash of having unimaginable power suddenly wink out of existence, leaving her little more than a vacant shell.

Her nose was pressed into Stacy's perfect corkscrew curls, and she could smell the Witch's expensive, lightly scented shampoo. Holly opened her eyes, and the first thing she noticed was that Stacy's stilettos somehow didn't have a lick of mud on the heels.

Of course, she thought dryly, but she wasn't sure she could ever feel true animosity for Stacy again. She was enormously grateful that Stacy was everything she wasn't.

At last Stacy dropped her arms, and when they separated, Holly's powers sprang back like a black flame flickering to life, but they felt normal rather than overwhelming.

"You can keep your ghosts," Missy said to Connor and Erikson, breaking the hushed silence. Her cheeks were pale. "That was enough for *me*. Holly, are you all right? Your eyes were completely black. No whites. It was like a horror movie."

"How did you know?" Aunt Rose asked Stacy. Her white braid had fallen down her back, and she seemed to have aged ten years, her cheeks sunken and her eyes disturbed.

"We felt the blast of power all the way at our farm," Stacy answered as one of her brothers helped her stand. It was obvious he was in pain by the harsh line of his lips and the way he was blinking as if he were staring into a sharp light, and Stacy was rubbing her manicured fingertips over her temples. She and her brothers edged away, trying to put some distance between themselves and Holly's family. "We knew there was trouble."

"The trouble was that we had to get rid of a ghost, and then Holly went all power trippy on us," Missy said.

"Thank you for coming." Aunt Daisy faced the three Witches, a faint smile on her lips. "There is a certain beauty in balance, isn't there? Each of us is here on this earth for a reason."

"Maybe ya'll aren't *so* bad," Missy said grudgingly.

Winter touched Holly's shoulder. "Are you all right?"

Holly nodded, but she was too embarrassed to look anyone in the eye. She'd lost all control, had given in entirely to her Wicked powers. What would she have done if Stacy hadn't stopped her? Connor had seen her use wind to rescue a puppy, but this—this was on an entirely different level of terrifying.

Holly took a deep, shuddering breath just as she was yanked into a pair of arms. She stiffened against Connor, but he wasn't having any of that. He rubbed her arms and her neck until she finally relaxed and snuggled into his embrace. She pressed her ear to his chest, where his heart beat steadily.

"You were brilliant," he murmured. "Absolutely brilliant."

"I lost control. Aren't you frightened of me? *I* am."

"You can ask me as many times as you need to, but the answer isn't going to change. I'm scared of a lot of things, Holly, but you'll never be one of them."

CHAPTER THIRTY-EIGHT

Erikson was sleeping at the motel complex, so that night Holly joined Connor in his little trailer bed, and they made lingering love while covered in the scent of wood smoke. Holly told herself she wasn't going to ruin things by pushing him away and losing what little time they had left together. She was already in love with him; a few more nights of intimacy and pleasure weren't going to make it any less painful when he hooked up the trailer and drove away.

The next morning he was already gone when she woke up, but he'd left a daisy on the pillow next to her. When she walked into the orchards that afternoon, things felt different. A weight had lifted from her shoulders, and she sensed a change in the atmosphere. Perhaps Miller's presence had been haunting the farm for so long that they'd become inured to the niggling feeling that not all was quite right. Now that he was gone, the difference was so obvious she didn't know how they could have missed that something evil was contributing to their apple farm's decline. Everything felt calmer, more hopeful. Brighter.

For the next three days, Connor and his crew filmed a reenactment of the councilman dustup, excluding all references to witches. Instead, they focused on the councilman's rage over his death, which was caused when he ingested a poisoned apple—the implication being that the apple had been poisoned bait for pesky wildlife.

Every night Holly slept with Connor in his trailer, where they laughed and shared secrets until eventually they stripped out of their clothes and made love. Despite her initial desire to keep their relationship quiet, she'd realized that doing so would mean having to sneak around and lose precious time with him. Besides, after the ghost banishment, it had been obvious that she and Connor had become more than former enemies.

The night before he was scheduled to leave, Holly found her aunts sitting together on the swing by the herb garden, swaying in companionable silence. Connor was in a meeting with his crew, and Holly was cooking dinner while she impatiently waited for the meeting to end. She'd come into the garden to collect rosemary for her dish, when she spotted the aunts, their shoulders touching and worry lines bracketing their mouths. Aunt Daisy's gloved hand was curled on her thigh, and Aunt Rose's eyes had the faraway look of someone deep in thought.

"Are you two all right?" Holly asked, walking over to crouch before the swing. She slipped her hand into Aunt Daisy's. Her aunts had spent a decade shouldering the worry of raising three headstrong girls. It was time Holly helped share the burden. "Is something bothering you?"

Aunt Daisy rubbed her thumb over the back of Holly's hand, the touch of thin leather familiar on Holly's skin. "We're troubled by how much power was used to expel Councilman Miller."

"You're worried it alerted the Shadow Council?"

Aunt Daisy nodded. A chickadee hopped across the garden, bleating its signature call as another bird encroached on its territory.

Holly set the bundle of rosemary on the ground by her knee. "They haven't made contact yet, and it's been days since it happened."

Aunt rose pressed her lips together. "When they come, there won't be any warning."

When, not *if.*

Holly withdrew her hand and cupped her chin in her palm. "The power usage was certainly unusual, but I didn't hurt anyone. Why would the Council care?"

"Oh, Holly." Aunt Rose sighed and looked fondly at her. "The Shadow Council is beholden to no governing body. There is no court to approve their decisions, no centralized Wicked organization to rein them in. Like any shadow squad, they have functioned for centuries by making sure no one challenges their power."

Holly let that sink in. "Are you saying they've kept their control by eliminating anyone who threatens their organization?" Threats like her and her sisters?

Rose nodded. "At the beginning the Shadow Council did what it needed to do to keep Wickeds safe. Over time and unchecked, they became corrupt and power hungry."

The aunts had raised Holly and her sisters to fear the Shadow Council discovering their powers. They'd impressed upon the girls how important it was that they remain as "normal" as possible. And all this time Holly had thought it was because of what she'd done to her mother, that she'd proven she and her sisters were dangerous and unstable. But now . . . "Is that why you've been so adamant that we remain out of the spotlight? Our family has always lived 'small' because of Autumn's vow, but you both took it a step further. I always thought you were afraid the Shadow Council would see us as a threat to others, but what you were really afraid of was that they would see us as a threat to *them*."

Aunt Rose and Aunt Daisy shared a speaking look. "We're sorry, Holly," Aunt Rose finally said. "If your mother had been alive, she might have found a better way than restraining your powers. We did the best we could to protect you."

Tears stung Holly's eyes. "I'm sorry I killed her. I ruined everyone's life that day."

Aunt Rose reached forward to stroke the top of her head. "It wasn't your fault."

Holly sprang to her feet. "I'm an adult; you can admit the truth. If I hadn't created that storm, she never would have lost control of her car."

Her aunts' faces went slack with stunned silence.

"Holly . . ." Aunt Rose's voice trembled on her name, a whisper of horror threading the vowels. "Don't tell me that's what you actually believe."

"How could I not? None of you ever blamed me, but I'm not an idiot. I started that storm. *I* was the reason she crashed."

Aunt Daisy pressed her gloved hands to her eyes, and when they came away the leather was damp. "My dear child, we didn't tell you the truth because we didn't want you to live in fear. If we'd known you held yourself responsible . . . You did not kill your mother, Holly."

"I appreciate you saying that, but—"

"*You* did not kill your mother, Holly," Aunt Daisy repeated.

The emphasis on *you* halted Holly's objections, and suddenly she knew, as if the pieces had always hovered close, but were only just now falling into place to reveal the larger picture. In that moment she understood how her aunts could know so little about their powers and other Wickeds, and yet be experts on the Shadow Council. She understood why her aunts had been terrified the Shadow Council would target the girls, and why they'd been so desperate to keep Holly and her sisters' strengths a secret.

A crushing weight lifted from Holly's chest while another, more ominous mantle settled over her shoulders. Her throat felt lined with cut glass when she whispered, "The Shadow Council killed my mother."

"Lilac was always the powerful one. Not as powerful as you girls, but of the three of us she inherited the most talent. She was strong and she was tired of hiding away. She saw how the Witches lived, and she wanted a brighter future for the Wickeds—a future that involved a centralized government and communities. A future that didn't hinge on the whims of a select council of fear." Aunt Rose touched her necklace, where a rose quartz sat against her skin. Drawing strength from it, she continued. "She'd even gone so far as to start having phone calls with Stacy's mother. They'd begun to put aside their rivalry, were even tentative friends. Lilac wanted to learn from the Witches, and she wanted to bring you girls out of the shadows so that you could have better lives."

Holly was stunned. "Mom was friends with Stacy's mom?"

Aunt Rose nodded. "They found their way to common ground before your mother's 'accident.' I think that is the way it was always supposed to be: Wickeds working in harmony with Witches."

Holly turned that over in her mind. She'd only remembered her mother's disdain for the Witches; she hadn't been aware of the budding truce. She thought of her own feelings about Stacy and how they'd begun changing. Was it possible that she and Stacy could find common ground as their mothers had?

"After the Council murdered your mother, Daisy and I knew if they discovered you girls had ten times her power it would be only a matter of time before they came after you as well. We didn't have the skill set to teach you how to handle your power, so we tried to suppress it."

"There can be no question of their knowledge now," Aunt Daisy said solemnly. "If the Witches felt your power, the Shadow Council did."

Holly's cheeks whitened. Had she put her entire family in danger? "What do we do?"

"We need to regain some of what we've lost," Aunt Rose said firmly. "It is time we take up where Lilac left off and step out of the shadows. We need to connect with other Wickeds and relearn what our family has spent so long forgetting. Perhaps answers will come with the knowledge. Until then . . ."

They looked at each other but didn't finish the sentence.

They didn't have to. Holly understood perfectly. Until her aunts either discovered a way to help Holly and her sisters hide their powers again, or she and her sisters learned how to fully control and conceal them on their own, they would be targets for a ruthless council that answered to no one. A council that had already murdered their mother.

Holly clenched her fists.

CHAPTER THIRTY-NINE

Later that evening, Holly shared what she'd learned with her sisters and the Grimms. The news was troubling, but when she asked Winter if she'd had any visions of the Shadow Council, Winter only frowned and shook her head.

"Are they powerful enough to conceal themselves from visions of the future?" Erikson asked.

"I don't know. I barely know anything about this curse," Winter snapped. "None of us do."

"There's something else," Connor said before Winter could stomp out of the room. "Your secret isn't as hidden as you thought. There is a reason Erikson and I chose your apple farm. Someone sent us a photo of Daisy using her power to decay a barrel of apples."

Holly listened to Connor, her jaw slack, and then stared at the creased photocopy of the picture he pulled from his pocket.

"That must've been taken from the blackberry brambles," Missy said, looking over Holly's shoulder at the picture. "Someone was sneaking around our property at night."

"Or it was taken by someone who was already in the house," Winter snarled. "Someone who wouldn't raise an alarm by being on the property."

Missy whipped around. "Are you accusing me of something? I swear to God I'll—"

"No," Connor cut in, nodding thoughtfully as he made eye contact with Winter. "She's thinking of Jeremy, aren't you?"

Winter's gaze turned to Holly, and she gave a one-shouldered shrug. "Sorry, Holly, but yeah. He had plenty of opportunities to take it. If it was him, he would have sent it when you two were still together, probably thinking that if Connor came to investigate the apple farm, he would get exposure as your boyfriend. Except then you dumped him, so he convinced Amy to go along with his stupid reality TV show idea."

Holly's ears burned with humiliation. How many other ways could she, the so-called protector of her family, put them in danger? "Do you think he knows what we are?"

"Doubtful," Erikson answered. "If anything, he suspects you're witches."

"Just like his great-great-granddaddy," Missy said sarcastically.

Holly's fingertips tingled. Jeremy had been boring, selfish, and manipulative, but this was leaps and bounds beyond shitty boyfriend behavior. He'd suspected her and her family of witchcraft, and so he'd taken photos of them when they were vulnerable. They'd let him into their home and trusted him, and he'd tried to expose them, to hurt them, and all so he could have a shot at being on TV and making a name for himself. Had he ever liked her? Or had "outing her" been his plan from the start?

She glanced at Connor. The parallels were too obvious to ignore. Connor had set out to expose her and her family as well, but the difference was that when he'd discovered what they were, he'd abandoned his plans for success and had committed to keeping their secret safe instead, whereas Jeremy was *still* trying to use her.

Holly spent the rest of the night cuddling with Connor, but he was quieter than usual. She wasn't sure if it was because of what she'd shared about the Shadow Council or because he was leaving the next morning. Maybe it was a little of both. She knew Connor cared for her, even if he didn't love her. He was probably concerned for her safety. Either that or he was relieved he wouldn't be around to be caught in the crossfire.

Despite her fervent wish that the night would last forever, light eventually streaked the dawn sky. Holly felt so sick about Connor leaving that she could barely exist in her own skin.

Charlotte had already said goodbye the day before, practically peeling out of the driveway after promising to send them a vegan meal subscription so they could experience proper vegan food. Both trailers were towed away, and the film crew finished restoring all that had been disturbed during filming.

By the afternoon, only Connor and Erikson remained behind. Erikson had volunteered to help Winter fix a cracked window in the barn, even though she had flat-out told him she didn't need his help, and Connor was hanging out in the kitchen with Holly, Missy, and the aunts.

Holly was lovingly drinking in her last moments with him when the house phone rang.

"I've got it!" Missy called. She jumped off the counter and answered the old-fashioned phone with the curly cord. "Celeste residence." Missy listened for a moment and then pressed the receiver to her shoulder. "It's for you, Holly."

Who would call for her on the house phone instead of her cell phone? The only person who'd ever regularly used the house phone was Jeremy when she didn't answer her cell phone "fast enough" for him.

"Hello?"

"Hello, is this Miss Holly Celeste?"

"This is she."

"Hi, Holly. This is Tyleneka Harris from NZT."

Holly frowned and met Connor's curious expression across the kitchen. NZT was a rival TV station of Connor's.

"Miss Celeste, I'm calling because we are extraordinarily excited about this concept, and we think it would add so much if you and your sisters consented to appearing on the show. The execs have already greenlighted the pilot, and the producer really wants to film on the apple farm. If you refuse, we can work around it, but then you won't have any say in the narrative told."

"I'm sorry, I have no idea what you're talking about."

The woman on the other end of the line paused uncertainly. "Jeremy O'Toole didn't tell you?"

"Didn't tell me what?" Holly asked, a little sharper than she meant to.

"Whoa, whoa." The woman chucked nervously. "Don't curse the messenger."

Holly's blood ran cold. It was don't *shoot* the messenger. Why would she have substituted it with *curse*?

"Mr. O'Toole contacted us with an exciting docuseries idea that takes a deep dive into your and your sisters' hidden lives as Wickeds."

Holly's heart seized in her chest. This couldn't be happening. They were supposed to be safe. Jeremy may have suspected them of witchcraft, but she had never told him about Wickeds, and she knew no one in her family had either.

That left only one person.

Holly stared at Connor Grimm, the man who had promised them their privacy and then turned around and shared their secret with the world. The betrayal she felt nearly forced her to her knees. How could he have done this? Had this been his loophole all along? He'd assured her he wouldn't expose them on *Grimm Reality*, but he'd never promised he wouldn't let someone else do it.

Had she meant anything to him, or had he only been trying to get close to her so she would open up to him and reveal her hand? Was he even worse than Jeremy?

Everyone in the kitchen must've sensed her devastation because Missy hopped off the counter, and Connor started toward her. Holly held up her palm, halting him.

"Miss Harris, I'm afraid Jeremy has misled you with a wild fantasy," she said in a husky voice.

"He told us he heard it from Connor Grimm himself. *Grimm Reality* has been a huge success, and our station would love a slice of the supernatural viewing market, especially as interest has multiplied over the years."

"It's not true," Holly said firmly, "no matter what Connor Grimm may have said."

Connor's head whipped up in shock.

The woman sighed. "I take it you won't be participating in the filming."

"No." Holly slammed the receiver on the wall and spun back to face Connor. "How could you?" she hissed.

"How could I what?"

She shoved past him and stormed out of the house. He called after her, but she took off at a run, sprinting into the apple trees and weaving down rows to lose him. The sky darkened as clouds blocked out the sun and rain began to fall. She had never felt so stupid, had never felt so taken advantage of.

Holly let out a howl of agony and it thundered. The steady rain instantly turned into a torrential downpour, as if the sky gods were tipping over buckets of water. She knew she needed to lock down her powers, especially now that she was on the Shadow Council's radar, but despair and betrayal thrummed through her blood with such force that she could barely see straight.

Holly thought she'd successfully lost him at the pumpkin patch, when Connor grabbed her arm from behind. Holly whirled around with such hurt and anger that she narrowly avoided gusting wind at him. "Don't touch me!"

He instantly let go. "What the hell, Holly?" he yelled over the rain. Water dribbled down his face and plastered his T-shirt to his chest. "What was that phone call about?"

"You! You promised me you wouldn't expose us and you *lied* to me." She took a step forward. "You *used* me, got me to open up, and then you sold our secret to *Jeremy O'Toole*! That was a TV network calling because they have the green light to run a docuseries on Wickeds."

She swallowed back a sob. "Do you know what you've done? Do you know what will happen to us now?"

Connor didn't back away from her enraged advance. Instead, his eyes narrowed and he said savagely, "I didn't tell that asshole *anything.*"

"The woman who called said you did. That's the only reason they're not laughing Jeremy out of the studio. He claimed you told him. How else would he know what we are? He only had a stupid picture that could've been faked, and a guess about witches!"

"I don't know," Connor ground out, "but I gave you my word that I would keep your secret. I would never in a million years share that kind of information with a weasel like Jeremy."

Holly wanted to believe him. Connor's character was nearly as reliable as the seasons. He would forever be curious to a fault, he would always ask questions and record stories, and until now she'd thought he'd always be a man of his word. But either Connor or Erikson *had* to have told Jeremy. There was no other explanation.

Rain pounded into the dirt at her feet, stirring the scents of earth and apples. "Erikson?"

"Never," Connor said fiercely. He was breathing hard from running after her, and his gray eyes were filled with rage and something wild and desperate. "When I told Erikson about you, we were all alone in the trailer and there was no—" Connor stopped abruptly, understanding flashing across his face.

"What?" Holly demanded.

"When I told Erikson, we were alone in the trailer, but when I turned around, the door was open several inches, and I could have sworn I'd closed it. Then a few minutes later, you had the altercation with Jeremy on the steps."

"You're saying Jeremy listened in on your conversation?" She injected as much doubt into her voice as she could manage, but already his theory made more sense than him selling the secret to Jeremy. Connor might not love her, but she knew for a fact he liked her more than her ex. The animosity between the two of them had been instantaneous from the moment they'd laid eyes on one other. The motive simply wasn't there.

Connor closed the space between them and gripped her hands. "I swear to you on my life, on my brother's life—on my stupid show's existence—that I never told Jeremy."

Holly turned her head away. "I believe you," she said flatly.

"Then why do you look like you still hate me?"

Holly sighed, suddenly so tired she could barely stand. The rain began to lighten until it was a soft drizzle. "I don't hate you, Connor, but the damage is done. You came to Wicked Good Apples even after I sent your goons packing, and you used our financial situation to leverage us into doing what you wanted. I asked you time and again to leave us alone, but you kept digging, kept sniffing, kept pressing until you got what you wanted, and this is the result. You know what will happen to us now. There will be people who pass Jeremy off as a quack, but there will be others that believe him, others that will start Wicked-hunting groups online and start blaming us for everything that goes wrong. At the very least, it will damage, if not destroy, our farm and reputation."

Holly tugged her hands from his and searched his eyes, both angry over his persistence that had led to this moment and terribly sad that it had to end this way. "Just leave, Connor." She took a step back. "There's nothing you can do. Even if you called up that studio right now and told them you never shared the information with Jeremy, they already love the idea. You got what you wanted: three ghost episodes and a quick fling. Now you can get back to your life."

His face was a blank mask when he said, "I don't want it to end like this."

She gave a humorless laugh. "Goodbye, Connor."

This time when she turned her back on him, he didn't run after her.

CHAPTER FORTY

Two months later

"Come on, Holly," Missy pleaded, tugging Holly into the living room with one hand while balancing a bowl of popcorn in the other. Winter was pouring cider into crystal glasses on the coffee table, and across the room on a shelf, Prickles was curled in a bed of soft rags. Someone had lit a candle, and even though it was August, the scents of fall clung to the air.

"I'm not interested," Holly said, freeing her arm. She'd watched the first two episodes of *Grimm Reality*'s deep dive into the ghost at Wicked Good Apples, and it had been more painful than she'd expected. Two months had passed since she'd seen Connor. He hadn't once texted her, hadn't once called. The only reminder that he'd ever been there were the ruts in the grass where his and Charlotte's trailers had been.

She had to admit he'd done a spectacular job producing the episodes, each one ending on a cliffhanger that garnered viewers for the next week. Wicked Good Apples wasn't open for the season yet, but Holly already knew it was going to make a massive difference in their sales. Missy had had the brilliant idea to open an online shop with Wicked Good Apples and ghost merchandise, and it had been such an instantaneous success that they were looking to hire on help.

Stacy had called and offered her more money, which Holly had sweetly declined. But then she'd texted Stacy after with a silly witch meme, and Stacy had responded back with a meme about an ugly wicked witch, warts on her nose and all. She and Stacy probably weren't ever going to be best friends—especially considering they physically couldn't stand to be near each other—but after the incident with Councilman Miller, Holly had a new respect for the role Witches played, for the balance they brought to Wickeds and vice versa. She might've still been a *tiny* bit jealous of Stacy's unrelenting perfectionism, but she didn't hate her. And in finding that friendly balance with Stacy, she felt closer to her mother than she had in years.

The Celestes hadn't heard a word from Jeremy or Amy, but according to town gossip they were in preproduction for their new television series. No one knew what the series was about—it was all being kept hush-hush—but Jeremy and Amy's social media pages promised it would be explosive.

Holly hoped Wicked Good Apples would make enough cash from this season to keep them going for a while, because once Jeremy's show aired, she didn't know what would happen. She suspected they might have to move, that the harassment and interest would be too much for them to stay here.

"No, you can't miss the last one. Come on," Missy insisted, grabbing her again and marching her toward the couch, where Winter was sitting with Aunt Rose.

Holly squeezed between them just as the opening credits for the final episode began. The song was catchy, the visuals jarring, and the hosts—Connor and Erikson—were ruggedly handsome, as usual.

How was it possible that it could physically pain her to see him? How was it possible that after two months she still hadn't fallen out of love with him? Whenever she painted in the hayloft, she thought of his silent acceptance of her studio of horrors. Whenever she was in the old apple orchard, she remembered their first night together under the moon. Whenever she held Prickles, she pictured how he'd thrown his body over hers to protect her from the exploding picture window.

She wanted to share every new joke she heard with him; she wanted him to taste each new batch of cider; she wanted to cry on his shoulder when everything felt bleak and overwhelming. It was the worst kind of longing, because they hadn't separated because of some silly argument. Yes, she'd been angry and disappointed with him when he'd left, but the roadblock that separated them was insurmountable. She loved her apple farm and he loved his show.

She loved him, and he loved . . . his show.

Idiot. Holly Celeste was an idiot.

The episode began, and Holly found herself drawn into the conclusion of the Councilman Miller hauntings, but even as Connor wrapped up that storyline, he introduced another. He stood at the edge of her apple orchard and spoke into the camera, the wind tousling his hair and pressing his jacket against his side. There, he told the audience there might be something supernatural at Wicked Good Apples that had nothing to do with ghosts.

The show went to commercial and Holly shared an alarmed look with Missy. What the hell?

After a tense commercial break where not a single one of them managed to choke down popcorn, the show picked up again. Holly watched, her heart in her throat, as Connor spun his hunt for the supernatural into the resolution of the ghost haunting. He raised all the points he had when he'd first arrived in their kitchen: rain during droughts, dry ground after storms, lack of apple diseases. He introduced the odd occurrences as solid reasons to suspect the Celeste women might be supernatural themselves.

There was another commercial break, and Holly wasn't sure she could stand to finish the episode. What had he done?

Missy downed her apple cider and shuddered. "I thought this was apple wine, Winter."

Winter ignored her. "Do you trust him, Holly?"

Holly thought about the question. Did she think Connor would betray her and her family, even though he had moved on and would likely never see her again? No, she didn't. It simply wasn't in his character. "Yes."

Winter nodded in satisfaction. "Then let's see what he has to say."

The show returned after far too many commercials. Connor reenacted the ghost exorcism with dramatic voiceovers, completely leaving out any accusations of witchcraft. Once the Councilman Miller story had wrapped up, he bounced back to his newest storyline: the *other* paranormal happenings at Wicked Good Apples.

"I came to Wicked Good Apples for more than a ghost," he said, the breeze tousling his hair as he stood among the rows of Macintosh trees. He had a few days' worth of beard growth, and combined with his jeans and rough work boots, it made him appear more outdoorsy than usual. "Before I chose this location, an anonymous contact sent me an intriguing photograph."

The photo of Aunt Daisy, black mist pouring from her palms over a barrel of apples, flashed on the screen. Holly gripped Missy's hand so hard her knuckles turned white. *Connor, what are you doing?*

"I decided to film there and dig around to find out if the photo was real or not. I wanted to prove that the paranormal existed beyond specters and Bigfoot. The photo, combined with the odd occurrences mentioned before, led me to believe I might finally do that at Wicked Good Apples."

He rubbed his chin and flashed a sheepish, boyish expression before directing the camera to what lay at his feet. "Do you see those blue tubes running across the ground?" The camera panned the watering system they'd installed a few years back, the blue lines winding through the tall grasses of the Macintosh orchard like snakes. "*That* is how the Celestes kept their orchard watered during the drought."

Not quite. The drought had been before the installation of the watering system, but no one would know that.

The camera flashed to Connor standing in a new location on their farm, one foot halfway in a ditch, the other knee bent. He'd taken off his jacket and the white polo was crisp against his tanned skin. "Drainage system," he said, gesturing along the ditch. Another scene, but this time Connor's back was to the pumpkin patch. He waved to the fields and forest that separated the farm from other dwellings, and explained that Wicked Good Apples was remote enough to have missed the apple disease. An interview with an expert arboriculturist was spliced in next, and a gentleman with an elflike gray beard testified that it was possible, even likely, that remote locations like Wicked Good Apples could avoid vegetative diseases completely.

With ruthless precision, Connor dismantled every single point of evidence he'd made earlier in the program for the existence of the supernatural on their apple farm.

At last, Connor stood in a laboratory with a forensic photographer, who leaned over a metal lab table with the photograph lying at the center. The man had bloodshot eyes and a bulbous nose, and he snorted with laughter when Connor asked him if the photograph could be real.

"It's clearly photoshopped," the "expert" said, shaking his head. "AI these days could trick anyone. Don't feel down on yourself."

In the final few minutes of the episode Connor stood in front of the camera again, the rolling Celeste orchards his backdrop, and talked to the audience in the friendly and authoritative way he had that made him the most lovable ghost expert in the country.

"After a thorough investigation at Wicked Good Apples, I can assure you there is nothing supernatural here . . . other than an angry councilman who we can only hope has finally moved on to another plane. I've been doing this a long time, long enough that I can admit when a hunch is wrong. This is just an ordinary apple farm." He gestured to the sun-gilded apple trees behind him. "If anyone tells you otherwise, they're yanking your chain."

Holly gasped and covered her mouth with both hands.

"Now that's a boss move!" Missy hooted.

"Yeah." Winter gave Holly a rare smile. "Your man just killed Jeremy's show in ten minutes flat."

Connor leaned closer to the camera and curved his lips into that sexy, trademark grin of his. "If you still want to experience something out of this world, you should try Wicked Good Apples' cider." A tray appeared in front of him with a glass of cider balanced on it.

Connor lifted the glass and raised it in toast to the audience. "Before we end, I want to thank all of you for tuning in to watch *Grimm Reality* these past ten years. You've made this show a success, not us. All we ever wanted was to expose the supernatural, and you've come along with us every step of the way. We hope you continue on that ride as Charlotte joins the team. You might recognize her as my former assistant." Charlotte popped into the picture, her grin wide and her hair threaded with lime-green highlights. "She's been with *Grimm Reality* since its inception. She's been to every haunting, every exorcism, and every unsolved mystery, and she'll be here for another hundred more." He clinked his glass with Charlotte's and then with Erikson's, who'd appeared at his other side holding his own glass. "To my last episode on *Grimm Reality* and to Charlotte's first as new cohost."

They drank deeply before the end credits began to roll.

Holly couldn't tear her eyes from the credits. Her heart was thundering in her chest. Had she just heard that right? Was Connor seriously retiring from his show? *Why?* He loved that show!

"Well, I didn't see that coming," Missy said. She waggled her eyebrows at Winter. "Did you?"

Winter was already edging toward the door. "More popcorn?" she asked. Holly glanced at the coffee table. Their bowls were still full. "Um, Holly, your boots are under the chair in the hallway," she added in a rush before slipping away.

"Wha—"

Holly's phone dinged with a text message. She stared suspiciously after Winter but grabbed her cell and opened the message.

Connor: *Meet me in the old orchard at eleven?*

It was 10:59.

Holly's heart gave a slow twist and she stood. "I need to . . ."

Missy grinned. "Yeah, I bet you do."

Holly sprinted into the hallway and fumbled for her boots—which she never would have found under the chair—and jammed her feet into them before bursting outside.

The August sky was still light enough that stars were only just beginning to twinkle on the purple horizon. The warm air caressed her bare arms as she jogged through the newer apple orchards. Fireflies blinked as they drifted over the tall grass, and apples bobbed on the branches as she slipped by.

When she reached the old apple orchard, Connor was already waiting for her, his hands in his pockets and a grin on his face. She ran toward him and threw her arms around his neck.

"Hey, Wicked," he said.

CHAPTER FORTY-ONE

Holly let go of him and backed up a step. For the first time, Connor truly understood the old adage *a sight for sore eyes*. He'd spent two months away from her, and seeing her now was like applying a balm to his bruised soul. Her hair was loose and she was wearing her high school track T-shirt. His eyes roved over her snug jean shorts to the bare length of her legs, and he wondered with some amazement what the hell he'd been thinking when he left.

"What are you doing here?" she asked happily.

"I'm not filming." It felt strange to say. He'd been committed to *Grimm Reality* for so long that it should have felt awkward and wrong, but even though it was strange, it felt right. "I'm officially retired. A publisher wants me to write a book about my experiences, and I couldn't pass it up."

Holly smiled up at him, the moonlight sliding in a gray wave down the back of her hair. "You'll write a great book."

He'd thought she might still be angry with him or reticent to see him after the way they'd left things. She'd been right about everything. He'd ruthlessly pressed his advantage when he'd discovered her financial situation. If he'd respected her original refusal to host the

289

show, then Jeremy never would have come so close to exposing her and her family to the angry and suspicious minds of the world. Connor hadn't given Jeremy the information deliberately, but it had been his fault all the same. The result had been that he'd nearly hurt the only woman he'd ever loved.

Because he *did* love her. He'd been in love with her from the moment she stood outside his motel room for twenty minutes in the pouring rain rather than admit defeat, but he'd been too stupid to know his own heart. He'd convinced himself nothing was more important than his show, that he was dedicated to a noble cause that he couldn't abandon.

Then Erikson had turned his whole fucking world upside down when he'd suggested they were doing more running than hunting.

"Once we wrapped up filming on the final episode, I went to Massachusetts with Erikson. To our childhood home."

"Oh, Connor." She took a step closer and slid her hand into his. It felt exactly right. "Did you see the ghost of the man who haunted you as children?"

"Not at first. We had to go back multiple times before he made an appearance. He was so much smaller and sadder than I remembered. When we were kids, he was frighteningly huge, but he was probably only in his early twenties when he died by suicide." Connor took a deep breath. "He told us his girlfriend found him and that she'd whispered into his ear she was pregnant. Some part of his consciousness heard her. He was elated and then consumed with such regret that he was never able to move on."

"Why did he show himself to you and Erikson when you were children?"

"I think it was more that we were able to see what others couldn't, not that he specifically chose to show us. But once he realized we could see him, he began appearing more often. I think he thought we looked like the family he could've had."

Holly squeezed his hand. "That's heartbreaking."

Connor nodded. It had been one of the saddest encounters he'd had. "His death was so long ago that his child is now dead, and we told him if he let go of his regret and moved on, he might be able to meet his child on the other side. I think he's finally at peace, and a part of me is too. It doesn't change how frightened we were as children or the strain it put on our parents, but we see it from another perspective now."

Connor rubbed his thumb over the back of her hand. "All this time I've been trying to prove how normal I am to the world instead of embracing the fact that I'm different. Erikson told me that," he muttered, "and the annoying bastard was right. I feel like that chapter of my life finally has closure. I've done what I set out to do. I've normalized ghosts to some extent, and I've faced my own. I'm ready to start a new chapter."

"Writing," Holly said.

"*You*, Holly, if you'll have me." Connor searched her green-rimmed eyes for any inkling to how she would receive the news that he was desperately and hopelessly in love with her. "You're my new chapter—and hopefully every chapter until the end of my story. I'm sorry I pressured you into the doing the show. I should've respected your caution. I want you to know that I have a friend at NZT, and Jeremy's show was canceled as of ten minutes ago."

Holly blinked up at him, but he couldn't read her expression.

Connor bent and picked up a soft brown bag with a leather strap and held it out.

Holly slowly took the somewhat ugly purse. "What is this?"

Feeling a little stupid, Connor said, "It's a hedgehog carrying case. That way you don't have to worry about leaving your purse open so Prickles can breathe."

When Holly lifted her eyes again, they were sparkling.

"What I'm trying to say," Connor said, cupping her cheek, "is that I love you. I love you with every cell in my body, every thought in my brain, every pump of my heart. If you were a ghost, I'd want you to haunt me for the rest of my life. I love *all* of you, and I want to spend the rest of my days knowing exactly how much I've pissed you off by how hard it's raining; I want to make love with you in every nook of the orchard; I want to be there to help ease the burden you carry."

Holly threw her arms around his neck. "I love you too, Connor Grimm."

Connor had no idea how he'd feel if or when she said those words, and he still didn't. Words simply didn't exist to describe how it felt to finally be whole. Connor was beginning to think the greeting card companies knew what they were talking about after all.

Holly tightened her arms around him. "I'm not the safest choice, Connor. We haven't heard a peep from the Shadow Council, but I don't believe they've forgotten us."

He may not have kept in touch with Holly, but he'd kept a vigilant eye on town happenings while he'd been gone, alert for even the slightest hint of trouble. "You're the *only* choice for me, Holly. Whatever happens, we'll face it together. I don't have paranormal powers, but I do have a mean right hook."

Holly grinned up at him and dragged his mouth down to meet hers. He kissed her with all of the longing and love and tenderness that had built up during their months apart. When he finally lifted his head, he said, "The first thing I ever said to you was that you were just the woman I needed. I had no clue how true that was."

Holly pretended to preen, and he laughed and kissed her again.

"This will make for a good story to tell our three daughters," she said, looking at him from beneath her lashes. "One older girl and a set of twins."

"Three daughters?" he repeated, a bit stunned at the thought.

"Three *Wicked* daughters."

A houseful of Wicked women. It sounded . . . "Perfect," he said.

EPILOGUE

Wicked Good Apples was a sensation. They were so busy they had to hire on four new staffers. Missy's merchandise store needed another two, and she was planning on opening the barn off-season for spooky wedding ceremonies, which would require even more help. It was a far cry from their pre-ghost break-even model, so they started The Apple Education Corp. to teach kids how to work the land and grow orchards. They also planned to fund scholarships for children living with extended family members. Balance was important.

"You can get married on Halloween!" Missy squealed from behind the counter as Holly rang up a purchase of pie filling.

Holly took the customer's card and couldn't help admiring the way the light from the window caught the sparkle of the black diamond ring on her left hand before she swiped the card through the reader. "No way, Missy. Practice your hosting skills on someone else."

Missy huffed but smiled at the customer before she returned her attention to Holly. "Well, when *are* you going to have the ceremony?"

Connor walked into the barn store at that moment and ducked behind the counter. He slid an arm around Holly's waist and pressed a quick kiss to her temple. "How's it going?"

"Missy wants to know when we're getting married."

Holly leaned her head back on his chest and felt his voice vibrate when he said, "Holly was thinking December 1ˢᵗ. She could make an offering and wear her frost crown, which she assures me is adorable."

"Oh, it totally is," Missy confirmed with a nod. "We're named after the winter season, so we're legit adorable as fuck in those crowns." Missy noted the woman with two kids browsing at the back of the store and winced. "I mean, adorable as bang-bang."

"Barely better," Holly said. She turned to Connor. "Did they love it?"

He grinned down at her with those gray eyes that Holly would never get enough of. "Yeah, they loved the proposal."

Missy popped a bubble of gum and hopped on the counter. "What proposal?"

"Connor wants to investigate hauntings in the West Virginian mountains and write a book on them. We think it could be a nice honeymoon this spring."

"Ugh, gag. You guys are so cute you kill me." Missy waved to a group of teens walking in. They spotted Connor and began squealing and shoving each other and hissing, "No *you* ask for a selfie."

"Well, that's my cue to go put out more sweatshirts and PopSockets," Missy said, sliding off the counter. "They're selling like hotcakes."

The teens approached Connor, and Holly gave him a wink before heading into the back to pull out more stock. At this rate they were going to run out of everything but apples by the time October came.

When she returned half an hour later, the store was empty save for Connor behind the counter, and Stacy, who was dressed in a tight skirt and sequin-studded heels, browsing the display of apple jellies. Stacy frowned with pain a split second before Holly appeared, but when she spotted Holly, she smiled.

"Stopping by to see how it's done?" Holly asked.

"Hardly," Stacy sniffed, but it was a far cry from the animosity that had existed between them when Holly had visited The Apple Dream all those months ago. Since Councilman Miller, the two had become almost friends, texting weekly, if not daily. "Actually, my brothers and I wanted to invite you to a Witch council meeting. We think it would be good for our kinds to communicate in a more official capacity. Are your aunts around?"

Connor splayed a hand on Holly's hip when she leaned against his side, trying to hide her nausea. "No, they left last week," she said. "They're traveling across New England to connect with other Wickeds and rediscover their roots. They've promised to be back in time for our wedding. I think the council meeting sounds like a great idea. I'll run it past Missy and Winter. Are you coming to the wedding?"

Stacy rubbed her temples and took a step back, fractionally easing both of their ailments. "I don't know how long I'll last, but I wouldn't miss it."

The back door rocked open, and Winter appeared, a toolbelt cinched around her waist and a pair of gloves tucked into her back pocket. When she spotted Stacy, she blanched and covered her mouth as if she were going to vomit.

Stacy took another step back, her heels clacking on the barnwood. "Text you later?"

"Only if you stop sending me cat memes."

"I'm a Witch. So, never."

Holly laughed as Stacy executed a perfect turn on her heel and strutted out the door.

Winter grabbed a bottle of water from the small cooler they kept behind the counter. "She coming to the wedding?"

"Yeah. I'm a little surprised, though. It won't be comfortable for her, but I'll seat her as far away from us as possible."

"I'm not surprised." Winter drank deeply and wiped the back of her hand over her mouth. "You two give us all hope."

Connor's lips grazed Holly's temple as she lifted a brow. "How's that?"

"You make the rest of us believe that someday, someone could love us the way we are. Wicked and all." Her cheeks flushed the moment the words escaped her lips, as if she were mortified by her own vulnerability.

Holly looked up and met Connor's loving gray eyes, then reached over and squeezed her sister's arm. "You know what, Win? I think there's a wicked good chance of that."

ACKNOWLEDGMENTS

Writing and publishing a book is always a team effort, and I want to give all of my thanks to the following people:

My agent, Emily Sylvan Kim, who has championed me from the start. Thank you so much for reading this book and liking the idea of Wickeds enough for me to write two totally different books on the subject (and for being cool when I ditched the YA version). Thank you for fighting for this book to be the best it can be. I could not do this without you!

My editor, Holly Ingraham, for loving this book and making it better with such insightful comments. Thank you for doing all you could to make it a success!

The folks at Alcove who have worked on putting this book into the world: Dulce Botello, Mikaela Bender, and Mia Bertrand in marketing; Stephanie Manova and Megan Matti in subsidiary rights; Thaisheemarie Fantauzzi Perez, Rebecca Nelson, and Pankaj Pandey in production; Jill Pellarin, copyeditor; and an absolutely beautiful cover illustrated by Dawn Cooper.

The 2024 debuts, fellow Alcove authors, and my Discord writer groups—I have found immense support in all of you. Thank you so much for your understanding and encouragement.

Acknowledgments

My family: my mother, father, sister, brother, in-laws (on both sides), aunts, uncles, and extended family—you have all showed up for me in a way I never could have imagined. You have supported me, bought my books, shared my books, asked libraries to order them, and generally been absolutely amazing and supportive. Thank you so much!

My friends, who have cheered me on and been the absolute best. Thanks for listening to all the "behind the scenes" stuff and for talking about my book to anyone who will listen.

All Mainers—I like to think Holly Celeste and her family would have had a wicked good life there if they really existed.

My children, who drew me the cutest pictures for my debut, and whenever I announce something awesome about publishing, are totally unimpressed. You are everything to me.

My husband, who has never once doubted me. You listen to me talk constantly about books, publishing, and my worries. You pick up slack so that I can find time to write. You are my support, my encouragement, and my love. You are the reason I believe in happily ever after.

Last, but certainly not least, all the readers. Sharing a book with the world is scary, and I appreciate every single one of you who has given my books a chance. Your kind words mean more to me than you'll ever know, and I hope to keep you entertained with stories for a long time to come.